JUSTIN GUSTAINIS

Known Devil

AN OCCULT CRIMES UNIT INVESTIGATION

ANGRY
ROBOT

ANGRY ROBOT
A member of the Osprey Group

Lace Market House,
54-56 High Pavement,
Nottingham NG1 1HW
UK

www.angryrobotbooks.com
Sliders

An Angry Robot paperback original 2014
1

A catalogue record for this book is available
from the British Library.

ISBN 978 0 85766 165 4
Ebook ISBN 978 0 85766 167 8

Set in Meridien by EpubServices

Printed and bound by CPI Group (UK) Ltd, Croydon, CR0 4YY.

"A cool mix of cop show and creature feature. Gustainis had me at 'meth-addicted goblins'."
Marcus Pelegrimas, author of the Skinners *series*

"A magical mystery tour of a murder case rife with supernatural suspects. Sit down for an enchanted evening of otherworldly entertainment!"
Laura Resnick, author of Unsympathetic Magic *and* Vamparazzi

"I enjoyed every page of Hard Spell. If Sam Spade and Jack Fleming were somehow melted together, you'd get Stan Markowski. I can't wait to see what Gustainis does next."
Lilith Saintcrow, author of Night Shift *and* Working for the Devil

"Justin Gustainis is a first-class writer; he's smart and he's fun, he moves quickly and he takes corners at speed. Every time you think you know where he's going, he makes a point of going somewhere else. His characters are sharp and vivid, his dialogue crackles with wit and tension, and when it comes to the scarier corners of the magical underworld, he knows his stuff."
Simon R. Green, author of the Secret Histories *and* Nightside novels

To Josephine Dougherty,
dinosaur fan and baby woman.
Hope you like it here, kid.

*"All sin tends to be addictive, and
the terminal point of addiction
is what is called damnation."*

WH Auden

*"Criminals do not die by the hands of the law;
they die by the hands of other men."*

George Bernard Shaw

"Revenge proves its own executioner."

John Ford

I've never had a lot of use for elves. In my experience, they're lazy and dumb – nothing like those drones in the stories, who supposedly work for the Fat Guy up north. I don't like elves, and elves with guns I like even less. And when those guns are pointed at *me* – well, it's like that Mafia guy on TV used to say: *fahgettaboudit*.

But first, a few words from my partner.

"So now him and this killer ogre are on top of the railroad car, dukin' it out, haina? Bond can't do any fancy karate moves with the train going forty miles an hour, but he's holding his own, against this thing that's about twice his size. You know how big fuckin' ogres can get."

"Yeah, I sure as hell do. So do you, comes to that."

Karl Renfer took a sip of lightly microwaved Type A.

"What Bond doesn't know, cause he's facing the wrong way, is that the train's coming up fast on a tunnel…"

Police union rules say we're allowed one coffee break per shift, along with half an hour for dinner. Karl and I were taking the coffee break in our usual spot, Jerry's Diner, although I was the only one at our table actually drinking coffee – Karl's beverage preferences are a little different.

It was just past 1am. Being open twenty-four hours, Jerry's place gets a fair amount of undead trade, so the menu includes Type A, Type O, and an AB negative plasma that Karl says is overpriced. I was content – if that's the word – with a cup of the dark roast that Jerry's is infamous for. It's not too bad with cream and sugar – a *lot* of cream and sugar.

Yesterday had been our day off. Karl had spent part of it checking out the new James Bond movie, *Skyfang*, and I was half-listening while he told me about it.

I gathered that Daniel Craig was fast replacing Sean Connery as Karl's favorite actor to play Agent 007. I could see his point. Yeah, I watch those movies, too – but unlike Karl, I only see them once.

We agreed that Craig was the first actor to play the role who looked like he might actually *be* a professional killer – and that's what Bond is, when you get down to it. I've known a few real life-takers in my time, and thought that Craig had the attitude down cold, so to speak. Even if he did have a better tailor.

It was just another Wednesday night, maybe a little quieter than usual. But that was before those two fucking elves came in and started waving guns around.

One of them used a chair to climb onto a vacant table and started yelling, in that high voice they have, "Nobody move! Everybody freeze!"

Good luck with that, shorty. Instead of acting like statues, everybody in the diner turned to see who the hell was making all the noise. Maybe that's what the elf had really wanted, anyway.

He looked typical for the species – around 4'6", with the blond hair and pointed ears that they all have. I've seen a few try to pass for human by dying their hair and wearing it long enough to cover the ears, but they can't do much about the fact that elves are what the PC crowd calls "vertically impaired".

This one was wearing jeans and a gray sweatshirt that said "College Misericordia" on the front. The part of my mind that wasn't focused on the Colt Python he was holding in both hands wondered if he might've come by the shirt honestly.

Even if he had attended Misery – as everybody calls it – I assumed the elf was a dropout. College Misericordia doesn't graduate thieves – at least not deliberately. It's true there are quite a few lawyers and politicians among their alums, but you can't blame the college for that.

The elf's partner in crime was wearing a navy blue sport shirt and khakis. They fit him pretty well – you can find clothing in all sizes these days, from Pixie Extra Tiny to Ogre XXXXXL. This guy was pointing some kind of automatic at Donna, the cashier, who'd gone pale enough to pass for a vampire's girlfriend.

"Open the register!" the elf yelled. "Put the cash in this – just the bills, no coins!" He tossed her one of those fabric tote bags that the crunchy granola types do their grocery shopping with. Donna fumbled the catch, and the bag fell to the floor at her feet. I thought the elf was going to have a coronary. *"Pick it up, bitch!* Put the money in it quick, before I blow your fucking head off! *Do it!"*

His buddy was still on the table, sweeping the room back and forth with the barrel of that big pistol. The Python fires a .357 Magnum cartridge, and it's got quite a kick – I wondered if it had knocked the elf on his ass the first time he fired it. Assuming he ever *had* fired it.

"Hands on the table!" he screeched at the customers. "Nobody move!"

Even from twenty-some feet away, I could see that the elf's eyes were bloodshot and bulging. I wondered if there was something coursing through his system besides adrenaline. If he'd been human, I'd have figured him for an addict of some kind. But apart from the fucking goblins – who've shown an unfortunate fondness for meth – human recreational drugs don't have any effect on supernaturals. Just as well – some of them give us more than enough trouble as it is.

Donna had finally got all the cash from the register into the canvas bag. The elf snatched it out of her hands, then turned and trained his gun on the customers, just like his buddy on the table was doing.

"OK now, listen up!" Like we were gonna ignore him, under the circumstances. "I'm goin' around the room now. When I get to your table, the men are gonna reach for their wallets slow and put 'em in the bag here. Then the bitches are gonna dump their purses out on the table, so I can see what you got inside. Anybody doesn't do what they're told, or who gives me *any* shit – I am gonna fuckin' *kill* you and everybody with you, too!"

He glanced toward the other elf, who was still on the table, nervously traversing the room with his gun.

"You cool, man?"

I thought he looked about as calm as Jell-O in an earthquake.

"Yeah, I'm cool. Go get the fuckin' money. I gotcha covered."

I wondered just how often these two losers had watched *Red Pulp Fiction*. Quentin Tarantino's got a lot to answer for.

"What're you packing?" I murmured, just loud enough for Karl to hear me.

"Straight silver. You?"

"Silver and cold iron, mixed."

Silver bullets are good against some kinds of supes, like vamps and weres. But they're useless on any members of the faerie family – including goblins, trolls, orcs... and elves. Karl's gun would be useless if the shit hit the fan in the next few minutes.

Cold iron, on the other hand, will take out any member of the faerie clan. The mixed load in my Beretta meant I'd have to double-tap each elf, to make sure he'd catch a bullet that would hurt him.

But our situation here was kind of complicated.

Cops are expected to protect the public at all times. That's why we all pack a gun when we go out, even off-duty. But the public, especially the portion of it currently inside Jerry's Diner, wouldn't be well served by a bloodbath.

Being undead gave Karl an edge that the elves didn't know about. He's faster than a human, and he'd be invulnerable to the bullets in the elves' guns – assuming all they were packing was lead. But they might have loaded some silver rounds, too.

Since we didn't know what the elves' ammo was, the smart move was for Karl and me to sit there like chumps and let those two little fuckers rob us, instead of risking a gunfight with all these civilians so close.

But that posed a problem, too, and it was going to arise when the elf with the bag got to our table. Even if Karl and I were meek as mice, once we reached for our wallets the guns on our belts would become visible. God only knows what the elf, who was close to the edge already, would do when he saw our weapons. He might start shooting out of sheer panic.

Besides, anything somebody else did could set one of these twitchy bastards off – *anything*. One of the customers could sneeze, or faint, or scratch an itchy armpit. Even worse, somebody might get a phone call.

Karl and I were going to have to take action before something happened to push the situation out of control. We had to find some way to take these two assholes down, without anybody getting killed – especially us.

We didn't have long to think about it, either. The elf was just three tables away now.

Then inspiration struck. At least, I hoped it was inspiration and not a sudden attack of stupidity.

There were salt and pepper shakers on every table. When I was sure the two elves were looking elsewhere, I palmed the salt shaker and used my thumbnail to pry off the plastic stopper. About three ounces of salt flowed into my palm. I closed my fist, trying to hang on to as much of it as possible.

Some species of supes are repelled by salt. Others aren't. But nobody likes it you throw the stuff in their eyes.

I was looking at Karl again. Vampires have super-acute hearing, so I knew he'd hear me when I whispered, "Double play. When I say 'Please', take out the one on the table." Karl gave me a slight nod.

It wasn't long before the elf with the bag was standing in front of us. "Alright, come on, wallets," he said tightly. "In the fuckin' bag – let's go."

I slowly turned toward him, then made my face scrunch up like I was about to cry. Like a third-grader who's been called to the principal's office, I said, "Pleeease."

Before the elf could do more than gape at me, Karl's chair went over backwards as he came out of it vampire-fast. Half a second later, he was up on the table with the other elf before the little bastard even knew it.

The elf standing in front of me looked up toward his pal – he couldn't help himself. That's when I threw the fistful of salt into his eyes.

He screamed, dropped the bag, and brought his free hand up to cover his burning eyes. I reached over and grabbed his gun hand. Pointing the automatic away from me, I slammed his wrist down on the table, disarming him. With my other hand, I punched him in the throat.

I heard a scream from the other elf and looked up. Karl had the Magnum now, while the elf was holding his gun hand against his chest, moaning. No surprise there – a broken wrist hurts like hell.

My guy had gotten off easy. He was on the floor, eyes streaming, as he clutched his throat with both hands and tried to remember how to breathe.

I stood up and pulled out the leather folder holding my badge and ID. "Police officer! We're both police officers! Relax, folks, it's all over."

We read both prisoners their rights, put them in cuffs – much to the discomfort of the elf with the broken wrist. – and called for backup. I was going to be spending the rest of my shift back at the station house. I looked forward to interrogating these two idiots once they'd been processed into the system. I wanted to know why elves – who, despite being shiftless and stupid, are normally peaceful creatures – were trying to take down Jerry's Diner.

I never did finish my coffee. Small loss, really.

The paramedics checked both suspects out at the scene. With my guy, they gently rinsed his eyes with a boric acid solution, determined that he was breathing OK, and declared him fit to be arrested. The other elf's wrist was broken, just as I'd figured. One of the EMTs put an inflatable cast on it and politely asked Karl not to handcuff that arm again. So the two of them went off to Mercy Hospital's ER together, the elf's undamaged wrist cuffed to one of Karl's.

Karl hadn't complained about taking the damaged elf to the hospital. He wouldn't be allowed to take part in any interrogation, anyway. The Supreme Court had ruled in *Barlow v. Maine* almost forty years ago that anything a suspect said in the presence of a vampire – police officer or not – was inadmissible, since there was no way to establish whether vampiric Influence was used to induce cooperation.

Cops have learned to be careful about this kind of stuff. Nobody wants to see some scumbag's conviction overturned because his lawyer claims there was a vampire three doors down the hall while the scumbag was answering questions.

That meant the other elf was all mine – sort of. The Scranton PD policy says that no detective is ever supposed to be alone in an interrogation room with a suspect. A lot of other police departments around the country have the same rule. In years past, some cops had been careless or stupid and actually been taken hostage by supposedly harmless prisoners. So now you're supposed to have at least two detectives present to carry out an interrogation.

Since Karl was at the hospital with the elf he'd maimed, I'd have to get another detective to join me while I talked to our suspect, who hadn't yet asked for a lawyer. His name was Thorontur Carnesin, according to his driver's license.

Yeah, lots of them have driver's licenses. You won't be surprised to learn that they mostly drive subcompacts.

When I looked inside the Occult Crimes squad room, the only detective around was Marty Sefchik. I knew his shift would start in about an hour – which was when his partner, Carmela Aquilina, usually showed up. Unlike Carmela, Sefchik often came in early. I heard he and his wife didn't get along so well.

Sefchik was looking at the early edition of the *Times-Tribune*, but he looked up when I appeared in the squad room door.

"Hey, Stan, what's up? I hear you and Karl almost got taken off the count by a couple of fuckin' trolls with slingshots or something."

"They were doing a little better than slingshots, asshole," I told him. "One had a 9mm Walther, and the other bastard was packing a Colt Python."

He whistled. "Serious iron."

"Uh-huh. And they were elves, not trolls."

"Get the fuck outta here – elves? When did *they* get all badass?"

"I don't know, but I was just about to ask one that very question. Wanna sit in?"

"Fuck, yeah. Gotta be more fun than the paper."

"Almost anything is. OK, come on."

The interrogation rooms are ten feet by ten, with furniture consisting of a scarred wooden table and a few beat-up chairs. A big iron ring is screwed onto the top of each table, and a suspect under interrogation gets one wrist handcuffed to the ring. Having a hand free allows the suspect to write or hold paperwork, but makes it pretty hard to commit mayhem. And that table is bolted to the floor.

Thorontur Carnesin had been sitting bent over, with his head resting in the crook of his shackled arm. But he sat up quick enough when we came in. Sefchik and I each pulled up a chair across the table from him.

The elf didn't look too good. I wasn't surprised that he had the reddest eyes this side of Transylvania – not after the salt I'd thrown in his face. But he was sweating, and it wasn't warm in the room, which gets AC pumped in just like the rest of the building. I also noticed some tremor in his hands that hadn't been present in the diner. Otherwise, he wouldn't have been able to hold the damn gun steady.

If this had been a human, I'd have said he was strung out – needing a fix of something and needing it bad. But supes don't do drugs. Give or take the fucking goblins.

"How ya doin?" I said. "We've met before, although we weren't introduced. I'm Detective Sergeant Markowski, and this is Detective Sefchik."

"Yeah, hi," the elf said. His right hand actually moved a couple of inches from the shackle, as if he'd intended to shake hands. I guess he bore no ill will for what happened in Jerry's Diner.

The fact his right hand was shackled meant he was a leftie, like a lot of elves are. We always leave their pen hand free, in case they feel like writing a confession.

"You've been advised of your rights," I said. "I know that, since I'm the one who did it. You understand that you don't have to talk to us without a lawyer present."

"Yeah, yeah," he said. "I know. It's cool."

"Your name's Thorontur," I said.

"Yeah."

"People call you 'Thor'?"

"Yeah – how'd you know?"

"Lucky guess," I said. "Mind if we call you that? It's less of a mouthful than 'Thorontur'."

"Yeah, sure. Whatever. Listen, dude, you gotta–"

"Don't call me 'dude'. It's 'Detective'," I said.

"OK, sorry. Thing is, I'm feelin' real bad, OK? I gotta see a doc, have him give me somethin'."

"We might be able to help you with that," Sefchik said. "But, we call a doctor, you know, first thing he's gonna ask is what's wrong with the patient. So, how're you feeling bad, exactly? You got the flu, or something?"

"Naw, it ain't that. I need some meds, you know?"

A junkie. The little bastard was acting just like a human going through withdrawal. And that just wasn't possible.

"What kind of medication are we talkin' about, Thor?" I said. "You under a doctor's care right now?"

"No, dude," he said. "It's just that–"

My right palm slapped the table, hard. *"I told you not to call me 'dude'. I'm not gonna tell you again."*

Thor jumped a little, which is what I'd intended. "Sorry, uh, Detective," he said. "I didn't mean nothin' by it. It's just how I talk, you know?"

"Not in here, you don't," I said.

I was acting like a real hardass because I wanted psychological domination over this guy. Something very fucked up was going on here, and I wanted to know everything about it. Everything.

"Yeah, OK, Detective. Whatever you want."

"I'm glad to hear you say that, Thor. Because what I *want* to know is what's up with you, and I want it without a lot of bullshit."

I sat back in my chair to give him a little space.

"You claim you need some kind of medication," I said. "What exactly is it you think you need – and why?"

"Hell, I don't know the scientific name, or nothing, man – uh, Detective. We call it Slide."

"We? Who's *we*?"

"Me and Car. And some other dudes we know."

"Car's the guy who was with you in the diner tonight? The one standing on the table?"

"Yeah, that's him."

"What his real name?"

"Caranthir Helyanwe. But most of us just call him Car."

"So, you and 'Car' and your buddies take this stuff called 'Slide'," I said, "and now you're *hooked* on it?"

Drug-addicted elves. *Shit.*

"Nah, I ain't hooked on nothing. I can quit whenever I want."

The elf even *talked* like a fucking junkie.

"OK, you can quit whenever you want," Sefchik said. "So why don't you just quit it now?"

Thor licked his lips. "It ain't that I *need* it, OK? But I ain't had any in a while. I just *like* the stuff – that's all."

"A *while* – how long ago is that, exactly?" I asked. "When did you last have some of this Slide?"

The tongue ran over his cracked lips again. "I dunno. Couple days ago, I guess."

"And you like this stuff so much," Sefchik said, "that you and your buddy were willing to stick up a fucking diner just to get money for some?"

Another shrug. "Slide ain't cheap."

"What's it do for you, anyway?" I asked him.

He looked at me as if I'd just spoken in Polish. "Say what?"

"He means," Sefchik said, "How do you feel when you're using it?"

"It hits you in, like two stages, man… uh, Detective. At first, it's like fireworks are goin' off inside your head, you know? There's flashes of light, all different colors – some that ain't even been invented yet."

"How long does that usually last?" Sefchik asked.

"Oh, m… Detective, I don't fuckin' *know*. I never looked at my watch – hell, I probably couldn't have seen it, anyway, with all the colors goin' off inside my head."

"So, there's two stages," I said. "What happens after the flashing lights?"

"After that, you just feel gooood, you know? All relaxed and happy and shit. It's like you just got laid, but about ten times better."

"And how long does that go on for?" I asked him.

"Like I already told you–"

"I know," I said. "You don't check your watch. But give me a ballpark estimate – an hour, three hours, half a day, all day?"

He wiped a shaky hand over his face. "I dunno, maybe three hours, could be a little more. But that's about right, I guess."

Sefchik frowned. "How much per pop?"

"Twenty-five bucks."

"How do you take it?" I asked him.

Thor turned his sweaty face toward me. "Huh?"

I will not hit the suspect in the head. I will not hit the suspect in the head.

"Do you snort the shit, inject it, smoke it, stuff it up your ass – what?" I said.

"Me and Car mostly smoke it," he said. "But I know a couple guys who say snortin' gives you a bigger blast. I dunno; I never tried it that way. Look – can you guys, uh, Detectives help me out here? I need to see a doc pretty bad. I feel like I'm gonna jump out of my fuckin' skin or something."

I got to my feet. "Detective Sefchik and I are gonna step outside for a couple of minutes."

Sefchik stood up too and followed me to the door.

"You guys gonna call the doctor?" Thor asked. The need in his voice was unmistakable.

"We'll think about it," I said.

"Cause if you ain't, then I want a fuckin' *lawyer* in here! *He'll* get me to a doc. This is fucking inhumane treatment! I got my–"

Then we were in the hall, and I closed the door behind us, cutting off Thor in mid-rant. Sefchik looked at me, his face a study in disbelief.

"Elf junkies?" he said. "Is this asshole fucking *kidding*?"

"Does he *look* like he's kidding?"

Sefchik shook his head a couple of times. "I knew fucking gobs could get hooked on meth, and that's bad enough – but elves? What's next – werewolves shooting heroin? Vamps on speed? Makes my head hurt, just tryin' to think about it."

"Yeah, I know just what you mean."

"So, why'd you take a break?" he asked me. "Just want to vent a little? Not that I blame you."

"Nothing wrong with venting," I said. "But the main reason is I have to make a phone call, and I don't want my man Thor listening in on it."

I pushed a button on my speed dial, and a few seconds later Karl's voice said in my ear, "Hey, Stan."

"Hey," I said. "Where are you?"

"We're still in the waiting room at the ER. You know how it is – they give you a quick once-over, and if you're not actually dying, you can go sit and wait for a few hours. I figure an elf's busted wrist isn't real high on their priority list tonight."

"There's a couple of things I'd like you to do while you're down there."

"Like what?"

"When they finally get your little buddy into a treatment room, make sure the docs get a blood sample and send it to the lab."

"Lookin' for what, exactly?"

"I don't know," I said. "Anything that shouldn't be in an elf's blood, I guess."

"I'll take care of it. What else you need?"

"Since you're gonna be waiting a while, why don't you ask your pal about something called Slide."

"What the fuck's that?"

"I'm not positive, but I think it might be a drug that elves can get hooked on."

"Well, fuck me," Karl said. "You sure about this stuff?"

"No, I'm not. That's why I want you to talk to Car about it. You know that's his name, right?"

"Yeah, he told me. Guess he got tired of me saying, 'Hey, you'."

"Later on, I want to compare whatever you get from him with what I already heard from his partner, Thor."

"*Thor*, you said? Like that old pixie joke, 'I'm tho thor, I can hardly pith'?"

"That's the one. And listen, if you have to use a little vampire mojo to get him talking about Slide, that's OK."

"Seriously? I don't even know if it'll work, Stan – but if it does, anything I get from him's gonna be inadmissible in court. You know that."

"Doesn't matter. I don't want this for the DA's office – I want it for me, so I can maybe figure out what the fuck is going on here."

"OK, I'll see what I can do. We're gonna be here a while, anyway."

"Good. Besides, if Influence doesn't get you anywhere, you can always flash your fangs at him."

"I'll keep that in reserve, just in case."

I checked my watch: 4.22. Sunrise would be about ten after seven.

"Listen, if you're still there an hour from now, give me a call," I said. "I'll bring one of the other detectives over, or even a uniform, if I have to. He can take over custody of Car, and I'll give you a ride back here, so you can head home in time."

"Thanks, Stan, I appreciate it."

"No problem. OK, I gotta go back and see Thor. He was yelling about a lawyer when I left him, and I sure wouldn't want to violate his constitutional rights by denying him timely access to counsel."

"Heaven forbid. Alright, I'll talk to you later, dude."

"Don't call me dude."

Thor was as good as his word. Once he was sure I wasn't going to bring in a doctor to give him a hit of Slide, he clammed up and demanded a lawyer.

I took him back down to Booking, where they'd put him in a holding cell and give him a phone, just like the law requires. I was pretty sure that once his lawyer got here, Thor wasn't going to be nearly as chatty as he had been upstairs.

If Thor was a human going through withdrawal from heroin, a doctor might actually have do him some good – and we'd provide one. That's the law, too. Some junkie bouncing off the walls because his dopamine receptor cells were going crazy wasn't exactly a new phenomenon around here.

A doc wouldn't give a prisoner any heroin, but a dose of methadone wasn't out of the question, or maybe a strong sedative. Even if we had a fucking goblin going nuts because he can't get any of the meth he's hooked on – the medical community knows how to handle that, too.

But an addicted elf? Hooked on a drug that nobody's ever *heard* of? No doctor could be sure that any drug he gave Thor might not interact with the stuff already in his system and kill the little bastard. So Thor was going to have to sweat it out, literally, until a specialist in elf medicine could get a look at him.

I went back to the squad room and got started on the paperwork stemming from the arrest of the two elves at the diner. I was almost done when Karl called around 5.30, saying he was still stuck at Mercy's ER. Car hadn't even made it into a treatment room yet.

"OK, I'll find somebody to take over for you," I said. "We oughta be there in ten, fifteen minutes."

"Roger that." Karl loves that kind of talk.

Sefchik had started his shift by now, and he and Aquilina were out on the street somewhere. But McLane and Pearce were in the squad room, drinking coffee and waiting to handle the next call that came in. Lieutenant McGuire was in his glass-enclosed office at the back, and I told him that Karl was stuck over at the ER with sunrise fast approaching. McGuire said I could run over there and take one of the other detectives with me to relieve Karl.

Ten minutes later, Pearce was at the ER, handcuffed to Car, and Karl was riding shotgun in my Toyota Lycan as I headed back to the station house. I had a lot to tell him. Turned out, he had a few items for me, too.

••••

When I finished telling Karl about my interview with Thor, I said, "If I hadn't seen it with my own eyes, I'd have said it was bullshit. But there he was, right in front of me – an elf who was obviously strung out on *something*."

"I think you're being too hard on yourself, Stan. You were going on what you'd been taught at the academy, and they taught me the same thing: supes don't get hooked on drugs, apart from goblins, I mean. Now it looks like some motherfucker has come up with a new kind of drug, and that throws all the old knowledge into the wastebasket."

"A game changer," I said.

"Uh-huh – like the old game wasn't tough enough already." Karl shook his head. "Well, I got a couple of things from talking to my buddy Car that I can add, and one of them's gonna blow your mind. I know it did mine."

"I can hardly wait," I said.

"I'll start with the other one. Car told me that there's another street name for Slide, and he thinks this one came first. He says some of his homies call it HG."

I didn't take my eyes off the road to stare at him, but I wanted to. "HG," I said. "Seriously."

"That's what Car said."

"It sounds like some old-time movie director – *Ready when you are, HG!*"

"Turns out, I can give you a better idea of its etymology," Karl said.

"Etymology."

"Yeah – it means the study of word origins."

I looked sideways at him. "You been looking at those copies of *Reader's Digest* I keep in my desk?"

I saw his shrug from the corner of my eye. "I sneak one every once in a while."

"OK," I said. "So, enlighten me as to the, uh…"

"Etymology."

"Yeah. The etymology of 'HG'.'"

"Car says he's pretty sure it stands for 'Hemoglobin-Plus', on account of hemoglobin being the basic ingredient."

"Hemoglobin plus *what*?" I asked him.

"Car didn't know. He says nobody does."

"With a guy like Car," I said, "*nobody* probably consists of him and three other losers like him."

"Probably. We're gonna have to start working our street contacts, see if somebody out there knows more about this stuff."

"OK, so the name is one piece of news," I said. "What's the other item – the one that's gonna blow my mind?"

"Thing is, it could be just bullshit – considering Car was the source and all."

"Fine – I'll keep that in mind. It might keep my skull from imploding. So what *is* it?"

"Car says he knows a vampire who's hooked on the shit, too."

With dawn coming soon, Karl had to split as soon as we pulled into the parking lot behind the station house. My shift was over, too, but I still went inside to see McGuire.

I told him what Karl and I had learned from the two junkie elves. He was as disbelieving as I'd been, at first. But he agreed with me that it was something the unit needed to know more about. He said each shift of detectives would be told to ask their snitches about Slide and exactly who might be addicted to it.

When I got home, Christine's car was parked in the driveway. Since the sun was already well above the horizon, I knew she'd be in her basement bedroom by now, wrapped in a sleeping bag and literally dead to the world until dusk. I'd talk to her then.

I went upstairs and traded my detective outfit for a sweatshirt and jeans. Time was, I'd head off to sleep right after getting home from work, but lately I've got into the habit of unwinding for an hour before I go to bed. I have fewer nightmares that way.

I went into the spare bedroom and checked on my hamster, Quincey. His water bottle was mostly full, but the bowl was empty. I filled it with food pellets and put it back in his cage. That woke him up – hamsters are nocturnal, just like vampires and some cops I know. When he came over to the bowl, I rubbed his head with my index finger for a little while. He likes that.

Then I went to sleep – and had bad dreams anyway.

When Christine came upstairs, I was in the kitchen, eating some scrambled eggs. "Morning, honey," I said.

"Good morning, Daddy."

It wasn't morning, but we'd agreed that starting the day with "Good evening" sounded stupid – especially when I said it using my Bela Lugosi imitation.

Christine wore the outfit she usually slept in – sweatpants and a T-shirt. Today the shirt said in front, "Thousands of vampires go to bed hungry." As she went to the fridge, I saw that the back read, "Give generously when the vampire comes to your ~~door~~ window."

She got at least a dozen different "vampire-centric" shirts, and I'd asked her once where she bought them. She'd given me a wink and said, "The Sharper Image catalog, of course."

Christine got a bottle of Type A from the refrigerator, pried off the cap, and put it in the microwave to warm up. Then she sat down and poured the contents into the mug I'd put on the table for her, along with a placemat and napkin. Setting the table for a vampire is pretty uncomplicated, but I knew she appreciated the gesture.

"So how was work?" she asked, taking her first sip.

"Depends on what part you mean," I said. "Do you wanna hear about how Karl and I almost got held up by elves, or about when it got *really* weird?"

Her eyes widened a little. "Goodness," she said. "You mean I have to choose?"

"Naw, I'm having a sale tonight – two for the price of one."

"Hmmm," she said. "And what *is* the price?"

"Your opinion, when I'm done."

"You've got yourself a deal, Sergeant. Go for it."

So I told her about my shift, starting with when the two elves hit Jerry's Diner. Eventually, I got around to the new street drug, Slide.

The look she gave me when I finished was as skeptical as McGuire's had been – not that I blamed her.

"A drug that addicts supes..." She'd picked up that term from me and used it freely, even though some supernaturals consider it a slur. Christine knows I don't mean anything by it.

"That's what it looks like," I said.

"I knew about the goblins and meth, of course," she said with a frown. "I'm not likely to forget, after a bunch of them came over here to kill you a while back."

"That's over and done," I said. "And anyway, things didn't work out too well for the gobs that night."

"Just as well," she said. "Little green bastards."

"I never thought it possible that other species of supes could become drug addicts," I said. "But I trust the evidence of my own eyes."

"I trust your eyes, too," she said, "but, for gosh sake... So this stuff affects both elves *and* vampires?"

"The vampire angle's just hearsay, for the moment. It came from that asshole Car, and I'm not sure I'd trust him if he said bats fly at night. But elves... yeah, I'd say that's a certainty."

She drained the mug and put it down. "Goblins and elves are both part of the faerie family. Think there's a connection there? Some kind of genetic thing?"

"Your guess is as good as mine," I said. "And for the moment, guesses are all I've got."

"I don't imagine that state of affairs will continue for very long – now that Detective Sergeant Markowski is on the case."

Some of that was kidding, but only some. Despite knowing me better than anyone alive – or undead – my vampire daughter seems to think I'm pretty cool. How many dads can say *that*?

"So," I said, "I take it that this is the first time you've heard about this HG stuff?"

"Absolutely. There hasn't been even a whisper. What's HG stand for, again? Hemoglobin-something?"

"Hemoglobin-Plus, according to the elf."

"Plus what?"

"That's the mystery, or one of them. It must be something pretty potent, since hemoglobin all by itself isn't addictive to anybody."

"Well, it is to *me*," she said.

"Fuck that. You're talking about nourishment, honey. Calling blood addictive to vampires is like saying humans are addicted to food. I mean, in a literal sense I guess that's true – without it, we'd die."

"The ultimate withdrawal pang."

"It's still not the same," I said.

She laughed softly.

I looked at her. "What?"

"Stan Markowski, once the scourge of the undead from Scranton to Shickshinny, defending vampirism. There was a time when you didn't talk like that."

I turned my head and looked out at the night that was pressing against the window. "There was a time when I didn't know better."

After finishing my eggs, I said, "I'd appreciate it if you'd ask around the… community about this HG shit when you have a chance."

"I'll be happy to," she said. "But if somebody's actually using this stuff, it's pretty unlikely they're gonna just admit it – at least to me."

"Maybe not, but it could be somebody heard about another vampire getting hooked on this stuff. You know people like to gossip."

"And vampires, like corporations, are people, too," she said, giving me a toothy smile.

"Yeah," I said, "but a lot more talkative."

On the way to work, I passed a couple of new billboards that had gone up just since yesterday. One said "SLATTERY FOR MAYOR" and, underneath that, "The man for REAL change." Three blocks farther on, another billboard reminded me that six of the eight people sitting on the City Council were up for reelection this year, too. But the ad wasn't paid for by them, even though they were shown in it. The faces of all six were lined up in a row, each with a red X across it. Below that, in big red letters, it said, "THROW THE BUMS OUT!"

I thought that was strange, since I was pretty sure that four of the councilors running for re-election were Democrats and the other two were Republicans. Who would call members of their own party bums?

Then I got a little closer and saw the smaller print saying that the billboard was brought to us courtesy of the fine folks at the Patriot Party. Now it made sense.

The Patriot Party didn't like anybody – except for fellow Patriots, that is. They were new on the local scene, and while I don't usually pay much attention to politics, I knew that the Patriot Party combined fiscal conservatism with a social agenda that some people found kind of disturbing. They were backing Philip Slattery for the mayor's seat, and supporting a whole slate of candidates for City Council.

Everybody wants lower taxes, including me. That's just what the Patriots promised – I think they wanted to cut the property tax rate in half. That would make a lot of people happy, but the big drop in revenue which would require serious cuts in city services.

The Patriots were fine with that, especially if the services that got cut involved poor people, unwed mothers, or people with substance abuse problems. Supporters of the Patriot Party apparently believed that poor people deserved to be poor, unwed mothers were sluts, and drunks and druggies had brought their problems on themselves and shouldn't expect taxpayers to help them cope.

The Patriots also weren't real fond of gays, and they were especially down on supes. Their members contained quite a few Bible-thumpers, who had declared supes to be "abominations before the Lord". They usually accompanied this claim with a bunch of quotes from the Old Testament – like the one from Exodus that says, "Thou shalt not suffer a witch to live."

But some other members of the Patriot Party made a more legalistic argument. They said that a "citizen" was defined someplace as "a man or woman living under a particular legal jurisdiction". Since supes weren't human, their argument went, they couldn't be considered citizens and therefore had no basis to claim civil rights.

I wondered if that meant supes didn't have to pay taxes, either. Karl and Christine would love that part of the program, if not the rest of it.

The PP seemed to have money to spare, considering how many billboards and commercials they'd bought. There was even a Super PAC, the Coalition for American Morality or something, that was running TV and radio ads in support of the Patriots, and putting out some other ads that said some real nasty things about Mayor D'Agostino and the incumbent City Council members.

Fucking politicians.

When I got to the squad room, Karl wasn't at his desk. That was unusual, since he usually gets in before I do. Then I saw him standing in the doorway of McGuire's office, talking to the boss. Karl looked my way for a moment and I heard him tell McGuire, "Here he is." Then he closed McGuire's door and headed my way, walking fast.

When he reached me I asked, "Something up?"

"Not much – just a war. Come on, let's go."

House of God.

That's what they call it – the Catholics do, anyway. Considering how many churches there are around the world, God's got more houses than Donald Trump.

St. Mark's Church towered over its South Side neighborhood like a skyscraper over a bunch of mud huts. As usual, God had used an architect who thought big and liked stone.

I wondered if He'd looked out the front window recently. Was He pissed that a little piece of Hell had been left within a hundred feet of His front door? Could be that He was amused. They say that God created everything – and I guess that means He made irony, too.

Karl and I made our slow way down the middle of the street, trying not to step in any of the blood. At least we didn't have to worry about traffic, since both ends of the block were closed off by police barriers. Behind the yellow sawhorses, reporters screamed for access, forensic techs waited impatiently, and neighbors just stared in shock and disbelief. It was a typical crime scene – even if this particular crime was anything but typical.

Even though it had been dark for hours, everybody could still get a good look at the carnage. The forensics people had set up enough lights for a film set. Difference was, these actors weren't getting up for another take, no matter who yelled "Action!"

I looked over my shoulder and said quietly to Karl, "You doing OK?"

He nodded. "Yeah, I had something before coming on shift."

I'd been a concerned that he might be feeling edgy. Some vampires get that way in the presence of a lot of fresh blood – although Karl was used to it. He'd been to a lot of crime scenes.

Our slow progress eventually brought us to the tall man in the black raincoat. He stood, hands in his coat pockets, staring at one of the bodies as if he was trying to memorize it. He didn't look up as we approached. Lieutenants don't have to show up at crime scenes, but Scanlon does anyway. I think he likes it.

"Evening, Scanlon." He outranks me but doesn't act like it, usually. I used to work Homicide, and even though I've been in Occult Crimes for years, we still run into each other at crime scenes – especially those with a body count as high as this one.

Scanlon slowly turned toward me. "Stan." He looked over my shoulder, nodded, and said, "Karl."

"Lieutenant." Karl doesn't have the long history with Scanlon that I do, so he keeps it formal, usually.

I made a gesture with my chin toward one of the bodies. "They all vampires?"

"That's what my guys tell me. Once I noticed one body had fangs, I had them check all the others."

"No wood, though," Karl said. "Did you notice?" We both looked at him. "No arrows," Karl said, "or crossbow bolts, or any of the other things most people use to kill the bloodsucking undead at night, when they're not lying helpless."

They, I noticed, not *we*. But the way he'd said "bloodsucking undead" showed that he wasn't completely indifferent to what had happened. Karl's what you might call conflicted.

"Silver bullets for all of them, you figure?" I said.

"That, or maybe charcoal," Scanlon said. "We had a guy use a charcoal slug on a vampire last year, remember?"

"Forensics will tell us about the bullets," I said. "But there's something else I noticed."

Now I was the focus of attention.

"A couple of them are lying on their backs, and I recognize the faces," I said. "Both members of the Calabrese Family."

Scanlon made a disgusted sound. "Fangsters. Jesus."

"Looks like somebody set up an ambush with the Calabrese guys as the guests of honor," I said. "They got hurt pretty bad tonight."

"It wasn't a shutout, though," Karl said.

I turned toward him. "What?"

"One of these dead guys is wearing thin latex gloves," he said.

"Paranoid about leaving his prints?" Scanlon said.

"Could be," Karl said. "Or maybe he was part of the ambush and figured he'd have to reload eventually." Karl made a grimace that briefly displayed his fangs. "The bloodsucking undead don't handle silver bullets too well."

Scanlon looked from Karl to me. "Vampires... ambushing vampires?"

"Makes a certain amount of sense," I said. "Word on the street these last few weeks is that a gang from out of town had its eyes on the Calabrese territory. I figured if the rumors were true, it was only a matter of time before the new guys tried what you might call a hostile takeover."

Scanlon's head did a slow pan, taking in the crime scene and the six dead men it contained, all of whom had probably died tonight for the second time.

"A vampire gang war," he said. "Just what we fucking need."

I shrugged. "Could be worse."

He looked at me, eyebrows raised. "Yeah? How?"

"I'll have to get back to you on that."

Back in the car, Karl said, "Looks like the new kids in the neighborhood don't play nice."

"No, but they're playing to win," I said. "A couple more nights like tonight, and Calabrese is gonna start running out of soldiers."

"You heard anything about where these new guys're from?"

"Nothing I'm willing to put any faith in," I said. "One guy I talked to last week said he thought it was Philly – but it turns out that it was something he got from his cousin, who heard it from some other guy, who was banging a girl who once knew somebody who lived in Philly. Or something like that. You know how it goes."

"Confidential informants – you gotta love 'em," Karl said.

"Not when they only have shit to tell me, I don't. If we're gonna find out what's going on, we better get a little closer to the source."

"So, we going to see Calabrese?"

I thought about that. "No, not tonight. After what happened to his crew, he'll be hiding out for a while."

"Hiding out?" Karl showed his fangs in a grin. "Don Pietro Calabrese, *capo di tutti vampiri*, hiding from his enemies like a rabbit cowering in his hole? Say it ain't so, Stan."

"That's not what Calabrese will call it," I said. "He'll say he's gathering his forces, or planning strategy, or maybe even going to the fucking mattresses. Do wiseguys still say that?"

"Beats me," he said. "All I know about the Mafia, I learned from Francis Ford Coppola. If I wanted to mess around with those guys, I'd be in Organized Crime."

"Well, since Calabrese is likely to be unavailable for a while," I said, "we oughta pay a call on Victor Castle."

Although Pietro Calabrese was the Godfather of the local vampire "family", the wizard Victor Castle was the unofficial head of the city's whole supernatural community. I was never clear on exactly how he got the job – was there an election, or a vicious power struggle, or did Castle simply have better magic than anybody else who wanted the job?

Before Castle, the position of local "supefather" had been held for a long time by an old vampire/

wizard named Vollman. But he'd died last year, at the hands of his own son.

Victor Castle has a lot of business interests in town, but he usually hangs out at the rug store he owns on the west side. Like a lot of businesses, Magic Carpets, Mystic Rugs was usually open at night, catering to customers who didn't come out during daylight hours.

When we walked into the store, Castle greeted us himself instead of sending one of his flunkies. Apart from the expensive suit he wore, the man who'd come into this world as Vittorio Castellino didn't look much like the big deal he apparently was. Average height or a little less, bit of a gut on him, and a lot of bald scalp glistening in the overhead lights.

Castle never seemed to know what to do with his hands. As we approached, he was fiddling with the large gold signet ring he wore on his right pinky finger. I never knew whether the ring was some kind of badge of office or just something that Castle wore as a complement to his thousand-dollar suits.

"Sergeant Markowski," Castle said. "Good evening." He turned to Karl and with a slight nod said, "Detective." There was usually a hint of tension between those two, and most of it originated with Karl. My partner was a vampire, but he was a cop first. I figured Karl was reluctant to pay homage to a guy who he might have to arrest someday.

Castle studied us for a couple of seconds, turning the ring around and around. Then he said, "Why don't we talk in my office?"

Castle's inner sanctum was done in dark wood, including a huge desk that looked like it might have been real mahogany. Rugs, rolled up and tied tight, were standing in three of the corners, and fabric samples of different sizes were tacked to each of the walls. Larger carpet samples, about a foot square, were stacked all around the room.

Despite the general sloppiness of the office, Castle's desk was nearly immaculate. All that rested on it were a fancy-looking clock encased in Lucite, a closed ledger, and one of those Tiffany-style desk lamps that provided the only light in the room.

A couple of comfortable-looking chairs faced the desk, and Castle gestured for us to sit down. Then he plopped into his leather desk chair and said, "And what can I do for the Occult Crime Unit this evening?"

It's been well established that human pupils dilate in response to sudden emotional change, and I was watching Castle's eyes closely as I said, "It's about HG."

All that got me was a frown of perplexity that might even have been genuine. His pupils didn't change at all.

"Since you seem intent on being mysterious," Castle said, "I'll have to ask you what *HG* refers to, Sergeant."

"It's the street name for a new drug," Karl told him. "It's short for 'Hemoglobin-Plus'."

Castle's heavy eyebrows nearly came together as he frowned. "Plus what?"

"That's the secret ingredient," I said. "At least, it's a secret for now. I take it all this is news to you."

"You're quite correct," Castle said. "But why are you asking me about some street drug? Humans become addicted to such things, not supernaturals – well apart from those degenerate goblins, and I think we've just about got that under control now."

"That's what we used to think, too," I told him. "But the evidence of our own eyes, along with a couple of interrogations, says that at least one species of supernatural is capable of getting hooked on the stuff."

"That's very interesting," Castle said, the way you do when humoring somebody. He was looking at me as if I'd just told him that I'd seen a six-foot cockroach walking down Mulberry Street, wearing an evening gown and playing the bagpipes.

Castle's gaze went to Karl – maybe to check whether he was smiling at what might be a tall tale. "What species are we talking about, exactly?"

"Elves," Karl said. "Two that we know about for sure, anyway."

We told Castle about how our coffee break the night before had been rudely interrupted by two elves packing heat, and what followed afterward. It took a while.

When Karl and I were done, there was a silence in the room so total that I could hear the electric clock on the desk ticking. Finally, Castle said, "I can think of no reason why the two of you would concoct a story like that. So I am inclined to take your account at face value."

"That's good to hear," I said. "I'd hate to think we've been wasting our time – not to mention yours."

"We're not kidding around," Karl said. "You're right that we've got no reason to do that. But if it *was* all a big joke, I'd say you haven't heard the punch line yet."

"Really?" Castle looked like a man who was developing a bad headache. "Then by all means deliver it, Detective."

Karl leaned forward a little. "There's an unconfirmed report that at least one vampire is hooked on the stuff, too."

Castle just looked at him. "Cross-species addiction," he said softly. Then in a normal voice, he told us, "I was about to say, as a reflex, that such a thing is impossible. But then, until a few minutes ago, I would have held that drug-addicted elves were an impossibility, too." It looked like Castle's headache had taken a turn for the worse.

He sat there for a little while, staring at the banker's lamp and drumming his fingers softly on the desk. Then, without taking his eyes off the lamp, he said, "What you've said concerns me on two different levels. One is the idea of a drug-addicted supernatural species other than goblins. My second concern is that until you officers told me, I had heard absolutely *nothing* about this."

"Could be that none of the junkies have been driven to crime before," I said. "Last night could've been the first time – hell, it must have been, otherwise *I* would've heard something."

"You don't understand, Sergeant," Castle said. "It doesn't matter whether last night's incident was the first or the hundredth. If elves are getting addicted to this 'HG', then I should have known about it before it resulted in armed robbery. I am *supposed* to know – I am *boyar*."

"Is that your title?" I said. "Some cops refer to you as the 'supefather'."

He smiled with half his mouth. "The Mafia term? Well, I suppose it's not a bad analogy, as long as you keep in mind that the supernatural community is not made up of..." He let his voice trail off.

"Criminals?" Karl said.

"Yes, Detective," Castle said, with a little more force in his voice. "Even if some of our number may have committed unlawful acts, they are *not* representative of our community."

"Hell, I know that," I told him. "If all the supernaturals, or even most of them, weren't law-abiding citizens, there'd be chaos in this city. My job would be impossible."

"Thank you for that," Castle said. He sounded less pissed off as he said, "I should not speak of this to outsiders, but you two already know so much, it seems pointless to conceal the rest from you." He folded his hands over his stomach and tilted the chair back a little.

"The fact is," Castle said, "there have been subtle challenges to my leadership lately. Nothing concrete, no overt defiance. And yet, sometimes when I give orders they are not obeyed or not carried out correctly. There are always excuses, of course. No one meant to disobey my commands, there was a misunderstanding, amends will be made, and so forth. And yet..." He shook his head.

"Once is happenstance," Karl quoted. "Twice is coincidence. The third time, it's enemy action."

Castle looked at him. "Oh, that's right. The James Bond fan. It may surprise you, detective, but I also have read the works of Mister Ian Fleming. Mostly, I regard them as light entertainment, but sometimes, as in your present example..." The fingers were drumming again, softly as tears falling on a coffin. "Sometimes, they contain words of wisdom."

The rest of our shift was fairly quiet, which gave Karl and me some time to talk with McGuire and the other detectives passing through about the latest scourge to afflict our fair city.

I may be the last person alive to refer to Scranton as "our fair city," and even *I* don't mean it. Well, not really.

I got McGuire's OK to knock off a little early, since I wanted to talk to Christine before she went downstairs for the day – I was hoping she might have found out something about vampires using HG. But I didn't get to talk to her – not that night.

It wasn't really my fault. I'm a cop – what am if I supposed to do if I'm driving home from work and hear the rattle of gunfire a few blocks away?

I arrived on the scene a few minutes later. Leaving my car around the corner from where the action seemed to be, I got out and tried to creep close enough to see what was going on without being either spotted or shot. This was a neighborhood full of warehouses, so I wasn't surprised that a 911 call hadn't already brought other cops to the scene.

It was still dark enough for me to see muzzle flashes, even though dawn was less than a half hour away. There seemed to be four guns involved. Three of them, located in different places around the street, were firing at a big car parked at the opposite curb. Somebody crouching behind that car was responsible for the fourth series of muzzle flashes. I couldn't see more, because the street lights in this area had been shot out long ago.

When I'm working, Karl and I keep a selection of special equipment and weapons in the unmarked police vehicle we use. But I don't carry any of that stuff in my personal vehicle, because I don't expect to get into gunfights when I'm off duty. One thing I do keep in there, however, is a set of night-vision binoculars. A lot of supes see real well in the dark, and I hate to be at a disadvantage, even when I'm not expected to be out enforcing law and order.

I ran back to the car, opened the trunk, and took out the binoculars. I flicked the "On" switch, hoping that the batteries were still fresh enough for the thing to function. The slight, rising whine of the device booting up meant that I was in luck.

I went back to my vantage point, looked through the dual eyepieces, and scanned the street. Everything was sharp and clear, even if I did seem to be looking at it through a green filter.

The big car I'd caught a glimpse of earlier was a Lincoln Continental, and there was what looked like a dead guy lying on the street near the driver's-side front door. I focused on the license plate and saw that it read "BATDAD1".

I recognized the tacky vanity tag – the Lincoln belonged to Don Pietro Calabrese, the Vampfather himself. The corpse on the ground probably wasn't the Don – if it had been, the shooters would have left by now. Nobody sticks around just to finish off the chauffeur. The gunfire from behind the Connie was probably coming from the Don himself.

And that meant the guys trying to finish him off were most likely members of the same bunch who'd taken out four of Calabrese's men earlier in the evening. Whoever these guys were, they didn't seem inclined to let any grass grow under their feet.

So it looked like vamps shooting it out with vamps, again. And judging by the three-to-one odds, I figured the new gang's hostile takeover of the Calabrese territory was just about ready to succeed. I wasn't sure how I felt about that.

I hustled back to the car, got on the police radio, and told the dispatcher what was happening and where. She said, "Wait one, Sergeant," and a few seconds later I was talking to the watch commander, Captain Fisk.

I explained the situation as I understood it, trying to be as brief as possible.

When I was done, Fisk said, "So, you've got four vampires exchanging gunfire in the street?"

"I haven't got a close enough look at any of them to either spot fangs or recognize their faces, sir. But I know that's Calabrese's car, and I also know that an out-of-town vampire gang took out four of Calabrese's people earlier tonight."

"Yes, I saw the incident report," Fisk said. He's a good cop, but a little too by-the-book for my liking. The rules and operational policies are important, sure, but so is flexibility and the ability to improvise when you have to. Fisk would never grasp that, even if he stayed on the job a hundred years.

"Standard procedure when supernaturals are involved in a situation like this is to call in SWAT," he said. "But I happen to know that the unit is already involved in a hostage situation involving some werewolves on the north side of town. I'll try to get in communication with Lieutenant Dooley and see if he can cut loose some of his people to deal with the situation you've got there."

The Sacred Weapons and Tactics unit consists of cops, a few of them clergy from different faiths, who are specially trained and equipped to deal with dangerous situations involving supes. They were just what the gunfight around the corner needed, except for one thing.

"That could take a while, Captain," I told him. "And I've got a feeling that by the time SWAT gets here, the action's gonna be all be over and the perps long gone. The ones who are still standing, I mean."

"Can't be helped, Sergeant. You say you've got a night-vision device?"

"That's affirmative, sir."

"Then get back in position to observe what happens, and take your radio with you. For their own safety, I'm going to order regular patrol units to stay clear of the area."

"Yes, sir."

"I'll let you know when SWAT is rolling," Fisk told me. "In the meantime, you are to *take no action* except to observe and report as necessary. Understand me?"

"Yes sir – I'm not to engage the perps, but to watch what's going down, and to report developments to you."

"That's affirmative. Now get moving, Sergeant. Fisk out."

I thumbed the radio off and sat there behind the wheel, trying to think.

If I followed Fisk's orders, Calabrese was going to die in the next few minutes, and the fangsters who'd killed him would get away clean. I might get a license number as they left, but any wiseguys – human or vampire – learn in their first ten minutes on the job always to use stolen cars when they're planning to commit a crime.

I had no love for Don Pietro Calabrese, who was a professional criminal and therefore a scumbag. He'd been a human scumbag until about twelve years ago. That's when he was diagnosed with pancreatic cancer – inoperable and almost certainly fatal. So he'd paid a vampire to turn him.

The guidos are all nominally Catholic, and the Church, with its usual tolerance, declared more than fifty years ago that all supes were *anathema* – cursed by God. So, choosing to become a vampire was considered a mortal sin. Of course, extortion, drug running, prostitution, and murder are also mortal sins, and guys like Calabrese aren't troubled by those. And vampirism offered the very substantial benefit of allowing him to avoid God's judgment indefinitely.

Having Don Pietro Calabrese lying dead in the street wouldn't send me into mourning. But he was at least a known quantity to local law enforcement, who'd worked out some grudging compromises with him over the years.

On the other hand, all we knew about the new bunch was that they were hungry for territory and vicious enough to go after it with the kind of public, in-your-face violence that Calabrese had abandoned years ago. Blood in the streets was bad for business.

That old adage about "better the devil you know than the one you don't" is something cops understand very well, even if we don't always like it.

Besides, if a cop was to save Calabrese's ass tonight, the Vampfather *might* be grateful enough to tell that cop exactly what the hell was going on with this attempted takeover. That information could save more lives in the near future.

The thing about these Mafia guys, alive or undead, is that most of them still have some old-fashioned notions about honor. They believe in vengeance, alright, but they also recognize an obligation when they incur one.

All this heavy philosophy went through my mind in about fifteen seconds, and the conclusion I reached – about the benefits to law enforcement from me saving Calabrese – was the reason I was about to risk my career by disobeying Captain Fisk's orders. My decision had absolutely nothing to do with the fact that I *hate* just sitting back and watching scumbags tear up the streets of my town with gunfire. Absolutely.

I ejected my usual load of mixed silver and cold iron from the Beretta and replaced the clip with one that was silver from top to bottom. That gave me fifteen rounds, each one deadly to vampires – and then I thumbed an extra silver slug from the clip of mixed ammo I'd just removed. I jacked a round into the Beretta's chamber, then removed the clip and added the cartridge I'd just scavenged. Sixteen. Sometimes one extra bullet can make all the difference in the world.

Usually, for a human to take on a bunch of vampires – in a gun battle or unarmed – means an express ticket to the morgue, since vamps are so much faster and stronger than the rest of us. But I'd taken on vamps before.

I could've called Karl for backup, of course – and he'd have come running. But it was bad enough that one of us was risking unemployment by defying the watch commander, without putting Karl's job on the line as well. Besides, dawn was coming soon.

So it looked like I was doing it alone.

I figured if I was going to have any chance of survival against three vampire gangsters, I'd have to take a page out of Che Guevara's book on guerrilla warfare, which I'd read in high school. It was a phase.

Che called it the "war of the flea". You bite the dog and then take off before it can scratch. Do it right, and you live to bite another day.

I made my cautious way back to the scene of the gun battle. It looked like Calabrese was holding his own, since muzzle flashes were still coming erratically from behind his parked Connie.

The night-vision binoculars would help me, but only to a point. They would allow me to see exactly where the bad guys were, but I couldn't look through the eyepieces and the sights of the Beretta at the same time. That meant I'd have to locate the fangsters with the night-vision device, but shoot at them without it. Kind of like a nearsighted guy viewing the bull's-eye of a target with his glasses on, then taking them off before squeezing off a shot.

I scanned the street to see if the three vampires who'd been firing on the Connie were still in the same positions. They hadn't moved.

The one closest to me was about eighty feet away, squatting behind a big Buick. Peering at the green-tinted image, I tried to fix in my mind where the vamp was, relative to the outline of the car. That was probably all I'd be able to see with my naked eye. Looked like he was about three feet from the rear bumper, and maybe a foot below the roof – except when he popped up long enough to fire a round at Calabrese. He did that while I was watching: stand up quick, take aim over the Buick's roof and fire, then squat back down behind cover.

I turned off the night-vision device and put it down carefully on the concrete next to me. I took a minute to let my eyes adjust to the dark, then drew a bead on what I could see of the Buick, which wasn't as much as I'd hoped. I tried to keep my hands steady, and waited.

Muzzle flash. I knew exactly where the vampire gunman was at this moment. More important, I was pretty sure that I knew where he was going to be three seconds from now. I sighted on the point where his gun barrel had briefly lit the night, then dropped my aim about three feet. I took in a breath, let half of it out, and fired – twice.

The moment I squeezed the trigger, I was violating not only Captain Fisk's orders, but also established Department procedure. A cop isn't supposed to shoot a suspect, even an armed one, without first doing the "Police officer! Drop your weapon and put your hands in the air!" routine.

I could just imagine the response of one of those vampire gangsters out there if I'd tried that crap on him, and I'm still too young to die. So when it's a choice between following procedure and staying alive, I'll go with common sense and take my chances with the bureaucrats later. As my old partner, Paul DiNapoli, used to say, "Better to be tried by twelve than carried by six."

After getting off those two shots, I didn't stick around to evaluate my marksmanship. The flea had taken a small chunk out of the dog – or so I hoped – and he'd better change position before he got scratched but good.

I grabbed the binoculars and scuttled back about twenty feet, dropping down behind somebody's silver Nissan. I raised up just enough to see over the top of the trunk, trying to expose as little of myself as possible, and saw one of the remaining bad guys do something stupid. I guess not everybody in the new vampire gang was a battle-hardened veteran of the streets.

The sky was brightening a little with false dawn. That and my darkness-adjusted eyes gave me a pretty good view of what this idiot was doing. *He actually stood up*, gun in both hands, searching the area where my two shots had come from. I wasn't there anymore – I'm sure his vampire night vision told him that. But he must've known that I wasn't far away. The barrel of his pistol kept moving back and forth as he sought somebody to shoot at.

He might've found me, too – if Calabrese hadn't fired from across the street and put a bullet through the dumb bastard's head.

Two down. What was the third vampire going to do now? If he was smart, he'd jump into his car and get the hell out of here.

Turned out he wasn't quite that bright. But he *was* smart enough to get behind me.

The guy must've hit the vampire afterburners and sprinted clear around the block in order to go from a few hundred feet in front of me to about twenty feet behind me. Probably took him all of six, maybe seven seconds – after all, it was a pretty big block. But I figured all that out later.

It was when I heard that crisp, metallic noise coming from behind me – the distinctive double click of the hammer going back on a pistol – that I knew I was about to die. There's nothing else in the world that sounds quite like that, and I guess for a lot of guys it's the second-last sound they ever hear.

It had to be the third vampire behind me. Another cop would have announced himself, if only so that I wouldn't do a Wild Bill Hickok and blow him away before I was sure of my target.

I decided that I was going to try to stand up and turn. The odds against my accomplishing either of those things made the Tri-State Powerball seem like a good investment. But I wanted to die standing upright if I could, instead of squatting there like some Cub Scout trying to take a dump in the woods.

I was barely halfway out of the crouch when I heard the sound of the shot that killed me.

It didn't, of course – but I was pretty confused for a moment. I even had the crazy thought this was some kind of "Occurrence at Owl Creek Bridge" moment. In that final instant, everything slows down so much that you can fantasize a whole different chain of events – before reality catches up with you and breaks your neck.

Then I figured out that it just wasn't my night to die, and I decided to just stand up, turn around, and work out what the hell had happened.

I'd had most of it figured right. There *was* a body on the ground a couple of car lengths behind me. I recognized him as one of the vampires I'd seen through the binoculars earlier, and the only way he could've gotten behind me like that was by sprinting around the block with vampire speed. The one thing I'd had wrong was which one of us was about to die.

Life can feel pretty damn good, especially when you were sure you were about to lose it. But once I got my mind working again, I wanted to know who had just killed the vampire gangster. Because there was nobody else around. Nobody.

He could've been nailed by a sniper from one of the windows, but who would do that? And why? It couldn't have been Calabrese, that much was certain. He was too far—

Calabrese. Shit.

I scuttled down the length of parked cars ahead of me, being careful to keep below the line of sight from across the street. It would be pretty ironic to get myself killed by the Vampfather after everything I'd just gone through to keep the bastard alive.

When I was directly across from the Lincoln, I stopped, took in a big breath, and yelled, "*Calabrese!*"

Nothing. Not a sound. I hoped they hadn't managed to nail him after all.

"*Calabrese!*" I yelled again. "*It's Markowski. Detective Sergeant Stanley Markowski. Do you recognize my voice?*"

Far too many seconds passed – maybe three – before somebody from across the street came back with, "*Maybe I do. What do you want?*"

"*The three vampires who were shooting at you are dead. You got one, and I nailed the other two.*" I hadn't killed the third vampire, but this was no time for complicated explanations.

"*Say that's true,*" the voice from behind the Connie yelled. "*What do you want – flowers?*"

Snide bastard. "*Conversation. The face-to-face kind.*"

No response.

"*Calabrese, I'm gonna stand up now. Then I'm gonna cross the street toward you, my hands empty and in the air. I'd appreciate it if you wouldn't shoot me, especially since I just saved your life!*"

Another few seconds of silence gave way to, "*OK, but be quick about it! I don't got a lot of time!*"

That was for damn sure. Not only was the sky getting brighter by the second, but I could finally hear sirens in the distance. Sounded like SWAT was on the way, but too fucking late to do any good.

I stood up, sidled between two parked cars, and walked slowly across the street, hands in the air. I won't say that my gut didn't tighten some as I walked slowly toward an armed criminal who had probably killed more people in his time than I've had meals. It was in Calabrese's best interest not to shoot me, and I was pretty sure he knew it, too. But still, my gut was tight as I crossed that street, and it stayed that way until I saw Calabrese stand up slowly and put his gun away.

He'd been fifty-two when the cancer had driven him to choose the world of the bloodsucking undead, and now he'd look that age forever – or until somebody put a silver bullet in his brain or a wooden stake through his heart. He had salt-and-pepper hair, wide-set brown eyes, and a thin mustache in the middle of a face that was no harder than your average concrete wall.

When I was within twenty feet or so, he said, "What?"

That was the Mafia version of a cordial greeting.

"I wanna talk. Not now – tonight. Tell me where and when, and I'll be there."

"Talk about what?" He wasn't stupid – dumb guys didn't get to be where he was – but I guess suspicion was second nature to him.

"You know what," I said. "Everything that's been going on, and what you're planning to do about it."

"And I should tell you all that shit, because…"

"Because I just saved your ass, that's why."

"Yeah? And you'd have been in such a big hurry to save my ass, like you put it, if I didn't have information you wanted?"

"Doesn't matter," I said. "You're alive, aren't you? Or, at least, still among the undead. And if I hadn't come along, you probably wouldn't be."

He stared at me with eyes that had probably looked dead even before he became a vampire. After a second or two he said, "Yeah, OK. Maybe."

He glanced toward the horizon and immediately turned away, since the first rays of sunlight were just becoming visible.

"Look," he said, "I gotta get the fuck outta here – *now*."

"I know," I said. Like a lot of vampires with money, Calabrese had a car with ultra-dark tinted windows, including the windshield. He could probably drive the Connie even in broad daylight – for a while, anyway.

"Tonight," I said. "Name a place and a time. If you're not gonna be there, have somebody waiting who'll take me to where you are."

He seemed to like that idea. "Alright – Ricardo's, around 10."

"Fine with me," I said. Ricardo's was one of the best Italian restaurants in town. I hadn't known that the Vampfather owned it, but I can't say I was surprised. And he *must* have owned it – no way was he going to meet me someplace he didn't control.

Calabrese hurried over to the other side of the Connie, stepping over the body of his driver in the process. He yanked open the door and said, over his shoulder, "See ya." Then he surprised me a little by adding, "And thanks."

Then he slid behind the wheel, slammed the door, and started the engine. I stepped back a few paces to give him room, but even so he only missed me by a few feet as the Connie pulled away from the curb, tires screeching, and took off down the street.

The sirens were very close now. I looked around, counting the corpses. The vampire gang had gunned down Calabrese's driver, who lay at my feet. Calabrese himself could take credit, if that's the word, for another of the stiffs. A third guy was mine, and the last one came courtesy of – who? My guardian angel? In grade school, the nuns used to tell us that everybody had a guardian angel, but none of them ever mentioned that mine might be packing heat.

The black SWAT van was up the street and heading my way fast, siren screaming and lights flashing like a meth junkie's nightmare. I stepped into the middle of the street and started waving my arm back and forth to flag them down. It was almost time to start the long process of explaining what had happened here. Some of it would even be the truth.

JUSTIN GUSTAINIS   59

I had the feeling that I wasn't going to get home for quite a while. I was right, too.

The story that I concocted was pretty good, if I say so, myself. At least, it was good enough to convince Dooley, the SWAT team commander, along with Captain Fisk, my boss Lieutenant McGuire, and a couple of clowns from Internal Affairs.

In my version of events, I'd followed Captain Fisk's orders to the letter – or tried to. I'd gone back to the gun battle with the intention of observing and reporting, nothing more. But then one of the vampires had spotted me, despite my best efforts to be discreet. He'd loosed off some shots in my direction, and I'd had no choice but to defend myself by returning fire.

One of the other attackers had been dispatched by whoever had taken cover behind the big car across the street – a Cadillac, I thought it was, or maybe an Oldsmobile. No, I hadn't been able to get a look at the license number or the shooter, who had taken off while I was trying to avoid being shot by the third vampire. That individual had been shot by person or persons unknown. Then the sun came up, SWAT arrived, and order was restored to the universe.

I got pretty good at answering the questions that always followed my little tale – maybe because I got so much practice in the six hours that followed.

How did the vampire you shot manage to spot you, since you were observing from cover?
Hard to say, for sure. But in order to see what was going on – as I'd been ordered to do – I had to expose myself, at least a little. And don't forget that vampires

have damn good night vision. They also hear pretty well, too – maybe he caught the sound from the night-vision binoculars when I turned the device on.

Why is it you can't tell us anything about the driver of the car, who left just before SWAT arrived?

He was using the car for cover, don't forget. And I wasn't at a good angle to see him when he popped for a second or two in order to get a shot off at his attackers. And by the time he left the shelter of the car's body to get behind the wheel, I was too busy trying to get a fix on the third attacker before he got a fix on me.

So, you killed one of the vampires in self-defense, and you saw the mysterious shooter behind the big car drop another one of them. That leaves two dead vampires unaccounted for.

One of them was down before I got there. He was laying on the street, near the big car. My guess is he was killed in the ambush set up by the three other shooters – an ambush that was also supposed to get the guy who was firing from behind the car when I got there.

OK, that's one. What about the other vampire?

I have no idea. I know who *didn't* kill him – me or the shooter behind the car. Beyond that, I've got no clue.

He was shot in the back. Are you sure you didn't have anything to do with that?

Take my weapon. Fire a test bullet from it, and compare that to the slug you dug out of the vampire. I'm pretty sure they won't match. I also resent the implication that I'm a back shooter.

The vampire you admit that you killed – you say he shot at you first. Where did the slugs go that he fired at you?

Beats me – they whistled past my head and headed off down the street. They could be anywhere up to two blocks away, I guess – unless they lodged in some car that the owner already drove away.

And that's how it went, over and over, for six goddamn hours.

"So, why'd you lie?" Christine asked me.

"The answer to that depends on which particular lie you're talking about."

We sat at the kitchen table, each of us having our own version of breakfast. I'd had all of three hours of restless sleep, and had to go to work soon. Fuck it – that's why God gave us coffee.

"I mean, I get the story about you shooting that fangster because he opened up on you first," she said. "If you told them that you'd just up and shot the guy, you'd get fired."

"At least," I said.

"But how come you didn't tell them that what's-his-name, the Mafia guy–"

"Calabrese."

"Yeah, him. Why didn't you just explain that there was an ambush set up, and Calabrese was the target? They killed his driver, he shot back, and then you came along and intervened – in self-defense, of course. Then, once the gunfight was over, he drove off before you could stop him."

"That last part's not what happened," I said. "I already told you that I deliberately let him go."

"That's right, sorry. I'm starting to get what you said really happened confused with the cover story. But why didn't you tell them about Calabrese?"

"Because they'd arrest him, that's why."

"How come?" she asked. "He was the victim, right? The other guys attacked *him*."

"That hasn't been established in a court of law. He killed a guy – and it isn't self-defense until the DA, or a judge and jury, say that it is. The guys in Organized Crime would love the chance to bust a guy like Calabrese, even if the charges didn't stick in the long run. They'd do it just for the nuisance value."

Christine picked up her mug and took another swig of her breakfast blood. "OK, so they arrest him – that's his problem, not yours."

"But if that happens, I lose my leverage," I said. "Right now, he thinks he owes me for saving his life, which he does – sort of. I think I can use that gratitude and get him to open up about this gang war. But if I save his life and *then* get him arrested, Calabrese would probably figure those two things cancel each other out. I'd never get a word out of him."

"What do you figure he knows?"

"If he knows anything at all about what's going on, that's more than I do. And, besides, if I don't rat him out to my fellow officers, that gives me even more leverage."

She looked at me, frowning. "How come?"

"Because I can always go back and change my story. And if I tell the truth and give them Calabrese's name, he *will* get arrested."

"But if you did that – went to the other cops and said, 'Look, fellas, I'm real sorry, but I lied about that gunfight. Here's what *really* happened,' you'd be in serious shit with the Department. Wouldn't you?"

"Yeah, but I'm betting that Calabrese won't take the chance."

She swirled the remaining liquid in her mug and studied the little whirlpool that resulted. "This cop stuff gets pretty complicated sometimes, doesn't it?"

"Yeah, but it's nothing that a master detective like your old man can't handle."

"I hope you're right, Daddy. I really do."

Even though dead tired, I came in to work half an hour early. I wanted to talk to Karl and McGuire – separately – before things got busy.

Karl's usually early, too – and tonight was no exception.

As quickly as I could without leaving anything out, I told him what had happened since he'd seen me last. When I was done, he sat there rubbing his chin.

"You took a big chance," he said. "Not telling them that Calabrese was involved, I mean. That could come back to bite you on the ass big-time."

"It's worth the risk, if it'll move us forward on this case. Shit, all we've got right now is a big, fat pile of nothing."

"It's just a *case*, Stan," he said. "How many do we handle a year – two hundred? Three hundred? It's not worth risking your job over."

"It's not just *any case*, dammit! This new bunch that's trying to move in on Calabrese has started a fucking *war*. Who knows when it's gonna end, or how?"

"What the fuck does it matter, really – they're all fangsters."

I just looked at him.

"Far as I'm concerned," he said, "we oughta just let 'em kill each other. If I could, I'd FedEx each side a case of silver slugs, just to help move things along."

I wondered how Karl would feel if it were human criminals fighting it out in the streets. Sometimes I think he tries a little too hard to prove that he's more cop than vampire. But I have the good sense to keep that thought to myself.

What I said instead was, "See if you still feel that way when a stray shot from one of those silver bullets kills a five year-old kid."

Karl broke eye contact with me then, but he didn't say anything.

"And it's not like it doesn't matter which side wins," I said. "This new bunch – whether they're from Philly or East Buttfuck, New Jersey – they don't give a damn about what happens to Scranton. Far as they're concerned, it's 'Fuck the city, fuck the cops, and fuck the citizens.'"

Karl gave me half a smile. "Maybe 'fuck the cops' especially."

"Yeah, maybe," I said. "Sure, Calabrese is a scumbag, but he's invested in the welfare of this town. His business interests, both legit and criminal, are here. He's got family all over town, too."

"Is that 'family' with a small 'f' or a capital one?" he asked me.

"Both," I said. "He was born here, you know, which means he's got relatives everyplace – not to mention what the guidos call 'brothers in blood'. Can you see him doing this kind of cowboy bullshit?"

"He *is* doing it," Karl said mildly.

"Only in self-defense."

The smile I got from Karl this time was full-bore, fangs and all. "Sounds like you're his biggest fan."

"No fucking way," I said. "I just know the difference between a mean dog and a mad one."

"Nice turn of phrase," he said. "You come up with that one yourself?"

"I probably heard it on TV someplace." After a couple of seconds, I asked him, "So, are you coming with me to Ricardo's tonight or what?"

"Shit, I wouldn't miss it for the world."

Then I went back to McGuire's office. He had a sour expression on his face, as if his ulcer was acting up again and the Tagamet wasn't helping. Not a good sign.

"Boss," I said, "I got involved in some shit last night on the way home. I thought you oughta know about it."

"Have a seat," he said. "I already heard a couple of things about that today, through the rumor mill. I was waiting for you to come on shift so I could get all the details."

I shifted in the hard wooden chair, even though I'd just sat down. "Maybe I should tell you what I told Captain Fisk, Internal Affairs, and everybody else."

The lines in his face deepened, and I had a feeling it wasn't the ulcer bothering him. He nodded slowly and said, "OK, we'll start with that."

So I ran through the mixture of truth, half-truth, and lies that I'd gotten so good at telling over the last twelve hours.

When I was done, McGuire stared at me for a couple of seconds. Then he said, "You look like shit. Want some coffee?"

Even if I wasn't dead tired, I wouldn't have turned down a cup of the boss's java. He makes it from these Jamaican Blue Mountain beans that he grinds at home, and a cup of it is enough to restore your faith in a benevolent God.

As I was taking my first sip, McGuire said, "So, that's the version you gave to Captain Fisk and everybody else. Now – what *really* happened?"

I drank some more coffee before answering him. "It might be better," I said, "if you could honestly tell a review board that you never knew the answer to that question."

He sat back, using a thumb and forefinger to massage the bridge of his nose. McGuire keeps a fancy-looking Howard Miller table clock on his desk. Even though it's electronic, the thing still makes a soft ticking sound – you can hear it on those rare occasions when the place is quiet. I counted twenty-two of those ticks before he said, "Fuck it, I've lied to review boards before – and, no, you don't get to ask me about that."

"Wouldn't dream of it," I said, even though I was curious as hell.

"I can't do my job, part of which involves keeping my detectives out of trouble, without knowing what's going on," he said. "So, off the record, then – what happened last night?"

"OK," I said. "I was driving home from work when I heard the sound of shots from a few streets over…"

I told him all of it, right up to the arrival of the SWAT team on the scene. He asked questions along the way, and I answered them truthfully. I might withhold information from McGuire occasionally, but I won't lie to him – he deserves better than that. He might be a tough boss, but he's saved my ass more than once when he could've saved himself a lot of trouble by hanging me out to dry.

When I'd finished, McGuire said, "Is that what you were talking to your partner about so intently when you first came in?"

"That's right," I said. "Karl thinks I'm being stupid for withholding information from the brass."

McGuire shook his head. "Stupid, no. Crazy – maybe."

"Nice to see a diversity of opinion," I said.

"Is there anybody out there who's likely to get in front of a grand jury someday and testify that what you told the captain is a crock of shit?"

"I doubt it," I said. "Calabrese couldn't do it without incriminating himself, and all the other potential witnesses died at the scene."

"I can think of one who didn't," he said. "Your so-called guardian angel."

"Oh, yeah – him."

McGuire looked through the glass into the squad room, which was starting to get livelier as other detectives showed up for the start of the night shift. "Have you considered the possibility that it could be Karl? I seem to recall he's watched your back in the past, without letting you know he was doing it."

"There's no way he could've been aware I was in trouble from that far away," I said. "Besides, he would've told me by now if it was him."

"If you say so, OK. I agree with you that it probably wasn't some other cop – he'd have stuck around to get the kudos for saving a fellow officer's life."

"And that's the same reason I don't think it was one of Calabrese's guys. He'd want the boss to *know* that he helped get him out of a tight corner."

McGuire spread his hands. "So, who does that leave? Who's gonna show up in the middle of a gunfight, pop some scumbag who's about to pop *you*, then disappear without so much as a word?"

"Yeah, who *was* that masked man?" I said. "He never gave me a chance to thank him."

"You didn't hear anybody calling out a hearty 'Heigh-ho, Silver!' did you?" McGuire almost grew a smile for a second, but then changed his mind.

"The only silver I remember was the slug that went into that vamp's back," I said.

"Well, if you ever find out who it was, be sure to let me know. In the meantime…"

"In the meantime," I said, "I have a dinner date."

It was a little after 10pm when Karl and I got to Ricardo's Ristorante, which is on the lower end of Moosic Street. Despite being a Polack, I love Italian food, and Ricardo's serves the second-best veal scaloppine in town – right after the place owned by my old buddy, Large Luigi.

The restaurant's in a two-story building made of red brick. The terrace outside the front door is open in warmer weather, for those who like sharing their food with the local bugs. I prefer to eat inside, where the only insects I'm likely to encounter have two legs.

The front is wide enough to have room for three identical canopies made out of maroon fabric running across the front. Each one had a fancy-looking black "R" in a circle, and under that it read, simply, "Ricardo's."

The place was said to have the best wine cellar in the Wyoming Valley – not that Calabrese would care. He never drinks the stuff.

Two guys were hanging around the entrance, wearing dark suits that were almost cut well enough to conceal the gun bulges under their arms. As Karl and I approached, they took a couple of steps toward us.

"You gentlemen have reservations?" one of them asked, flashing a little fang in the process.

I already had my badge folder ready in my hand – I'd figured that guys like these might react badly if I were to reach under my jacket suddenly. I held it up and said, "Yeah – right here."

"Me, too," Karl said, displaying both his badge and fangs.

"Hold it!" the other goon said, with a raised palm. He looked a little older – in human terms, anyway, and I guess he was the one in charge. More politely, he said, "Sorry to bother you, officers, but it isn't too hard to manufacture police ID these days. Mind if I take a closer look?"

It took some guts to do that – I'll give him that much. I suppose the sight of Karl's fangs had spooked them, since they were at war with another gang of vampires. And maybe not everybody in the underworld knew that the SPD now had an undead cop among its members.

I handed him the leather folder that proves I'm a cop. He looked at both the badge and ID card carefully, and compared the photo with my face. Then he handed it back, said, "Thank you, officer," and turned to give Karl the same treatment.

That surprised me, since my own ID had apparently passed inspection. But the guy might've had specific instructions from Calabrese, and fangsters who disobeyed the boss's orders have been known to come to a bad end. Or maybe the guard just didn't believe there were vampire cops.

The guy handed back Karl's ID folder and said, "Thank you, officers. Please go on in." He made a gesture toward the door that was almost gracious. Not bad for a thug.

Inside, a red-haired hostess gave us a quick once-over and said with a smile, "Good evening, gentlemen, and welcome to Ricardo's. Table for two?"

"We're here to see Calabrese," I told her.

She tried to look puzzled, but wasn't a good enough actress to make it work. "I'm sorry, sir, did you say Calabrese? Is that someone dining with us this evening?"

"You know who he is," I said. "It's alright – we're expected. Tell him it's Markowski and Renfer."

For a moment I thought she was going to continue her little charade, but then she dropped the smile, said, "Wait here, please," and headed off into the dining room.

In less than a minute she was back, and so was the professional smile. "If you gentlemen would follow me, please?" I noticed she didn't pick up any menus to take with her.

The dining room continued with the motif from outside. Red brick columns were used to support crisscrossing ceiling beams that looked like polished mahogany. Every table was occupied, and the room hummed with the noise from a couple of dozen quiet conversations.

The hostess led us to a corner table that was well away from the windows. On the way, Karl and I received hard looks from several pairs of men in dark suits who were sitting at tables scattered around the dining room. I assumed that Calabrese was paying for their dinners, which mostly came in glasses.

Three other men were with Calabrese, although only the boss had his back to the wall. Two of them were anonymous soldier types, but I recognized the third one as Louis Loquasto, who was the *consigliere*.

Loquasto was a slim guy with gray hair, wearing a sharp suit and an even sharper expression. He was the only member of the Calabrese Family who hadn't crossed over into the world of the undead. Calabrese probably considered it an advantage to have a trusted associate who could move about in daylight.

As we reached his table, Calabrese said something I couldn't hear, and the two soldiers got up and left. Loquasto stayed where he was.

I nodded at Calabrese. "You're looking pretty good for somebody who almost met true death a few hours ago."

He looked at Karl sourly, then back at me. "You didn't say anything about bringing a friend."

"Neither did you," I said. "But you don't hear *me* complaining."

Calabrese took a sip from the tall glass of red liquid he had in front of him and gestured toward the two empty chairs. "Sit down, if you want."

When we were seated, I nodded at Loquasto. We all knew each other, so introductions weren't needed. Calabrese said, "You guys want a drink, something to eat?"

"I wouldn't mind a cup of coffee," I said. I was going to need a lot of that, just to get through my shift tonight.

Karl nodded toward Calabrese's glass. "I'll have whatever you're having."

Calabrese made a slight gesture, and a waiter appeared at our table immediately. "A pot of coffee" – I guess Calabrese had noticed the circles under my eyes – "and another one of these." He touched his glass.

It came as no surprise that we were served quickly. Once the waiter had gone, Calabrese looked at me. "You said you wanted to talk – so talk."

"You've got some vamps from out of town trying to muscle in on your business."

He snorted. "How's about you tell me something I *don't* know."

"That's kinda what I was hoping to get from you – some things I don't know," I said. "Like who these new guys are."

Calabrese started to speak, but Loquasto laid a gentle hand on his boss's forearm. "Perhaps before you say anything, we should consider the possibility that one of these gentlemen is wearing a wire."

I looked at Loquasto. "Maybe we oughta consider the possibility that you're full of shit, Counselor. If I wanted to take down Don Calabrese, I didn't need to come in here with a microphone under my shirt to do it."

Loquasto rattled the ice cubes in his glass, but didn't take a drink. "Is that right?" he said.

"Yeah, that's exactly right – all I had to do was sit on my hands this morning and watch while the three fangsters who had him trapped eased his transition from Undead to True Dead with a couple of silver bullets in the brain."

I stirred some sugar into my coffee. "Instead, I killed two of them *and* let him leave the scene afterwards."

I was exaggerating my body count by fifty per cent, but there was no reason why these guys had to know that.

Calabrese pulled his arm from Loquasto's grasp. "Forget that wire bullshit," he said.

Then he turned to me. "These motherfuckers making a move on me are out of Philly – the Delatasso Family."

"Philly, huh?" Karl said. Not exactly next door." Philadelphia's about a two-and-a-half hour drive south from Scranton.

"Compared to the kind of action they've got down in Philly," I said, "Scranton's got to be pretty small potatoes."

"It ain't Charlie Delatasso who's trying to expand," Calabrese said. "It's the son, Ronnie."

"With his father's blessing, of course," Loquasto said.

"Sounds like a young man in a hurry," I said. "How old is he, anyway?"

"Thirty-nine, I believe," Loquasto said.

"Eldest son?" I asked.

"*Only* son," Loquasto told me.

"I don't get it," Karl said. "Why would he take all the risks involved in starting a war – and so far from home, besides? Shit, all he's gotta do is wait."

"That's right," I said. "Sooner or later, the old man's either gonna croak – from either too much linguine or multiple gunshot wounds – or get sent up for a long stretch. Either way, the kid gets to take over."

Calabrese gave me an indulgent smile. "Didn't you know?" he said. "Delatasso the elder came over, about four years ago."

I stared at him. "Came… You mean he's undead?"

"That's exactly what he is," Calabrese said.

"Our sources say Don Charles had a heart attack," Loquasto said. "Apparently you were right about all the linguine. He recovered eventually, but the close look he got at the Grim Reaper frightened him – enough so that he took steps to postpone indefinitely any future visits."

I nodded slowly. "I think I begin to see the problem."

"Me, too," Karl said. "The old man, if he's careful, could live a long, long time. And even if junior got turned, too, he still has to wait… and wait."

"Oh, he has been," Loquasto said. "Delatasso told everyone in his Family that they could either change, or leave. That edict included his son, who, as you pointed out, Detective, will nonetheless have a very long wait before he can take over the business."

"Unless he takes steps to move things along," I said. "That's not exactly unheard of."

"Not gonna happen," Calabrese said. "In some Families, maybe. But from what I hear, Ronnie is everything a father could want in a son. He loves his old man – worships him, even."

"There's a more pragmatic issue for young Mister Delatasso to deal with as well," Loquasto said. "His father is very popular among his soldiers and the other members of the Family. Apparently the Don has been generous in distributing the profits of his various enterprises among his employees. I also understand he possesses a great deal of personal charm."

"So," Karl said, "if the kid bumped off his old man and tried to take over…"

"He would likely face vengeance at the hands of his father's former associates," Loquasto said. "All of which makes a takeover very unlikely."

"So Junior's feeling his oats and wants to make a name for himself," I said. "And to do that, he's gotta branch out."

"And the little cocksucker picked Scranton," Calabrese said.

I refilled my coffee cup. The stuff they served here wasn't as good as McGuire's Jamaican Blue Mountain, but it wasn't half bad.

"Waging a war's expensive," I said. "And over a hundred miles from home, too. It must be costing the old man a fortune."

"It would, if he were paying for it," Loquasto said. "His preference is for Ronnie to stay at home and help run operations there – he held quite a responsible position, I understand. Charlie has not forbidden his son from engaging in this attempt at expansion, but he has declined to bankroll it."

"What the fuck's the kid doing, then," Karl said, "putting it on his MasterCard?"

"The source of Ronnie's funding is something of a mystery," Loquasto went on. "But it seems abundantly clear that he has found a backer." He gave an expressive shrug. "Perhaps in one of the other Northeast families."

"The fucker probably promised them a cut of the profits on that new drug," Calabrese said. "That'd get their attention."

Louis Loquasto was probably the only man, living or undead, who could get away with the hard look that he gave Calabrese right then. The Don had just said something he wasn't supposed to – and judging by the expression on his face now, Calabrese knew it, too. Maybe the attempted assassination attempt last night had affected him more than he wanted to admit. Even vampires have nerves, you know.

Things at the table went very quiet. I let the silence go on for a little while before saying, in a conversational tone, "Oh? And what new drug might that be?"

Calabrese looked at Loquasto. The *consigliere* was usually a hard man to read, but this time the small shrug, combined with his facial expression, said clearly, *You might as well – we can't go back now.*

Calabrese hesitated a few seconds longer before he looked at me and said, "On the street, they call it Slide."

I can't say I was exactly blown away when he said "Slide". It was pretty damn unlikely that *two* new drugs were being sold in this town.

"Sounds like that name's something you guys recognize," Calabrese said.

"I heard it for the first time just a couple of nights ago," I said, "from an elf I was questioning. We busted him and one of his buddies when they tried to take down Jerry's Diner. Turns out they wanted the money to buy more of this Slide."

"Our sources tell us that it's been on the street for about a month now," Loquasto said.

"Something like that's not supposed to exist," I said. "A drug that addicts multiple species of supes."

"Yes," Loquasto said. "We find it very puzzling – not to mention unprecedented."

"I know that elves can get hooked on it," I said. "I've seen *that* with my own eyes. But I also heard a rumor that it has the same effect on vampires – I didn't know whether to believe that one or not."

Calabrese and his *consigliere* exchanged a look. Whatever passed between them ended with Calabrese saying, "Yeah, it affects us, alright. And fuckin' weres, too."

Karl whistled softly, which must have been hard to do through his fangs. Then he looked at me and said, "Worse and worse."

I said to Calabrese, "And this shit is coming from the new guys – the Delatassos. Not you."

"You got that right," he said grimly.

"Takes some pretty big balls," I said. "Selling stuff like that, right under your nose."

"Yeah, well, there's one thing about having big balls," Calabrese said. "They're easy to find when you're ready to cut 'em off."

"So that's how the war started?" Karl asked. "Delatasso Junior sent some people into town, who started pushing Slide. And you... objected."

Loquasto started to say something diplomatic and non-incriminating, but Calabrese interrupted him. "Yeah, we *objected*, alright," he said. "We got hold of two of those guys, tied 'em up good, then left the fuckers in a field to meet the sunrise."

I swallowed. Vampires exposed to sunlight burst into flame. What Calabrese had done, or ordered someone to do, was the equivalent of pouring a gallon of gas over somebody, then dropping a match on him.

"How'd you know they worked for Delatasso?" Karl asked.

"We had a little conversation before they went out to that field," Calabrese said. "One of my guys poured some holy water on them until they felt like talking. It didn't take long."

Of course it had been Loquasto. He was the only member of Calabrese's crew who could handle a vessel containing holy water, and I bet the screams hadn't bothered him at all. Loquasto might not be a blood-drinking monster – but he was a lawyer, which was close enough.

If I'd needed any reminder of what I was dealing with, Calabrese had just provided it. Not that it changed anything – it was either deal with him or try to reach an accommodation with the Delatassos, if they took over. And Ronnie Delatasso didn't sound like the reasonable type.

"Did you ever consider just letting the Delatassos sell Slide in Scranton, in return for paying you a hefty commission?" I asked. It was too late for that now, of course – I just wanted to see Calabrese's reaction.

"No fuckin' way," he said. "You let those bastards get a foothold, and before long you're the one who's on the outside, looking in. And besides..."

Calabrese hesitated, and I wondered why. He hadn't exactly been shy about saying what he thought, so far.

After a few seconds, he said, "For the sake of discussion, say that we do a lot of business involving... illicit pharmaceuticals – heroin, coke, crack, even marijuana."

"Not meth?" Karl asked him.

"Naw, that shit's too hard to make, and dangerous besides. Independent operators handle that, and we let 'em. They can sell it to the fucking goblins – they're animals, anyway."

Calabrese drank some more blood from his glass. "But all that other stuff is for humans. If they wanna put it in their veins, or their noses, or their lungs – that's their problem. But I'm not gonna sit back and let our own kind get hooked on this new shit, like a bunch of fucking warm-bloods." He looked at me. "No offense."

I just shrugged. You can only be offended by those you respect.

"So you're OK with pot, coke, and heroin," Karl said. "But Slide's bad, because supernaturals can get hooked on it."

"Fuckin' A right," Calabrese said. "It's bad for morale, bad for discipline, and bad for business."

"Speaking of business," I said, "You got hit pretty hard the last couple of nights. You gonna be able to keep these guys from taking over?"

"I got plenty of soldiers left," Calabrese said. "Besides, the Delatassos lost a few, too." He grinned. "Thanks to you and me."

The urge to put my fist through his face was growing stronger, and I didn't know how much longer I'd be able to resist it. I drained my coffee cup and pushed my chair back.

"I assume it doesn't matter to you," I said, "whether the Delatasso soldiers are in the ground or in jail."

Calabrese spread his hands. "Don't make any difference to me, long as they're off the streets."

I nodded. "I'll see what we can do about that. In the meantime, it might be good if we had a way to stay in touch."

Calabrese looked at Loquasto and nodded. The *consigliere* produced what looked like a business card and wrote something on the back. Handing it to me, he said, "That's my private number. You can reach me there anytime, day or night."

I put the card in my pocket and stood up. "Thanks, Counselor," I said. Then I looked at Calabrese. "There's not gonna be a war in the streets. Not in this town – I won't let it happen."

He gave me a sharp-edged grin. "Hey – I'm a man of peace, Detective. Ask anybody." Then he stopped smiling. "Maybe you'd better talk to the other guys – and good luck with that."

"Being lucky is one of the things I do best."

Back at the squad room, Karl went to brief McGuire on our meeting with the local Mafia, and I went downstairs to see Rachel Proctor, the Department's Consulting Witch.

When I got to Rachel's office, the door was open, as it often is. She was sitting with her back to me, watching something on her laptop. I figured I'd better announce myself – startling a witch is never a good idea, even one who practices white magic like Rachel.

I rapped on the frosted glass that makes up the door's top half. Without looking up, she said, "Come on in, Stan."

Rachel's body may be a size 2 – she barely tops five feet and is lean as a whippet – but both her brain and heart are generously proportioned. Whatever the Department pays her, it's not enough.

As I got closer, I saw that she was looking at one of those "TED Talks" lectures that Christine is always telling me about. "Who's doing this one?" I asked her.

"It's some professor from MIT, going on about the physics of magic," she said.

"I didn't know you were good at physics," I said.

"I'm not – maybe that why this thing is giving me a headache."

"How'd you know it was me at the door – witchcraft?"

"Uh-uh. You're the only one who ever knocks."

She logged off the computer and then swiveled her chair around to face me. "What can I do you for, Stan?"

"You ever hear anything about Slide?" I asked her.

"Slide? Isn't that a dance? I think I saw David Hasselhoff try it on *Dancing with the Sidhe* a while back."

"It might be a dance," I said, "but it's also a drug – a bad one."

She sat back and looked at me, all levity gone from her face. "A street drug, by the name."

"Uh-huh. Brand new – or damn nearly."

"I would have thought that modern science had already figured out just about every way there is to fuck people up with chemicals," she said. "What's this one do?"

"Not much – unless you're a supe."

"A drug that affects supernaturals? Get *outta* here…"

"I'll leave if you want – but I'd rather stick around and talk about this drug."

"Still funny as a cold sore, I see." She gave me a tiny smile, which is more than my feeble witticism was worth.

"We're not just talking about goblins here, are we?" she asked.

"No – elves, for sure. And I have on good authority that it works on vamps and weres, too."

"Goddess between us and all harm," she said softly.

"And maybe other species of supes, too," I said. "I don't know anything about that – but then, until two days ago, I'd never heard of Slide, either."

"What are the effects of this stuff?"

"I can tell you how it affects elves – at least, according to the elf who told me about it."

"So, tell me about the elves, then. For starters, how do they ingest it?"

"My guy told me that he and his pals smoked it," I said . "Although he claims to know some elves who shoot up with it, too."

"What happens after it's in their bloodstream?"

"He described it as being like fireworks going off inside your head – every color in the universe, and some from outside it."

Rachel tapped her chin a few times. "Sounds like an LSD trip, although that stuff affects different people in different ways."

"It's not a hallucinogenic like acid," I said. "You don't start seeing purple vultures coming out of the walls, far as I know. Just the flashing lights, at first."

"Then what?"

"Euphoria that apparently goes on for hours."

"And what happens after that?" she asked. "Is there an emotional letdown – a crash – or do they return to normal, or what?"

"The elf didn't say, and I forgot to ask," I said. "Shit. But I can try to talk to him some more about it, if you think it'll be helpful."

"'Try?'"

"He's probably lawyered up by now, which means he may not have a lot to say anymore – to me, at least."

Rachel stood up and went around to perch on the edge of her desk, arms folded, staring at the floor. After a few moments, she said, "Are you sure it's physically addictive, Stan – not just habituitive?"

"Oh, it's addictive, alright. My new buddy Thor–"

"Who?"

"Sorry. That's the elf we busted. He was showing all the signs of a strung-out junkie: sweating, hands shaky, and a good amount of physical discomfort. Kept yelling for a doctor to come in and 'give him something'."

"Sounds like he's got a monkey on his back, alright."

"Besides, when's the last time you saw somebody commit armed robbery to get money for marijuana?"

Rachel's eyebrows shot up. "Armed robbery?"

I told her how Thor and his pal tried to take down Jerry's Diner while Karl and I were on our coffee break. When I was done, she said, "I see what you mean about the robbery. That's certainly an act of desperation, which usually accompanies addiction. Not the kind of thing you see with marijuana smokers."

"True – but I did know a pothead who tried armed robbery, once."

"Really?"

"Yeah," I said. "He took down a bakery – guy had the worst case of munchies I'd ever seen."

She shook her head. "You just don't quit, do you?"

"Sorry – it's reflexive."

"If you didn't come down here just to tell bad jokes – and I hope you didn't – then why *did* you stop by, Stan? I mean, it's good to know about this new drug, but what do you want from me?"

"I want to know if you can cure it."

She showed me the kind of look you give to a slow third-grader. "You can't cure a drug, Stan – it's not sick. It simply *is*."

"I meant, cure the addiction."

She put her hands into the pockets of the long skirt she was wearing and took a slow stroll over to the window. Looking through the dirty glass, she said, "Addiction is an individual matter and has to be treated individually. Some magic practitioners have been able to treat addicts successfully, but many other people get good results from the more mundane arts, such as psychotherapy."

She turned from the window and looked at me. "You know how many therapists it takes to change a light bulb, Stan?"

"How many?"

"Oh, just one – but the bulb has got to *want* to change."

I winced. "What's that, Rachel – payback for all the dumb jokes I've inflicted on you?"

"Maybe," she said with a smile. "If so, it represents only a down payment." Then she dropped the smile and said, "But it does contain a core truth about curing people – whether through magic, therapy, or medicine. The patient has to desire to be cured. And with addiction, you know, that's not always the case."

"But if you had an addict who wanted to stop using whatever drug he was hooked on, you could help him kick it?"

"I haven't done a lot of that kind of thing myself," she said. "But yes, probably. Of course, I've never tried to cure a supernatural. Goblins tend to take care of their own, for better or worse. And until ten minutes ago, I didn't even know that the other members of the community were vulnerable to addiction."

"I don't know if all the other varieties of supernaturals are capable of getting hooked on this shit. The only species I know about for sure is elves – but the intel about vamps and weres comes from a pretty reliable source."

"Mind if I ask who?"

"Don Pietro Calabrese, his own self."

Her eyes widened a little. "The Vampfather? And you think he'd tell you the truth about *anything*?"

"He would, when it's in is best interest," I said. "As it seems to be this time."

"I hope you're right," she said. "OK, I'll send out some feelers among the local witches about this new drug – if I hear anything useful, I'll pass it on."

"Thanks, Rachel, I appreciate it."

I was heading for the door when she called me back. "Stan!"

"What?"

"If you have the opportunity, I'd really like to get a sample of this Slide to study. I want to see if I can figure out its chemical properties – might help if I have to attempt any curing spells later."

"Alright," I said. "I'll see if I can get some for you."

"Thanks. What are you going to do, in the meantime?"

"Try to stop a war."

So an elf and a goblin walk into a bar – sounds like the start of a joke, right? But what happened at Fred's Original Bar and Grill that night was no joke – especially as far as Fred was concerned.

Once Karl and I got back to the squad room, we briefed McGuire on our conversation with Calabrese and Loquasto. The boss made notes as we spoke and said he was thinking about putting together a briefing for all shifts of detectives, to let them know that their jobs had become even more complicated.

Not long afterward, a call came in, and Karl and I caught it. Normally an armed robbery isn't the business of the Occult Crimes Unit, but this one seemed to be a little unusual. It wasn't until we talked to Fred that we found out just how unusual it was.

Fred was actually Frederick Tapley, Junior. He'd inherited the bar from his old man, Fred Senior, who'd died about twelve years ago. Why the father had bothered to call the place Fred's Original Bar and Grill was beyond me – I didn't think he'd had to worry much about people ripping off the name.

It was a little after 3am, which meant the place had closed for the night about an hour ago. That's one way you can tell the "human" bars from the "supe" bars. Although the law says you can drink wherever you want, regardless of species, most people – as well as those who aren't – tend to prefer the company of their own, especially when they're relaxing. So, although bars catering to supes tended to stay open until dawn, the ones with a mostly human clientele usually closed around 2.

I know the owner of every supe bar in town, but I'd never met Fred Tapley before, since his place catered to humans. He was a big guy, with a thick mustache and brown hair combed forward in a vain attempt to hide a hairline that was not so much receding as it was in full retreat. A couple of Robbery detectives, Pryce and Dalton, were already taking his statement. After exchanging nods, Karl and I joined them – I figured it would save Tapley some trouble, and save us some time, by not making him tell the story twice. Dalton performed introductions, then told Tapley to go on with what he was saying.

"I got the last customer outta here just before 2," Tapley said. "That was Ritchie Patinka, one of my regulars. When he comes in, which is most nights, he always stays till closing. I guess I can understand why – his wife is the original psycho bitch from hell – but I ain't gonna let him spend the night here, for Chrissake. So, like, ten minutes later, I'm sweepin' up, when there's a knock at the door. I yell, 'We're closed! Come back tomorrow!' and go back to my sweepin'. But the knockin' don't stop. So, in case the guy didn't hear me the first time, I take in a good breath and this time I fucking bellow it: 'WE'RE CLOSED. GO HOME!'"

"But the knocking didn't stop?" Pryce asked him.

"Fuckin' A right, it didn't. It keeps on, like I never said nothing at all. I figure it's some drunk who got kicked outta another bar at two o'clock and decided to try his luck here, 'Closed' sign or no 'Closed' sign. So, I figure I'm gonna have to tell him to his face. So I pick up Fats, in case he's gonna be, like, belligerent, and go to the door."

Dalton looked at him. "Fats? I thought you said you were alone."

"I was," Tapley said. He took a couple of steps over to the bar and picked up a two-foot-long piece of sawed-off pool cue. "This is Fats – short for Minnesota Fats. I keep it under the bar, in case somebody gets a little too feisty, you know? Usually just showing it is enough to quiet a guy down, even if he *is* half in the bag. I've only had to use it for real a couple of times."

"Alright, fine," Pryce said. "So you and Fats here go to the door, and…?"

"And I open it, of course. Well, there's a fuckin' elf standing there. And the second thing I notice is that the bastard's got a greenie with him."

"You mean a goblin?" Pryce asked.

"Yeah, right – a fuckin' goblin. Like I said, that's the second thing I notice. The first thing is the cut-down shotgun the elf is holdin' – and it's pointed right at my chest."

"Did either of them say anything at that point?" Dalton asked him.

"Yeah, the elf tells me, 'Back the fuck up.' So I do. Then he says 'Drop the bat.' Stupid bastard doesn't even know the difference between a bat and a pool cue."

"I assume you complied anyway," Pryce said.

"Bet your ass I did – I wasn't gonna get myself shot. Not over what was in the till, or even ten times that."

I decided to make a contribution to the interview. "What about the goblin?" I asked Tapley. "Was he armed, as well?"

"Yeah, he had one of them knives they carry, must've been a foot and a half long. But I was a lot more worried about the shotgun."

"Did he say anything?" Karl asked. "The goblin, I mean."

"Aw, he made some kind of noises. If they was supposed to be words, I couldn't make any of 'em out."

"Tell us what happened then," Pryce said.

"The elf says open the register. So I do. He's standing next to me the whole time. In fact, I thought about grabbing the shotgun, since the little bastard was so close. But then I figured if I try it and miss, they end up cleaning my guts off the walls. Fuck that."

"Good decision," I said.

"Yeah, whatever. So, I open the register, and the elf hands me a paper bag. 'Put the bills in here,' he says. Then he makes me lift up the drawer, so he can get at the compartment underneath, where I stash the big bills. I don't get a lot of big spenders in this joint, so there's only a couple of fifties in there. He gets those, too."

"What's the goblin doing while all this is going down?" Karl asked him.

"He's just standing the other side of the bar, holding that knife and shifting his weight from one foot to the other, like a kid who gotta go to the bathroom real bad."

"Then what?" Dalton said.

"So then the elf tells me to lie on my face, with my hands over my ears. This is when I start to get real nervous, cause I figure he's either gonna shoot me or beat my head in with my own pool cue. So as not to leave witnesses, you know?"

"But he didn't, since you're standing here talking to us," Dalton said. "So, what *did* he do?"

"Well, I can't hear nothin', but I can feel the vibration in the floorboards that tells me they're walkin' around. Then, after a few seconds, I can't feel that no more. I wait a little longer, just to be safe, then I take my hands away from my ears, and I can't hear a thing. I get up, real slow, and sure enough, they're gone. So I find my phone and call 911."

"You're supposed to call 666 when supes are involved," I said.

"Oh, yeah," Tapley said, "I forgot. Anyway, it worked – you guys are here, right?"

Pryce asked for descriptions of the perps but didn't get much that was useful. The elf was short – *duh* – and wearing a dark-colored T-shirt. The goblin looked like a goblin. He was green and furry.

The guys from Robbery were making arrangements to have Tapley come over to police headquarters later and look at mug books when Karl and I decided we'd learned as much as we were likely to, and left.

Outside, Karl shook his head. "Elves and goblins working together. Jeez."

"Only one of each, so far," I said. "But you're right, it could be the start of a trend that's gonna catch on big-time unless we do something about it."

We got into the car, and as I started up, Karl said, "And what exactly did you have in mind to do, oh wise man?"

"The crimes are caused by addiction to Slide, right? Slide is being pushed by members of the Delatasso family. Stop them, we stop the drug from circulating. Eliminate the drug, and we get rid of the crime."

"So we're gonna do Calabrese's dirty work for him?" Karl didn't sound too happy about it.

"No, we're doing the City of Scranton's work. It just happens that Calabrese's goals and the city's goals converge this time."

We'd gone a couple of blocks when Karl said, "Remember that rule you told me about once, 'Locken's First Law'?"

"'You can do everything right and still lose,'" I quoted. "Yeah, so?"

"So, let's say we succeed beyond our wildest dreams. We drive the Delatassos out of Scranton for good, and the supply of Slide dries up to nothing. Then what've we got?"

"Peace and quiet?" I said.

"No, just a different kind of noise. What do you think's gonna happen when all these addicted supes can't get a fix, no matter how much money they steal to pay for it?"

"They all go into rehab?" I knew that wasn't what he meant.

"No, they all go fucking apeshit – sticking up drugstores to find something that's similar to Slide, and tearing into bloody pieces anybody who so much as looks at them sideways. It would be like every dog in town suddenly went rabid."

"Say you're right," I told him. "What're we supposed to do, then? Let the Delatassos sell their shit wherever they want? I know some people who wouldn't care for that much – one of 'em's named Tapley, and another one's named Donna, not to mention everybody else who was in Johnny's Diner the other night."

"I'm just raising the question." Karl said. "I never claimed I had the answer."

"Yeah, well, there's only one answer to your question that I can think of," I said.

"I am all attention."

"Shut the fucking Delatassos down as soon as we possibly can – that won't eliminate your 'mad dog' problem, but it'll keep the impact to a minimum."

"As soon as possible," Karl said, with a slow nod. "That means we're gonna have to cut some corners."

"Shit," I said, remembering all the lies I'd told the brass yesterday, "we've already started."

But before you can cut corners, you have to know just where the corners are. So back at the squad room, Karl and I sat down with McGuire to talk about the legal status of Slide.

"Somebody's selling that shit, but we can't even bust them for it, can we?" I said.

"Not right now, you can't, no," McGuire said.

I gave a sigh. "I was kinda afraid of that."

"Why the fuck not?" Karl said. "Selling addictive drugs is illegal, right? Everybody knows that."

"I wish it was that simple," McGuire told him. "'Addictive' is a medical term, not a legal one."

Karl frowned at that. "Say what?"

"Lots of stuff's addictive," McGuire said. "Tobacco, alcohol, and caffeine, for instance. But none of them is illegal, you might have noticed."

"Because they're not 'controlled substances'," I added.

"Exactly right," McGuire said. "Something's a controlled substance because there a law that says it *has* to be controlled. Shit, a hundred years ago *cocaine* was legal, before they knew how bad it could fuck people up. Heroin, too – all that shit. It just took time for the law to catch up with the menace."

"And cause Slide's so new, there's no laws on the books banning it." Karl shook his head. "Fuck."

"Yeah," I said. "Fuck."

"Wait a minute," Karl said. "We've busted goblins for meth before."

"Yeah, that's because meth was already illegal before the goblins ever got hold of it. It was the only drug that addicted supes – well, one species of supe – as well as humans."

"Or so we thought," McGuire said.

Karl looked at McGuire, then at me. "And we don't even know if Slide has any effect on humans, do we?"

"Nope," I said. "And if it turns out that there's no human addiction..."

"It could be years before Congress, or even the state legislatures, get around to banning it," McGuire said. "You know how it is."

"Yeah, I know how it fuckin' is," Karl said. "Stuff that only involves supes doesn't exactly get a high priority with the government."

McGuire had the good grace to look a little embarrassed. Karl was speaking nothing but the truth. Supes were still considered second-class citizens by a lot of people – some of them government officials.

"Course, since this stuff seems to be causing supes to rob *humans*," Karl said, "maybe it'll get some politicos' attention a little quicker."

"Could be," McGuire said. "But for now, Slide's as legal as soda pop."

"Well, fuck me," Karl said.

I shook my head slowly. "Sorry," I said. "I kinda like you, but not that way."

"What we need to do," I said, "is get our hands on some Slide."

Karl and I were sitting behind our desks in the squad room, facing each other. He understood what I meant, but he pretended not to. "What's up with that, Stan – you lookin' for a new kind of high?"

"Not exactly," I said, "but you're pretty close."

He gave me raised eyebrows.

"For one thing," I said, "I want to have the shit tested, to see if it does have any effect on humans. If it's as addictive for them as it is supes, we might see some quicker action on making it illegal."

Karl made a disgusted sound. I don't think he disagreed with me – he just hated the fact that I was right.

"I'd like to get some Slide for Rachel. She wants to see if magic might work in curing somebody who's hooked on the shit."

"Well, good luck to her, then." Karl glanced at his watch. "Looks like it's almost quitting–"

That was when McGuire came out of his office and yelled, "OK, listen up!"

The room got quiet fast, and then he said, "We just got a call, and I want everybody on it."

"What's up, boss?" Sefchik asked him.

"A report of multiple shots fired in the 400 block of Moosic St. Get in your cars – now!"

"Shit!" I said.

Karl looked at me. "That's Ricardo's."

"Looks like the war's not over yet."

The other detectives were already out the door. We stood up, and Karl turned to McGuire, who was still standing outside his office. He pointed his chin toward the window, then pointed to his watch. "Lieutenant..."

It was still dark outside, but the sun would be up in less than an hour. That was what Karl meant, and McGuire knew it. He nodded at Karl and said, "Yeah, I know. OK, head on home." Then he looked at me. "You're riding alone on this one, Markowski."

As we walked toward the stairs that led to the parking lot, Karl said, "Try not to do anything stupid and get yourself killed, OK?"

"Do my best."

"I mean, you've still got my DVD of *Thunderblood*, and Christine might not be in a hurry to give it back. She might even decide to keep it."

"Yeah," I said. "She just might."

In the parking lot, I caught up with Sefchik and Aquilina and asked if I could ride with them out to the crime scene – if that's what it was. No sense in taking another car out just for me – especially since the police department had been hit by another budget cut this year by the City Council.

Once I was in the back seat of their car, I called Christine. I knew she was still at work, and so wasn't surprised to get her voice mail. I waited for the beep, then said, "Hi, honey, it's your old man. We've had some shit hit the fan at work. Nothing to worry about, but it looks like I won't be getting home until you're sacked out. So, sleep well, and I'll see you at breakfast."

On the way to Moosic Street, I told Sefchik and Aquilina what I'd learned about Slide and the Philly fangsters who were peddling it in town.

"Christ, that's just what we need," Aquilina said from behind the wheel. She never took her eyes off the road. "A new drug on the streets, addicted supes going crazy, and a gang war, to boot. God, I love this job!"

We arrived at Moosic Street a couple of minutes later. The end of the block containing Ricardo's Ristorante had a couple of black-and-white units straddling the street with their lights flashing, to keep out civilian traffic. That was as close to the action as the uniformed officers were likely to get. Department policy said that when vampire perps were suspected, regular patrol units were supposed to secure the area, keep their distance, and wait for the specialists from Occult Crimes to arrive.

Two more cars from the squad, headlights still on, had got there ahead of us. They were parked more or less in front of Ricardo's Ristorante, diagonally from the sidewalk. Cops at crime scenes don't *have* to park at crazy angles that nobody else would imitate – we do it because we *can*.

I was noticing trivial stuff like that because there was nothing else to look at. No suspects in custody, no bodies, no wounded vamps – *nothing*. That street was cleaner than a nun's asshole.

The restaurant itself was shut tight, with no lights showing anywhere. I thought that was unusual – places like Ricardo's usually stay open until dawn, at least. But maybe Calabrese didn't want the restaurant to be known as a supe hangout – or maybe they'd just closed early tonight.

The only things moving in that block of Moosic Street were seven detectives, who were milling around and looking at each other with "What the fuck" expressions on our faces.

I glanced around at the others. I was the only sergeant in the bunch, and that meant I was Ranking Officer on Scene – at least until some Lieutenant or higher came along and relieved me. I hoped it wouldn't take long for that to happen. In the meantime, I figured I'd better act like I knew what I was doing.

"Alright, everybody!" I said. "Looks like I'm ROS for the time being, so we might as well get to work." The other detectives all looked at me, but nobody gave me an argument.

"Aquilina, Sefchik, see if you can get somebody to answer the door at Ricardo's, and don't forget to check around back. The rest of you start the canvass. A lot of the neighbors aren't gonna want to come to the door at this hour, but keep your thumb on the buzzer until they do. You all know what kind of questions to ask, so let's get started."

Nobody ever answered the door at Ricardo's that morning, and our canvass of the neighborhood turned up exactly zip. None of those living in the apartments overlooking the street saw anything, knew anything, or thought anything – or so they said. Even the two people who'd called 911 about shots being fired told us that they'd heard the gunfire, yes, but hadn't looked out to see where it was coming from. They had said so very earnestly, and the detectives interviewing them had just nodded, as if they believed every word.

It's a pain in the ass when witnesses won't talk, but I couldn't really blame the civilians for clamming up. Who wants to get on the wrong side of a bunch of criminals – hard guys with guns who aren't afraid to use them?

So we had no witnesses, and no forensic evidence, either. Whoever had cleaned up the scene had been fast but thorough – they hadn't left so much as a shell casing behind. There were bullet holes in some of the buildings, but the bullets would be so badly fragmented that ballistics tests would be impossible. Several fresh-looking stains in the street were probably blood, but that stuff was useless without somebody's DNA to compare it with. And I had a feeling that the guys whose blood had seeped into that asphalt were never going to be seen again.

It took about two and a half hours to reach the conclusion that this so-called crime scene was going to be about as fruitful as a dead apple tree. Lieutenant Russo from Homicide had taken over by then, and he finally turned us loose. Since my shift was already long over, I didn't have to go back to work. I'd been feeling hungry the last hour or so, so I decided to stop for something to eat on my way home.

I didn't go to Jerry's Diner this time – I had a hankering for something that wasn't served with a light coating of grease. Fortunately, Wohlstein's Deli and Eatery downtown serves everything on their menu all day long.

Whoever wrote "A thing of beauty is a joy forever" must have been thinking of Manny Wohlstein's turkey club sandwich – and if not, he should have been. I was halfway through mine when I saw the ghoul come in and take a seat at one of the corner tables.

You can't ID a ghoul just by looking – although if you get close enough to smell their breath, it's what you might call a dead giveaway. But this one I recognized. He goes by "Algernon", and he's the brother of a guy everyone calls Barney Ghougle, a local undertaker and one of my most reliable informants.

I knew who Algernon was because he's got a little problem that sometimes gets him into trouble – a habit of taking his cock out in front of people and waving it around. I hoped he'd be able to resist the impulse as long as he was in Wohlstein's – I was off duty. Besides, I'd seen ghoul cock before and hoped never to have to look at any again.

Taking another bite out of my sandwich, I began to wonder what the hell Algernon was doing there. Wohlstein's offers a large menu, but they don't serve the kind of stuff that ghouls eat. Just as well, really – a menu item like *Human thigh, sliced thinly and served au jus* would probably turn off a lot of human customers, me included.

All of the waitresses are Manny's daughters, and the tall one, whose name is Clara, stopped at Algernon's table, order pad in hand. The ghoul said something that I couldn't hear, but Clara went away and returned a minute later with what looked like a glass of iced tea. She said something to Algernon, who shook his head, and she went off to her other tables.

I continued eating but kept an unobtrusive eye on Algernon. I was waiting for him to drink some of his iced tea. But although he tapped the straw out of its paper wrapper and put it in the plastic tumbler, it never touched his lips. He just sat there, staring off into space.

After a while, one of the busboys came over to Algernon's table. I didn't recognize him, but that meant nothing. Manny has four daughters but no sons, so busboys come and go. But I did think it was strange for a busboy to wipe down a table while the customer was still sitting there.

The busboy, was a slim, red-haired human in his early twenties. He gave the table a quick once-over with a damp rag and said something to Algernon without looking at him. Then he turned, stashed the rag in his apron, and walked across the dining area to the men's restroom. Half a minute or so later, Algernon stood up and went in there, too.

The two of them were in the bathroom together for a couple of minutes, then the busboy came out and went directly into the kitchen. I started counting silently to myself, one thousand *one*, one thousand *two*... When I got to ten, Algernon came out and headed for the door without returning to his table.

I knew what I'd just witnessed, as any cop worth his badge would. Restaurants are prime locations for drug dealing – always have been. You've got people coming and going all the time, and nobody pays much attention.

Sometimes the restaurant owner is in on the action, other times not. I'd known Manny Wohlstein for years, and I'd have bet my pension that he had no idea how one of the employees was supplementing his salary. If Manny ever found out, I hoped the busboy had some *very* good health insurance – the kind with catastrophic coverage.

Ordinarily, this kind of thing was none of my business. I'd just drop a word to a guy I know in Vice, Gus McDorman, and let him deal with it. But one of the parties in the transaction I'd witnessed was a supe, which meant that the drug for sale had almost certainly been Slide. And that *made* it my business. The only question was what I was going to do about it.

It didn't take me long to make up my mind.

Manny Wohlstein can usually be found in his office at the back of the restaurant, but I decided against paying him a visit. The busboy might see me and ask somebody who was in there talking to his boss. All of Manny's daughters knew me by sight, and I didn't want one of them putting the busboy on his guard by telling him that Manny was talking to a cop.

I finished my sandwich, paid the check, and went out to my car. The Yellow Pages app on my phone gave me the deli's number, and I called it.

"Wohlstein's Deli," a cheerful female voice said. "How can I help you?"

"I'd like to speak to Mister Wohlstein, please."

"Can I say who's calling?"

I was pretty sure the voice belonged to Naomi Wohlstein, and I didn't want her saying my name where the busboy might overhear it.

"This is Lou Pastorelli," I told her. "From Mid-Atlantic Produce Distribution."

"Just a minute, Mister Pastorelli."

Then Manny's voice was saying in my ear, "This is Manny Wohlstein. What can I do for you?"

"Manny, it's Stan Markowski. I'm sorry for giving Naomi a false name, but I didn't want her saying my right name out loud. I'd rather you didn't say it, either."

"Why do you want me to do that?" His voice sounded wary.

"I'm calling to ask about one of your employees, who's still in the building. I didn't want him to hear you say my name, in case he's heard it before. I don't want him to start wondering why you're talking to a cop."

"You said 'him', so this isn't one of my girls you're asking about."

"No, of course not."

"Alright, then." Manny's voice relaxed a little, and I could hear that old desk chair of his creak as he leaned back. "So how can I help you, Mister... Pastorelli?"

"We can drop the charade as long as he's not close enough to overhear you."

"And who would that be?" Manny asked.

"You've got a busboy, early twenties, red-haired, tattoo on the inside of one arm."

"Oh, sure, that's Roger Gillespe. Not to worry, Stan. He never comes back here, except to pick up his check, and that's on Friday. He couldn't overhear us even if he had ears on him like an elephant."

"Great," I said. "How long has this Gillespe worked for you?"

"He's been with us over a year, I know that. Could be as long as eighteen months. You want I should look it up?"

"No, that's OK; it doesn't make much difference. But what I *would* like you to look up is his schedule, and whether he's gonna be working tomorrow."

"That I can do." I heard the chair creak again, then the sound of a file drawer opening. "This busboy of mine – he's in some kind of trouble, Stan?"

"Not necessarily," I lied. "That's something I'm still trying to find out. Could be he's just an innocent bystander who might be a useful witness in a case I'm working."

Manny's got a temper, and I knew he'd have trouble controlling it if I told him his busboy was dealing drugs right there in the restaurant. Even if he didn't fire the kid – or break both his arms and *then* fire him, which was more likely – he'd act differently toward Gillespe, which might spook the redhead into a disappearing act. And that bastard wasn't going anywhere until we'd had some conversation.

Manny came back on the line. "Stan? Roger works six in the morning till two in the afternoon. His days off are Monday and Tuesday, which means he should be here tomorrow – unless he calls in sick, which he doesn't do often, it looks like."

"Have you got a home address for him?"

I listened to papers rustle for a second or two. "Yeah, here it is – 144 Spruce Street, Apartment 9."

"Terrific. Thanks, Manny. I'd appreciate it if you wouldn't let this guy know that we've talked. In fact, it would be good if you didn't give him any indication that something's up."

"Not a problem, Stan. I hardly see him anyway, except for two minutes on payday."

"I'll be done with him before then," I said.

I finally got home around noon. As I undressed, I told Quincey about the latest developments in the case. The little guy always seems interested in what I have to tell him, which is more than I can say for some of the people I know. I went to bed and grabbed about five hours' sleep.

Over breakfast, I told Christine what I'd learned in the last twenty-four hours. It didn't amount to much.

She looked at me over the rim of her mug. I noticed she'd slept in a T-shirt that said in front, "'For the blood is the life' Deut. 12:23."

"What are you going to do about this busboy?" she asked.

"Talk to Karl about him," I told her. "Then we'll see."

"Whatever his customer base is, he's not selling to vampires – not at work, anyway. Manny doesn't have vamp food on his menu."

"How do you know?"

"I know," she said. "Word gets around – about the places we're welcome, and the ones where we're not."

"Manny's not prejudiced," I said. "If he doesn't sell blood, it's probably some kind of religious thing."

"Maybe," she said, and took another sip of warm Type O, her favorite. "But the result's the same."

I couldn't think of anything to say about that.

Christine put her mug down. "I went for a walk last night, during my break," she said. "Came across something interesting."

"What was that?"

"A Patriot Party rally. They were holding it at Abington High School's football field."

I smiled a little. "Home of the Fighting Warlocks."

"That's the place. They've done some renovations since I was there last. It looks nice."

"Good turnout?"

She nodded. "The bleachers were packed."

"The Patriot Party's gone from zero to sixty in, like, six months," I said. "And they're local, not part of some bigger movement, far as anybody knows."

"Maybe they'll catch on," she said with a shudder. "But I hope not."

I drank some of my coffee, which wasn't remotely as good as McGuire's. "Yeah, they don't care much for supes, do they?"

She snorted. "That's putting it mildly. Phil Slattery, their candidate for Mayor, was speaking when I passed by. He called supernaturals 'a cancerous growth that threatens our city's purity.'"

"I never could stand a politician who mixes his metaphors," I said.

"I wish that was the worst you could say about him. But he's quite the rabble-rouser – got a standing ovation when he was done and everything. That was when I decided it was time for me to get back to work, before the audience noticed me and turned into a lynch mob."

"That bad, huh?"

"At least," she said.

"Good thing you can fly, if need be."

"Good thing I didn't have to."

I got to work a few minutes early and was catching up on my email when Karl plopped down into his desk chair opposite mine.

"I thought vampires were supposed to be silent as death," I said, without looking up.

"We are," he said. "When death is the objective. But since it's just you, I figured it was OK to be my old, noisy self."

"Works for me," I said. "It beats having to jump halfway out of my chair every time you appear from out of nowhere."

While Karl's computer was booting up, he asked me, "So, what went down at Ricardo's Ristorante last night?"

"Not a damn thing, far as I can tell."

He tilted his head a little. "False alarm?"

"All depends on how you define your terms," I said.

I explained how we'd found nothing in the street outside Ricardo's except some bullet holes that would surely prove worthless as evidence, and some fresh stains on the street that might have been blood – the lab report hadn't come back yet.

"Sounds like Calabrese won that round," Karl said.

"How do you figure?"

"If the Delatassos had taken out a bunch of Calabrese's soldiers again, what incentive would they have to clean up after themselves? They'd want plenty of evidence lying around, just like last time. They probably figure all the carnage is gonna intimidate Calabrese into giving up."

"Yeah, and good luck with that," I said.

He nodded. "I don't figure you could scare Calabrese with anything less than a nuclear bomb – and it would have to be a *big* bomb to do the job."

"That's a pretty good theory you came up with, though – that the lack of bodies means a win for Calabrese. You should share it with McGuire."

"OK, if you think it's worth the effort."

"Everything's worth the effort at this point," I said. "But I'm not done with my story yet – it gets better. We canvassed the neighborhood and came up with absolutely shit, as you might expect. So, after a couple of hours, they finally let us leave. I was in no hurry to go home, since Christine was already sacked out, so I headed down to Wohlstein's Deli for something to eat...."

I told him about the busboy who I'd observed in what had to be a covert business transaction with Barney Ghougle's brother, Algernon.

Karl shook his head a couple of times. "Stupid fuck. First indecent exposure, now street drugs. Looks like Algernon's bucking for a slot in the Loser Hall of Fame."

"He'll get my vote," I said. "But I'm a lot more interested in that busboy, Gillespe."

"Yeah, he's a link in the chain – the first one we've come across so far."

Thor and Car, the two gun-toting elves, had hired attorneys and now weren't saying anything to anybody. I figured the DA would eventually offer one of them a deal that would have the little bastard singing like a drunk on karaoke night, but it hadn't happened yet. Like everything else in city government, the District Attorney's office is understaffed and underfunded.

"And since God, or whoever's in charge, has seen fit to gift us with this link," I said, "it would behoove us to follow it and see where it leads."

"Well, whether it fucking behooves us or not, we can't just bust the guy," Karl said. "The shit he's selling is legal, remember?"

"I wasn't planning to bust him," I said. "But I do think he should be questioned."

Karl looked at me as if I'd just said I believe in the Easter Bunny. I don't, of course – although, far as I'm concerned, the jury's still out on the Great Pumpkin.

"We can't pick bring some guy in to question him about something that's not a crime, Stan. You know that, well as I do."

"I never said anything about bringing Gillespe *in*," I told him. "And as for questioning, I figured I'd leave that up to you."

He leaned back in his chair. "OK, now the light dawns. You're talking about one of those more *informal* Q-and-A sessions."

"Uh-huh. Preferably carried out in the back seat of our car while it's parked in an alley someplace."

"Nothing we get out of him would be admissible in court," he said slowly. "On the other hand..."

"On the other hand, it might bring us one step closer to the Delatassos. And if need be, once we find the next link, we can repeat the informal procedure with him."

"I like the way you think," Karl said. "One thing we have to–"

That was when McGuire opened the door to his office and stepped out. "Markowski! You and Renfer got one!"

Moments later, McGuire was back behind his desk, while Karl and I stood in front of it to get our marching orders. "Black-and-white units are already at the scene," he said, "along with the fire department and somebody from the State Police bomb squad. But I wanted you two on it as well."

Karl and I looked at each other before Karl said, "On what, boss?"

"It looks like somebody blew up Victor Castle."

Even before we got to Evelyn Avenue, I could hear them: the whooping, screeching, and honking sounds made by about a hundred car alarms going all at once. A sound wave can set off lots of different makes of car alarms, if it's strong enough. Anybody living near an airport could tell you that.

Then we turned the corner and drove straight into the middle of a Hieronymus Bosch nightmare.

The street was full of police cars, ambulances, and fire trucks, not to mention the van belonging to the State Police bomb squad – all parked at crazy angles. Their flashing red-and-blue lights sent strobe-like shadows skittering across the storefronts and apartments that lined the street on both sides. Broken glass from what had been hundreds of windows threw back the flashing lights crazily, as if the street and sidewalks themselves were on fire.

Somebody had given this part of Scranton its own version of the Nazi *Kristallnacht* – the Night of Broken Glass. According to what I saw on the History Channel, a night like this had signaled the beginning of the organized persecution of Germany's Jews. I hoped the rampant destruction I was looking at wasn't going to be a sign of some new kind of terror.

We parked as close as we could get to the scene – which turned out to be two blocks away from the outer ring of yellow crime scene tape. Karl and I made sure our badges were in plain view, and started walking. There were no flames visible up ahead, and no water running through the gutters, so I guessed the fire trucks had been called as a precaution and had decided to stick around, just in case.

Up ahead, I saw an ambulance start up and slowly drive away. I noticed the driver wasn't using the lights or siren, which meant he was headed for the morgue, not the hospital. There's never any hurry when your passenger is already dead.

I saw a guy over near the bomb squad van who I recognized. Chris Dennehy and I used to run into each other at crime scenes back when I was in Homicide, although I hadn't seen him in a while. Death by explosion isn't an M. O. you come across very often on the supe squad.

We went over there and I stuck my hand out. "Chris," I said. "Been a long time." I had to raise my voice so that he could hear me over the din caused by all those car alarms.

"How ya doin', Stan," he said as we shook. He was speaking louder than normal, too.

I saw him looking over my shoulder. "This is my partner, Karl Renfer," I said. "Karl, meet Chris Dennehy. He's a Statie who gets blown up for a living."

"Not if I can help it," Dennehy said, and shook hands with Karl. As he let go, I saw a puzzled look on his face – maybe because Karl's grip, like every vampire's, is colder than a banker's heart. Dennehy might have realized then that Karl was undead – but if so, he was smart enough to let it go.

"Have they got a positive ID on the body yet?" I asked.

"Yeah, one of the guys who works in the rug store was in back when the bomb went off, so he wasn't hurt . He looked at the body for us. When he got done puking, he confirmed that it was Castle."

I made a head gesture toward the street. "How d'you figure it went down, Chris?"

He looked toward what had once been the front of Mystic Rugs, Magic Carpets, narrowing his eyes against the flashing lights. "Looks like the bomb was in a trash can in front of the store. Nailed

Castle from about twenty feet away, along with a lot of the surrounding real estate."

Karl looked at him. "Radio-controlled, right?"

"Had to be. No way somebody could've cut it that fine with a time bomb."

I nodded agreement, then said, "Can you think of any local experts who might have been able to put something like this together?"

"Uh-uh. Only guy from around here who was good at stuff like this was Mickey McCormick," he said, "and he spread himself over two city blocks in Hazelton last year, in what I can only assume was some kind of on-the-job accident."

I took a slow look around at the broken glass and scorched pavement. "Whoever he was, he used something pretty powerful. You don't get results like this from a couple of cherry bombs taped together."

"Judging from the blast pattern, I'd say it was some kind of plastic," Dennehy said. "C-4, maybe even Semtex. We might have something more definitive on that in a couple of days." He shrugged. "Or not. You know how it goes."

"A remote detonator and Semtex," Karl said. "Not exactly amateur night, is it?"

"It's professional work, alright," Dennehy said. "And since Mickey McCormick's in the ground, probably buried in a shoebox, I'd say somebody brought in out-of-town talent."

"Where you gonna find somebody like that?" I said. "I'm pretty sure they don't let bombers advertise on Craigslist."

"Best bet's one of the big cities," Dennehy said. "And even then, you'd have to know the right people to talk to. There's two pros I've heard of in New York, although they mostly do work for the Five Families. And if you looked hard enough, you could probably find bomb specialists in Boston, Chicago…"

"Maybe even Philadelphia," Karl said.

"So, when you said Philly, you were thinking of the Delatassos," I said to Karl. "Right?"

"Course I was," he said.

We were on our way to a bar – but not because either one of us wanted a drink. Drinking on duty's against department policy, anyway.

But Renfield's is more than just a place where you can get any drink known to man – as well as a few that most men wouldn't *want* to know. As the biggest supe bar in town, it's often been a good source of information for Karl and me. You get an interesting mix of customers at Renfield's, and some of them have been known to be talkative, given the right incentive.

I glanced at Karl. "Why would the Delatassos want to take out Victor Castle?"

He shrugged. "Could be he was trying to fuck with the Slide trade. When we told him about that stuff the other night, he wasn't a happy camper, remember? I don't know what pissed him off more – that somebody was selling shit like that in Scranton, or that he hadn't heard about it yet."

They say that bad news travel fast. You may also have heard the expression "the dead travel fast". So you can just imagine how fast bad tidings travel among the dead, the undead, and the formerly dead. The news of Victor Castle's murder had gone through the local supe community like a prairie fire.

I realized that as soon as Karl and I opened the front door of Renfield's. For one thing, the place was packed – pretty unusual, even for Saturday night. But when catastrophe strikes, the members of any community will tend to draw together – whether to mourn, to commiserate with each other, or just to gossip about what had happened and share details that are mostly rumor, fantasy, or speculation.

And if the size of crowd didn't tell me that news of Castle's death had already spread, what happened when Karl and I came in would have made it crystal clear. We hadn't taken more than a couple of steps into the room when the level of conversation went from what I'd call "medium-loud" to what anybody would have to describe as "silent as a fucking tomb".

That wasn't normal. Sure, they knew Karl and I were cops, but we'd been coming into Renfield's together for more than a year without any problems, not to mention all the times before that when I'd drop by with my old partner, Paul DiNapoli. And these days, Karl was even what you might call a member of the supe club.

Our footsteps sounded loud in the silence as we made our way to the bar. I don't know if the customers were expecting us to make some kind of announcement, or start arresting people, or even shoot up the place. But once it became clear that none of that was going to happen, the level of tension slowly eased. By the time we reached the bar, the buzz of conversation had started again. Over the next few minutes, it gradually returned to its former level.

Tending bar was a thirtyish brown-eyed blonde with a pug nose and a perky manner. I was a little surprised to see her on a Saturday, since she usually works weeknights.

"Hi, Sam," I said. "Where's Elvira?"

The regular weekend bartender has a persona based on that campy sexpot who hosts a TV show in LA devoted to bad horror movies. The cleavage alone probably gets our local version a lot of tips.

"She took some vacation time and went back to Minneapolis – I guess her mom's pretty sick," Samantha said. "What can I get for you, Stan?"

"Club soda for me and a…" I glanced toward Karl.

"Type O, lightly warmed," he said.

I was a little disappointed when she didn't just twitch that cute nose of hers and cause the drinks to appear by magic. But I knew that Samantha wasn't a real witch – she just played one on the job. And magic doesn't work like that, anyway.

As she moved off down the bar, I said to Karl, "I'm a little surprised you didn't order that 'shaken, not stirred'."

He gave me a half-smile. "I save that for when I want a Bloody Mary."

As you might imagine, the Bloody Marys in Renfield's are made with real blood.

I slowly turned in my stool and scanned the room, looking for my favorite informant. I could've used the big mirror over the bar to check the place out, but that's not always reliable. On any given night, some of Renfield's patrons won't necessarily reflect in mirrors.

When I heard Sam's voice behind me say, "Here you go, fellas," I turned back around and reached for my wallet, since Karl had paid the last time.

Dropping a ten on the bar, I asked Sam, "Barney Ghougle been in tonight?"

"Not so far, Stan. In fact, I don't think I've seen him all week."

That was too bad. Most ghouls love gossip the way pigs enjoy mud, and Barney Ghougle was usually hip-deep in it. If anybody had any scuttlebutt about what had been going on in town lately, it would be him. Then I noticed a sometime informant of mine sitting in a corner. Robin was alone but probably wouldn't be for long.

Looking at that corner table, all you'd see was a tall brunette in a tight blue dress who sat there sipping a drink and oozing sex appeal. If that's what you saw, you'd be partially right. She *was* a beautiful woman – but only some of the time.

Robin was a succubus – which meant that, like all of her kind, she was also an incubus. A succubus/incubus can take on either a female or male aspect at will, each one extremely attractive and highly desirable. Whether you were male or female, gay, straight, or bi, Robin could be exactly what you wanted – for the right price, of course. She was believed to be the most successful prostitute in town, if not the whole Wyoming Valley. A few more good years, and she'd probably be able to *buy* the Wyoming Valley.

Every cop who's been on the job longer than ten minutes knows that prostitution goes on. But in Scranton, like a lot of towns, we mostly leave the working girls alone. As long as they're discreet and don't cross over into something like robbery, blackmail, or drug dealing, they can ply their trade without being harassed by the law. There's enough *real* crime – involving humans and supes alike – to keep the police busy without us becoming guardians of public morality as well.

Due to the size and variety of her clientele, Robin came across a lot of information – some of which was even true. I caught her eye and made a slight gesture with my chin in the direction of the restrooms. Then I said to Karl, "I'll be back in a couple minutes. See if you can find anybody who's feeling talkative." Then I slid off my stool and headed toward the men's room around the corner.

Two minutes later, I was standing at one of the urinals when Robin came in. There was nobody else in the place – I'd checked the stalls, just to be sure – but even if another guy came in, he wouldn't have noticed anything unusual, since Robin now looked like a man.

Hell, Robin *was* a man – a dark-haired, good-looking guy with nothing remotely feminine about his features. Even the clothing was different – the male version of Robin was wearing designer jeans, a chambray shirt and a sport coat that probably cost what I make in a month. I'd never understood how the physical transformation could be accompanied by a change in outfit, but I guess magic is magic. If you can shift from one gender to the other in a matter of seconds, changing your wardrobe is a pretty small trick by comparison.

I was standing at one of the urinals, pretending to take a leak, when Robin walked up to one a little to my right and unzipped his pants. I assume that what he pulled out was a porn star-size schlong, to be consistent with the rest of his studly persona, but I didn't check. As Guy Rule Number Four clearly states: "You *never* look at another man's dick in a public restroom." I hear there are some towns where that rule has exceptions, but Scranton isn't one of them.

Robin must've known Rule Number Four as well. He kept his eyes looking straight ahead as he said, quietly, "What's on your mind, Sergeant?"

"Lot of bad shit going down lately," I said. I kept my voice down, as well. No sense broadcasting this conversation to anyone on the other side of the door.

From the corner of my eye, I could see the smile that briefly creased the handsome face. "'Bad shit going down.' How Seventies. I didn't think anybody said stuff like that anymore."

"Yeah, well, some of us do."

"Perhaps if you could be a little more specific...."

"Alright," I said. "We've got a gang war going on, with Scranton as the prize. The Delatasso Family from Philly wants in, which means they have to move Calabrese out."

"I understand that it's not Delatasso Senior who's behind the hostile takeover attempt – it's his son, Ronnie."

"Yeah, I'd heard that, too."

Robin finished his business at the urinal and went over to the sink. "The smart money says that Calabrese is going down," he said.

"Yeah? How come?"

"The reason varies, depending on who you talk to. Some say the Vampfather has had it too easy for too long. He's gone soft."

I bet the two guys that Calabrese staked out to greet the sun would disagree, I thought.

"What else do you hear?" I asked.

"That Delatasso the elder isn't bankrolling Junior. But Ronnie seems to have found a sugar daddy somewhere – he's got all the money he needs. Enough to put a lot of soldiers on the ground, anyway."

"Anybody know who the sugar daddy is?"

"There's a lot of speculation, but not a lot of facts to hang it on."

"What kind of speculation?"

"One of the New York families, or maybe a family from some other city, or the CIA, the DEA, the FBI, some eccentric billionaire." He shrugged those well-tailored shoulders. "It's all smoke."

Robin tossed the wad of paper towels he'd been using in the trash and said, "Will there be anything else this evening, Officer?"

"Slide," I said. "Also known as Hemoglobin-Plus."

"Yes, I've heard about it. So?"

"So, who's selling it?"

"The Delatassos, of course. You *must* know that much."

"I do," I said. "I mean who *specifically*?"

"Vamps – some vamps, anyway." He thought for a few seconds. "Elves, too, or so I hear. There's even been a rumor that some humans are dealing the stuff."

That last one was more than just a rumor, but I decided to keep the fact to myself.

"Where's it come from, do you know?" I asked him. "I mean, who makes it?"

"I haven't the faintest," Robin said. "I remember that one of my… clients told me he'd heard that it first showed up in Australia, a year or so ago. But then, my clients are sometimes full of shit."

Mine, too, I thought. *Let's hope that you're not one of them. Not this time.*

Aloud I said, "I guess you heard about Victor Castle."

"Of course I have. Everyone has. It's a damn shame."

I gave him raised eyebrows. "It's a shame, because...?"

"Because he was a good guy," Robin said impatiently. "Not a prick, like Vollman. Pity he wasn't more vigilant – Castle, I mean. He should have seen this coming, or something like it."

"Why's that?"

"Because not everybody in the community agreed that he *was* a good guy." He shrugged again. "Or maybe it didn't matter. Maybe he was just in the way."

"In the way of who?" I said. "Or what?"

"I don't know, exactly," Robin said. "And if I did, I probably wouldn't say."

I gave him a hard look. "You're not usually so shy about sharing information, my friend. You scared of something?"

"Maybe I am," he said. "Maybe you should be, too."

Before I could think of a comeback to that, Robin turned away and walked the two steps to the door. His hand on the knob, he looked back at me, his handsome face as grim as I've ever seen it.

"I've been around a very long time, Sergeant," Robin said. "And one of the things I've learned is – when the winds of change start blowing, you either bend or you break."

Pulling the restroom door open, he said to me, "Take care you don't get broken, yourself."

Then he was gone.

••••

"'Take care you don't get broken,'" Karl quoted as he drove us toward Spruce Street. "What the fuck does *that* mean?"

"Something to do with those winds of change, I guess."

"So somebody took out Castle because he – or she – wanted to be the *capo di tutti supi*. If we can pin a murder rap on the bastard, fine. But otherwise, why should we care?"

"Well, you might care, a little," I said. "Being one of the *supi* and all."

He thought about that for a second. "OK, maybe as a vampire it matters to me – a little, like you said. But as a cop, I can't see how it makes much difference who's in charge. As long as he's somebody we can do business with, that is."

We'd gone another couple of blocks before I said, "But what if he's not?"

He took his eyes off the road just long enough to give me an odd look. "Say *what*?"

"I mean, say the new guy isn't interested in doing business with us. Maybe he's some kind of supe separatist and sees all cops as the enemy."

He frowned. "I didn't think we had any of those around here."

"Me, neither. But there's a first time for everything, I guess."

Ever since supes began "coming out of the coffin" after World War Two, most of them have wanted nothing more than to integrate with human society. And they've been successful at it, too – with a few exceptions, on either side.

There are the supe haters, and some of those assholes are organized into groups, like the KKK used to be. And there are some supes who consider humans an inferior species and want nothing to do with us – until they get hungry, that is. Put those two groups within sight of each other and you could have a scaled-down version of a race war.

Race war. Something about that phrase sent a thought skittering across the back or my mind, but before I could grab it for a good look, Karl said, "This must be it, up here – on the corner."

"Let's go by it slow. I want to see if they have off-street parking." The idea that had been trying to get my attention a moment earlier was gone now.

We drove past the small apartment building that Roger Gillespe, busboy and Slide dealer, apparently called home, then turned the corner on to Penn Avenue, to get a side view. There was no room behind the building for cars to park. That meant Gillespe's vehicle – assuming he owned one – would have to be parked on Spruce Street, since there was no parking allowed in this section of Penn.

"Go around the block and back to Spruce," I said to Karl. "I saw an open parking space – looks like it has a clear line of sight to the front of the building. We'll see him when he comes out to his car."

"What if he's walking?" Karl said.

"Then he'll have to walk right past us, if he's on his way to work – and he oughta be. Manny said the kid's shift starts at 6."

I could have called the Motor Vehicle Bureau to find out if Roger Gillespe had a car registered in his name, along with the make and model, but I didn't. When you ask Motor Vehicles for that kind of information, they take down your name and shield number. Same thing if a cop does a search for that stuff online. In case anything went wrong in the next few minutes, I didn't want my interest in Roger to be part of any official record.

I just hoped that the guy hadn't spent the night someplace else with his girlfriend, if he had one. Or boyfriend.

It was 5.42 by the dashboard clock when the front door of the building opened. The street lights showed me a slim young guy with red hair who came out, bounced down the three steps to the sidewalk, and turned left. He walked maybe fifty feet and stopped next to the driver's door of a dark blue Volkswagen Geist that was parked at the curb. He reached into his pants pocket, as if searching for keys.

"That's him," I said. "Let's go."

Roger Gillespe didn't even have the Geist's front door open when we pulled up next to him, parked at an angle to prevent his car from going anywhere, even if he did get started up. He was still gaping at us when I rolled out of the passenger seat and showed him my badge.

"Police officer!" I said. "Don't move!"

Karl was out too, his Glock pointed at Gillespe from across the hood of our car.

"Take your hand out of your pocket – slow!" I told him. "And it better be empty when I see it."

He complied, so I said, "Turn and face the car, hands on the roof. Do it!"

As I began to frisk him, I said, "You got anything in your pockets I need to know about – any needles or sharp objects?"

"No, man, I got nothin' like that." His voice, deeper than I would have expected for his size, was unsteady. Not surprising, considering the big pile of shit he'd just found himself dropped in.

In the left-hand pocket of his jeans I found what I'd been looking for – a half dozen zip-lock plastic baggies, the small ones that are called "snack size". Each bag was about half full with a gray-looking granular powder.

I slipped the bags into my jacket pocket and finished the search, but none of his other pockets contained anything interesting. Then I took the handcuffs off my belt.

As I pulled his hands behind his back, one at a time, I said, "Roger Gillespe, you are under arrest on suspicion of trafficking in illegal substances."

He tried to look at me over his shoulder. "But that's not... I mean, I don't...."

"Shut up and face front," I said.

When the cuffs were locked in place, I said, "You have the right to remain silent," and went on with the rest it, reciting the same Stoker warning that I must've said a thousand times over the years.

"Do you understand these rights as I have explained them to you?" I asked him. That's part of the routine, too – even if it didn't apply in Roger's case.

"Yeah, sure," he said, "But you don't–"

"I sure as hell do," I said. "Come on – get in the car."

A few seconds later he was in the back seat, I was in front, and Karl had us rolling out of there.

We didn't take Roger Gillespe back to the station house for booking and interrogation. We skipped the booking entirely, and the interrogation took place behind the loading dock of a warehouse that I knew wouldn't open for business until 8 o'clock.

As soon as Karl shut off the engine and killed the lights, Gillespe said, "What're you guys doin'? This ain't the police station! What the fuck's goin' on?"

I took off my seat belt and twisted around so that I was facing him. "This is us, giving you the chance to stay out of jail, Roger."

"Jail? They can't send me to jail – that stuff you took off me is *legal*. Ask anybody!"

"Oh, we will, Roger," I said. "But first my partner here has a couple of questions for you."

"I don't need to answer no fuckin' questions – you already said so. I want a lawyer!"

"Look at me when I talk to you, Roger," Karl said quietly. He'd tilted the steering wheel up to give himself room and was turned facing the suspect now.

Roger made eye contact with Karl and started in surprise – but he didn't look away.

"Listen to me, Roger," Karl said. "You hear only my voice, and you're going to do exactly as I say. Aren't you?"

Roger swallowed a couple of times. "Yeah, sure. Whatever you say." His voice was calmer now, and he kept his eyes on Karl.

Karl had told me a while back that he'd been practicing with the mental-control ability that vampires call Influence, and said he was getting pretty good at it. I saw now that he'd been telling the truth.

"That Slide you've been selling," Karl said. "Where do you get it?"

"I buy from a guy called Larry."

"What's his last name?"

A shrug. "He never said. I never asked."

"How'd you meet him?"

"At a party – at some guy's house in Dunmore."

"When was this?"

"'Bout four months ago."

"How did he approach you?"

"He already knew my name, and my job at the deli. He asked if I wanted to start making some real money."

"Selling Slide."

"He called it HG, but yeah. He said when supes get a taste, they always want more. And there's lots of supes in this town."

"You try it yourself?"

"Larry said it has no effect on, like, humans." Another shrug. "I snorted some, anyway. All it did was make me sneeze."

"How much do you get for it?"

"Fifty bucks an ounce. That's what one of them little bags holds."

"What do you pay Larry for the stuff?"

"Twenty-five an ounce."

"How do you take delivery?" Karl asked him.

"I meet him every Friday, in the food court at the mall. Noon sharp. He always sits near Taco Bell."

"What happens at the food court?"

"I slip him an envelope with the cash in it – enough to pay for last week's supply. He fronts me the money, a week in advance. He's got a bag with him, from one of the stores in the mall. He puts it on the table. We shoot the shit for a couple of minutes, then he gets up and leaves. He don't take the bag."

"What store is the bag from?"

"It ain't always the same."

I muttered to Karl, "Description of Larry."

"What's this Larry look like?" Karl asked.

"Black hair, dark eyes. 'Bout average height. Looks like he lifts weights some."

"How old you figure he is?"

"Pretty old – at least forty."

Karl gave me a look, eyebrows raised. He was asking if I still wanted to end this the way that we'd discussed. I nodded.

He turned back to Gillespe and said, "Roger, that Slide that you were carrying is gone – you can't remember what happened to it."

"Can't remember."

"And Larry – he's gonna be pretty pissed when you can't pay him for last week's supply."

"Yeah, he'll be pissed. *Real* pissed."

"He might do something bad to you, when he finds out."

"Something pretty bad."

"Your best bet is to leave town, before he finds out."

"Gotta get out of Dodge – quick."

"You're gonna pack a couple of bags, throw them in your car, and start driving – west."

"Drive west. Yeah."

"And you're never coming back to Scranton," Karl told him. "It's not safe for you here anymore."

"Can't come back. It's not safe."

"And you're gonna forget everything that happened since you came out of your building this morning. You never met us. This little talk never happened."

"Yeah, sure. Never happened."

We dropped Roger Gillespe back where we had picked him up. He got out of the back seat and slammed the door without giving us a second glance. Then he walked toward the entrance to his apartment building – moving quickly, like somebody with a lot to do in a short time.

"We'd better do some hustling ourselves," I said to Karl as he drove us away from there. I looked at my watch. "The sun'll be up in–"

"Nineteen minutes," he said calmly. "Plenty of time."

When we were a block away from the station house, he said, "Well, we got one Slide dealer off the street. Didn't even have to arrest him – for real, anyway."

"We got more than that," I said. "We also have six ounces of his product, obtained at no cost."

"Just think of the money we saved. It's better than coupons."

Once Karl was on his way home, I went back up to the squad room. I needed to tell McGuire what we'd learned at the bombing scene and at Renfield's.

When I'd finished, McGuire sat back in his chair and said, "Doesn't give us a lot to go on, does it?"

"My thoughts exactly," I said. "But I did get one thing."

"What's that?"

"Sixouncesof Slide, dividedintoone-ouncepackets."

His eyes narrowed. "Do I even want to know where that came from?"

"Not to worry, boss," I said. "It's not like I was carrying heroin. Slide's legal, remember?"

He made a face, like I'd just reminded him that he was going to die, someday. "So, why are you carrying it around at all?"

"I want to have Louise send some to the State Police Crime Lab for analysis. If we can figure out what the shit actually is, maybe we can get a handle on where it comes from."

"What good you figure that's gonna do?"

"Maybe none – but I won't know until I get some answers. I'm also thinking about sending some over to a couple of profs I know at the U. One's a biologist, and the other one's in the Chem department."

"How come? The crime lab's pretty good."

I shrugged. "Second opinion – and quicker results, too, probably. I'm also going to leave some with Rachel. She said she'd take a look at it, see if magic might have any effect on its addictive properties."

"Not a bad idea," he said. "Can't do any harm, anyway."

"That'll leave me with two ounces," I said.

"Got any big plans for those?"

"Well," I said, "Karl's got a birthday coming up. And since he's a supe and everything...."

"Get the fuck out of here, Markowski. Just get out, and go home."

I got out, but I didn't go home – not immediately, anyway.

My first stop was the desk of our PA, Louise. I left one of the packets of Slide with her and told her to send it on to the State Police Crime Lab.

"You might also add a request that they rush it," I told her.

She looked up at me. "You figure that's likely to make any difference?"

"Sure," I said. "But then, I put out cookies and milk for Santa every Christmas Eve."

"Doesn't everybody?"

I went downstairs to see Rachel.

Once I explained what I'd brought her, she held the plastic baggie up to the light and shook it gently.

"So this is the famous – or should I say infamous – Slide," she said.

"Also known as 'HG', or 'Hemogoblin-Plus.'"

"Is that the base ingredient?" she asked. "Blood hemoglobin ?"

"Beats the hell out of me," I said. "All I know is that's what the dealers call it."

"And a drug dealer would never lie about the contents of the shit he's selling."

"Course not. Is an ounce gonna be enough for you to work with?"

"I should think so."

"I've got a couple of spares, so let me know if you need more." I nodded toward the baggie on her desk. "You going to be able to do anything with that?"

"I have some tests in mind, as well as a couple of spells I want to try," she said. "But with magic, as in life, results are not guaranteed."

"Yeah, I hate that about life – and about magic, too."

"Another neurotic heard from."

I gave her a hard look that I didn't mean, and she knew it. "You saying I'm neurotic?"

"Yes, but you're in good company – most of the human race, I expect."

"Good to know I'm special," I said.

"You understand the difference between a neurotic and a psychotic, don't you, Stan?"

"Maybe."

"A psychotic thinks that two plus two equals five. Or maybe nine. A neurotic *knows* that two plus two is four – but can't stand it."

"You know, I really can't stand jokes like that," I said with a smile.

"Who said I was joking?"

The sun was up by the time I left the building. Christine would already be home and at rest by now, so I decided to stop by Jerry's Diner on the way home. I hadn't been in there since the robbery attempt a few nights ago.

No way was I going to drink any of Jerry's notorious coffee at this hour, since I hoped to get in some sleep before sundown. But I found myself with a hankering for one of their ham and cheese omelets. I also wanted to see how Donna, the cashier, was doing.

The possibility that she might not have come into work never occurred to me. Unless it was her day off, Donna would be there. She's descended from a long line of coal miners and is tough as a three day-old bagel.

When I walked in, she was behind the register.

"Hey, Stan. Crushed any elves lately?"

"Not since the other night, but the week's not done yet. How you doing, Donna?"

"You mean after all the excitement? Ah, I'm OK. Takes more than a couple of diffies with guns to shake *me* up." *Diffy* is a term some people use when referring to elves. Others consider it as bordering on an ethnic slur. Donna's got lots of good qualities, but she's never been what you'd call politically correct.

"I'm glad you didn't let it get you down," I said.

"Me?" She snorted. "Not hardly. But tell me – them little bastards aren't back on the street, are they?"

"Nope. They didn't make bail, neither one of them. They'll be in County until trial, which won't be for three, maybe four months."

At arraignment, the judge had set bail for Thor and his buddy Car at $10,000 each. A bail bondsman could have got them released for ten percent of that, but neither elf could come up with the deposit. I guess if one of them had a thousand bucks to spare, he wouldn't have had to stick up diners.

"I was about to ask where's Karl," Donna said, "but then I realized..." She made a head gesture toward the nearest window and the sunlight streaming in through it.

"Yeah, he's home by now," I said. "I had to stay a little later at work and talk to some people. Then I was heading home myself, but I realized that I'd probably sleep better with one of Jerry's omelets in my stomach."

"I never can get to sleep on a full stomach, myself," she said. "But if it works for you, enjoy."

So I had my omelet with ham, cheddar, and mushrooms, and liked it just fine. Then it was time to go home, so I went around back to where I'd parked my car – and found that I had somebody waiting for me.

••••

It was a couple of bodies, actually – two guys who were leaning against my car. That pissed me off, a little. I mean, the Lycan's nothing special, but it's *mine*, dammit, and I resented these two treating it like a fucking park bench.

One was tall and broad in a blue suit, and the other one was average height and broad in a gray suit. The suits weren't handmade, but they hadn't been bought off the rack at JC Penney, either.

"You're Markowski, right?" gray suit said.

That pissed me off some more. I try not to get all self-important, but I'm kind of fussy about respect. Other cops get to call me "Markowski", and friends call me "Stan". As far as I'm concerned, civilians can use "Detective", "Sergeant", or "officer" until I tell them different. I figured the chances of these two being cops were almost as good as the odds of us ever being friends.

"You know who I am," I said. "Congratulations. Who're you?"

"Just a couple of fans," blue suit said, with a smile that was close to a nasty grin. They both pushed themselves off the car and slowly walked toward me.

"If you want me to pose for pictures, I'm gonna have to say no." I unbuttoned my sport coat and pushed it open, for quick access to the Beretta on my hip. "But I'll give you guys an autograph, if you want." These two weren't vampires – not standing in the light of the morning sun like that. But a silver bullet will drop a human as quick as it will a vamp – and cold iron will, too.

Blue suit's laugh was as nasty as his smile. "Autograph – that's pretty good. Dontcha think, Joey?"

Gray suit, whose name appeared to be Joey, said, "You don't need the gun, Sarge. We just want to talk a little."

Sarge. *That's three.*

"So, talk," I said. "And stand there while we do it, your hands in plain sight."

They stopped walking forward. "No, problem, Sarge," blue suit said.

"OK," I said. "What's on your mind?"

"Well, we hear you've got an interest in this new stuff that's on the street," Joey said.

"What stuff is that?" I wanted to hear him say the name.

"They call it by different names," he said. "Some people call it HG, or so I–"

That was when I heard the small sound from behind me. It was nothing much, probably the sound of loose gravel moving under somebody's shoe, but it was enough to tell me that I was in serious trouble.

I started to turn, very fast, my right hand pulling the Beretta from its holster. But I wasn't fast enough to avoid the impact of something hard on the back of my skull, and the next thing I knew the ground rose up to smash me in the face. Then somebody's knee, with the weight of a good-sized body behind it, came down on my spine. I would have screamed aloud if I'd been capable of any sound at all.

I heard voices, coming as if from a long way off.

"Get his wallet, and don't forget the watch, too," one of them said. "They said make it look like a robbery."

Rough hands went through my pockets. I was vaguely aware when they found and removed

my wallet and unbuckled the watch from my
wrist. Then I felt a tug as the Beretta came out of
its holster.

"Use his own gun," a voice said. "And hurry the
fuck up, before somebody comes."

I thought I heard the hammer go back on the
Beretta, but I might have imagined it. But I didn't
imagine the sound of the shot that followed, or
the two more shots that came almost immediately
afterward. Shooting me three times did seem kind
of excessive – overkill, even.

*Wait – I'm supposed to be dead. So why am I making
dumb jokes? If this is what the afterlife's like, it really sucks.*

I was still trying to figure it all out when the dim
light in my head slowly narrowed to a pinpoint and
then went out completely.

The pain woke me up. Or maybe the pain had been
there all along, patiently waiting for me to become
aware of it. My head hurt, my nose throbbed, and
my back felt like a company of Irish clog dancers
had been using it for a practice stage.

"I think he's coming around," somebody said.
The voice was female, but not familiar.

No sense making a liar out of her, so I opened
my eyes – or tried to. The lids felt like they were
stuck together with Super Glue. Finally I got them
separated, but a second later I was closing them
against the light. I tried again, opening my lids
slowly to let the eyes adjust. After a few seconds, I
was actually able to see my surroundings. The first
thing I was able to make out was a pleasant-faced
woman – mid-forties, black, very thin, wearing green
hospital scrubs – standing at the foot of my bed.

No, it wasn't a bed. I was on one of those hospital gurneys with steel rails along the sides. Half of it had been raised, to put me in a seated, upright position. I saw that I was in one of the treatment bays in Mercy Hospital's ER. I'd been here plenty of times – sometimes as a visitor, and other times, like now, as a reluctant guest.

"Welcome back to the world, Stanley," the woman in scrubs said. "Or do you prefer Stan?"

"Stan's fine," I said. My voice sounded like I'd been gargling with drain cleaner. "Who're you?"

"I'm Nurse Jenkins," she said. "You're at Mercy Hospital. How are you feeling?"

"Tell you the truth, I hurt like hell."

"Where's your pain located?"

"Back of my head's pounding like a motherfu… uh, I mean it's really pretty bad."

She gave me a gentle smile. "You can say 'motherfucker' if you want, Stan. I've heard the word before – in this job, I hear it quite frequently."

"Good to know."

"On a scale of one to ten, how bad would you say the head pain is?"

"Hard to be objective, when you're a tough guy like me," I said. "But I'd give it about a six."

"OK," she said, and made a note on the clipboard she was holding. "Do you have pain anywhere else?"

I moved around a little, and winced. "My back hurts some, too. Not as bad as the head, though."

"How bad is it?"

"About a four, I guess."

Another notation. "We'll have that checked out. What's the last thing you remember?"

I thought for a few seconds. "Somebody with his knee in my back, going through my pockets. Oh, and shots. Three shots. Seems like none of them got me, though."

"No, you're not exhibiting any gunshot injuries." She looked at me for a moment. "You're a police officer, is that right?"

"Uh-huh. Detective Sergeant Stanley Markowski, at your service," I said. "Well, I *could* be at your service, if my head didn't hurt so much."

She gave me another half-smile and wrote on the clipboard some more. "No retrograde amnesia," she said. "That's a good sign – probably means you're not concussed."

She flipped through the papers on the clipboard and paused at one. "The head X-ray that was performed when you were brought in shows no damage to the skull. You're a lucky man."

"I'll try to keep that in mind."

"Any dizziness?"

"No."

"Ringing in the ears?"

"No."

"Try not to blink for a second." She produced a penlight and shined it in one of my eyes, then the other.

"OK, good." She turned the penlight off, then asked me, "What day is it?"

"Um… Sunday . I think. At least, it was, last I remember."

"What's your mother's first name?"

"Eleanor."

"Who's President of the United States?"

I told her, then added, "Don't blame me, though – I didn't vote for him."

She smiled at my feeble joke and said, "I'll let Doctor Reynolds know you're awake. He should be in to see you shortly."

Nurse Jenkins walked away, her tread muffled by what looked like expensive running shoes. She slid the privacy curtain open a few feet, slipped through the gap, and closed it behind her.

I thought I was alone now. But then I remembered that Nurse Jenkins had said something like "He's awake now." Who had she been talking to? That was when I turned my head to the left, which hurt like hell, and saw Lieutenant McGuire sitting in the corner.

He was sprawled in a low-slung armchair that had seen better days, holding a tattered copy of *Reader's Digest*. As I watched, he tossed the magazine onto a table and stood up.

"I just finished the 'Increase Your Word Power' quiz," he said. "Only got seven out of ten."

"That's better than I usually do."

"Do you know what a fucking 'clowder' is?"

"Sounds like something you'd order in a seafood restaurant," I said.

He tossed the magazine aside, stood up, and came over to stand a few feet from my gurney. "It's the term they use for a bunch of cats," he said.

"Yeah? I'll try to work that into conversation, next time I'm talking to Karl. He'll be impressed." My voice sounded better now.

McGuire looked at me for a few seconds. "Your guardian angel's been putting in some overtime."

"You mean, because I'm not dead?"

"Because you're not dead, and because three other guys *are*."

"The ones who jumped me? I only saw two of them, but the third guy left me a souvenir." I gently touched the back of my head and found it covered with a thick bandage that had been taped in place.

"They were all carrying ID that turned out to be fake, but we ran their prints, and the State Police got back to us pretty quick." He took a notebook from his pocket and flipped through some pages. "Avery Dalton, Peter Amico, and Steven 'Thumbs' Milbrand. All three of them leg-breakers from downstate, each one with a rap sheet as long as my arm."

I looked at McGuire. "How far downstate are we talking about?"

"Philadelphia."

I nodded, and then the pain taught me that I shouldn't do that. "Wiseguys?"

Even though the Delatasso family was headed by a vampire, that wouldn't prevent them from having some "warm" members. A lot of vampire gangs had humans on the payroll, to guard their resting places during the day.

"Uh-uh," McGuire said. "Day labor. The kind of muscle loan sharks hire to beat up on some guy who's a couple of weeks behind on the vig."

"All the way from Philly? Shit, they could've hired somebody local and saved themselves some money."

"Maybe not," he said. "Even the dumbest scumbag in town is smart enough not to kill a cop, except out of desperation. They know the kind of heat that brings – every cop in Scranton would be on the case, whether assigned or not. And we'd never stop looking."

"On the other hand, if they use imported labor..."

"Exactly," McGuire said. "They blow into town, do the job, then go back to whatever shithole they crawled out of. None of the locals can snitch on them, because nobody knew they were even here."

"Except it didn't work out that way."

"Not this time. At the sound of the shots, some of Jerry's customers came running out to see what was going on."

"That's either very brave or extremely stupid."

"Whatever it was, they went around back and found four guys on the ground. Turned out the only one still breathing was you. The other three each had a bullet in the head."

"Three shots, three kills," I said.

"Yeah, I know. Whoever was back there knew how to use a gun. Had steady hands, too."

"Are you about to ask me if I was the shooter?"

McGuire gave me a thin smile. "Don't need to. Your weapon hadn't been fired."

"Good to know."

"Besides," he said, "the clip in your Beretta was your usual load of silver, alternating with cold iron – I know, because I checked."

"So...?"

"So while I was waiting for you to come to, I got an email on my phone from Homer Jordan at the Coroner's Office. Must be a slow day, because he's finished the autopsy on one of the Philly boys already. The slug that killed the bastard was lead."

"Which explains why you started out talking about my guardian angel."

"Somebody nailed those three goons before they could kill you. At least, I'm assuming that was their plan. Can't see them coming all the way up here from Philly just to lift your wallet – although one of them did that anyway. We found it in his coat pocket, along with your watch."

"They wanted it to look like a mugging," I said. "I vaguely remember one of them saying that. They were gonna shoot me with my own gun, too – make it look spontaneous, I guess."

"You heard them talking?"

"Yeah – they must've assumed I was out cold. Or maybe they figured it didn't matter what I heard, since they were about to put a bullet in my head."

"Instead, somebody put a bullet in *their* heads," McGuire said. "You see anything, hear anything, that'll give us a lead on the shooter?"

I shook my head – another painful mistake. "All I remember is the sound of the shots and wondering why I wasn't dead – the second time that's happened to me recently."

"You're thinking about those vamps who were trying to kill Calabrese the other night – especially the one who got behind you."

"Yeah," I said. "Somebody got *that* guy in the head, too."

"We'll compare the slug from the vamp with the ones they dig out of today's casualties," McGuire said. "Although the first time, the shooter used silver – for obvious reasons."

"Won't matter," I said. "The striations will still be identical – assuming it was the same gun, both times."

"And if there's no match, what does that prove? Diddly-fuck. Your guardian angel could have more than one gun. Maybe he carries one with lead, and another one loaded with silver. That way, he's ready for everything – or she is."

"Question is, who's doing this – and why? Not that I'm complaining, you understand."

"If we had the 'who', we'd have the 'why'," he said. "Or if we figured out the 'why', it'd probably give us the 'who'."

"Stop," I said. "You're making my head hurt worse than it already does, and that's saying something."

"Don't complain," McGuire said. "If it weren't for whoever's been watching your back, you wouldn't be feeling anything right about now."

They decided to keep me overnight, "for observation." What they wanted to observe wasn't exactly clear. Maybe they were afraid I'd develop subdural hematoma – a term I picked up from doctor shows on TV.

McGuire made it very clear that he didn't want me going all TV-detective-hero on him and checking myself out of the hospital prematurely because the Forces of Evil were on the march, and only I could stop them.

"The Forces of fucking Evil are *always* on the march," he said. "They'll still be there, day after tomorrow. In the meantime, you're gonna stay here until the docs are sure you're not about to fucking die on me. Got it?"

McGuire's the only guy I know who can make compassion sound like he's threatening your life. He went on. "I'll ask the Captain to put a uniform on the door to your room, once they get you settled."

"You figure the Delatassos have a 'B' team waiting in the wings?"

"Could be," he said. "If not, he can at least keep the reporters away – unless you've decided you like giving interviews to the media?"

"Fuck that shit," I said.

"That's kinda what I figured."

While I was waiting for the people in Admissions to process my paperwork and assign me a room, I called Christine. It was just past 2 in the afternoon, and I knew that she was still resting. But I wanted to leave a message on her voicemail so she wouldn't panic when she came upstairs at sunset and found that I'd never made it home from work.

Hi, honey – this is your old man. Listen, do not freak over what I'm about to tell you, OK? I'm in Mercy Hospital, but only for observation. I'll be out tomorrow. I ran into a little trouble and got whacked upside the head. But you know what a thick Polack skull I have – there's been no damage, apart from a lump that feels like it's the size of a billiard ball. No skull fracture, no concussion, no subdural hematoma. In other words: nothing to worry about. But apparently it's SOP to keep head injury cases for twenty-four hours, and that's what they're doing with me.

So, listen, on your way to work tonight, could you drop off my toilet kit? It's in the big suitcase in my closet. And bring a change of clothes, too, will you? Nothing too dashing – I'll have to go to work in them.

I appreciate it, kiddo. I'll see you sometime tonight. Love ya. Bye.

I don't think I own an article of clothing that anybody would call "dashing", but I wanted her to understand that I needed work clothes, not jeans and a T-shirt.

Before the orderly wheeled me upstairs – I told him that I could walk OK, but apparently the wheelchair was SOP, too – I stopped at the hospital gift shop and picked up a paperback book, along with a copy of the *Times-Tribune*. When the lady in Admissions had told me the cost of getting TV service in my room, and that insurance wouldn't cover it, I decided that reading would pass the time just as well, and cheaper.

Fifteen minutes later, I was in a private room, sitting up in bed and wearing one of those idiotic hospital gowns that are cleverly designed to rob you of any dignity you might have left after getting poked and prodded downstairs.

McGuire had said that the ER nurse in charge of Intake had taken my gun when I'd first arrived and given it so someone for safekeeping. He'd found out who had it, and waved his badge around until they gave my Beretta to him. He'd slipped it to me when no one was looking, just before the orderly came to wheel me up to my room. "You never know," he'd said. "You might get a visitor who isn't the friendly type."

My clothes were now hung up in the little locker they have in each room, but the Beretta was under the sheet next to my right leg. Just in case.

The book I'd bought was *Sematary Danse*, the new exposé of the funeral industry by that true-crime writer, Stephen King. I'd been wanting to read it for a while, but I decided to look at the paper first, in case anything important had gone down while I'd getting beaten up by hired thugs.

There was no story about all the excitement that had taken place behind Jerry's Diner, and I hadn't expected one in this issue. The *Times-Tribune* is a morning paper.

But it would be front-page news tomorrow unless a war broke out, and my luck never runs that good. *Three Dead in Attack on Police Officer*, the headline would read. And the local networks would have the story for their evening broadcasts.

I was glad that McGuire was going to have somebody on the door to keep the media jackals away. The last thing I needed right now was some asshole with a hundred-dollar haircut sticking a microphone in my face.

The Patriot Party had a full-page ad on page three, reminding me that the election was about a month away. The tone hadn't mellowed any since I'd last seen their advertising. They were still attacking Mayor D'Agostino without mercy, although it looked like they'd found a new horse to ride: crime in the streets.

LAW AND ORDER?
GANG WARFARE THROUGHOUT THE CITY
TERRORIST BOMBS DESTROYING LIFE
AND PROPERTY
DRUG-ADDICTED "SUPES" RUNNING RAMPANT
IS THIS THE MAYOR'S IDEA OF
LAW AND ORDER?

All of this was in what looked like thirty-point type.

As far as I knew, the only life that the "terrorist bomb" had taken belonged to one of those supes that the Patriot Party disapproved of, but my experience has been that political advertising and the truth have a nodding acquaintance at best.

I must have dozed off, because the next thing I remember was a tapping noise that turned out to be somebody knocking on the door of my room.

"Yeah – who is it?"

The door opened just wide enough to admit the head and shoulders of a uniformed cop who I vaguely recognized.

"You got a visitor, Sarge," he said. "Says she's your daughter."

I glanced toward the window and saw that night had fallen. "It's OK, officer," I said. "Let her through."

A moment later, Christine was in the doorway, bearing both a suitcase and a worried expression. I wondered why she was just standing there, but then I remembered.

"Hi, honey," I said. "Come on in."

She set the suitcase down at the foot of the bed. "I'd run over there and throw my arms around you, like a good daughter should," she said. "But my guess is that it might hurt like hell."

"You're right – it probably would," I told her. "Apart from this goose egg here, my back is sore from where some bastard dropped to his knees on me while I was down. There's no permanent damage – just lots of colorful bruises that are very sensitive to pressure."

She bent over the bed and kissed me carefully on the cheek. "I'd offer to have a few words with the assholes who did this you," she said as she stepped back. "But my guess is, right about now, they're just finding out that Hell doesn't have cable TV."

"I've heard that it does," I said, "but all they get down there is reruns of *Here Comes Honey Boo-Boo*."

When she finished laughing at my dumb joke, I asked her, "How come you know about all that? Did McGuire call you?"

She picked up a chair from the corner, put it next to the bed, and sat down.

"Nobody called me," she said. "But the *Times-Tribune's* web page is updated on a regular basis, remember? You're the front-page story right now"

"Shit, I forgot about the digital edition."

"I noticed that the story didn't have any quotes from you," she said.

"That's the main reason that uniform is at the door," I said. "To keep the goddamn media out of my face."

"I figured that would be your attitude, and I managed to help out a little."

"Really?"

"Really. I shared an elevator with a reporter and camera guy from Channel 22," she said. "When I realized who they were coming to see, I, uh, *convinced* them that there was no story here, and they might as well leave. They took the same elevator car back down."

"That's my girl."

"I figured that cop was outside in case whoever sent those three guys after you decided to send a few more."

"Well, yeah – that, too."

"That's why I used some vacation time and took tonight off," she said. "I'll be right here, in case something happens. Unless you've got some hot babe coming over later to cheer you up. If that's the case, I can wait in the hall with your brother officer while the cheering-up is going on."

"Even if I knew where to find a hot babe," I said, "the way I feel right now, anything she did would probably finish the job those guys started behind Jerry's."

"You don't know any hot babes?" she asked with a half-smile. "What about what's-her-name, that blonde cop from Wilkes-Barre?"

"Lacey Brennan."

"Yeah, that's her name. What about her? I thought you guys had a thing going."

"That's kind of up in the air right now," I said. "Anyway, she's in Wisconsin, visiting her sister."

"That doesn't sound too good."

"We'll see," I said.

"Well, once you're feeling better, let me know if you're in the market. I bet I could fix you up with one of the warm girls at work." She gave me a full-on smile, complete with fangs. "I know a couple of cute vamps, too, if you feel like a walk on the wild side."

"I'll keep that in mind," I said, and decided to change the subject. "McGuire says that the three guys who jumped me are muscle-for-hire up from Philly."

She gave me a look. "Philly. The Delatassos?"

"Seems like," I said. "I can't think of anybody else in Philly I might've pissed off recently."

She chewed her lower lip for a few seconds. "Why humans? If they waited until dark, they could've sent vamps after you."

"Misdirection, maybe. Killing a cop brings down a lot of heat. Maybe the Delatassos didn't want it focused on them."

"You're sure killing you was the objective – they weren't there just to rough you up or something?"

"No, it was a hit." I told her what I'd heard the goons say to each other while I was semi-conscious.

She nodded slowly when I was done. "So they intended to take you out. Sounds like they would've succeeded, too, if not for – who?"

"That's a question I've been giving a lot of thought to," I said. "The answer's been pretty fuckin' elusive. I can't think of–"

Another knock sounded on the door. The uniformed cop stuck his head in and said, "Your partner's here, Sarge."

"OK, thanks," I said – then, in a louder voice I called, "Come on in, Karl."

Karl Renfer had brought me a small plastic baggie that turned out to contain a Reese's Cup, two Snickers bars, and a pack of Lance cheese crackers. "Just in case the food in this place is as bad as I hear," he said, then looked toward my other visitor. "Hey, Christine."

"Hey, Karl." A look passed between them, and I wasn't sure how to read it. Then I remembered that Karl had, out of necessity, spent a day in my basement with Christine a few months back. He'd been working until almost sunrise, and hadn't had time to make it home.

During the daylight hours, a vampire is literally a corpse. But neither Karl or Christine had ever mentioned how much time they'd spent together downstairs once the night had returned. They'd never brought it up, and I'd never asked.

And I sure as shit wasn't going to ask now.

Instead, I said to Karl, "Is this an official visit, officer, or are you just here on a goodie run? Not that I'm complaining."

"Nothing official," he said. "Once I found out what had gone down this morning, I took a couple hours' personal time. McGuire said you weren't in bad shape, considering, but I decided to see for myself."

"I've been worse," I told him.

"Yeah, I can tell," he said. "But there is one thing that's been bothering me a little since I got here, though."

"What's that?"

He looked down at the bed. "Is that a gun under your blanket, or are you just glad to see me?"

"McGuire got my Beretta back for me," I said. "A little extra firepower never hurts."

"Speaking of firepower," Karl said, "I had an interesting email waiting when I got in to work tonight. From one of my snitches."

"Do tell," I said.

"Is this secret stuff?" Christine asked. "Should I go out in the hall?"

Karl gave her a smile and a shrug. "Don't see why. Your old man's gonna tell you all about it later, anyway." He looked at me. "Right?"

"Yeah, most likely," I said.

"Since he trusts you, I trust you," he told Christine. "You might as well stick around. Besides, you're the only one in here who's easy on the eyes."

They exchanged that look again, and I made myself stop wondering what it might mean. Christine's love life is none of my damn business, as she'd be the first one to tell me. Neither is Karl's.

But – my daughter and my partner. Dear sweet merciful Jesus.

"So you got this email..." I said to Karl.

"Yeah, from a guy who's kinda on the fringes of the Calabrese organization. He picks up interesting gossip once in a while. He trades it for small favors, or just the chance to bank some goodwill." He paused.

"Come on, Karl," I said. "Stop milking it. What's the guy say?"

"He tells me that Calabrese has brought in some out-of-town talent to help in this war with the Delatassos."

"Philadelphia?" I asked. "Don't tell me we've got more thugs from Philly in town."

"No, this one's from Boston. And he's no run-of-the mill thug. Word is, Calabrese hired John Wesley Harding."

There was silence in my little room until Christine broke it by saying, "John Wesley Harding? Wasn't he some desperado in the Old West?"

"Hardin," Karl said. "You're thinking of John Wesley Hardin. This guy's name is the same, except for the 'g' at the end."

"*Desperado*'s not a bad description, though, from the stories I heard," I said. "Dude's supposed to've killed more people than the Black Death, although that's an exaggeration. Probably."

"Is he warm?" Christine asked.

"He was," I said. "Still is, as far as I know. Maybe that's why Calabrese hired him. Could be he wants somebody who's as deadly in daylight as he is at night. That'd be pretty useful in the kind of war Calabrese is fighting."

"Wonder if one of Harding's parents was a Bob Dylan fan?" Karl said.

"Well, what *I'm* wondering," Christine said, "is whether he's Daddy's 'guardian angel'."

Karl looked at her. "You mean whoever iced those three guys this morning?"

"Them, as well as the one who took out the Delatasso fangster who got behind me, that night Calabrese got cornered," I said. "I agree with McGuire – it seems pretty unlikely that I've got *two* guardian angels. I think it's pretty amazing that I have even one."

"Well, whoever he is, it's probably not Mister Harding," Karl said. "My source says that Calabrese just hired him, and the dude hasn't even hit town yet."

"Your source could be wrong," Christine said. "That ever happen to you?"

"Sure, all the time," Karl said. "And if his information was off by just a few hours, then, yeah, it could put Harding behind Jerry's Diner this morning, in time to save Stan's ass. But it still doesn't explain the Delatasso guy who got nailed in the street last week."

"Why not?" Christine asked.

"Because if somebody on Calabrese's payroll had killed that shooter who'd got behind me," I said, "Calabrese wouldn't have been shy about saying so. In fact, he'd probably have told me that it wipes out whatever obligation he might have incurred when *I* saved *his* ass."

Christine frowned. "So, we're back to square one," she said. "Either there are two different 'guardian angels' involved here–"

"Which seems unlikely," I said.

"Which seems unlikely," she agreed. "Or it wasn't this Harding guy at all. So we still don't know who's doing it."

"Yeah, I can't even send him a 'Thank You' card," I said. "Too bad. I had a nice one all picked out."

Nobody spoke for a little while, then Christine said, "We were talking about Lacey earlier. It just occurred to me that she makes pretty good guardian-angel material, Daddy. She likes you, and you told me that she's pretty handy with a gun. What do you think?"

"Hmmm. I never thought of that," Karl said.

"Absolutely not," I said. "No fucking way."

Christine tilted her head a little to one side. "How come you're so sure?"

"Like I told you – Lacey's in Wisconsin, visiting her sister."

"Maybe she came back early," Christine said, "and hasn't told you yet."

"No chance," I said. "If she was back in town, she'd have let me know." I paused for a second. "Probably."

That prompted another exchange of meaningful looks between Christine and Karl – something I was starting to get tired of.

Karl looked at me. "You and Lace ever figure out what kind of relationship you guys want?"

"We're still working on that," I said. "That's one of the things she said she wanted to think about out in Wisconsin."

Karl nodded as if he understood, although I was pretty sure he didn't.

"Besides," I said, "if Lacey was watching my back like that, she'd want me to know about it. She wouldn't be pulling this Lone Ranger crap and disappearing once her work was done."

"OK," Christine said. "If you say so. It was just a thought."

"You're probably right, Stan – it's not Lacey who's your shadow," Karl said. He gave me a half-smile.

"Hell, I bet she doesn't even know what evil lurks in the hearts of men."

"Of course she does, Karl," I said quietly. "She's a *cop*, isn't she? She knows." I looked toward my vampire daughter. "We all know."

"So, who's gonna replace Victor Castle," I asked Christine, "as the *capo di tutti supi*?" I noticed sirens in the distance, but that's a pretty common sound around a hospital.

"It's anybody's guess," she said. "No clear candidate has emerged, as they say."

"I was in the hospital when Castle took over from the late Mister Vollman, so I never got around to asking you about the process. How does the supe community choose a leader, anyway? Is there a series of... primaries or something?"

The sirens were louder now, and there were more of them. But the sound didn't seem to be getting any closer to the hospital.

Christine gave me a small smile. "It's nothing so organized," she said. "What usually happens is–"

That was when music started coming from Karl's pocket – the first thirteen notes of the James Bond theme, to be exact. Karl had just received a text message.

He doesn't get them very often, so he pulled out his phone, thumbed an icon, and looked at the screen. From his expression, I was pretty sure he wasn't reading birthday greetings from his mom, and my suspicion was confirmed when he said, "Aw, *fuck!*"

As he put the phone back in his pocket, Christine and I both said, "What?" at the same time.

"There's been another bombing," he said to Christine, then looked at me. "Ricardo's Ristorante."

The sudden jolt of adrenaline started the bump on my head throbbing all over again as I asked Karl, "How bad?"

"McGuire didn't say – you can't put a lot of info into a text message, anyway. But when's the last time you heard of a bombing that *wasn't* bad, Stan?"

"Yeah – I withdraw the question." I threw back the blanket and sheet and swung my legs slowly over the side of the bed.

"Where do you think *you're* going?" Christine asked, but before I could say anything, she went on, "Never mind, I know where. But *why*, Daddy? The fucking bomb already went off, right? And there's gonna be a gazillion cops and firemen and paramedics and gosh knows what – all over the place. Why do *you* have to be there?"

"So I can find out what the fuck is going on!"

I stood up, and the pounding in my head immediately shifted from second gear into third. I glanced back at the sterile-looking hospital bed, and at that moment it looked like a really good place to be. But I turned away from it and started walking toward the suitcase that Christine had brought me.

"I don't mean to throw you out, honey," I told Christine. I picked up the suitcase and tossed it on the bed. "But unless you want to embarrass us both by seeing your old man naked, maybe you'd better leave. I'll see you when I get home, unless it's after sunrise. In that case, I'll talk to you at breakfast."

She made an exasperated sound, but her voice was calm as she said, "I don't suppose arguing's gonna do any good, huh?"

Karl answered her before I could. "You've known him longer than I have, babe. What do *you* think?"

Babe. I wondered if it was too late to have that talk with Christine about the bats and the bees.

Yeah – about twenty years too late. Maybe more.

Christine gave him one of those *What can you do?* expressions, then turned to me and said, "I guess I'll see you at breakfast, Daddy – if not before."

She stepped closer and kissed my cheek. "Be careful – there's likely to be a lot of broken glass out there."

"I will."

I wondered if Karl was going to get a kiss, too – but apparently they weren't willing to do that in front of me yet. He got a friendly nod and "'Bye, Karl," and then she was gone.

I dropped the hospital gown, then opened the suitcase and began to pull clothes out of it. Getting dressed doesn't usually pose a challenge for me, but this time was a little different. The first time I bent over, I was afraid my head was going to explode. Then I started hoping it *would* explode and put me out of my misery.

With a little help from Karl, I managed to make myself presentable. I filled the empty suitcase with the dirty clothing I'd been wearing when they brought me in, closed it, and said, "OK, let's go."

"You want a wheelchair, get you as far as the front door?"

I looked at him. "You figure they're going to have any wheelchairs at the fucking crime scene?"

He shrugged. "I could borrow one from here."

"Yeah, and I can just hear the other guys from the squad when I show up looking like you just sprung me from the Shady Rest Old Folks Home. I might hear the end of it in ten, maybe fifteen years. Fuck that shit – no wheelchair."

"Then at least let me carry the damn suitcase."

"Fine – take it."

As we passed the nurses' station, one of the ladies in scrubs glanced up at us from her clipboard, then did a double take. "Mister Markowski! What are you doing out of bed? I need you to–"

With his free hand, Karl held his ID folder out and growled, "Police business." Then he flashed her a little fang. I'm not sure which impressed the nurse more, but after a second, she picked up the clipboard again and began studying it like she was trying to memorize every damn word.

When we came through the sliding doors of the front entrance, Karl said, "Wait here – I'll bring the car around."

"I can walk to the fucking car, dammit! Stop treating me like some kind of invalid."

Karl turned and faced me. "Stan – I'm a member of the bloodsucking undead, right?"

"Yeah – so?"

"So, I can't see myself in a mirror. But I'd still bet fifty bucks that right about now *you* make *me* look good. Just stay put while I get the fucking car, OK?"

Before I could come up with a suitable retort, Karl turned and started walking away. Then a few seconds later the vampire afterburners kicked in and he disappeared into the night.

Fucking undead showoff.

We hadn't gone very far from Mercy's parking area when I started to wonder why Karl was driving like a little old lady on her way home from a Sunday social. Then I got it: he was trying to avoid the many bumps and potholes, to cut down on any bouncing around that would make my head hurt worse than it already did.

"Karl."

"What?"

"I know what you're doing, and I appreciate it. I really do. But nobody ever died from a goddamn headache, and I want to get to the crime scene ASAP – so will you fucking *move*?"

He glanced at me. "Yes *sir*."

Karl pressed down on the accelerator while reaching under the dash with one hand. He flicked a switch, and the red LED lights behind the grille started flashing their get-the-hell-out-of- the way message. Then he found the toggle that controls the siren.

The high-pitched wailing noise that began an instant later cut into the back of my head like the business end of a Black & Decker Model 12V. And like the Energizer Bat, it just kept going, and going, and going.

Be careful what you wish for, Markowski.

I did my best to keep the pain off my face, but that's the thing about having a vampire partner – he can sense changes in your heart rate, and sudden agony will definitely kick things up a notch or two.

Karl gave me another sideways look. "Pretty bad, huh?"

"I'm alright – just drive."

Eight long minutes later, we arrived at the scene of the restaurant bombing – or as close as we were able to get. What looked like dozens of official cars

and vans were blocking Moosic Street, all with their
own lights going – red, blue, or yellow, depending
on the department responding. The effect that light
show had on my pounding head made me want
to squeeze my eyes shut and keep them that way
– for a week, maybe. But Karl and I had a three-
block hike in front of us, and I wasn't going to do
it like some kind of blind man. So, squinting like
the second lead in a spaghetti western, I got out of
the car.

The walk was slow going, what with the police
and emergency vehicles parked at crazy angles and
the immense crowd of gawkers standing around,
probably hoping to see a dead body being carried
away – or, better yet, a headless corpse.

Finally, we came to the barrier of yellow crime-
scene tape that extended from one side of the street
to the other, uniformed cops standing behind it
every fifty feet or so. The one we approached, a
red-haired patrolman named McHale, knew us
by sight and lifted the tape so Karl and I could
duck under it. Bending over like that achieved
something I wouldn't have thought possible – it
made the pounding in my head even worse. When
we'd straightened up, I said to Karl, "Let's wait
here a minute or two, see what's going on." Truth
was, I just wanted to stand still and see whether
the pain would back off a bit – just receding from
"Intolerable" to merely "Pretty Fucking Awful"
would've been OK with me.

Karl looked at me, but all he said was, "Sure,
Stan."

If McGuire had been there, I was prepared to
listen to a bunch of "I told you not to act like some

TV hero" crap, but I guessed he'd stayed back at the station house. Maybe my night was improving – a little.

Christine had been right, back at the hospital. There was nothing I could do here that all the other professionals on scene couldn't do, and probably better. But there were things I wanted to know. Besides, I couldn't stay in a hospital bed while every other cop in the city was on the streets working this case. I just *couldn't*.

After a while, the pain did let up a little – enough for me to focus on the scene before us. And quite a scene it was.

This section of Moosic Street was brightly lit, but all of the illumination came either from the headlights of emergency vehicles or the dozen or so HMI lights that had been rigged by the police and fire departments. None of the usual light sources were worth shit at the moment.

Up and down the street, tall wooden lampposts were either bent in half, their lights smashed on the ground, or just knocked flat by the explosion. Most of the power poles had gone down, too, taking the electrical wires along with them. Several loose wires lay on the asphalt, still live, sparking and hissing like wounded dragons.

What I could see of the street – the part that wasn't covered with debris or puddles left by the fire hoses – had depressions in the asphalt, as if a T-Rex had stomped through, on his way to eat Dixon City. Broken glass was everywhere, and the air was thick with the odor of gasoline, burned rubber, scorched metal, and several other smells that I couldn't identify.

"Blood," said Karl, the mind reader. "There's a lot of blood in the air."

"You gonna be alright?"

"Yeah, I'm fine," he said quickly. Maybe a little too quickly.

"Look – Scanlon's here," I said, as much to change the subject as anything else.

"I'm not surprised. Lot of work for him and his boys tonight."

Hugh Scanlon made his careful way toward us, stepping over or around the worst of the debris, avoiding the puddles made by the fire hoses. He kept his hands in the pockets of the light topcoat that he seemed to be wearing every time I saw him.

When he reached us, Scanlon stopped and looked me over. "I heard you were dead," he said finally. "Looks like the reports are only half right."

"Yeah, I get that a lot," I told him.

"Me, too," Karl said.

Scanlon gave him a look and turned back to me. "I've heard about six different stories about you," he said. "You know how cops are – they gossip worse than a bunch of old ladies."

I gave him raised eyebrows. *"They?"*

"I just listen," he said with a shrug. "That doesn't count."

"If you say so," I said.

"One version says that you were jumped by a bunch of guys behind Jerry's and managed to take out three of them before they finally took you off the count."

"I think I'll encourage that one," I said. "The first part of it, at least. Makes me sound dangerous."

"Yeah, whatever," Scanlon said. "Another story has you in Mercy Hospital, deep into a coma due to a fractured skull." He leaned a little to one side to get a better look at my bandaged lump. "Looks like they weren't far wrong," he said. "About the fractured skull, I mean."

"I'm doing OK," I lied. "They say I don't even have a concussion. Just some bruises, a big lump, and frequent visits from the Headache from Hell."

The sudden whoop of an ambulance siren sent a fresh jolt of pain through my head. When it had receded a little, I said, "Look, I dragged myself out of my bed of pain because it seems like the gang war's escalating. I want to know what the fuck happened here and why."

"Short version," Scanlon said. "The answer to your first question is 'car bomb', and I'm guessing the answer to the second one is 'to kill a bunch of folks'."

"Well, duh," Karl said, which earned him another look from Scanlon.

"How many dead?" I asked him.

"They're still bringing bodies out," he said. "Nine that we know about, so far."

"They're all human, aren't they?" Karl said.

"How the hell do I know?" Scanlon said. "That's for the Medical Examiner's people to figure out."

A third-story parapet that had run across the front of an apartment building directly across from Ricardo's suddenly came loose and fell to the sidewalk with a crash. I was glad nobody had been standing underneath it. There'd been enough dying on this street tonight already.

"My point is," Karl said, "that I'm pretty sure none of them were vampires."

"Yeah?" Scanlon said. "And you reached this conclusion how, exactly?"

"Because you can't kill vampires with a bomb."

Scanlon and I both stared at him, then we looked at each other. "He's got a point", I said.

"Does he?" Scanlon frowned. "Look, I freely admit this isn't my area – I mostly deal with humans who kill other humans." He looked at Karl again. "You're telling me you can sit a vampire on top of a ton of TNT, set it off, and the vampire just gets up and walks away once the smoke clears?"

"Yeah, pretty much," Karl said.

"But the vampire'd be blown into a million pieces," Scanlon said. "Do they all get –"

"No, he wouldn't," I said. "A human would be in a million pieces. The vampire wouldn't discorporate like that. He'd probably be blown a fair distance by the blast, and he wouldn't feel so great for a while – but, yeah. He'd get up and walk away."

Scanlon shook his head slowly. "How the fuck is that possible?"

"Who the hell knows?" I said. "How are vampires possible? How is magic possible – and lycanthropy, and all the rest of it? It just *is*."

"Wait a second," Scanlon said. "What about that case down in Louisiana a few years back? Some religious nut turned himself into a suicide bomber directed against vampires. He made up an explosive vest, then hung a bunch of silver jewelry all over it. Showed up at a party some vamps were having, and *boom*. That killed a few, as I recall."

"Yeah," Karl said, "but that was the silver shrapnel that did it, not the explosion itself."

"Maybe that's what happened here," Scanlon said.

"No way," Karl said. "If there was that much silver around here, I'd be able to feel it – and I'm not getting anything at all like that."

I tried to make myself think, despite the insistent pounding in my head. "This is fucked up," I said.

"What was that word your partner used a minute ago?" Scanlon said. "*Duh*?"

"No, what I mean is, if you're waging war against a gang of vampires, why would you use a weapon that's not gonna kill any vampires?"

Karl looked at what had once been the front of Ricardo's Ristorante. "I think you're right, Stan," he said. "What's the point?"

"The *point*?" Scanlon made an impatient gesture that took in the whole street. "Maybe the fucking *point* is to make sure that nobody ever comes near this joint again, even if they *do* get it rebuilt someday. That bomb might not've hurt Calabrese's body, but it sure as shit put a big, fat hole in the middle of his wallet."

"Maybe," I said. "Maybe not."

"What the fuck's *that* mean? Scanlon said.

"Think about it, Scanlon," I said. "The restaurant wasn't a money-maker for Calabrese – my guess is, he barely broke even on the place. And since this was his headquarters, he wouldn't have had any of his illegal operations going on in there, so blowing the joint up probably wouldn't even affect his main income stream."

"And if Calabrese hasn't got a ton of insurance on this place," Karl said, "then the bastard isn't half as smart as I think he is."

Scanlon spent a few seconds with his eyes closed, rubbing the bridge of his nose with two fingers. Behind him, the work of cleaning up the devastation continued.

EMTs brought out the dead and injured as soon as the Fire Department could locate them. Cops were trying to secure the crime scene so that evidence could be systematically gathered from it later. Men and women in yellow hardhats from PG&E went around deactivating the live electrical wires before somebody stepped on one and got fried. And clergy from several faiths were ministering to those among the injured who the EMTs didn't think were going to make it as far as the hospital.

"Let me see if I understand this," Scanlon said at last. "Whoever set the bomb off wasn't trying to kill vampires with it, cause you can't kill vamps with a bomb."

"That's right," Karl said.

"And they didn't do it to destroy the business," Scanlon went on, "since Calabrese doesn't use the place to make money."

"Seems that way," I said.

Scanlon looked at me, then at Karl, then back at me again. "Then why the fuck did the Delatassos *do* it?"

"That's a hell of a good question," I said. "But I've got one that might be even better."

"Which is…?"

"What if the Delatassos *didn't* do it?"

As Scanlon walked away, I noticed Dennehy from the State Police bomb squad standing a couple of hundred feet away, giving orders to some of his people.

"Come on," I said to Karl, and we made our slow, careful way over to where Dennehy was standing.

I stumbled once and Karl tried to take my arm, but once I'd glared at him, he let go again. We came up on Dennehy just as he was finished deploying his troops – four guys and a woman, all dressed in identical blue jackets that read "State Police BDU" on the back.

"Don't forget to check for fragments buried in the sides of buildings." He practically had to yell to be heard over the noise from all the other people and vehicles in the area. "You see anything unusual, dig it out and bag it. We'll figure out if it's relevant later. OK, get to work."

As the four bomb techs trotted away, Dennehy turned toward Karl and me. "I wish I could say it was good to see you fellas again, but under the circumstances..."

"Yeah, I know what you mean," I said.

Dennehy looked at me for a few moments, his head tilted a little to one side. "Christ, what happened to you, Stan?."

"It looks worse than it is," I said. "I just got jumped by some guys early this morning. One of them whacked my head with something hard, probably a gun barrel. But I've got that thick Polack skull. I'm OK. But we came over to ask you about this bomb."

"What d'you want to know about it?"

"Anything you can tell us," I said. "I realize you haven't had much time to investigate yet."

Dennehy sneezed a couple of times, then blew his nose on a big bandana handkerchief. "It's the dust," he said. "Always irritates my sinuses at these scenes. I tried wearing a respirator once, but the other guys kept asking me if I was still beating up on Batman, so I gave it up."

"The bomb, Chris," I said. "What about the bomb?"

"OK, well, for starters – it had a lot more juice than the one that did in what's-his-name..."

"Castle," Karl said. "Victor Castle."

"Yeah, him. You can see by the amount of damage that it was a much more powerful explosion this time – not the kind of charge you could fit in a trash can, that's for damn sure."

"What was it in, then?" I asked him. "Any ideas?"

"Car bomb, most likely." Dennehy pointed up the street in the direction of what had once been Ricardo's Ristorante. "That car there, specifically."

A couple of hundred feet from the restaurant's entrance was something that might once have been an automobile. It was lying on its roof – at least, I *think* it was. Looking at that twisted, burned pile of metal, it was hard to say for sure.

"You figure plastic explosive, like the last time?" I asked.

"Most likely," he said. "Big difference between this bomb and the last one, though – I mean, apart from the amount of explosive used."

"How do you mean?" I said.

"That other one – very precise. You can't use words like 'surgical' when talking about bombs, but the one outside the rug store had a very specific objective – to take out that one man. The other damage was incidental. But this...." Dennehy waved his arm in a gesture that took in the whole scene. "This is more like the kind of stuff you see in the Middle East. The fuckers who set it off don't really have a specific target in mind. They just want to cause as much damage – to people and structures both – as they can."

Karl and I glanced at each other. "That's very interesting," I said.

"The first time, it was a hit, pure and simple," Dennehy said. "But what we had here tonight was fucking terrorism."

"You think so?" I just wanted something to say while I tried to get my mind around what I'd heard.

"Goddamn right it was," Dennehy said. "And you know what Lenin wrote about terrorism?"

"The Russian revolution guy?" Karl asked him.

"That's the one. Lenin said, 'The purpose of terrorism is to terrify.'"

"Sounds about right, but a little obvious," I said. "What's your point?"

"My point," Dennehy said, "is this: *just who were these fuckers trying to scare?*"

An hour or so later, we were back at the car. The trip to the crime scene hadn't given me a lot of useful information, but it sure had been a rich source of questions.

"Where to?" Karl asked. "Back to Mercy?"

"No, fuck that. If I was gonna drop dead from that whack on my head, I'd have done it by now. Take me home, will you?"

"Home it is, then," he said, and started the engine.

"Wait," I said. "Where's my car, anyway?"

"Should be in your driveway. One of the guys from the squad drove it over to your place from Jerry's earlier today."

The route Karl followed to my place took us past Saint Peter's Cathedral. Karl averted his eyes from the large crosses on the front door, but did it without a lot of drama. I didn't say anything – I've seen him do that a hundred times since he joined the ranks of the undead.

We'd gone a block past the cathedral when Karl said, "Remember what Victor Castle told us a while back – that he thought a vampire's aversion to religious symbols was just psychological? We *believe* we're supposed to be scared of crosses, and so we are."

"Yeah, I remember."

"Think it's true? Or is it because we really *are* spawn of the devil?"

I shifted in my seat, which didn't help my head any. The issue Karl had raised was one I tried not to think about too much.

There was a time when I was wary of vampires, because the popular culture said they were monsters – a view that the Vampire Anti-Defamation League has been fighting for decades. Then a vampire killed my wife, and I came to hate the creatures. That was why I'd requested a transfer to the Occult Crimes Unit – I figured it would give me the chance to kill a few vampires in the line of duty and thus get away with it.

But now my partner and best friend, as well as my daughter Christine, were vampires. More than that – each of them was undead because I had made it happen. It was either that or stand by helplessly and watch them die.

Karl and Christine *weren't* evil – I was convinced of that. But I also knew that if you waved a cross – or a Star of David, or some other religious symbol – in the direction of a vampire, he'd run from it. Or she would. And if religious symbols represent God, vampires being afraid of them meant… what?

The academic types have a name for my current attitude towards vampires: *cognitive dissonance*. That's a fancy way of saying that somebody holds conflicting attitudes toward something – or somebody.

"I don't know if Castle was right or not," I said to Karl. "But that *spawn of the devil* stuff is bullshit."

Another couple of blocks went by before Karl said, "I've been spending some time with Doc Watson, talking about all that shit."

I didn't know what to say about that, so I settled for "Uh-huh."

Terence Watson, MD, is a local psychiatrist who's been a lot of help to the Scranton PD over the years. I'd last run into him about a month ago, in the frozen foods section of Wegmans. Doc and I had chatted briefly, but he didn't say anything about having Karl as a patient. Of course, he wouldn't. Doc Watson's very big on preserving confidentiality – maybe that's why so many people trust him.

"Doc seems inclined toward Victor's Castle's opinion on the cross issue," Karl said.

"Seems?"

"You know how it is – or maybe you don't. He doesn't tell me much. Just asks questions and lets me come up with my own answers."

"So you're working toward the point where you can look at a crucifix without wanting to run like hell?" I said.

"Something like that."

"How's that working out?"

"I'm not there yet," Karl said. "Maybe I will be, someday."

"Here's hoping," I said.

"Yeah."

Karl had been right about my car. When we got to my house, his headlights showed the Toyota Lycan, sitting in the driveway. As we came to a stop, I checked my watch: 3.18.

"You going back to work from here?" I asked him.

"Yeah, might as well see if McGuire's got anything for me to do as a solo, or maybe I can go out with one of the other teams. If not, there's always paperwork to catch up on."

Karl put the car in park and looked at me. "You gonna take tomorrow night off?"

"Fuck, no – I'll be in for my shift. You can tell McGuire as much, too."

"I dunno, Stan. I mean, no offense, but you're not movin' around too good right now. Maybe some rest is just what you need."

"I'm *gonna* get some rest. I plan to keep vampire hours today – sleep from sunrise to sundown, and I may even get to bed earlier than that, after I talk to Christine."

"OK, good, but I still think–"

"Karl, listen. The fucking city is coming apart at the seams, right? We got bombs going off, supes doing crimes to get high, fangsters shooting it out in the streets, and God knows what all. And by the way, I know what you're thinking."

He gave me a flash of fangs in a quick grin. "Is that right?"

"Yeah – you're thinking that I've got some kind of Matt Dillon complex–"

"Who?"

"*Gunsmoke*. Before your time. Anyway, you think I've got some kind of hero thing going on, where

I figure that only *I* can stop all the bad shit that's been goin' on. Right?"

"Well, I wouldn't have put it quite that way – but that's because I never heard of *Gunsmoke*."

"I should've used a James Bond example – but, anyway, you're wrong. I don't figure I'm going to stop it alone. Shit, maybe it can't be stopped by anybody. But all I know is, I've got to *try*."

Karl made an "I give up" gesture and said, "Alright, OK. Fine."

"Scranton's my town, Karl. I've never lived anyplace else. And I'm *not* gonna spend tomorrow night at home watching *Zombie Survivor* on TV while the whole place goes to hell in a handbasket. I *can't*."

"I said OK, didn't I? I believe you, Stan – don't get aggravated."

"Yeah, I guess that could be pretty bad for a guy in my condition, huh?"

"Fuckin' A," Karl said. "Goddamn fuckin' A right."

"OK, I'll see you at nine tonight. Thanks for the lift."

As I reached for the door handle, he said, "I'll wait until you're inside before I take off."

I turned back and looked at him. "I'm all grown up and everything, Karl. Besides, I've got my Beretta."

"You had it with you this morning behind Jerry's Diner, didn't you?" He gave an embarrassed shrug. "I'm just sayin'."

I like Karl pretty well most of the time, but there are moments when I hate him – especially when he's right. Like now.

I drew in breath to say something sarcastic, but what came out was, "OK, Karl – and thanks."

••••

I closed the kitchen door behind me and made sure it was locked. Christ, Karl had got me paranoid now – although I'd always thought that the philosopher Allan Konigsberg had a good point when he said "Being paranoid doesn't mean that they're not really out to get you."

I could hear the TV playing in the living room – I'd already known that Christine was home, since her car was in the garage. I was about to call out "It's me!" when the TV shut off. She'd heard me come in, as any vampire would have. A moment later, Christine appeared in the doorway between the living room and kitchen.

She looked at me for a second before saying, "Hi."

I think she'd been about to say something involving the phrase "death warmed over" but changed her mind. Good for her.

"Hi, yourself." I pulled a chair out from the kitchen table and sat down, although "collapsed into it" is closer to the truth.

Christine went to the freezer and removed what looked like a gallon-size freezer bag filled with ice cubes. I was pretty sure it hadn't been in there yesterday. She wrapped the bag in a clean dishtowel and handed it to me. "Here," she said. "Try this on your head."

"Thanks, honey." I took the ice pack and pressed it gingerly against my lump. She'd been right – after a little while, the pain started to ebb a bit.

"So how was your night?" she asked, but then quickly added, "If you don't feel up to talking, it's alright. You can tell me about it later."

"No, I'd rather do it now," I said. "Talking will help take my mind off the way my head feels. The ice is helping, though – that was a good idea. No wonder you're my favorite daughter."

She pulled out a chair opposite me and sat down. "So, tell me – what's been going on?"

I told her everything I'd seen and heard at the crime scene, leaving out only the couple of times when I'd nearly passed out from the pain in my head.

When I'd finished, she remained in the position she'd assumed for most of my account – elbows on the table, face cupped in both hands. Finally, she put her hands down on the table. "Talk about a fucking mystery."

"You mean, how vampires can't be killed by an explosion? Yeah, that's–"

She shook her head. "No, I mean all of it. A car bomb goes off in front of Calabrese's restaurant, but it couldn't have harmed the Don or any of his guidos."

"Uh, I think that's considered an ethnic slur."

She looked at me with her eyebrows raised. "What, *guidos*? And since when did you get all politically correct?"

"I'm just sayin'."

"OK, so the bomb wouldn't have killed Calabrese or any of his Mafia murderers. Better?"

I shifted the ice pack around a little. "More accurate, anyway."

"And the bomb didn't do any serious harm to his business interests. You'd think the Delatassos would know both those things."

"Yeah, you would, wouldn't you?" I said. "Makes me wonder if the Delatassos had anything to do with it."

"But, shit, if *they* didn't do it, who did? Who'd be mad enough to car-bomb Calabrese, and dumb enough to think it would do him serious harm?"

"You figure that one out, be sure and let me know. I can probably get you hired by the Police Department as a detective."

"Oh, boy – Karl and I could work the night shift together."

I asked myself if I wanted to pursue that subject – her and Karl together, I mean – and myself got back to me immediately: *No fucking way, Markowski. Not now. Maybe not ever, but especially not right now.*

While I was congratulating myself on my good judgment, Christine said, "I didn't go right home after I left you at the hospital tonight."

"Oh? What'd you do, instead?"

"Stopped off at Varney's for a drink."

Varney's is another supe bar, but it tends to attract mostly vampires, instead of the kind of mixed crowd you find at Renfield's. I didn't know where Christine was going with this, so I just said, "Uh-huh."

"You were wondering, earlier, who's going to replace Victor Castle."

"I still am," I said. I took the ice pack off my bump and put it on the table in front of me. "You hear something?"

She took the dish towel from around the plastic bag of cubes and re-wrapped it more neatly. "I don't know if you've heard about this, but once a week, Varney's has open mike night, although they don't call it that."

Despite my throbbing head, I couldn't keep the smile off my face. "Vampire stand-up comedy? Really?"

"No, I've never heard anybody using it to tell jokes," she said. "Half the times I've been there on Thursdays, nobody got up at all."

"What did they do, the rest of the time?"

"It varies. Sometimes it's just a bunch of announcements – somebody's looking for a house sitter, somebody else is trying to unload a used coffin, stuff like that. Other times, you've got one of the community up there whining about how tough life is for a vampire these days."

"And is it?" I asked. "Tough, I mean."

She shrugged. "You have good nights and bad nights, just like anybody else. In my experience, whining doesn't help much."

"No, it usually doesn't," I said.

"One time, they had a poetry slam." She did a face-palm. "God, that was awful."

"But that's not what happened last night."

"No, last night we got to hear from Dimitri Kaspar about how supes, especially vampires, have been taking shit from the Man for too damn long, and it's time we stood up for ourselves."

"There's a vampire named Casper?" I said. "Like the friendly ghost in the comics?"

"He spells it differently, and from what I hear, he's not all that friendly. There's a story about how one time some human made a 'friendly ghost' joke in front of him." She studied the pattern in the dish towel as if it were the most interesting thing she'd ever seen. "Supposedly, Dimitri tore the guy's throat out so fast, he didn't even realize he was dead until he hit the floor."

"That's murder," I said.

"It's just a story, Dad. Anyway, if it really happened, I don't guess anybody who saw it is going to be in a hurry to testify against Dimitri Kaspar."

"Probably afraid the same thing would happen to them."

"That'd be my guess," she said.

"So what makes you think this sweetheart wants to succeed Victor Castle?"

"He said so. He told us that Castle was weak, and had been collaborating with the fascist police to keep supes from gaining true equality with the bloodbags."

I gave her a look. *"Bloodbags?"*

She had the grace to look a little embarrassed. "It's a… term some in the community use for humans."

"Never heard that one before," I said.

"I expect you're going to be hearing it a lot – especially if Dimitri Kaspar has his way."

"I was going to ask you just how the leader of the supe community gets chosen. Is there some kind of election, or what?"

She made a face and shook her head slightly. "Nothing that formal. But at some point there'll be a meeting, and each of the different species of supe will send a representative."

"You mean one from the vamps, somebody from the weres, a witch, a troll, and all that?"

"Right. And each one expresses the consensus of his species as to who should be leader. Or hers. Way I hear it, everybody sends a rep, except the fucking goblins."

"It being impossible to get a bunch of goblins to agree on pretty much anything," I said.

"Yeah, that's about it."

"So when is this big conclave supposed to take place?"

"No date's been set yet. It probably won't be until after Victor Castle's memorial service, which is this weekend."

"But this Dimitri Kaspar is an early favorite?"

"I don't know if you could call him a favorite," she said. "But nobody else has stepped forward so far. Maybe they're afraid to. And I hear that Dimitri's been spreading a lot of money around – buying goodwill, I guess."

"He's rich?"

"Not as far as I know," she said. "I think he works for the Postal Service. But he's got money from someplace."

"And money's the lifeblood of politics – even among supes, I figure."

"You figure right," she said. "But who's gonna give a bunch of it to Dimitri Kaspar? I mean, whiskey tango foxtrot?"

Military radio code for WTF or "What the fuck?" I wondered if she'd picked that up from Karl, who's been known to say it occasionally.

"Yeah, I know," I said. "Seems all I've been getting lately is a bunch of questions I don't have any answers to." I looked up toward the ceiling. A little louder, I said, "If God's taking requests tonight, some enlightenment would be greatly appreciated."

I kept looking a few seconds longer, but the ceiling didn't dissolve in a flash of bright light to admit a Heavenly messenger bearing the solutions to all my problems. I should be used to that by now.

I went to bed soon after that, even though it was still a while before dawn. Christine said she'd see me at breakfast.

I fell asleep while my head was about a foot above the pillow and slept like the undead for a few hours. But after that, whenever I changed position, the lump on the back of my head would give out a jolt of pain that woke me up. I'd fall back asleep, until my next movement repeated the process and brought me back to the surface again. It was frustrating, but I was so exhausted that I stayed in bed until sundown, when the alarm I'd set got me up.

By the time I got downstairs, Christine was up, drinking a cup of lightly warmed Type O, which is her favorite. I knew what it was, because the empty bottle was still on the counter. She'd put it in the recycling bin later.

"Good morning, Daddy."

"Morning."

She peered at me in the harsh light from the kitchen fluorescent lights. Of course, she could have seen me even if the room had been pitch black.

"Well, you look a little bit better," she said.

"Only a little bit?"

"I'd say you've made the transition from 'death warmed over' to 'death over easy'."

"Any improvement's better than none, I always say."

She'd made a pot of coffee for me, which I thought ought to qualify her for canonization – even if the Pope does hate vampires. That won't last forever, and neither will he.

As I sat down with my steaming cup, she said, "Would you like me to make you some eggs?"

Although my stomach was empty, the thought of eggs made me want to break out in dry heaves. "No, but thanks."

"Solid food doesn't appeal right now, huh?"

"No, not hardly."

"Try to eat something later, OK? And not junk from the vending machine at work."

"Yes, Doctor."

I left the house an hour earlier than usual – but not because I was eager to get to work. The way I was feeling, it was likely to be a *long* shift tonight, and I had no desire to make it even longer. But before I headed for the station house , there was somebody I needed to talk to.

The Brass Shield Bar and Grill sits on Mulberry Street, on the edge of downtown. If you heard the name and guessed that it was a cop bar, you'd be right. Alcoholism is a big problem in my profession because of all the stress, not to mention those things you see on the job that burn themselves into your mind – images that you'd give anything to be able to forget, if only for a few hours.

And even those on the force who haven't made booze into a problem often like a couple of drinks to help relax before they go home. It cuts down some on the domestic violence, I figure – although there's a lot of it that still goes on anyway. When you spend eight hours ready to fight or shoot at a moment's notice, it can be hard to let it all go as you walk through the front door and call, "Honey, I'm home."

That's not meant to be an excuse, by the way. I never laid a violent hand on my wife all the years we were together, and I despise men, cops or not, who come home and use somebody they swore to love and cherish as a punching bag. But that's why cops are drawn to the booze – some cops, anyway. And when cops drink, they mostly like to drink among their own.

I walked in and headed for the bar, nodding at several guys who I know pretty well. Frank Murtaugh, the owner, waited on me himself and I asked for a bottle of Stegmaier that I could pretend to drink while waiting for the guy I was there to see.

I found an empty booth near the back and sat down. I had a sip of the beer, the only one I planned to take. I wasn't on duty yet, but I would be in an hour. And the pain in my head was making it hard enough to concentrate without adding alcohol to the mix.

I'd been waiting maybe five minutes when *consigliere* Louis Loquasto slipped into the seat opposite me, holding a glass of what looked like a double bourbon on the rocks. His elegant suit was blue this time, and I would've bet that its price tag could've put some kid through college for a year – at a state school, anyway. I'd figured Loquasto's drink was just a prop, like mine, to avoid drawing undue attention, but then he brought the glass to his lips and took a good-sized pull from it.

"Looks like you needed that drink, Counselor," I said. "Life getting a bit stressful for you lately?"

"I find your infantile sense of humor difficult to endure at the best of times, Markowski," he said. "Which these demonstrably are not."

"Is that why you wanted to meet here – because nobody in his right mind would bomb a bar full of cops?"

"The thought had crossed my mind. Now, you said you wanted to talk – so talk."

"I said I wanted to talk to your boss, remember?"

"Mister Calabrese is otherwise engaged. But you may be sure that I will relay to him the details of this conversation, although it has been singularly uninteresting thus far."

Lawyers know more ways to say "Fuck you" without ever using those exact words than any bunch of people I've ever met.

"Somebody set off a car bomb outside of Ricardo's Ristorante last night," I said. "You know anything about it that I don't?"

"Detective, the sum total of what I know that you don't would probably fill the Scranton Eagles Stadium."

Arrogant prick. "Maybe we could focus on the bombing and leave all that other stuff for some other time – like maybe some Friday night when we're knocking back a few brewskis at the Polish-American Club."

Maybe to hide the distaste that had appeared on his face at the thought of hanging out with me socially, Loquasto took another pull from his drink. Setting the glass down, he said, "Some of our people saw the arrival of the car containing the bomb."

"Did they, now?"

"They didn't know what it was at the time, of course. The car, which was described as a late-model blue Mazda Skinwalker, stopped in the street outside the restaurant, blocking one lane of traffic."

"Probably stolen," I said.

"Yes, I expect so – although I gather so little was left of it after the explosion that identification would likely be impossible, anyway."

"So this car parks in front of Ricardo's – then what?"

"Almost immediately, what appeared to be a gnome got out from behind the wheel, dashed across the street, and hopped into the passenger seat of another car that had apparently been waiting, its engine idling."

"A gnome." I realized that I'd just taken another swig of beer without really thinking about it.

"That's what our people say. Short, nimble, white beard. He even wore that little conical hat they're known to sport."

"You trust the accuracy of the description your guys provided?" I asked him.

"By and large, yes," Loquasto said. "They are reliable people, or they would not be in Mister Calabrese's employ. Further, each was questioned separately – and provided essentially the same account."

I nodded slowly. My head protested the movement, but not quite as loudly as it had been doing yesterday.

"In that case, somebody's fucking with you."

He gave me the kind of look you'd expect from a duchess who's just been patted on the ass by one of the help – but I don't think his heart was in it. After a couple of seconds, his face lost its haughty expression and returned to its default setting of cold and hostile. His voice was flat when he said, "Explain."

"Don't take it personally," I said. "They're fucking with me, too. Maybe they're fucking with all of us."

"Is that your idea of an explanation?"

"No, but this is: *gnomes don't wear conical hats.*"

Loquasto scratched his jaw. "I was under the impression that such headgear was a trademark of the species."

"You and lots of other people," I said. "It's a cultural stereotype, like vampires wearing capes or witches riding brooms. Maybe once upon a time, in Europe or wherever, gnomes actually used to wear those stupid things. Stereotypes have to start someplace, I guess."

"But the gnomes don't do so any longer – that's what you're telling me."

"Exactly. I've met quite a few gnomes over the years, Counselor. They might wear baseball caps in the summer or stocking caps in the winter like the rest of us. When the weather's nice, lots of them don't wear anything on their heads at all. But those conical hats? No fucking way."

Loquasto swirled ice around in his glass but didn't drink this time. "I see."

"For a gnome to wear one of those cones out in public would be like a black guy walking down the street with a bucket of fried chicken in one arm and a watermelon under the other one."

I know, I know. Some black people actually like fried chicken, with watermelon for dessert. So do I. But I was trying to make a point here, political correctness be damned.

"So, it's your contention," Loquasto said, "that the driver of the car bomb couldn't have been a gnome?"

"Not necessarily. Shit, you can find members of *all* species, including human, who'll do just about anything if the money's right. Maybe the guy was a gnome, maybe not. My point is, whoever sent him wanted us to *think* he was a gnome."

Loquasto gave me a dubious look. "Why on Earth would the Delatassos do something like that?"

I paused for a second – dramatic effect, I guess. *"Maybe they didn't."*

Loquasto stared at me, then picked up his glass and drained it. "I need another," he said. "You want another beer?"

"No, I'm good, thanks."

Loquasto was smart – he wouldn't be a Mafia *consigliere* otherwise. By the time he was back at our booth, he'd figured out what I meant and started considering its implications.

"How could whoever sent this faux gnome with a car bomb be sure that there would be surviving witnesses to describe him?"

"Last time I was at Ricardo's, my partner and I were braced by three guys from Calabrese's crew, all vampires. Are those guys out there all the time?"

"Ever since the war started, yes. Mister Calabrese stationed some soldiers at the door. They were in place for as long as the restaurant was open every night. Rotating shifts, of course."

"Vampire soldiers," I said.

"That's what the Family consists of now." He gave me a thin smile. "With a few notable exceptions."

"Vampire soldiers," I repeated, then said, "Vampires... wouldn't be killed in an explosion, no matter how powerful it was."

Loquasto stared down at his drink, as if he hoped to find the answers floating in the cheap glass along with the ice cubes. "Guaranteed eyewitnesses. Very clever."

He looked up at me. "Who's got it in for gnomes so badly that he wants to frame them for an explosion that's killed..." He pulled out his smartphone and tapped the screen a few times. "Eleven people so far, with four others on the critical list. Who hates gnomes that much?"

"I think you're being too narrow in your thinking, Counselor."

His eyebrows rose slowly. "Am I indeed? Then please enlighten me."

Ignoring the sarcasm, I said, "Could be that whoever's behind it isn't just trying to set up gnomes. Maybe his target is the whole supe community."

One thing I liked about Loquasto – one of the few things, actually – was that you didn't have to draw him a diagram.

"The Patriot Party," he said softly. "I know politics is a dirty business, but that's just... *absurd*."

I gave him half a smile. "Yeah, you'd think so, wouldn't you?"

"I've heard of placing bugs in someone's campaign headquarters, or breaking into a psychiatrist's office to look for dirt on your opponent, or using magic to alter the other side's billboards and campaign signs, but this..."

He took a big gulp of his bourbon. "And it isn't a national campaign, or even a state-wide one. They're not playing for the White House, or the Governor's mansion in Harrisburg. This is all to win an election in *Scranton*?"

"Yeah, I know. A buddy of mine named Ned, who teaches at the U, once told me, 'The reason that academic conflicts are so vicious is because the stakes are so low.'"

Loquasto used one hand to make an impatient gesture. "Very clever, I'm sure," he said. "But it makes no sense in this context. We're not talking about stealing someone's research, or messing up an assistant professor's tenure file, or some such nonsense. Eleven people are dead, Markowski, including two children who were sitting in their parents' apartment, watching TV. Nineteen more, wounded. Immense property damage. All so a bunch of proto-fascists can gain political control of Scranton?"

"Doesn't make a lot of sense, when you put it that way," I said.

I was suddenly distracted by a man's voice on the other side of the big room saying loudly, "*Yeah, well, fuck you, too!*" I looked over and watched a couple of half-drunk off-duty cops get into a shoving match that was quickly broken up by other guys sitting nearby.

"Unless it's supposed to be some kind of pilot project," Loquasto said, "in which case I fail to see–"

I looked back at him. "Wait – what did you say?"

He gave me an annoyed look. Probably wasn't use to being interrupted, especially by his social inferiors. "What I *said* was it might be some kind of pilot project, although why anyone would choose Scranton to run it in is quite beyond me. Why – what's the matter?"

"That phrase, 'pilot project'. Somebody else said that to me, a while back."

"Were they talking about our little problem?"

"No, probably not," I said.

"Then I suggest we stick to the matter at hand."

"OK with me," I said. "Does the matter at hand include John Wesley Harding?"

I don't know what I expected, throwing the name at him from out in left field like that, but I didn't get anything dramatic. He didn't gasp, or go pale, or spill his drink. All he did was blink, twice, as soon as I'd said Harding's name. It looked like the tip Karl had received about a certain Boston hit man had been true.

Loquasto took a sip of his bourbon with hands that were as steady as when he'd first sat down. He lowered the glass, gave me a tiny smile, and said, "I don't believe I'm familiar with that individual, Sergeant."

"Uh-huh. A usually reliable source told me that Calabrese has brought in a life-taker from Boston by that name."

Loquasto tried for a casual shrug. I have to admit, he pulled it off pretty well – but then, he would.

"Then perhaps you need to find some new sources," he said.

"Or maybe you need to remember that fucking with me is not in your best interest – yours, or Calabrese's."

Loquasto sat back and looked at me for a second or two. The shrug he gave me this time was less elegant and more on the irritated side.

"Let's say, for the sake of discussion, that your information is correct," he said. "What business is it of yours?"

"It's my business if this war between your boss and the Delatassos is about to get a whole lot worse."

"Worse than what happened on Moosic Street last night?"

"I thought we were operating on the assumption that the Delatassos had nothing to do with that," I said.

"I never operate based on assumptions, Sergeant. I much prefer facts."

"Yeah? OK, here's a fact for you." I leaned forward across the table. "Just because I cut Calabrese a little slack once doesn't mean he should start expecting a free pass from me. Not now, not ever. If Calabrese – or anybody who works for him – gets caught shooting up the streets, then he's going down. One way or another."

"I'll be sure to pass that information along," he said in a bored voice, as if I'd just told him it might rain tomorrow.

Loquasto began sliding out of the booth. "This has been an illuminating conversation, Sergeant Markowski," he said, and stood up. "Perhaps we'll have another one sometime. Do have a good evening."

He turned and walked to the door without looking back. I waited, half-expecting to hear gunfire or another explosion as a sign that the Delatassos had tracked him here. But the street outside remained quiet.

At least he'd paid for his own booze.

My conversation with Loquasto had taken longer than I'd planned, which meant that Karl beat me in to work. As I pulled out my desk chair, I saw that he was busy on his computer – whether paperwork or another game of "Angry Bats" I didn't know.

"Hey," I said.

"Hey, yourself," he said. "Don't sit down – Rachel wants to see you."

"Rachel Proctor?"

"I don't know any other Rachel around here," he said. "Do you?"

"Guess not. What's she want?"

"Didn't say. But I'm pretty sure that she's down in her office now."

"OK, I'll go see what's up. Buzz me if we get a call to go out, will you?"

"Ten-four on that, Sergeant."

Normally I'd walk the two flights down to Rachel's office, but I decided that the elevator would make my head hurt less than bouncing on the stairs. I was pushing the button for Rachel's floor when it occurred to me that Karl hadn't once looked up from his computer during our brief conversation. What was his problem?

Rachel's office door was open and I could see she was at her desk, writing something on a pad. She looked up at my knock.

"Hi, Stan."

"Hi, Rachel. Karl said you wanted to see me about something."

She hesitated a moment before speaking, and I thought, *Why the fuck is everybody in this place acting weird tonight?*

"Yes, that's right," she said, finally. "Come on in."

As I approached, I saw that the usual clutter had been cleared away from the top of her desk. A clean white cloth had been dropped over it, and I could see that Rachel had laid out there some items of we laymen like to call "magic stuff".

What looked like a perfectly round circle had been drawn on the cloth in some kind of orange ink or paint. Inside the circle was a squat yellow candle, unlit. Two small ceramic bowls held small amounts of powder – red in one dish, blue in the other. In between the bowls was a small bottle with an ornately carved stopper. It contained a clear liquid with what looked like tiny flakes of metal floating in it. Next to the bottle was a small knife with a handle that might have been ivory, or maybe white bone. Its four-inch blade was shiny and looked very sharp.

"What's all this stuff?" I asked her.

"It's for an experiment I'm conducting," she said.

"Something to do with Slide?" I'd given her some samples to work on, although neither one of the dishes contained any of the stuff, far as I could tell.

"Not directly," she said. "Bear with me a few moments, will you?"

She lit the candle with a disposable lighter – not exactly a magical implement, but still the modern equivalent of the traditional flint and steel.

"OK, now," she said. "Watch closely."

So I stood there and looked on as she mixed the powders together by pouring them back and forth from one bowl to the other. I suppose the number of passes she made had some magical significance, but I didn't count them. She chanted softly the whole time, in a language that I vaguely recognized as ancient Greek but didn't understand. You could even say that it was all Greek to me.

When the powders had been mixed to Rachel's liking, she removed the stopper from the bottle and poured the liquid into the bowl. "Now," she said," looking up at me, "time for your contribution, Stan." She picked up the little knife. "I'd like a single hair from your head."

My first reaction was wariness – but that was just habit. Give a black witch a bit of your hair, fingernail clippings, even some spit – anything that's an integral part of you – she can end up owning your soul.

I had to remind myself that this was Rachel, certified practitioner of *white* magic, trusted consultant to the police department and – so I liked to think – a good friend, despite all the trouble I'd gotten her into in the past.

Hoping she hadn't noticed my momentary hesitation, I said, "Sure, no problem. What've you got in mind, anyway?"

"I'd rather not say right now, Stan. It could spoil the spell. But I'm pretty sure you won't be displeased with the result."

I shrugged, which sent another jolt of pain through my head. I was going to have to train myself to stop doing that, at least until my lump finally faded away.

"OK, if you say so," I told her. "But I can just yank one out for you if you want – you won't need to cut it off with that thing."

"I'm afraid use of the knife is part of the ritual," she said. "I promise I'll be careful."

"Go on, then." I learned forward – but for the sake of my head, I did it slowly.

She was as good as her word. It took just a second or two before she said, "Got it, thank you."

I straightened up and saw that she held a single strand of hair between her fingers. As I watched, she dropped it into the bowl containing the powder and liquid. Then she used the knife blade to carefully stir the mixture, chanting softly the whole time.

After a while, she picked up the bowl and carefully poured off the small amount of remaining liquid, leaving her with a purple-colored paste.

"Good," she said. "Now, Stan, would you take your sport coat off, please?" She pointed to a nearby chair. "You can put it over there, if you like."

I gave her a look, but the pleasant expression on her face didn't alter. So I turned away, unbuttoned my jacket, and slipped it off. *This is Rachel, dummy. Just relax – whatever she's doing, everything's gonna be fine. Probably.*

I wished my mind hadn't felt the need to add that last word, but I've learned that there are damn few certainties in life. Anyway, "probably true" is the standard most of us use for almost everything we do.

I folded my jacket and draped it over an arm of the chair, and when I turned back around Rachel was right there, standing less than a foot away. She'd come up behind me, and I'd never even known she was there.

Getting careless, Markowski. That could get you killed, one of these nights.

"Rachel, what're you–"

"Hush," she said, placing her left hand on my shoulder.

Given the height difference between us, Rachel needed to tilt her head back quite a ways to look me in the eye, and that's what she did now as she said, "Kiss me, Stan."

"Come on, is this some kind of–"

"No questions. Just kiss me."

Since I was male, straight, and not insane, I did what she asked, even though bending my head forward like that hurt like a bastard.

My God, her lips were sweet. I've kissed a few women over the years – not as many as I would've liked to, but still – and I've never had a woman's lips pressed against mine that tasted and felt like Rachel's.

The small part of my mind that was not reveling in the sensations my mouth was receiving started wondering why Rachel was still keeping her right hand down by her side. As if bidden by my thoughts, her right arm suddenly came up, the hand reaching for the back of my neck.

Then that part of my mind still capable of rational thought remembered the knife she'd been holding a few moments ago. If you hit the right spot at the base of the skull, right where it joins the spine, you can kill a man with a knitting needle, let alone a razor-sharp blade.

I could have died, right at that moment – and if it been Rachel's intention to kill me, that's exactly what I would have done. But instead of the knife, what I felt on the back of my head was Rachel's bare hand – which she then pressed, very hard, against that throbbing lump that had been making my life so damn miserable.

In the space of half a second, the pain raced up the scale from "pretty damn bad" through "fucking awful" to reach a level of agony that would have impressed even the head torturer for the Spanish Inquisition.

But before I could even scream, the anguish just... *stopped*. It didn't fade gradually, which is what I'm used to. Instead, it was as if somebody had found the pain switch on my skull and flicked it to "Off."

That was when Rachel stepped back, a little breathlessly. I saw now that her right hand was smeared with some of the purple paste that she'd made up in the bowl. That meant a glob of it was probably smeared on the back of my head, but I was in no position – or mood – to complain.

"You…" I began, but couldn't think what to say next. I tried again. "You did… something…"

"Yes, I did," Rachel said with a grin. "Feel the back of your head, Stan. Go ahead – the pain won't return, I promise."

I put my hand back there, felt what had to be some of the purple paste. It was cool on my fingers, and gritty. What I *didn't* feel was the lump on my skull that had been put there by a gun butt belonging to a recently deceased thug from Philadelphia.

I just looked at Rachel, whose grin was still in place. Finally I took my hand away from the back of my head and used it to dig around in my pocket for a handkerchief to wipe the goop away.

"You used a spell," I said. My grasp of the obvious was not reduced at all by my recent ordeal. "A healing spell."

"Well, Karl said you were in a lot of pain, and too damn stubborn to take some time off in order to heal. He asked me to see what I could do to help you out."

She went back behind her desk and used the cloth covering it to wipe the remaining magical goop off her hand. "There's no magic I've ever heard of that would make you less pigheaded, so I figured the only alternative was to heal your injury."

"What I know about healing spells," I said, "they're not something you can just pull out of the air."

"Quite right," she said. "I've been working on this one most of the day."

"Not to sound ungrateful – because I'm not, believe me –but I hope McGuire doesn't find out you spent your time working on that instead of the stuff they pay you for."

"Whether I was wasting the city's money depends on your point of view, Stan. One could make the case that I've performed a signal service for the Occult Crimes Unit by restoring one of its most valued officers to full capability."

"Most valued?" I asked. "Really?"

The grin made another appearance. "Well, *somebody* must think so. Karl might – on your good days, anyway."

"Do you think we could sit down?" I said. "I'm feeling a little... I dunno... lightheaded."

"That should pass pretty quickly," she said. "But, sure, have a seat."

I moved my sport coat off the arm of the chair and flopped down. Rachel blew out the candle and sat down behind her desk.

"Would you like a bottle of water? You look like you could use some hydration."

I hadn't realized that I was thirsty until she said that, but now I felt parched. "That'd be great – thanks."

She swiveled in her chair and produced two plastic bottles of water from the mini-fridge behind her. When she gave me one, I cracked the top and raised the bottle in her direction. "Here's to... I don't know. Witchcraft, I guess."

"I'll drink to that," she said, and did.

That water was the second-sweetest thing I'd tasted since coming into Rachel's office tonight. After I'd had a couple of long swallows, I asked her, "So why the subterfuge? Why not just say, 'Get your ass down here, Stan – I've got a cure for your headache'?"

"I was afraid you'd go all macho and say that you could handle the pain just fine, thank you very much, and you didn't need anybody casting spells to make you feel better."

"What made you think I'd react like that?"

"We've known each other how long, Stan? Five years?"

"Yeah, more or less."

"*That's* why."

"Oh."

"I didn't want all the work I spent preparing this spell going to waste, just because you were suffering from a case of testicular poisoning."

"I don't think I've ever heard it put quite that way, but maybe you've got a point" I said. "OK, that explains why you didn't tell me. But what was up with that kiss?"

She laughed a little. "Oh, yes, I suppose I should apologize for that."

"I was just asking a question, Rachel – not complaining."

That earned another brief laugh. "Well, the kiss served two purposes, actually – one mundane, the other magical."

"Which one of those covers knocking my socks off?"

"I'll have to think about that. Anyway, the mundane reason was a simple distraction. I didn't want you ducking away when I put that salve on your injury."

"Assuming I was gonna be all macho about it."

"Yes, assuming that."

"And the magical reason?"

"A healing spell involves the transfer of positive energy from the practitioner to the patient. There has to be a generation of what another religion's tradition would call 'good karma'. I should add that I put on some lipstick with a mild enchantment on it, to make you want to stay with the kiss for a while."

"I'm not sure that was necessary, but I'd say it served its purpose pretty well."

"Yes, and a good thing, too. If the kiss hadn't worked, my only other option was to increase the positive energy of the spell in a more... extreme way." I swear she actually blushed as she said that last part.

"Extreme? You mean... *sex*? You and me?" If I wasn't such a tough guy, I think I might have been blushing a little myself by that point.

She gave her head a toss. "Well, it was either that or give up on the spell – and, as I said, I had spent a lot of time on it." She took her time drinking some water, then said, "White magic draws its strength from nature, from the earth itself. And the earth is, as you know, the ultimate life force."

"I think I read that someplace."

"Well, that's why generation of the life force is sometimes called for, especially in healing spells."

"So, if the kiss hadn't worked, you were prepared to...?" I let my voice trail off rather than say what I'd been about to, which was "fuck my brains out." That seemed a bit crude, considering the circumstances – and the company.

"Fuck your brains out?" said Rachel, another mind reader. "I'll just say that I would have given it serious consideration, and leave it at that. Let's be glad that it proved unnecessary."

"I know what you're saying," I said, "but I'm having a little trouble being glad about something like that."

"As far as the Scranton PD is concerned, it might well have raised some ethical issues." She put her water bottle aside and started gathering up the magical materials from her desk. Without looking at me, she went on, "Not to mention emotional ones, quite possibly."

That's the advantage of having a bottle of water in your hands – drinking from it gives you something to do while you're trying to figure out what to say to something like that. But the best I could come up with was "Yeah, quite possibly."

"Anyway," she said, "the spell worked, and you're feeling more like your old self, which was the object of the exercise. There's too much weird shit going on right now not to have you at your best."

"'Weird shit' is right. Speaking of which – how's your research on Slide been coming along?"

"No breakthroughs so far," she said. "Although I've learned quite a bit about its properties, which is a good first step. The work, as they say, continues."

I finished off my water and put the bottle aside. "Rachel," I said, "I don't know how to say 'Thank you' for what you did."

"I'd say you just managed pretty well."

"Alright, then," I said, and stood up. I braced myself for the pain that would follow, then remembered that there wouldn't be any – not any more. "Duty calls."

I was almost to the door when she said, "Stan...?"

I turned back. "Yeah?"

"You should know that I wouldn't have used that healing spell on just anyone – at *any* level of intensity."

I looked at her. She stared back. Neither of us spoke, but when the silence started getting awkward, I said, "Is this something we should talk about?"

"Maybe," she said. "But not right now. Go out and bust some bad guys, Stan."

"Count on it."

As I sat down at my desk, Karl looked up for the first time since I'd seen him tonight. "Looks like you're moving around a little better than you were before," he said.

"Yeah, Rachel worked some magic and made my fucking lump disappear. My head doesn't hurt at all now."

"Glad to hear it," he said, and went back to whatever he'd been doing at his computer.

"You wouldn't know anything about that, would you?" I asked him.

He looked up again, his face a study in innocence. "Course I would," he said.

"Really?"

"Sure – you just told me about it, remember? Jeez, Stan, maybe that knock on the head fucked you up worse than you thought."

I decided to give it up. "Guess there was no call for us while I was downstairs."

"Nope. Slow night – so far. There is one interesting thing, though."

"What's that?"

"You see the paper today?"

"No, I haven't had a chance," I said. "Why?"

He handed me the front section of the *Times-Tribune*. I saw that another judge from Luzerne

County was being charged with corruption and lying under oath. I'm surprised they even bother to put that stuff on the front page anymore.

"Page three," Karl said.

I opened the paper and found that the good folks at the Patriot Party hadn't been letting any grass grow under their feet. They'd taken out another full-page ad, characterized by their usual restraint and statesmanlike approach to the problems facing our city. This one was expressing their sober concern regarding of the recent bombing outside Ricardo's Ristorante.

"*OUTRAGE*" was centered at the top of the page in letters that had to be two inches high. The rest was pretty much what I would have expected, even if the print was a little smaller. "*Another bomb explodes!*" it read, followed by "*More human lives snuffed out! More human property damaged!*" The worst property damage had been at Ricardo's, which was owned by a supe – but I guess the Patriot Party wasn't going to let facts get in the way of a good rant. The ad continued. "*How much longer will this go on?*"

Further down, there was some text claiming that the bombing represented the latest atrocity in the ongoing supe gang war – I noticed it was "supernatural gang war" and not "vampire gang war", which would have been more precise. The ad said a gnome was a suspect in the bombing, which caused me to wonder just where the Patriot Party got its information. I hadn't had the chance to tell anyone what I'd learned from Loquasto, and I doubted that he or anybody else in the Calabrese family was spreading that information around.

The thrust of the ad was the same theme the Patriot Party had been playing for some time now: the city was going to hell, the supes, who were all either gangsters or drug addicts, were responsible, and the city government had been too inept or too corrupt to stop it. Blah, blah, blah.

I folded the paper and put it back on Karl's desk. "I can't exactly say I'm surprised. Are you?"

"Not about that shit, no," he said. "But I got an email from a guy I know who works at the *Times-Tribune*, and what it said did surprise me a little."

"And that was...?"

"The text of that ad, all laid out and ready for uploading, was emailed to the *T-T* at 7.29 pm yesterday. They just made the deadline for the next morning's edition – the cutoff time for ad copy is 7. 30, he tells me."

"OK – has this joke got a punch line?"

"Fuckin' A," Karl said, "and it's a doozy. You know what time the bomb went off?"

"No, I didn't hear the blast. Don't forget, Mercy Hospital's on the other side of town from Ricardo's."

"I wasn't sure of the time myself," Karl said. "So I checked the 911 log. The first call reporting the explosion came in at 7:17."

After a couple of seconds, I reached over and retrieved the paper from Karl's desk. I wanted another look at that ad.

There was a lot of text, and most of it was very specific to the bombing at Ricardo's. This wasn't a bunch of boilerplate that could be pulled out of a document file and turned into ad copy in no time at all.

I put the paper down and looked at Karl. "Somebody at PP headquarters works pretty fast, don't they?"

"Maybe too fast."

"Uh-huh. And there's something about this mess that I haven't told you yet. Before I racked out this morning, I called that number that Loquasto gave me."

"The *consigliere*."

"That's the guy."

I gave Karl the details of my conversation with the Calabrese Family's *consigliere*. When I'd finished, he looked at me as if I'd just told him that the Girl Scouts were going to be selling hash brownies along with their cookies this year.

"That's just... fucking ridiculous," he said.

"It sure would be nice to think so."

"The fucking Patriot Party is going around blowing shit up so that they can blame it all on supes and sweep the election? Stan, I knew those guys were assholes, but ... come *on*."

"I know, I know," I said. "It's crazy. Except that it's been done before."

"Where?

"Germany," I said. "The Thirties, soon after Hitler was elected Chancellor. One night the Nazis burned down the Reichstag, which was their Parliament building. Burned it to the ground. Then they found some Communist doofus and hung the whole thing on him."

"Why that guy?"

"Because, like I said, he was a Commie, and the Commies were the Nazis' biggest political rivals. As a result of the public panic over the fire, the Communist party was outlawed and the Nazis gained absolute power – which they hung onto until the end of the war."

"OK, I see the parallel, assuming what we're thinking about the Patriot party is true," Karl said. "But, dude, this is Scranton. Not Nazi Germany. *Scranton.*"

"I know," I said. "But when I was talking to Loquasto about this earlier, he said something that had a weird association for me, but I don't know why."

"What'd he say?"

"Just like us, he was trying to get his mind around the idea that somebody would do all this bad shit just to get political control of Scranton. And then he said something like 'Maybe it's a pilot project.'"

"Pilot project," Karl said. He chewed his lower lip, which is a tricky thing for a vampire to do. Then he said to me, "Maybe we better go see McGuire."

After Karl and I had finished talking, McGuire sat back in his chair, the worn springs creaking under his weight. He studied Karl, then spent a few seconds looking at me.

"I suppose I could order both of you to see the department shrink," he said. "He's probably seen a lot of cops with paranoia and has some ideas on how to treat it."

"Doc Watson, you mean?" I said. "Yeah, he's pretty good. He'll probably have Karl drinking Type O laced with clozapine. He'd still be paranoid, but it wouldn't bother him so much."

The look McGuire gave me said he thought I was about as funny as diarrhea. It's a look I've seen from him more than a few times.

"Alright," he said. "Assume, for the sake of discussion, that the two of you aren't bat-shit crazy.

What do you plan on doing about this... *conspiracy* you think you've stumbled onto?"

"We were hoping you might have some advice for us, boss," Karl said.

"I hope you weren't thinking about arresting somebody," McGuire said. "Right now, you haven't got enough probable cause to justify a fucking traffic ticket."

"We don't need probable cause to bring somebody in for questioning, though," I said.

McGuire raised an eyebrow at me. "Who've you got in mind?"

"How about the head of the Patriot Party...?" I looked at Karl.

"Slattery," he said. "Phil Slattery."

"You're assuming he's the head of the party," McGuire said, "because he's their candidate for Mayor?"

Karl frowned at him. "You're saying he isn't? If not, then who is it?"

"I didn't say that Slattery wasn't the head honcho," McGuire said. "But there's a rumor floating around City Hall, something about a power behind the throne."

"Slattery hasn't got the throne yet," I said.

"Just an expression," McGuire said. "But there's some guys in the Mayor's office who think there's somebody behind the Patriot Party, pulling the strings."

Karl shook his head. "And you called *us* paranoid," he said quietly.

"Has this somebody got a name?" I asked McGuire.

"Fuck, no," he said. "Like I told you, it's just a rumor."

"We can't bring a rumor in for questioning," I said. "Which brings us back to Slattery."

McGuire put his feet up on the open top drawer of his desk, a sign that he was expecting this discussion to take a while. "We call Slattery in here for questioning," he said, "and his campaign's gonna scream bloody murder. They'll claim the mayor's using the police to harass him."

"Let him," Karl said. "Doesn't look to me like the Mayor's office has got a whole lot left to lose at this point. According to the last poll I saw, the Patriot Party's expected to kick serious ass in the election."

"Anyhow, that sword cuts both ways," I said. "If Slattery balks, he could be handing the mayor a nice campaign issue: 'Why won't the PP cooperate with a legitimate police investigation?' he could say. 'What's Slattery afraid of?'"

McGuire pursed his lips for a second. "OK, that could work," he said. "But say we get him in here – so what? He'll have his lawyer with him, for whatever that's worth – I hear Slattery's pretty sharp all by himself. What do you expect the guy to say that's gonna do this investigation any good? He won't even be under oath."

"That's right," I said. "He won't be under oath. He won't even be under arrest."

"Not without probable cause, he won't be, and we sure as shit haven't got any," McGuire said.

"Which means we won't be reading him his rights beforehand."

McGuire didn't say, "Well, duh!" but the look he gave me got the point across pretty well, anyway.

"The *Barlow* decision says you can't have a vampire anywhere around a suspect who's being questioned by the authorities," I said. *"Once he's been read his rights."*

My boss isn't stupid, and neither is my partner. They were both looking at me now, and their expressions said they thought I might actually possess an IQ higher than two digits. I tried to enjoy the experience, since it happens so rarely.

"Nothing Slattery says'll be admissible in court," Karl said, but not as if he was disagreeing with my idea.

"It wouldn't be admissible, anyway, since we're not gonna read him his rights," I said.

"He won't come alone," McGuire said.

"No," I said. "We've already stipulated that he's not stupid."

"So whoever's with him," McGuire said, "his lawyer or his bodyguard or his mother or whoever the fuck he brings, is probably gonna figure out pretty quick what we're doing."

"Yeah, the boss is right," Karl said to me. "We might get only one question under Influence."

"In that case," I said, "we'd better make it a good one."

McGuire said he'd do his best to get Phil Slattery down to headquarters some night for questioning, but nothing was likely to happen until tomorrow at the earliest. It was already after 11pm, and I agreed with McGuire that guys like Slattery probably weren't available to anybody as unimportant as a cop at that hour of night.

For a while after that, Karl and I sat at our desks in the squad room and tried to figure out what to ask Slattery, assuming that Karl would be able to use vampire Influence on him.

"Should we assume that Slattery or his people are gonna shut everything down once they figure out that I'm using Influence?" Karl said.

"We should probably assume the worst," I said, "which is that we'll only get one crack at him, if that. But what the hell – we could also have some backup questions prepared, in case somebody on Slattery's side has a sudden attack of the stupids and lets him keep talking."

"You figure that's likely?"

"No, but I can dream, can't I?"

"Something else just occurred to me," Karl said. "What if Slattery says, 'You cops wanna talk, then come to me. I'm not going down to police HQ – not until I walk in as mayor, anyway.'"

"That would kinda complicate things, wouldn't it?"

"Just a little," Karl said. "There's a good chance one of Slattery's people would figure out that I'm undead before I ever get near him –- which means I never *would* get near him."

"Discrimination against supes is illegal," I said.

"Yeah, I bet that matters a great big bunch to the haters in the Patriot Party."

"Good point," I said. "It's probably as little account to them as sparrows' tears."

I figured Karl would recognize that I was quoting the last line from *You Only Live Twice*, and the grin he gave me showed I was right.

"Hey, not bad, Stan," he said. "Your taste in reading is improving."

"Even *I* get tired of *Reader's Digest* sometimes."

I went to the front of the squad room and poured a cup of coffee that I didn't really want, just to give myself a chance to stretch a little and think. By the time I got back to my desk, I figured I might have an answer to the problem Karl had raised.

"So, alright," I said to Karl. "Let's say Slattery's people give us that 'You come to us' bullshit. So we tell them, 'Sure – we'll be happy to come over there to talk to Mister Slattery. We'll have to work it into our busy schedules, though. And we can't guarantee that we won't show up in the middle of the candidate's next press conference. Wonder what all those reporters would make of a couple of detectives showing up to talk to the Big Man himself?'"

Karl thought about that for a bit. "That might just do the trick. Slattery's got a big lead in the polls, but I don't guess he's willing to chance any bad publicity this close to election day." He gave me an approving nod. "Pretty good, Stan – you're developing a devious mind. I like that in a partner, even if he *is* warm."

I was about to thank him for the compliment when McGuire stuck his head out of his office door and yelled our names.

When we were standing in front of his desk, McGuire said, "We've got a report of another explosion."

"Aw, *fuck*," I said. "How bad is this one?"

"Not like the car bomb at Ricardo's, I'm glad to say. In fact, Scanlon says it might not be the same kind of bomb at all."

"Scanlon's there already?" Karl asked.

"Yeah, and he says there's a couple of dead vampires at the scene – so you two better get over there."

The address he gave us turned out to be in the 1800 block of Spruce Street. Using the flashing lights and siren, we were there within ten minutes. This time out, the siren didn't bother me at all, thanks to Rachel. I'd been remembering the sweet taste of her lips when Karl brought the car to a halt, and my thoughts came back to the present.

The yellow crime scene tape marked off an area in front of Cassidy's Bar and Grille – a place that I knew drew a mixed clientele of humans and supes. Despite what McGuire had told us, I was expecting something along the lines of the devastation we'd seen outside of Ricardo's, or at least the kind of damage that that had accompanied Victor Castle's murder. But all the klieg lights showed us was a lot of broken glass from Cassidy's front windows and numerous small holes in the masonry – along with two dead bodies sprawled in the middle of the street.

There was also a hell of a lot of gore – splashes of blood, hair, and tissue spread out from the bodies at a wide angle and for maybe fifty feet behind them. It was as if somebody had been using a machine gun and hadn't been worried about conserving ammunition.

Scanlon was about twenty feet from the corpses, staring as if he expected them to get up and tell him what the hell had happened.

"When we got word there was another explosion, I was expecting something a lot worse than this," I said by way of greeting. "Not that I'm complaining."

"I had the same kind of reaction myself when the call came in," he said. "But this was no car bomb – we can be thankful for that."

"What's Dennehy think?" I asked him.

"Bomb squad's not here yet," he said. "But I got a couple ideas of my own. Come on."

He led us away from the bodies and toward the sidewalk on the opposite side of the street from Cassidy's. Although the area was still within the area cordoned off by crime scene tape, it wasn't nearly as well lit as the area around the corpses.

Before I could ask him, he said, "The crime scene people are short of lights tonight. There was a bad car crash on the South Side, and they had to take some of the kliegs over there. But check this sucker out."

From his coat pocket, Scanlon produced what I assumed was a flashlight, thick around the middle but less than a foot long. Then he clicked it on, and I found myself squinting against a sudden glare that was far brighter than I would ever have expected from something so small. Karl can see in the dark, but even he seemed impressed as he said, "What the fuck, Lieutenant?"

"Nice, isn't it? One of those new quartz tactical flashlights. Puts out 860 lumens, whatever that means."

"I think that's tech-speak for *pretty fuckin' bright*," I said. "How come Homicide gets those and we don't?"

"Homicide doesn't,' he said. "I bought it myself from a catalog. Set me back eighty bucks. Now, take a look over here."

We'd reached the curb, and Scanlon's super-flashlight gave a clear view of what there was to see: a lot of scorched asphalt, a chunk of what looked like melted green plastic, and a small piece of shiny metal in a V shape.

"This was the *bomb*?" Karl asked, disbelief clear in his voice. I didn't blame him.

"I don't think it was a bomb at all," Scanlon said, "in the accepted usage of the term. I'm pretty sure that this here is what's left of a Claymore mine, after it's been detonated."

"That's military ordnance, isn't it?" I said.

"It sure is," Scanlon said. I figured he'd know. Scanlon was in the Army when he was younger, and I knew he'd served in the Transylvanian war, although he never talked much about it. He probably used Claymores himself or saw them used.

"I thought a mine was a round thing that you hide just below the surface of the ground," Karl said. "Somebody who doesn't see the detonator steps on it, or drives over it, and *boom*."

"They still use those," Scanlon said. "But this is a different kind of weapon." Scanlon brought out his smartphone. "I looked it up on the Internet for you," he said, and handed the phone to Karl. "Here."

I looked over Karl's shoulder, even though I'd seen pictures of a Claymore before.

The photo on Scanlon's screen showed a curved rectangle of green plastic, on its side, with "FRONT TOWARD ENEMY" stamped on it in big letters. It had a small metal attachment on top that looked like a rifle sight, and from the underside protruded two pairs of scissor legs that would stand the thing upright. The shiny piece of metal that lay on the road in front of us looked an awful lot like one of those legs.

Karl scrolled down to see the details. "Seven hundred steel balls embedded in plastic explosive," he read aloud. "Kill zone is fifty meters wide, extending back more than a hundred meters."

He handed the phone back to Scanlon. "Pretty impressive. Thanks, Lieutenant."

I said to Scanlon, "McGuire said that the vics were vampires – that's why we were sent over here."

"They are," Scanlon said. "I checked for fangs, and they've both got 'em."

"Then this impressive weapon here" – I nodded toward the asphalt in front of us – "should have been worth shit, since we all know that explosive devices don't kill vampires."

"You're right – they don't," Scanlon said. "Unless they've been specially modified." He took something small and round from his coat pocket and tossed it to me underhand. "With these."

As I tried to get a close look in the uncertain light at what I was holding, Scanlon said to Karl, "I could have given that to you, but it would have been kind of like pulling a nasty practical joke – and I have no use for people who do shit like that."

I was holding a metal sphere about the size of a pea, and when I heard what Scanlon said to Karl, I was pretty sure I knew what it was. "Silver?"

"Seems to be," Scanlon said. "Technically, that little item should be in an evidence bag. But there's so many of them back there – embedded in the building, the road, the vics, and God knows where-all – that I figured it wouldn't hurt to hang on to one."

"A vampire-killing Claymore mine," I said. "What *will* they think of next?"

"You got any ID on the vics yet, Lieutenant?" Karl asked.

"Philadelphia addresses on both of their driver's licenses," Scanlon said. "Those could be bogus, of course – we'll check with DMV in the morning. And their prints will go out on the wire, too. Their fingertips were about the only parts that didn't have holes in them. Well, one guy did lose a finger in the blast, but his other nine are intact – more than enough for an ID if he's ever been fingerprinted."

"I'm guessing both of them will have prints on file," I said. "They've been busted a few times, most likely."

Scanlon took the little silver ball back from me. "Delatasso Family, you figure?"

"Makes sense, all things considered," I said.

"Yeah, it does. And while I was waiting for you guys to show, I radioed one of my detectives back at the station house and told him to check NCIC. I was wondering whether there's been any reported thefts of Claymore mines lately. You don't exactly pick those things up at Vlad-Mart."

"And the fact that you're telling us about it," I said, "means your search rang the cherries somewhere."

"Uh-huh," Scanlon said. "A National Guard armory in Newton, Massachusetts reported a case of Claymores missing two months ago. But since they only do their weapons inventory once a year, there's no way to nail down precisely when the theft occurred."

"Newton," Karl said. "Is that anywhere near Boston?"

"Hold on."

Scanlon consulted his phone again. It seemed that damn thing would do everything but walk the dog for you. There was probably an app for that, too – but Scanlon wouldn't have bought it, because his apartment building doesn't allow dogs.

"Looks like Newton's about ten miles west of Boston," Scanlon said after a minute or two. "Was that just idle curiosity, or do you know something?"

"We know something," I told him. "Whether it's relevant you'll have to decide for yourself."

Karl told Scanlon what his confidential informant had said about Boston hit man John Wesley Harding, and I added that the Calabrese *consigliere*, Loquasto, had all but confirmed it for me earlier in the evening.

"Hit man from Boston, Claymore mines stolen from near Boston, modified Claymores used to take out a couple of Delatasso soldiers in Scranton," Scanlon said. "Could be a coincidence, I suppose."

"You see that a lot in our business?" I asked him.

"Not so much, no," he said. "If this guy Harding has got any kind of a rep back home, Boston PD's Organized Crime Unit should have something on him – maybe even a picture or two. I'll talk to a guy I know on the force there, see what he can turn up."

"Anything you get, we'd appreciate a copy," I said.

"Oh, good," he said, "because I always feel like crap at the end of my shift unless I've done at least one favor for the Occult Crimes Unit."

Sarcastic bastard.

After everything that had happened – official and unofficial – so far tonight, I was hoping that the rest of our shift would be quiet. It was quiet, alright. For a couple of people, it was quiet as the grave.

As luck would have it – whether good luck or bad you can decide for yourself – our route back to the station house took us down Penn Avenue, right past the apartment building that Roger Gillespe had called home. I might have forgotten about that fact, if it wasn't for those flashing red lights coming from around the corner on Spruce Street to serve as a reminder.

As we approached the corner, I said to Karl, "Slow down. I want to see where all the action is coming from."

Karl looked sideways at me but did as I asked. "You thinking it's what's-his-name, Gillespe?"

"No – I'm hoping that it isn't."

Yet another one of my hopes hit the ground with a thud as we reached the corner and I saw the squad cars parked in front of Gillespe's building, along with the ambulance. Each vehicle had its red lights going, and I bet Roger Gillespe's neighbors just loved *that* – especially the ones who had to get up the next morning.

"Find some place to pull over, will you?" I said to Karl. "I've got a bad feeling about this."

"You're not the only one," he said.

Karl found a parking space, and we walked the half-block or so back to what was clearly a crime scene. Our badges got us past the uniform who was stationed at the yellow tape to keep the morbidly curious away, and they got us in the front door of Gillespe's building, as the two uniforms standing there stood aside to let us pass.

"Which apartment?" I asked one, a tall guy with a big nose named Zawatski, who's a third-generation cop. I'd been seeing him at crime scenes for years.

"It's number nine, Sarge," he said. "Upstairs."

"Have they got an ID on the vic?"

"Not that I know of, but the name on the lease is ...." He pulled a small notebook from his pocket and checked it. "Gillespe, Roger J."

I didn't exactly fall down with shock. That's the problem with my bad feelings – they're almost always right. I asked Zawatski, "Who's ROS?" I wanted the name so that I'd know what kind of lies to get ready, if any.

Zawatski stowed his notebook away. "Homicide dick named Eisinger."

Behind me, I heard Karl mutter, "Great. Just fucking *great*."

"Thanks," I said to Zawatski.

The other uniform opened the door for us, and Karl and I went past him and started up the stairs. Nate Eisinger was the kind of cop who would probably refer to black people as "niggers," except Scranton's African-American population is so small, he doesn't get much chance. But there's no shortage of supes in this town, and Eisinger doesn't exactly have warm and fuzzy feelings about them, either.

Maybe he'd keep his bigoted opinions to himself once Karl and I got to apartment nine , either because 1) I outranked him, 2) racist remarks to another cop could get him brought up on charges, or 3) Karl might be tempted to tear his throat out.

Once we got to the second floor, it wasn't hard to figure out which apartment had belonged to Roger Gillespe, since only one had a uniformed cop standing in front of it. As we walked down the hall, I said softly to Karl, "Don't let Eisinger get under your skin. It'll only make him happy."

"I'll try to make sure he stays miserable, then."

Whether he recognized us or just saw the badges hanging over our jacket pockets I don't know, but the uniform at the open apartment door just nodded at us and stepped aside. Past the door was what I assumed to be the living room of the late Roger Gillespe, former busboy and drug dealer.

The big-screen TV mounted on one wall, along with the DVR and fancy-looking DVD player hooked up to it, were the only signs that Gillespe had been earning more than a busboy's salary. Otherwise, the place was a dump, with peeling wallpaper, a puke-green carpet that was worn through in several places, and furniture that Goodwill probably would have turned down. It wasn't a big room, and it felt crowded. In addition to Karl and me, the small space now contained another bored-looking uniformed cop, a couple of forensics techs crawling around on their hands and knees, and Detective Second Grade Nathan Eisinger, the pride of the Homicide Squad, who was writing something down in a small notebook. Roger Gillespe was there, too, but I didn't think the extra company bothered him.

He lay on his back, arms spread wide, as if he'd been held down while he died. His eyes were bulging and red – it looked like every blood vessel in them had burst, which is probably just what happened. A thin stream of blood had trickled down from his nose to stain Gillespe's lower face as well as the torn blue "AC/DC" T-shirt that he wore.

You can't judge a book by its cover, or a werewolf by his fur. And just because Nathan Eisinger looks like he could've been a poster boy for the Waffen-SS, with his crew-cut blond hair, square jaw, and blue eyes the color of Delft china, doesn't automatically make him a racist, fascist, low-rent asshole. In Eisinger's case, I'm sure it's just a coincidence.

He finished what he'd been writing, looked up, and saw Karl and me for the first time. His pale eyebrows went up theatrically. "Well, if it isn't the Supe Squad! Welcome to our little crime scene," he said with the exaggerated courtesy that's always intended as an insult.

I said, "Eisinger," and Karl just nodded.

"So what brings you two... detectives over here this evening? One of the neighbors thinks she saw a ghost?"

I just shook my head, and Eisinger went on. "Because I sure didn't call for you – no reason to. The *corpus delicti* here" – he nodded toward the body on the floor – "ain't one of your supes, far as I can tell."

Corpus delicti has nothing to do with a corpse, even though it sounds like it should. The term refers to the legal doctrine that you have to be able to prove a crime's been committed before you can charge somebody with it. Eisinger knew that as well as I did. He was misusing the term deliberately, for the same reason he threw in "ain't" despite being a college grad. He thinks it makes him sound like a real street cop, somebody not to be messed with.

I've never heard Scanlon say stuff like that, but then he doesn't have to. He already *knows* he's tough.

"No, we already made sure," Eisinger said, and took a couple of steps toward the corpse. "Ain't no

skinner – we checked that with a moonlight test."
"Skinner" is a term some people use for "werewolf"
– although if you say it in front of one, you're going
to have a fight on your hands, whether the moon's
out or not.

Looking down at the body, Eisinger said, "You
can sniff his breath without needing to puke, so I'd
say that rules out him bein' a baby-muncher."

There some urban legend that says ghouls like to
hang around outside abortion clinics so that they
can feast on the undeveloped tissue that's discarded
every day. Except that clinics don't throw that
material out with the trash – and even if they did,
most ghouls wouldn't have any interest. They've
got too much class – which is more than I could say
for Eisinger.

Then he slipped on a thin white evidence glove
and dropped to one knee next to Roger Gillespe's
still form. Peeling back the upper lip, Eisinger said,
"And this shows he wasn't no leech, either."

He looked up at Karl as he finished saying that,
and his face had the kind of smirk you want to
wipe off with a blunt instrument. "That's enough,"
I said, and my voice might've had a bit more snap
to it than I'd intended.

"Oh, gosh, that's right," Eisinger said, playing
all naive. I thought he sounded about as innocent
as Adolf Eichmann. "I completely forgot that one
of the bloodsucking undead was among us." He
looked at Karl. "No offense intended, Renfer."

I felt Karl tense up next to me, but his voice was
calm and businesslike as he said, "None taken –
and it's *Detective* Renfer."

"Then I sure am sorry," Eisinger said, *"Detective."*

Before this got out of hand, I asked the question that had prompted me to come in here in the first place. "Gillespe here – how did he die?"

"Coroner's report isn't out yet," Eisinger said. "Hell, they ain't even done the autopsy, which you should know, since the dude is still lying here on the floor."

I looked at him. "What, in your professional opinion, was the deceased's cause of death?"

He gave me an exaggerated shrug. "Well, I'm no pathologist, but I'd say those plastic baggies that are jammed down his throat had something to do with it. Looks like there's at least a dozen of 'em stuck down there. You want, I'll send you one as a souvenir, once the post is done."

"Don't bother," I said.

"What's your interest in this dude, anyway?" Eisinger asked. "Him being human and all."

"He was one of our CIs," I said, which I guess was technically true. Roger Gillespe had given us information, and we had kept his name to ourselves, even if it wasn't for the usual reasons of confidentiality. "Well, thanks for the info," I continued, keeping most of what I felt out of my voice. I turned to go, but then noticed that Karl hadn't moved. He was looking intently at Eisinger.

"Detective," Karl said softly.

"What?" Eisinger looked at Karl, and I saw their eyes lock. The two of them stood, in what someone else would have taken to be a stare-down, for at least half a minute.

Then Karl said, in that same quiet voice, "We've all done things that we're ashamed of, things we hope nobody ever finds out."

"Yeah," Eisinger said dully.

"Why don't you tell us," Karl said, "about the one thing you've done in your life that you're most ashamed of. Say it nice and loud."

Another few seconds went by before Eisinger said, in a monotone that was still loud enough for everyone in the room to hear, "When I was fourteen, I started fucking my sister, Kathy. She was twelve. I said I'd kill her if she ever told anybody. It went on for over a year, two, three times a week – whenever our parents left us alone together. I made her do everything – oral, anal, the whole nine yards. And then one day she got one of my Dad's guns and shot herself. Right in the heart. But she never told on me. Not even in the note she left."

"Thanks, Detective," Karl said, and broke off eye contact. "Thank you for sharing." Then we got the hell out of there.

As we went down the stairs, I said quietly to Karl, "What the fuck was *that*?"

"Two things," Karl said. He kept his voice down, too. "One of them was payback – and don't tell me the bastard didn't have it coming."

"I wasn't planning to," I said. "But what was the other thing?"

"Practice."

We didn't say anything as we walked back to where we'd parked the car. Once he was behind the wheel, Karl clicked the button that would unlock the door on my side. I got in as he was buckling his safety belt. I got my own seatbelt on and waited, but Karl didn't start the engine. Instead, he sat there, staring straight ahead.

I didn't ask what was bothering him – I knew it was the same damn thing that was bothering *me*. After a couple of seconds, Karl said, "He wasn't supposed to *be* there!" As he said "be," Karl slammed the steering wheel with the butt of his palm.

"I know," I said.

"He was supposed to be halfway to fucking *California* by now, not dead on the floor of his fucking *living room*!" He slammed the wheel twice more for emphasis as he said that.

"Karl."

"*What?*"

"You're gonna break the steering wheel, you keep that up." Vampires are a lot stronger than humans, but Karl sometimes forgets that – especially when he's pissed off.

"Oh, right. Sorry. But *dammit*, Stan..."

"Yeah, I know. I know."

After a couple of seconds went by, I said, "Is it possible your Influence didn't work?"

"Didn't *work*? Shit, you heard the kid, Stan. He spilled his guts to us that night, and he didn't do it cause we offered him a candy bar. It worked, alright."

"I was thinking more of what you told him to do later," I said. "The post-hypnotic suggestion, or whatever the hell vampires call what you did. Maybe it... wore off after a couple of hours or something. Can that happen?"

Karl looked away. "Fuck, I don't know. Anything's possible, I guess. I never said I was an expert at this stuff."

"You did pretty well back there with Eisinger – which was pretty fucking ingenious, by the way.

How'd you know he was going to say something like that?"

"I didn't," Karl said. "But everybody's got some kind of dark secret they carry around with them. A guy like Eisinger, I figured it would be particularly nasty – and I was right, too."

"Good work," I said. "But you've earned yourself an enemy for life. You know that, right?"

"Fuck it – I don't figure he was all that fond of me before, anyway," Karl said. "What with me being one of the bloodsucking undead and all."

"You've got a point."

"Anyway, what I did back there was short-term. I don't know if I've got that other stuff down, yet – what you called 'post-hypnotic suggestion'."

"Is there anybody you can ask about it?"

"Maybe, but what's that matter now?" Karl said. "It's not gonna do Roger any fucking good."

"I was thinking for future reference," I said. "In case you need to do it again sometime."

"You mean with Slattery?"

"Maybe – assuming we get a crack at him."

Karl sighed, which is a good trick for somebody who doesn't need to breathe. "Yeah, alright. There's some older vamps I could talk to about it. Hell, I could even ask Christine, I guess. She's been undead a while, haina?"

"Seven years," I said. "No – closer to eight." I tried to keep what I was feeling out of my voice, and I think I succeeded. On the other hand, with a vampire, you never know for sure.

It had been almost eight years since I had convinced a vampire to bring Christine across to the world of the undead. It was either that or watch her die of leukemia. Selfish of me, maybe – especially since Christine had been unconscious from the painkillers and couldn't give her consent. But after losing her mother, I just couldn't stand the idea of being without the one person in my life who still loved me. After the change, Christine and I both had some issues to deal with, but we'd resolved them pretty well by now. I hope.

"I'll ask her about it next time I see her," Karl said.

Yeah, when the two of you aren't busy fucking.

I didn't say that out loud, of course. And as soon as the thought entered my head, I tried to push it out again. Guess I still had a few issues of my own.

Karl started up the car. "I suppose we oughta tell McGuire about what happened to Roger."

"Yeah, along with the news that there's a hit man in town with access to Claymore mines."

"Yeah," Karl said. "He's especially gonna love *that* part."

Back at the squad room, we brought McGuire up to speed. As Karl had predicted, nothing we had to say made the boss very happy.

"I was in the Air Force, not the Army," McGuire said. "But even *I* know what a Claymore mine is. Never heard of one being modified to kill supes, though."

"Word is that John Wesley Harding's got himself quite a reputation," I said. "Guess it had to come from somewhere."

"Guys like that, their rep usually comes from the body count they rack up," McGuire said. "Not ingenuity."

"Maybe in Harding's case, the one leads to the other," Karl said.

McGuire took a swig from his coffee and put the mug aside. "And speaking of ingenuity, I guess you could apply that term to what happened to that informant of yours, Gillespe."

We'd never told McGuire about the vampiric Q-and-A session we had with Roger Gillespe the other night, since it probably violated five or six department regulations. So in discussing Gillespe's death just now, we'd explained our interest by saying that the guy had been one of our regular street sources of information. Which was true, really – except for the "regular" part.

"You mean the way they killed him?" Karl asked.

"Uh-huh," McGuire said. "That thing with the baggies must've taken some time and trouble, even if they did have a couple of guys to hold Gillespe down. Shit, they could've just shot him in the head and been done in about two seconds. I'd say somebody's trying to send a message."

"Maybe you're right," Karl said. "But what message? And who's it intended for?"

"The use of the baggies to kill him suggests that Gillespe was dealing," McGuire said. "If that was the case, could be the stupid bastard tried to stiff his supplier. Or maybe he found his own source and decided to go into business for himself. In the drug trade, either of those things can get a guy killed."

"So you think the message was intended for the other dealers?" I said. *"Here's what happens when you fuck with us."*

"Wouldn't be the first time that kind of thing's been done," McGuire said. "You ever hear of a Colombian necktie?"

Karl and I both shook our heads, although I thought the term seemed vaguely familiar, like something I'd read about, years ago.

"The Colombian cartels," McGuire said, "who control the wholesale end of the cocaine trade, have a way of dealing with people who piss them off. Been using it since the Sixties, I think. They slash the guy's throat, and once he's dead they take his tongue and yank it out through the wound so that it's lying against his throat. Hence the term 'Columbian necktie.'"

Karl made a face. "I wonder if somebody's gonna come up with a cutesy term for the way Roger Gillespe was killed."

"If it happens often enough, somebody probably will," McGuire said. He shook his head. "They'll probably start calling it the 'Scranton Appetizer' or something. Not the kind of fame the city needs."

"There's another possibility," I said. "Could be that his supplier found out he'd been talking to us." Roger Gillespe had only done so once, and involuntarily, but I thought it best not to mention that. "So maybe the message to the other dealers is *Here's what happens when you open your mouth to the wrong people.*"

"And at the same time," Karl said, "it's a big fat 'Fuck you' to the cops who make use of guys like Roger for information."

"It might also fit in with something else that happened tonight," McGuire said.

We both looked at him, but instead of explaining, he nodded toward the squad room behind us. "Pearce and McLane caught it. You can get the details from them. Once you've heard what they have to say, let me know what you think."

We went over to where McLane and Pearce were sitting, each one busy on his computer. Like Karl's and mine, their desks were pushed together, facing each other.

I said to them, "The boss says you guys have a case that might fit in with something we're working on. Mind telling us about it?"

"Sure, why not?" McLane said, and I noticed his partner nodding. "Gotta be more fun than filling out these goddamn forms."

Karl and I got our own chairs and rolled them over close to Pearce and McLane's desks. Once we were seated, I said, "Lot of weird shit going on lately, even by the standards of the Spook Squad."

"Tell me about it," Pearce said. He's a big guy who used to box in the Golden Gloves. If his build didn't give that away, his nose would – it's been broken more times than a hooker's promise.

"You're talking about the gnome, right?" McLane asked. An awful case of acne as a teenager had left his face severely pockmarked. In another age, you'd figure him for a smallpox survivor. When he said "gnome", I felt my pulse go into overdrive. I glanced toward Karl before telling McLane, "I don't know – the boss didn't tell us. He just said your case would interest us. And if it's about a gnome, I'd say he was right."

"Well, that's what the vic was, no doubt about it," Pearce said. "Four feet tall, more or less, white beard, big nose – he fits the profile to a T."

"Then there was the name on his driver's license," McLane said. "Pedric Bonbink."

"Yeah, that's a gnome's handle, alright," I said.

"So what happened?" Karl asked.

"He lived in the basement unit of this building over on Adams Avenue, the Cody Apartments," Pearce said. "Know it?"

Karl looked at me. "Didn't we question a guy who lived there, couple of years ago?"

"Yeah, that's right," I said. "We thought he might be involved in a fairy dust smuggling ring that was operating in town, but nothing came of it."

"Well, something sure as hell went down there, this time," McLane said. "The super gets a call from one of the other tenants, who says there's a really nasty odor coming from the basement. So he goes down there and sure enough, it smells like a boat full of mackerel that's been left out in the sun all day. The gnome's the only one living in the basement. The super bangs on the guy's door. Gets no answer. So he uses his master key, lets himself in, and almost pukes because the smell is so overpowering. Then he gets a look at what's causing it, runs outta there, and calls 666."

"So the call gets routed to McGuire, and he sends us over there," Pearce said. "The super was right about the stench – I've smelled some pretty nasty shit on this job, and I damn near heaved my guts out once we got inside that apartment. And that's *before* we got a look at the gnome's body."

"Yeah, dead gnomes rot a lot faster than humans, or any other supe species I know of," I said. "And they tend to smell a *hell* of a lot worse."

"The corpse didn't look so bad, actually," McLane said. "We've seen a hell of a lot worse. The gnome was on the floor, with a bullet hole in his forehead, right between the eyes. Looks neat as you please – until you take a gander at the exit wound, which took out most of the back of his skull."

"You get a look at the round that killed him?" Karl asked.

"There was a bullet hole in the wall, behind where the gnome had been standing," Pearce said. "We knew the guys from Forensics would throw a fit if we dug it out ourselves, so we waited for them to do it. They took the slug with them to the lab for ballistics, but let us have a look at it first."

"Nine millimeter," McLane said. "Cold iron."

"No surprise there," I said. Gnomes are one of the many species of faerie, and all of them are vulnerable to cold iron. That's why there's a fey wing of the county jail where each cell's bars are made of iron, not the steel that's used elsewhere.

"No, but here's something that is kinda surprising," McLane said. "We waited around while Forensics tossed the place, looking for evidence. And guess what they found in Pedric Bonbink's closet?" He waited, as if he really wanted us to take a stab at it.

"If you're gonna make me guess," I said, just to get it over with, "I'll say a blue pinstripe suit from Brooks Brothers, size Extra-Extra-Small."

That got a laugh from the other three, but not much of one.

"Not bad, but you're wrong," McLane said. "What they turned up was a red conical hat – the one you always see in cartoon drawings of gnomes. You know – the kind that *real* gnomes hate with a fucking passion."

Karl and I looked at each other. "Well, now," I said.

"We thought you'd find that interesting," Pearce said. "We did the interviews with those vamp goombahs who were outside Ricardo's when the bomb went off – the only living witnesses, if you can call them living." He glanced at my partner. "No offense, Karl."

Karl just nodded, his face impassive.

"We interviewed them separately," McLane said. "And each one said more or less the same thing. That the driver of the bomb car, who jumped out and got into another vehicle that drove off just before the explosion, was a gnome – complete with that red fucking hat. Now, what does that sound like to you?"

"A little too good to be true," Karl said.

"More than that," I said. "It sounds like somebody's cleaning house."

We spent the next couple of hours in the squad room, catching up on paperwork while we waited to be sent out on a call. But when McGuire called us into his office, it wasn't to give us an assignment – he gave us a big chunk of bad news instead.

Inside the office, we didn't even have a chance to sit down before McGuire said, "I just heard from Slattery's campaign manager. In order to show his respect for the forces of law and order who keep our city safe" – McGuire kept most of the sarcasm out of his voice – "Mister Slattery has agreed to come to police headquarters, accompanied by his attorney, of course, to answer questions pertaining to our investigation."

McGuire took a second to look at Karl and me before he went on. "I've been told that because of his busy campaign schedule, the time of his appearance is not negotiable. Slattery will be here three days from now – *at 11am*."

••••

"Well, shit," I said.

"Yeah, that's one way to fucking put it," McGuire said bleakly. "Pretty much puts the kibosh on our little plan to get Slattery and Karl in a room together, doesn't it?"

"Where does this asshole get off telling the police what time we're going to talk to him?" I said.

"There's no arrest warrant out for him," McGuire said with a shrug. "He's not under indictment for anything, either."

"Yeah, I know," I said, "but we still get to bring people in for questioning – on *our* terms. The law says so."

McGuire nodded. "Sure it does. And if we exercise our power under the law with Slattery, what do you figure is gonna happen?" Before I had a chance to say anything, McGuire answered his own question. "It'll go down like this," he said. "Slattery calls a press conference to tell the world how even though he offered to cooperate with the ongoing criminal investigation, the city government is using its police power to harass its political opponents in an effort to stifle the democratic process and blah, blah, blah. Shit, it might even win him some votes."

"You're probably right, boss," I said, "but I still think that you–"

"Maybe we can do it anyway."

As soon as Karl said that, McGuire and I turned our heads to stare at him.

"I read an article, couple months ago, about a vampire who was able to stay awake during the daytime," Karl said, "instead of turning into a corpse at sunrise, the way we all do."

"How'd he manage that?" I said. "Or she."

"Magic," Karl said. "Dude had a witch cast a spell that let him keep functioning during the daytime. He still had to stay out of the sun, though – that didn't change."

"What kind of magic are we talking about here?" McGuire said. "White or black?"

"White, definitely," Karl said. "All legal and aboveboard. I doubt they'd be writing about it in *Supe* magazine otherwise. It's illegal to advocate the practice of black magic, boss – you know that, same as I do."

"So this vampire that got the spell cast on him – he doesn't have to rest during the day anymore?" I said.

"Nah, the spell's not *that* good," Karl said. "It only worked for one day, and the witch who did it had to spend a lot of time in preparation. I guess she did it as kind of an experiment in thaumaturgy. It's not a consumer magic item yet – not by a long shot. Maybe it never will be."

"But it worked at least once," I said. "That's what's important."

McGuire asked Karl, "Far as you know, did the vampire who did this suffer any ill effects?"

"The article didn't mention any," Karl said. "Except that the guy was really wiped out by the end of the next night, same as you might be after pulling an all-nighter." He gave us a pointy grin. "Guess you could say he was dead tired."

I sat there rubbing the bridge of my nose for a little while, then said, "I figure there's a couple of things we need to do pronto."

"I assume one of them involves getting a copy of that article Karl's been talking about," McGuire said.

"You assume right." I turned to Karl. "Have you still got your copy of the magazine at home?"

"I doubt it," he said. "I don't usually keep stuff like that around once I've read it. But *Supe*'s got an online edition that I can access cause I'm a subscriber. They should have all the back issues in there."

"Good," I said. "How about you track down the article and print off three copies – one for me to read and one for the boss."

"What're you gonna do with the third one?" he asked me.

"Take it with me when I go downstairs to see Rachel."

Rachel Proctor leaned back in her creaky desk chair and shook her lead slowly. "I've never heard of anything like that being done before, Stan," she said. "I'm not even sure it *can* be done."

"Then take a look at this," I said, and handed her the article that Karl had downloaded from *Supe* magazine. She put on her glasses and read it slowly, her concentration so intense that I could almost feel it. I sat there in front of her desk, tried not to fidget, and kept my mouth shut. That's something I should try more often – keeping my mouth shut, I mean.

Finally Rachel looked up and tossed the article onto her desk.

"Sounds interesting in principle," she said, "but it's kind of short on specifics. *Supe* is usually a decent enough source for news, but it's no academic journal. It's hard to know how much of this story is accurate."

"There's academic journals for magic?" I said. I'd never thought about it, but I guess it made sense. They've got professional publications for every other field. Christine had once showed me an article that had appeared in the online edition of something called *Vampirology*. The title was "Free Choice vs Influence: Ethical Issues in Recreational Exsanguination." Or something like that.

"Sure," Rachel said. "The *Quarterly Journal of Thaumaturgy* is one of the big ones. Then there's *Critical Studies in Sorcery*, the *Annals of the American Academy of Witchcraft*, and a whole bunch of others."

"OK," I said. "I guess I can see how an issue of *Supe* doesn't belong in with that crowd."

"On the other hand," Rachel said, "it so happens I've heard of the witch who carried out this experiment. Annabelle Araguin has made quite a name for herself in thaumaturgical research circles over the last few years. So it's possible that this article is actually on the level."

"How fast can you find out? Like I said, we haven't got a lot of time."

Rachel shrugged. "I can send her an email right away. But how fast she responds is up to her."

"You know this Annabelle ...?"

"Araguin. Yes, slightly. We've met at conventions a few times."

I used to smile at the idea of witches attending conventions, until Rachel set me straight. All fields have their own professional meetings, she'd explained, and witches were nothing if not professional. I knew *that* much – you've got to be licensed to practice magic, and that license is a lot harder to get than the kind that lets you drive a car.

"Have you got her email address?" I asked.

"No, but I should be able to find it online easily enough. I'm sure she's got a website. Most practicing witches have one."

"Of course they do," I said. "How soon can you track her down?"

"As soon as you get out of here and let me start looking."

I stood up. "I'm practically gone already," I said, and headed for the door.

Our shift ended about ninety minutes later, and I checked in with Rachel before leaving.

"No joy yet," she told me. "I got Annabelle's email address without too much trouble, and sent her a message. She hasn't replied, but it is pretty damn late for people who don't keep the kind of hours that you and I do."

"How about a phone call?" I asked.

"I'm working that angle, too. Her number's unlisted, which isn't surprising. But I've sent out some more emails to people who might know her, asking for the phone number. No responses yet, but, again…"

I nodded. "Most people are still in bed. Well, I'm heading home, but if anything develops, don't hesitate to call – no matter what time it is."

"You'll be the first to know."

I went home, spoke with Christine briefly, then went to bed and slept for eight hours straight. Normally, that's a good thing – but this time, it meant that Rachel didn't have any news worth reporting.

When I got to work, there was no message from Rachel waiting for me. I was about to go down to her office when McGuire sent Karl and me out on a call. There'd been a near-riot at Eric's, one of the local dance clubs, the night before.. Word was, every male patron in the place had tried to rush the stage during the final number, performed by a local band called the Banshees. After a certain amount of head-scratching, management had finally decided that a supernatural influence had been at work, and called the Occult Crimes Unit.

The band members weren't really banshees, of course. Those Irish spirits are harbingers of death, and nothing else. Their singing, although beautiful enough to break your heart, isn't something anybody looks forward to hearing. Besides, it hasn't got much of a backbeat.

As soon as I learned that only the male patrons had been involved in the disturbance, I thought I knew what we were dealing with. Karl and I had a conversation with the band members in the club's dingy dressing room before they went onstage, and it didn't take long to find out that I'd been right.

The Banshees' bass player was a crew-cut blonde who called herself Scar, but whose real name, I finally got her to admit, was Meredith Schwartz. She didn't usually sing, I learned, but last night they'd let her take lead vocal on the final song of their set.

I turned to Meredith. "You're a Siren, right?"

She locked eyes with me for a couple of seconds, then looked away. "Ain't no law against it," she muttered. She wore a sleeveless black top, and I saw that her upper right arm bore a large heart tattoo – not the valentine kind, but an anatomically correct human heart, valves and all.

"Of course not," I said. "There's no law against *being* anything. It's the stuff you *do* that can get you in a shitload of trouble."

"There's a city ordinance against Sirens singing in public places – or at least, in front of any audience that includes males," Karl said. "You guys know that – or you ought to."

"And if you're wondering why that ordinance exists," I said, "what happened in the club last night should give you a pretty good idea." Looking at the three male members of the band, I asked, "How come you guys weren't affected by her voice?"

After a moment, their leader, a beanpole named Artis Bowdin who went by the name of "Daddy Longlegs", shrugged and said, "Earplugs, man. We always wear 'em when we play. Nobody wants to end up stone deaf, like, ten years from now. You know?"

"If you let Scar sing lead again, going deaf is gonna be the least of your problems," Karl told them. "Incitement to riot is a felony, no matter how you do it. And you guys could also be sued for any damages that result, either to the audience or the joint where you're playing."

"We're not going to bust you this time," I said. "And the club management says there wasn't enough wreckage to worry about – not much more than they get on an average night, anyway. But if this happens again, you guys are gonna find yourselves in a world of hurt. Understand?"

Nobody gave me an argument, which was probably the closest this bunch was ever going to get to "Yes, officer, whatever you say, sir."

As we turned to leave, Daddy Longlegs said, "Hey – we got a gig next week at Susie B's. You got any problem if Scar sings at that one?"

Susie B's is the city's biggest lesbian bar. For reasons nobody's ever been ever to explain, women are immune to the Siren's song.

"Sounds OK to me," I told him. "Go wild."

"Just be sure they keep all the windows closed while you're playing," Karl said. "Wouldn't want guys who were driving past to crash their cars against the front of the building, would we?"

When we got back to the squad room, our PA, Louise the Tease, handed me a message slip that read, "See Rachel Proctor, ASAP."

"It took a while, but I finally hit the jackpot," Rachel told me. "Unlike most people I know, Annabelle isn't compulsive about checking her email. I never was able to dig up her phone number on my own, but when she saw my message, she got back to me right away and suggested I call her. Which I did."

"And how did that go?"

"Quite well, actually. Once I explained to her the seriousness of the matter – without telling her too much, I hope – she sent me a PDF of an article she's written that's already been accepted for publication in the *Journal of the American Magical Association*. That's the most prestigious journal in the field, although Annabelle's article won't see print for another couple of months."

"And this PDF she sent – it contained the spell?"

"Uh-huh. I've read through it once already," Rachel said, frowning. "The mathematics and symbology are pretty involved, but thank the

Goddess for computer programs that handle most of that stuff."

"So, can you do it?"

"Keep Karl awake and functioning past dawn tomorrow?"

"That's what we need, yeah."

Rachel blew out a slow breath. "Maybe. If I put all other work aside and bust my hump for the next twenty-four hours or so, I might – *might* – have the spell ready in time, and if I do, it *might* even work. No guarantees."

"I'd appreciate it if you'd make the effort," I said. "I know it's a lot to ask."

She stared at me for a couple of seconds, a hand on one slender hip. "Explain to me again what's going to be achieved if I put myself through all of that – an activity for which I will almost certainly *not* be paid overtime."

I'd had a little speech prepared, in case this question should arise. I was going to talk about duty, and sacrifice, and the greater good, and blah, blah, blah. But looking at Rachel, I knew she'd see all of that as the self-serving bullshit it really was.

Then I remembered a scene from *All the President's Men*, that movie about the two reporters who broke the Watergate scandal all those years ago. As Richard Nixon said much later, "It wasn't biting all those people's necks that did me in – it was the cover-up afterward."

I'd seen the movie a several times, most recently on HBO a couple of weeks earlier. I thought about what the editor of the *Washington Post*, played by Jason Robards, had told his two star reporters near the end of the story. So I said to Rachel, "Well, there isn't very much riding on this, really – just the election, the future of our city, and maybe a few dozen lives – human and supe both." I tried for a casual shrug. "Not that any of that matters."

After a couple of seconds, Rachel gave a tired-sounding sigh. "Tell Karl not to go too far from the station house tomorrow night," she said. "I'm not sure when I'll be ready for him – but once I am, there won't be any time to waste."

"I'll tell him," I said. "And thanks, Rachel."

She gave me a crooked smile. "Thank me if the fucking thing works."

Twenty-six hours later, I was standing next to my partner in Rachel's office, saying, "I owe you a big one, Rachel. I've got some of an idea of how hard this must've been to pull off in such a short time" – how could I look at her haggard face and think anything different? – "and I want you to know I really appreciate it."

After looking from me to Karl and back again, Rachel said, "Why don't you wait and thank me in" – she checked her watch – "an hour and forty-two minutes." Rachel's habit of cynically telling us to postpone gratitude might've started to annoy me if I hadn't known about all the intense effort she'd put in for this thing to work. If it did.

"What happens then?" If I'd taken a second to think, I would've realized the answer to that question even before Karl and Rachel said, at the same time, "Sunrise."

The Q-and-A session with Slattery was scheduled to take place in what McGuire calls the Media Room, where us detectives go whenever there's a briefing that involves visual material. It's got a four-foot-square white screen on one wall and a projection system that's hooked up to both a Blu-ray player and an Apple computer on the opposite side of the room. I once had to watch a snuff film in there that still gives me nightmares. But the projector wouldn't be in use today.

McGuire told me he'd picked the media room because it was about the only place in the building big enough to hold the number of people who were going to be present. I was pretty sure he had another reason for the choice, too – the media room doesn't have any windows.

But there *were* windows between the Occult Crimes squad room and the media room, and covering them to keep out the sun would probably have roused Slattery's suspicions. So Rachel and I were in the media room with Karl well before sunrise, which was due to arrive in Scranton at 7.24 this morning, according to *Weatherwitch.com*. The three of us sat in the last row of chairs, with Karl in the middle.

"How you feeling, buddy?" I asked Karl.

"About like usual," he said. "A little hungry, since Rachel said it was better to do this on an empty stomach. But that's no big deal – I been hungry before. I'll survive."

I sure as hell hope so, I thought.

"Do you normally conk out exactly at meteorological sunrise?" Rachel asked.

"Beats the shit out of me, Rachel," Karl said. "I don't go by the clock."

"Then how do you know when it's time to close the coffin lid?" Rachel smiled. "Metaphorically speaking, I mean." She knew that most vampires don't spend the day inside a mahogany box these days, if they ever did. Karl used a sleeping bag, just like Christine did. I found that thinking about Karl, Christine, and sleeping bags put an image in my mind that I didn't much care to have there, so I banished it by focusing extra-hard on what Karl was talking about.

"It's hard to describe," Karl said. "You can feel it coming, getting closer you know? It's like when they give you anesthesia before surgery."

"When did you have surgery?" I asked. "You never mentioned that before."

"Ah, I got gang-tackled during a football game when I was in high school," he said. "Broke my leg in three places, and they had to operate on me to fix it – put plates in or something. So, yeah, I know what anesthesia's like."

"*Count backward from one hundred,*" Rachel intoned with a little smile.

"Yeah, kinda like that, except without all the counting," Karl said. "You feel yourself going, and the feeling gets stronger, and then" – he snapped his fingers – "you're gone."

"Well, if you start to experience that sensation, be sure and say something," Rachel said.

"So you can do what?" he asked.

She shrugged tiredly. "Catch you before you hit the floor, I guess."

I didn't tell them, but I had a back-up plan ready in case the spell failed. As a favor, Homer Jordan from the ME's office had loaned me one of those green plastic body bags that they use to transport bodies to and from the morgue. If Karl turned into a corpse at dawn, the way he usually did, I was going to get him into the body bag and find somebody stronger than Rachel to help me carry him out of the building and to the trunk of my car. The deadly sunlight would never touch him.

I don't remember a lot of what we talked about, the three of us, as we sat in that big, empty room, waiting for the sunrise. Somebody started a conversation about a TV program, but that didn't go anywhere. Small wonder – we all worked nights, and at least one of us hadn't seen any daytime TV for quite a while.

Then Rachel mentioned that she was a mixed martial arts fan. That surprised me a little, but then I've been accused of stereotyping people in the past. We got into a mild debate over whether supernaturals should have their own MMA league, and that went on until the moment when Rachel glanced at her watch, then looked up and smiled.

"What?" I asked her.

"Checked the time lately?" she said, the smile still in place.

I looked at my watch: 7.26.

Not wanting to put complete faith in either my Omega Spellmaster or the Internet's posted time for sunrise, I stood up and said, "Excuse me a second."

I turned left out of the media room and took the next right. Walking another twenty feet put me right in front of a window. I spent a few moments there, looking out at the sun rising over my city. This part of the building was still in shadow, dark enough for me to see my own reflection in the glass. I watch a smile sprout on my face and quickly grow into a full-out grin, like one of those high-speed films that shows a rose going from bud to bloom in only a few seconds.

Damn!

I walked back to the media room and resumed my seat. Trying to sound casual, I said, "Pretty sunrise out there. Looks like it ought to be a nice day."

Karl gave us a razor-sharp grin. "Shit," he said. "I never even noticed."

"Well, that was the object of the exercise," Rachel said. Although she still looked tired, her face had a glow about it now that made even exhaustion look kind of attractive.

"Eagle, this is Houston," I said, trying to imitate a super-serious space program guy. "Your mission is a *go*."

Phillip Kevin Slattery, the Patriot Party's candidate for mayor, was one of those guys some people refer to as Black Irish. Although his great-grandparents supposedly all came from County Cork, he didn't look like anybody who'd be invited to dress up like a leprechaun for next year's Saint Patrick's Day parade – besides, everybody knows they use real leprechauns for that.

Slattery's thick, carefully combed hair was the same dark brown as his eyes, and his complexion wouldn't have earned him a second look at any Sicilian's family reunion. I doubted he'd ever known a freckle in his life. He had a heavy beard growth that I'd bet he shaved twice a day to avoid looking like a common thug. That impression would have been misleading, anyway – as far as I was concerned, Phil Slattery was a very *special* kind of thug.

His blue pinstripe suit was good quality, and the shirt he was wearing – white with thin blue stripes – went with the suit well enough, but whoever had picked out that tie for him must have been either color-blind or demented.

The interrogation rooms that we use to question suspects were way too small for the number of people who'd be involved this time. Besides, the Media Room had the advantage of being windowless – good thing, too, since the sun was well up in the sky now, shining bright and clear.

Slattery had brought three men with him. The thin, balding one with wire-rim glasses had been introduced as Bob Franks, his campaign manager. He had the pinched look of somebody who has ulcers on his ulcers. The stocky guy with prematurely gray hair was somebody I already knew. Jerome Duplantis was a partner in Archer, Duplantis, and O'Brien, the biggest law firm in the city. I guess he was along in case we tried to violate Slattery's rights or something. His own suit made Slattery's look dowdy, but then Duplantis wasn't running for anything.

The last man's name, we were told, was Robert Brody. Slattery referred to him as "my personal assistant." In my experience, that's usually a fancy name for "gofer". but not this time. Brody had big shoulders and a narrow face, with blue eyes that were colder than a five hundred year-old vampire's – and I ought to know, since I've *met* a five hundred year-old vampire. He had a way of standing, with feet spread and the right foot slightly forward, as if he was waiting for someone to knock him down – or try to. Personal assistant, my ass – I know a bodyguard when I see one.

McGuire had ordered every detective on the squad who wasn't on the street that morning to be sitting in one of the media room's uncomfortable folding chairs, even if it meant he had to pay overtime to several of them. There were even a couple of guys from Homicide there, because McGuire had asked Scanlon for a few warm bodies to fill the seats. The chairs were laid out in twelve rows, with a central aisle running down the middle.

Most of those cops didn't have speaking parts in the little drama we were staging, but that didn't make them unimportant. For one thing, they would provide strength in numbers, which McGuire thought might intimidate Slattery and his people a little. Fat chance of that – the Patriot Party crew looked about as bothered as a bunch of cats at a mouse convention.

But more important, such a large group of detectives meant that introducing them all was impractical. We didn't want any of Scanlon's group to hear a name that might raise a red flag, and lying about who Karl was could come back to bite us later. Besides, McGuire and I had figured that a crowd this large gave us a chance that neither Slattery nor his entourage would notice one of the detectives in the room was a vampire. Karl knew enough to keep his fangs out of sight, and none of our visitors would be expecting one of the undead, anyway. It was broad daylight, after all, which meant that all vampires were asleep snug in their coffins. Everybody knew that.

Karl had remained in his back-row seat, just as we'd planned. I was down front, since I intended to take an active part in the questioning. As I took my seat, I resisted the urge to look behind me and see how Karl was doing. Being awake during daylight hours must've been a weird experience for him. I hoped he could make his Influence work under such unusual conditions.

Four chairs had been moved to the front of the room, and that's where Slattery and his crew were asked to sit. Once they were in place, McGuire got up from his front-row seat and turned to the audience of cops. "Alright, quiet down," he said, loud enough to cut through the buzz of a dozen quiet conversations. "We're about to get started." The low murmur of voices stopped almost at once.

McGuire then turned to Slattery. "On behalf of the Scranton Police Department, I want to thank you for taking time out of your busy schedule to come down and talk to us," he said. His voice held nothing but formal politeness. Me, I wouldn't have been able to deliver a line like that without wrapping some sarcasm around it – I guess that's one reason why McGuire is a lieutenant and I'm not.

"You're quite welcome," Slattery said. He took a slow, deliberate look around the room. "But I can't say I was expecting such a large group of inquisitors."

McGuire had sat down by now, and he didn't rise again as he said, "This is no inquisition, Mister Slattery. Most of these officers won't be asking you any questions today."

Slattery tilted his head a little to one side. "Then why are they here?"

McGuire was ready for that one. "My understanding is that, like me, they are concerned about the recent violent events and want to hear your views on what's been happening," he said smoothly, then made himself smile. "Although I'm pretty sure that some of them are fans of you and your party. I'm afraid you might be asked for a few autographs before you leave here today." McGuire paused, then took the big gamble. "Of course, if having so many police officers in the room makes you... uncomfortable, I can send most of them back to their duty stations before we start."

McGuire and I had talked about this earlier. It was important that he offer to clear the room before Slattery could ask him to, which he just might do. But now, if he said, "I want them out," people might start to wonder what he had to hide. After all, as a politico, he was used to speaking to crowds much bigger than this one.

Of course, if Slattery took McGuire up on his offer, we were screwed, blued, and tattooed. But I didn't think he would – and I was right.

"No, it's fine, let them stay," Slattery said with a tight smile. Then Duplantis, the lawyer, piped up.

"I want the record to show that my client is here of his own free will, Lieutenant," he said. "He is under no legal obligation to answer *any* of your questions, and is prepared to do so, for a limited amount of time, purely out of his sense of civic duty."

That was as fine a layer of rhetorical bullshit as I'd heard in quite a while – but then, for what Duplantis charged, it ought to be good.

"There is no record here, Counselor," McGuire said, still polite. "This meeting is not being recorded in any fashion, although I suppose I can't stop some of these officers from taking a few notes, if they want to. But if there *was* some kind of record,

I'd certainly want it to show my appreciation for Mister Slattery's… exemplary citizenship as shown by his willingness to come down here today."

Duplantis nodded with satisfaction, but I saw something glitter in Slattery's eyes. He was pretty sure that all this elaborate courtesy was McGuire's way of pissing on his shoes, but he couldn't say anything about it. How do you complain about somebody being polite?

"Right, then," McGuire said. "Mister Slattery, I'd like to start by asking you…"

Like McGuire had said, nobody was recording the session. But I'd asked Louise, our PA, to sit in. She shouldn't have been there, strictly speaking, because she isn't a cop. But she *is* a master – or maybe that should be mistress – of the arcane art of shorthand. I had her sitting in back, next to Karl, with instructions to keep the notebook she was writing on out of sight from the visiting politicos. After the Q-and-A session, she typed up her notes for me. Far as I could tell, she got down everything said in that room as accurately as if she'd been transcribing it from a tape recording. Louise is good – damn good.

This is the transcript as Louise typed it, along with my own snarky comments in brackets.

McGuire: Right, then. Mister Slattery, I'd like to start by asking you about your party's position on supernaturals. In your party platform, as well as in your speeches, you've got some pretty inflammatory statements.

Duplantis: I object to the use of the word inflammatory.

McGuire: I appreciate your diligence, Counselor. But we're not in court here, and the rules of trial procedure don't apply. Perhaps you could just let your client speak for himself.

Slattery: If anything I've said has upset people – good. Some people deserve to be upset. The Patriot Party doesn't indulge in political correctness. We say it like it is.

["Say it like it is." Reminded me of the hippies, back in the day – although Slattery was about as far from a flower child as you could imagine.]

McGuire: But you are aware that the law says that supernaturals are entitled to the same rights as anybody else, right?

Slattery: I respect the law – I've never said otherwise, even though, like many Americans, I regard the Supreme Court's decision in *Stevens v. US* to be misguided. But if the supernatural community expects the protection of the law, then they should be prepared to *obey* the law.

Markowski: Are you saying that all supernaturals are lawbreakers?

[Of course, that's *exactly* what he was saying – but I wanted to see if the son of a bitch would admit it.]

Slattery: It's Sergeant Markowski, right? You of all people should be aware of what's been going on in our city, Sergeant. Shootouts in the streets, bombings that destroy life and property, drug addiction, armed robbery – the list of crimes is practically endless.

Markowski: I know supernaturals break the law sometimes, just like humans do. That's what the police force is for, to deal with that kind of thing when it happens.

Slattery: Then when are you going to *start* dealing with it? So far, the police have seemed powerless in the face of this recent crime wave. It's like you're trying to stop a flood with buckets and squeegees. No disrespect intended, of course.

Markowski: No, of course not.

[Yeah, right.]

McGuire: Since you mentioned bombings, I'd like to ask you about that, Mister Slattery. Your party ran a full-page ad in the *Times-Tribune* the other day about the latest bombing, the one in front of a place called Ricardo's Ristorante. The ad claimed that it was just another example of supernaturals run wild with the police helpless to stop them. Remember that?

Slattery: Yes, of course. We got a lot of positive response to that one.

McGuire: I'm not surprised. Somebody clearly put a lot of thought into that advertisement. Your case was very effectively argued, I thought.

Slattery: Yes, we've got some talented people working for us. A couple of former journalists, in fact.

[Slattery smirked a little as he said that. Maybe he thought McGuire was a kindred spirit. If so, he couldn't have been more wrong.]

McGuire: I'm sure you do. But there's one thing that puzzles me. I'm told that your advertisement, all laid out and ready to print, was received by the *Time-Tribune*'s advertising department less than twenty minutes after the bomb went off. Considering all the specific detail about the bombing at Ricardo's contained in that ad, I don't see how it was possible for anybody, even those well-qualified ex-journalists, to put it together in such a short time.

Slattery: Are you suggesting that my campaign had something to do with that act of terrorism? Is that what you're implying, Lieutenant?

[Sounding really pissed now – although, since he was a politician, there was no way to tell if it was genuine.]

McGuire: I'm not implying or suggesting anything, Mister Slattery. I'm just asking a question. How is it possible to write an ad containing all that detailed information, not to mention layout and design, in something like fifteen minutes?

Slattery: Obviously, it isn't. Therefore, I'd have to say that you've been misinformed, Lieutenant. Whoever told you about the arrival time of our advertisement is either mistaken or lying. It's as simple as that.

McGuire: Well, here's the thing, Mister Slattery. The ad copy was sent as a PDF, attached to an email. You know as well as I do, when an email is received by somebody, the time when it arrives is included in the message heading. Well, the explosion occurred at 7.17, give or take a minute. Your campaign's email containing that advertisement was received by the *Times-Tribune* at 7.29 in the evening. Sounds to me like somebody was in a sweat to make the 7.30 deadline for getting an ad in the next day's paper.

Slattery: Emails can be tampered with, Lieutenant, as I'm sure you're aware. Some geek with the right technical background can make an email look like it came from Lee Harvey Oswald on November 22, 1963, if he wants to.

[Snide bastard.]

Markowski: I'm pretty sure they didn't have email back then, Mister Slattery.

[I can be pretty snide myself, when I want to.]

Franks: I think there's been quite enough of this. Mister Slattery did not volunteer his time to come down here and be badgered about some foolish

[That's when Karl made his move – the reason why this whole charade was happening in the first place.]

Renfer: There's just one thing I was wondering about. Mister Slattery, what do you expect to happen in Scranton if you and your party win the election?

[That was what they used to call the $64,000 question. And Slattery's answer turned out to be worth every penny. He frowned deeply and blinked several times, as if trying to resist what Karl was doing inside his head. Finally, he answered.]

Slattery: Helter-skelter, of course. The race war will start here, but we have no doubt it's gonna spread quickly, once other humans see that it's possible to take a stand against–

[That was when his campaign manager grabbed Slattery's arm, and he wasn't gentle about it.]

Franks: That's it! We're done here. Don't say anything more, sir. Not another word!

All four of the Patriot Party guys stood up and headed toward the door. Franks was in the lead along with his boss, still maintaining his death grip on Slattery's arm, as the group headed down the central aisle between the chairs on their way to the door. Behind them, the murmur of conversations started again, as the cops asked each other what had just happened. Several of them stood up and made their way into the central aisle as well, probably figuring that the show was over. They couldn't have been more wrong.

McGuire and I looked at each other but didn't have to say anything. We knew what had just happened. There was a lot we had to talk about, once the crowd had cleared.

One of the detectives who had already stood up was Karl, who had taken a few steps that put him next to the media room's only door. He wasn't blocking the way, but anybody who wanted to leave was going to have to pass pretty close to him.

This move wasn't part of the playbook that we'd worked out earlier, and I wondered what Karl had in mind. Maybe he hoped to get one more shot at Slattery with his Influence as the PP leader and his entourage left the room. But things didn't quite work out that way.

I turned in my chair, and watched as the Patriot Party foursome made their rapid way toward the exit. Franks, the campaign manager, must have noticed Karl standing near the door, because he let go of Slattery's arm and turned to say something to Brody, the bodyguard posing as an administrative assistant.

The instructions that Brody had received became clear a couple of seconds later. As the group reached the door, Brody put his wide body between Slattery and Karl – typical bodyguard behavior, even though Karl hadn't made any kind of threatening move. But then Brody did something that wasn't so typical of his profession: he reached inside his coat and came up with a crucifix, extending it out toward Karl they way all the vampire hunters do in the movies. I've done the same thing myself – for the simple reason that it works.

I was still in the front of the room and too far away to hear what Brody said, with all the other voices in the room competing with his. But from his posture and expression, I had no trouble guessing that it was something like "Get your ass back, bloodsucker!"

I sucked in a breath. We hadn't planned for this, either. Franks must've figured out that Karl was a vampire, even though it was common knowledge that no member of the undead could possibly be up and about this long after sunrise. I guessed that I wasn't the only Sherlock Holmes fan in the room, because Franks had clearly adopted one of the Great Detective's core principles: "When you have eliminated the impossible, whatever remains, however improbable, must be the truth."

Quite a few of the cops were milling around in the aisle now, asking each other variations on the "What the fuck?" question. I shoved my way through them, in a hurry to get to Karl so I could do something about that cross Slattery's bodyguard was using to threaten my partner. Brody was still standing in his Van Helsing pose, even though the tactic had already served its purpose: Slattery and the other three had slipped out behind him and were probably halfway to the front door by now. I didn't know what Brody intended to do – maybe the big man wasn't sure himself. I just knew I wanted to get that cross away from him before the situation went from bad to worse. But this seemed to be my day for surprises.

Karl had flinched from the crucifix at first, turning away and using his arm to shield his face, just like movie vampires have been doing since Bela Lugosi – the real ones have probably been doing it a lot longer. But then something strange happened.

Karl slowly turned back toward Brody and looked right at the cross that the bodyguard was pointing at him like a pistol. I couldn't see his face then, but Karl's body was tight with tension as he reached out his left hand and grabbed Brody's wrist.

I'd made enough progress through the press of bodies in the aisle that I was close enough to hear my vampire partner say, "That's a nice piece of religious art you've got there, Brody. Mind if I take a look?"

Karl must have tightened his grip as he spoke. Brody was big and tough, but his muscles and pain threshold were no match for vampire strength. After a couple of seconds, his hand opened involuntarily, letting the cross drop from his grasp. It was falling toward the floor when *Karl reached out his other hand and caught it.*

I stopped pushing my way through the crowd then and just stood still, watching. I don't think my jaw dropped, but it might've. The conversations in the room, which had been fading as more people saw what was going on, went completely silent, as if the talk had been coming from a TV that somebody had just turned off

Karl let go of Brody's wrist then, glanced down at the crucifix in his palm and said, "So, where'd you get it – Vlad-Mart?" Brody didn't say anything. He was staring at Karl as if a three-headed alien from the Planet Mongo had just beamed down in front of him and asked directions to the White House.

Karl looked down at the cross again. "It's nice work," he said. "Not too elaborate. I always thought less is more, myself." I think he was trying for a casual tone, but to me, at least, the strain in his voice was unmistakable. "I bet you had it blessed by a priest, too, didn't you? Maybe even the bishop himself."

Brody took a step back, stared at Karl a few seconds longer, then turned on his heel and walked rapidly out the door. In the silence, I could hear his footsteps in the hall outside, receding rapidly. He was not quite running.

The buzz of talk came back all at once, twice as loud as it had been before. I shook off the paralysis caused by amazement and made my way over to Karl. Now that I could see his face, the strain of what he'd just done was obvious.

He tried for a smile but it barely displayed the points of his fangs. Handing the little crucifix to me, he said, "Just as well it's not made of silver. That would've made things... difficult."

"Difficult," I said, and grinned at him. "Yeah, absolutely."

Karl's smile broadened into something more genuine. "Guess Doc Watson had it right, after all," he said.

I was about to say something clever involving a pun on "elementary", but I never got the chance – because suddenly Karl's eyes rolled back in his head, and he collapsed in a heap on the floor. I knelt to check his pulse before realizing just what a futile exercise that would be.

••••

"Rachel?"

"Ummpf."

She'd gone home around 8.30, pleading exhaustion. I could hardly have blamed her. But this call was absolutely necessary.

"It's Stan. Stan Markowski."

"Whaa? Stan who?"

"Rachel, Karl's dead."

There was silence on the line for three or four seconds, and when Rachel's voice came back there was no sleepiness in it at all.

"You don't mean *undead*, but dead for *real*?" she asked.

"That's the problem – I don't fuckin' *know*."

"What happened?"

I ran it down for her, starting with the arrival of the Patriot Party crowd and ending with Karl's swan dive to the floor of the media room.

"Karl handled a *crucifix*?" Her voice was as dubious as mine would have been, if I hadn't seen it for myself.

"Bet your ass he did," I said.

"Without any burns on his hand, or any other ill effects?"

"Nope, none at all – unless you count what happened there at the end."

"Handling holy objects," she said, as if to herself. Then, a little louder: "There's nothing in the spell that should have given him that kind of power. Although, I grant you, it's still experimental, so who knows?"

"I don't think it was the spell that did it." I briefly explained the sessions that Karl had been having with Doc Watson to see if his aversion to holy objects was only psychological.

"That's fascinating," Rachel said when I'd finished.

"Yeah, fascinating," I said. "But it doesn't do anything about the fact that right now, my partner's doing a pretty good imitation of *something that you'd pull out of a drawer at the county morgue.*"

More silence from the other end. "Rachel? You still there?" I shouldn't have raised my voice to her like that – but it had been kind of a stressful morning. I decided to start acting like a grown-up. Better late than never.

"Shut up – I'm thinking. Or trying to."

After a few seconds, she said, "Where's Karl now?"

"In the trunk of my car, zipped up in a plastic body bag."

"What're you going to do with him?"

"I was kinda hoping to get some advice from you on that question."

I heard her breath go out in a long sigh. "My Goddess, Stan, we're dealing with stuff here that nobody else has ever had to *think* about, as far as I know."

"Well, then, I guess it's time somebody started," I said. "I nominate you for the honor."

"My cup runneth under," she said. "Alright, let's try to think this through. There's nothing unusual about a vampire appearing to be a corpse during daylight hours, because he *is* a corpse – until sunset."

"When were you planning to tell me something that I don't already know?"

"Stan," she said tiredly, "stop. I know you're worried about Karl, and so am I. But please, just… stop."

I made myself take a deep breath and let it out slowly. "Yeah, alright. Sorry."

"Forget it."

"But what *happened*, Rachel? This was the day that Karl *wasn't* supposed to be a corpse, remember? He was supposed to be alive and kicking, all day long. What went wrong?"

"Any answer I might give to that is pure speculation at this point. Maybe the spell doesn't affect every vampire the same way. The one that Annabelle worked with was conscious and functioning the whole day, she said – but it's always a mistake to generalize from a sample of one. That's true in both science *and* magic."

I'd been about to say, "If you didn't know whether it was safe, then why did you *do* it?" when the truth stood up and hit me right in the mouth. *She did it because you and Karl asked her to, smart guy. Asked her – shit, you both practically* begged *her.*

So, instead of making a *complete* ass out of myself, I just said, "Uh-huh."

"Or maybe having to deal with that jerk holding the cross caused more stress than Karl's system could handle, considering the strain he was already under."

"Yeah, the cross was something none of us had counted on," I said. "But, Rachel, you should have *seen* him – taking hold of that goon's wrist, then catching the cross when it fell. I was so proud of him..."

"Yes," she said, "as well you should be."

I had to swallow a couple of times before I went on. Keeping most of what I was feeling out of my voice, I said, "It'd be nice if I get the chance to tell him that sometime. You think I will?"

"The simplest answer to that is also the most difficult," she said, "because it involves waiting. Make sure you're with Karl at sunset. Not to be blunt about it, but either he'll rise or he won't. Then we'll know."

"That's *it*?" I said. "That's the best you've *got*?" The promise I'd made myself to remain calm hadn't lasted very long.

"Well, there is one *other* method," she said, sounding like someone whose patience had just been used up. "The advantage of this one is you can do it right now, as soon as you get out to your car. But it does have something of a downside, as well."

"*What*?" I practically yelled. "What is it?"

"If Karl is still among the undead, then he still possesses all of a vampire's vulnerabilities. The sun's shining nice and strong today – from my window, I can hardly see a cloud in the sky."

I thought I could see where this was going, and I didn't like it.

"So what you do," Rachel said, "is open the trunk, unzip that body bag, and take hold of Karl's arm. Pull it out of the bag until the sun is shining on it. If it bursts into flame, you'll know that Karl's OK – apart from his arm, of course. I imagine it'll heal, eventually. Are you willing to do that to your partner, Stan? To your *friend*?"

"The *fuck* I am," I said.

"No, I didn't think so." We were both quiet for a bit, being pissed off at each other, but when Rachel finally spoke, the anger had drained out of her voice. "I knew you couldn't," she said. "I couldn't do it, either. So, I guess that means we wait, huh?"

"Yeah, I guess so," I said dully. "Shit."

"And if you think the hours between now and sunset are going to be one tiny bit easier on me than they'll be for you, Stan…"

"I know, Rachel. I know."

"You'll be with Karl then. Come sundown."

"Fuckin' A right I will be."

"Then when you, uh, know for sure, call me, OK? No matter... no matter what."

"Count on it."

I sat in McGuire's office, sipping from a cup of his excellent coffee and telling him what Rachel'd said about Karl. The coffee's rich taste aside, I was just grateful for the caffeine. I felt more tired than I had in a long time, and only part of it came from being short on sleep.

"Fine," he said when I was done, slapping a palm on his desk. "Just great. One of my detectives may or may not be deceased, and I won't even *know* until" – he glanced at his watch – "something like five fucking hours from now."

"*We* won't know," I said. I might've said that with a little more emphasis than I usually use with the boss, but like I said, I was tired.

McGuire stared at me for a second, as if he was wondering how I'd look with a shiny new asshole, but then blew out a breath between his lips and slowly sat back in his chair. "Yeah, alright. I know. It's not all about me."

"No, I'd say it was mostly about Karl."

He nodded tiredly. "Well, while we're waiting for the sunset to resolve that particular issue, there's no shortage of other ones to think about."

"Like what Karl got out of Slattery, there at the end."

"That'd be pretty high on my list, yeah," he said. "Helter fucking-skelter. Jesus. Never thought

I'd hear that again, except maybe on some TV documentary about the Sixties or something."

"Patton Wilson," I said. "He's back. Has to be."

"I heard that bastard was hiding out in Australia someplace."

"Maybe he was," I said. "Or that could've been a rumor he started himself, to throw the feds off his trail. Anyway, I'm betting he's in Scranton now. Or someplace close by."

"Close by," McGuire said with a slow nod. "That's right – he never was much for delegating, was he?"

"No, he wasn't," I said. "He's a very hands-on terrorist, is Mister Wilson."

"Terrorist?"

"I don't know what else to call the bastard. He wants to wipe out all the supes by starting a 'race war' between them and humans. If that's not terrorism, I guess it'll do until the real thing comes along."

"Yeah you got a point there. Last time, he just used that bunch of religious whackos he controlled–"

"The Church of the True Cross," I said.

"Yeah, them. But this time, he's doing what the military calls 'fighting on multiple fronts'."

"Multiple is right," I said as I rubbed my forehead. "It makes my brain hurt just trying to get a handle on it all."

"The Patriot Party's the easy one," McGuire said. "We got that straight from the horse's mouth not an hour ago."

"Wilson's gotta be behind the Delatassos, too," I said. "Delatasso Junior, anyway."

"The bombings, you mean?"

"That's one part," I said. "Those bombs have got the people scared shitless, and I don't blame them.

And since the bombing's all part of the gang war, supes get the blame, with the fucking Patriot Party right there to fan the flames. Just like the Nazis and the Reichstag fire."

McGuire's a World War Two buff, so I didn't have to explain to him what I meant. "For them, it was the Jews," he said slowly. "And for the PP, it's supes."

"With a similar result in mind," I said.

"You said the bombings were only one part of it," McGuire said. "Are you thinking what I'm thinking?"

"I am, if you're thinking about Slide," I said. "Drug-addicted supes are gonna commit crimes to get money. And every time they do, the PP gets something else to be outraged about."

"And if the Patriot Party wins the election..."

"Wilson gets a city government that's gonna do whatever he tells it to. Same thing if the Delatassos wipe out the Calabrese family and take over local organized crime. Then Wilson controls both the cops *and* the crooks."

"But the Delatassos are supes, too," McGuire said. "They're *vamps*, for God's sake."

"I figure Wilson's willing to overlook that – for a while," I told him. "Shit, the Nazis had an alliance with Japan, remember? And the Japanese weren't exactly what Hitler and his crew considered members of the fucking master race."

"Alright, fine," he said. "But let's put the history lesson aside. The important thing–"

"Wait! Wait a second – something just occurred to me."

He raised an eyebrow in my direction. "I don't suppose it's a miraculous solution to all our problems."

"Sorry, no. In fact, it's another problem – or it is if I've got things figured right."

"Then let's hope you're wrong," McGuire said. "But you better tell me anyway."

"I just remembered something Christine was telling me the other night. Now that Victor Castle's dead, that leaves a power vacuum in the supe community."

"You needed your daughter to tell you that? You must be slipping, Markowski."

"No, I figured that part out for myself. But what I *didn't* know is that there's a guy – a vamp – who's angling for the job. And it sounds like he's pushing pretty hard."

"Pushing how?"

"The usual combination of carrot and stick. The stick is what you might expect – he's known as a bad guy to cross, you should pardon the expression. Any supe who's against him runs into a world of hurt."

McGuire leaned back in his chair. "If that's the way he does business, I'm surprised we haven't encountered him before now. Or maybe we have – what's his name?"

"Dimitri Kaspar."

He shook his head slowly. "Doesn't ring a bell."

"The guy doesn't have a sheet, at least not locally. I asked the Staties to check their database, see if he's been busted anyplace else in Pennsylvania. But you know how that works."

He nodded. "They're going to get back to you – any day now."

"Yeah, that's about it," I said.

"Still, this Kaspar just sounds like a run-of-the mill punk, whether he's got fangs on him or not."

"I'd agree with you," I said, "except for the size of the carrot he's offering to those who go along with him."

"What kind of carrot are we talking about?"

"The usual kind – money. Apparently he's been spreading a lot of it around. But here's the thing, boss – this guy works at the Post Office, sorting mail. He should barely be able to make the rent every month, let alone throw cash around like he's been doing. Unless he's hit the lottery, there's only one explanation I can think of."

McGuire stared at me for three or four seconds. "You know, under other circumstances, I'd be inclined to say you were batshit paranoid."

"Yeah, but just cause we're paranoid doesn't mean that Patton Wilson isn't really out to get us."

McGuire let out his breath in a long sigh. "No, I guess it doesn't."

"The bastard's thorough," I said. "You gotta give him that."

"Alright," McGuire said. "Whether you're right about this vamp Kaspar or not, it's pretty damn clear that Wilson is back, and he's up to the same shit as last time – but on a much bigger scale. Question is: what the fuck are we gonna do about it?"

"Oh," I said. "You don't know, either?"

I got through the rest of the day somehow. I wouldn't have minded going out on some calls, even though I felt beat to shit, but McGuire said he couldn't authorize the overtime for half a detective team. He didn't mind if I hung around the squad room, though, so I spent a lot of time at my desk.

Lieutenant Crestwell, the squad's day-shift commander, came on duty at some point. McGuire must've asked him to leave me alone, because Crestwell didn't acknowledge my existence all day, beyond a nod when he first entered the squad room. That was fine with me – I was busy thinking about the return of Patton Wilson. I wish I could say that some brilliant idea occurred to me as I sat there, but brilliant ideas seemed to be in short supply for me lately.

That bastard Wilson was angling to be the power behind three thrones – the local Mafia family, the city government, and the Scranton supe community – assuming you want to dignify any of those positions with a word like "throne". Well, you couldn't fault Wilson for nerve – the guy had the balls of a brass ape. Unfortunately, he also had both brains and bucks in abundance – maybe enough to make his twisted ambition a reality. Unless somebody stopped him. Somehow.

I realized that Christine would be rising at sunset, and she'd expect to find me at home. If I wasn't there, she might assume the worst, so I called and left a message on her voice mail.

Hi, honey, it's your old man. Listen, I won't be there when you get up tonight, and I'm not sure if I'm gonna get home at all. Some crazy stuff's going on at work – I'll tell you about it when I see you, which may not be until tomorrow night. But there's nothing to worry about.

I hoped that last sentence didn't turn out to be a lie. I didn't know what, if anything, Christine had going on with my partner, but I still didn't relish the idea of telling her Karl wouldn't be coming around anymore – ever.

Apart from a shower and quick change of clothes in the locker room, I spent most of the day at the station house. But as the sun finally lowered over the city, I was in another part of town, standing behind my parked Toyota Lycan, with the trunk key in my hand – waiting.

Today's *Times-Tribune* and *Weatherwitch.com* both agreed – sunset was scheduled for 6.07. I checked my watch – it was coming up on 6.00. Of course, the jury was still out on whether vampires rise and sleep at meteorological dawn and dusk, or whether they're obeying some other, more fundamental, impulse.

6.04: No sounds or stirring from inside my trunk, where Karl Renfer slept. Whether his current state was going to last a couple more minutes or go on forever was the question that had my guts feeling like a tightly clenched fist.

6.06: I found myself wondering what kind of funeral Karl would have wanted, and pulled my mind away from that thought as quick as I'd yank my hand from a hot stove. I'm not one of those nitwits who think the "power of positive thinking" ever changed one goddamn thing, but I was *not* going to stand here and think about Karl being dead forever. *I was not going to do that.*

6. 07: Full dark now – at least, it seemed that way to me. The interior of the trunk remained as quiet as the grave, a metaphor I banished from my mind the instant it showed up. I thought about Rachel and wondered what she was doing right now – as if I didn't know. Wherever she was, she had the face of a clock or watch in view. She'd probably be trying not to stare at it, to distract her mind with other stuff – and failing, just as I was.

6.08. I was going to have to tell Rachel, eventually. After all, I'd promised. "Call me, either way," she'd said. McGuire would want to know, too. I wondered how long I should wait before deciding to make the call that both of them were dreading. It seemed that I should–

"Hey – what the fuck is going on here?"

That pissed-off voice came from inside my trunk, and it was the voice of Karl Renfer – loud, and clear, and alive. Well, undead, anyway.

"Just a second, Karl!" I yelled. I nearly pounded my fists on the trunk lid in relief, but had enough sense to realize that Karl might misinterpret the sound, not knowing where he was. "Everything's fine – just give me a second!" I started patting my pockets for the car keys, then realized that they'd been in my left hand the whole time.

I finally got the Lycan's trunk open, and the light came on to reveal the body bag, bent at a sharp right angle. We'd had to bend Karl at the waist in order to get him into my trunk, which isn't exactly roomy. Most Toyotas are compact cars, unless you want to spring for the Hexus, which is the luxury model, and I've never had that kind of money.

I could see slight movement from inside the body bag. Karl could have torn his way out of that thing in about a second, but I'd asked him to wait, and that's what he was doing.

I grabbed the tab of the big zipper and yanked it down all the way to reveal my partner, who was looking a whole lot better than when I'd zipped him in there six hours earlier. For one thing, his eyes were open.

He blinked at me a couple of times. "What the fuck, Stan?"

"I'll explain in a second," I said. "But first, let's get you out of there."

It took a little while to get him straightened out and completely free of the bag, but finally Karl was standing on the sidewalk next to my car, making a futile effort at brushing out the wrinkles his suit had developed during the day. He gave up after a few seconds and raised his head to look around.

"Hey, we're in front of my building," he said.

"I figured once you were out of there, you might want a change of clothes, maybe a shower and something to eat." Like any self-respecting vampire, Karl had a supply of blood in his fridge.

"You figured right," he said. "But what the hell was I doing in... *oh*."

"Remember what happened now?"

He slowly ran a hand through his hair, which was pretty mussed up from getting in and out of the body bag. "I'd just used some Influence to slip what's-his-name, Slattery, a question, right?"

"Uh-huh."

"I remember he answered, something about helter-skelter. Then all the PP guys walked out in a huff. I went over near the door, hoping for another shot at Slattery when he passed, but then his pet gorilla started waving a cross at me."

"How'd you feel, when he did that?"

Karl made a face. "At first, it was the same as always – I saw the cross and had the urge to be someplace else – *fast*. But then the stuff I've been working on with Doc Watson came back to me.

I used one of the relaxation techniques he'd had me practicing, and, shit – it *worked*. I was able to look at the cross, and then…" Karl shook his head in wonderment.

"And then you took it away from him, remember? You grabbed his wrist, made him let go of the cross, and then you caught it. *You held it in your hand, Karl.*"

He lifted his right hand and stared at it, turning it back and forth as if checking for damage. "Shit," he said again. "No burns, nothing."

"Guess Doc Watson was right, after all," I said, and we just stood there for a minute, grinning at each other like a couple of idiots.

Karl's grin slowly faded, then he said, "That's the last thing I remember – holding the cross."

"I'm not surprised," I said. "You kind of flaked out on us after that."

I told him what had happened, and explained how he'd ended up in a body bag inside my trunk for the last five hours or so.

"And you drove here just before sunset," he said.

"Yep."

"You must've been pretty confident that I was OK."

"Of course I was," I said. "Never doubted it for a minute." He looked at me for a second or two, not speaking, then gave me half a smile. Vampires are good at detecting lies, but the one I'd just told didn't seem to bother him very much.

Karl made a head gesture toward his apartment building. "Let's go inside," he said. "You can bring me up to speed while I clean up a little and get into some fresh clothes."

"Good idea," I said. As we headed up the sidewalk toward his building's front door, I pulled out my phone. "But I've got a couple of calls I need to make first."

What with one thing and another, we were over an hour late reporting for our shift. But McGuire didn't seem inclined to dock us for the time.

"Good to see you, Detective," he said to Karl as we walked in. "I was pleased to learn that I won't have to dig my dress uniform out of the closet again just yet. It was a little tight, the last police funeral I attended, and I haven't lost any weight since then."

Fucking McGuire – sentimental, as always.

"Sorry I flaked out on you, boss," Karl said as we sat down. "But at least we got something good out of Slattery. It wasn't a wasted effort."

McGuire twitched one side of his mouth. "Depends on what you mean by 'good'. It was interesting – I'll say that much. The only problem we've got now is what the hell to do about it."

"I don't guess it would do Slattery's campaign much good if word got out about his thoughts on helter-skelter," I said.

"I dunno," Karl said. "There's folks in this town who'd think that was a reason to vote for the son of a bitch."

"But there's plenty who wouldn't," I said. "Supes, especially."

"I think you can assume that Slattery's already lost the supe vote, Stan," Karl told me. "He wrote us off a long time ago."

"Anyway, there's no video of him saying it," McGuire said. "Nothing for the media to run with."

"There's about thirty cops who heard him say it," I said. "Including the three of us."

"Doesn't matter much," McGuire said. "Slattery would say we'd all been ordered to lie by the mayor, who wants to keep his job come election day. And there's something else."

We both looked at him.

"Maybe Slattery admits he said all that stuff about helter-skelter, OK? But then he says there was a vampire in the room who used Influence to *make* him say it – further proof that vampires have no place on the police force."

"Influence doesn't work that way," Karl said.

"You and I know that," McGuire said. "But do you think the average human living in Scranton knows it – or even gives a shit? People believe what they want to believe."

People believe what they want to believe. McGuire wasn't saying anything that I didn't already know, but there was something... *Shit.*

"You're right, boss," I said. "We haven't got any ironclad proof that Slattery said it. But, shit, who needs proof when you've got innuendo?"

McGuire shook his head. "I'm not following."

"It's simple," I said. "We just follow the advice of Lyndon Baines Johnson, a guy who knew a few things about politics."

Karl looked at me and said, "If you're waiting for somebody to feed you the next line, I'll do it – what'd Johnson say?"

"When all else fails, call your opponent a pig fucker – and let him deny it."

After a few seconds, McGuire said, "I think the light is beginning to dawn."

"I wish you wouldn't say stuff like that, boss," Karl said with a slight smile. "Especially after yesterday." Then he looked at me and said, "I still don't get it."

"Print media may be on its way out," I said, "but it isn't dead yet. Plenty of people still read the *Times-Tribune* every day. It's online, too – so even the geeks see it."

"Yeah, they do," McGuire said. "And if somebody were to leak the story to the *T-T*–"

"On deep background, of course," I said.

"Of course. I bet they'd run with it," McGuire said, "especially if they had the names of a few cops who were there, so they could confirm the story."

"I know a guy at the *Times-Tribune*," I said. "He's always pestering me for stories."

"Then maybe you oughta give him one," McGuire said.

"Yeah, I think I will."

"I love the idea," Karl said, "But we're not gonna sink Slattery's campaign with something like this."

"No," I said. "But maybe we can cause it to spring a leak or two."

"Then what?" Karl asked.

"Then we'll see," I told him.

Karl and I went downstairs to pay Rachel a visit – the first time either of us had seen her since early in the morning, when Karl was still defying the laws of nature by being awake after sunrise.

The custodians had been waxing the floors at this level, and the smell of polish was strong as we walked toward the open door of Rachel's office. We found her seated behind her desk, face buried in a big, old-looking book. Although an awful lot of written material has been turned into easy-to-read electrons these days, Rachel once explained to me that most of the old magical texts still only exist in paper form. When I'd asked why, she'd said, "Not enough of a market. The people with the skills don't have the interest, and the people with the interest don't usually have the skills. Besides," she'd said with a light laugh, "there's such a thing as tradition. Not to mention safety."

"Safety?"

"Sure. I'd hate to be in the middle of a tricky conjuration and have the battery of my Kindle pick that precise moment to fail."

Rachel looked up as we came in. I got a quick smile, but when she turned to look at Karl, the smile faded and her expression became unreadable.

As we approached, Karl said, "Hey, Rachel."

Rachel nodded slowly. "Karl." She pushed her desk chair back and stood up.

The witch and the vampire looked at each other for three or four seconds, before Rachel broke the silence. "I hardly know what to say, Karl. I'm certainly relieved to see you, although Stan called me as soon as he knew that you were back among the living. Well, not the living, but…"

"I know," Karl said.

Rachel brushed a couple of stray hairs out of her face. "I just… I'm sorry that my skills let you down, Karl. If it's any consolation, I spent most of today in gut-twisting uncertainty, until I heard you were OK."

"It doesn't make me feel better that you had a miserable day, Rachel," Karl said gently. "Why would I want that? I'm not mad. You did the best you could with a brand-new spell – and, hey, the darn thing worked, didn't it?"

"It worked, but less than perfectly," she said.

Karl shrugged. "Perfection's a pretty high standard. If everybody used that one, most of us would come up short. The spell did what it was supposed to – kept me going long enough to work a little Influence on Mister Slattery."

"Yes, Stan said you had been successful, but didn't go into detail. Maybe that part's none of my business?"

"You've been with us through most of this mess," I said to her. "No reason to keep you in the dark about the rest."

I told her what Slattery had said, and briefly mentioned some of the possible implications we'd discussed with McGuire. When I was done she shook her head slowly. "Patton Wilson. I should've known."

"We all should've," I said. "But you know what they say about hindsight."

"Yeah, looking out your ass is always 20/20," she said. "Now that you know he's the guiding hand behind all the recent hurly-burly, what are you going to do about it?"

"We're still working on that," Karl said.

"Rachel, I agree with Karl that we oughta be grateful the spell worked as well as it did," I said. "But have you figured out why it *didn't* last the whole day, like it was supposed to?"

"This is an area where actual data is scarce," she said. "But I have a theory."

"Theorize away," I said.

"It comes down, in a word, to stress," she said. "The spell was already putting considerable strain on Karl, since it had him going against his vampire nature by remaining conscious after sunrise. And then, on top of that, he's confronted by that oaf with the crucifix."

She turned to Karl with a grin. "Congratulations on the way you dealt with that, by the way. Strong work." She stood up and stuck out her hand.

Karl's grin was a mirror of her own as they shook. "Thanks – but nobody was more surprised than I was. I should call Doc Watson, let him know his therapy passed the acid test."

"I'd like to talk with you about that sometime," Rachel said. "The therapeutic process, I mean." She turned back to me. "Facing that cross, especially in the assertive manner he did, must have put more strain on Karl than even his resilient vampire system could handle. So the spell was broken, and Karl instantly reverted to his natural – or, rather, supernatural – state."

"I returned to life and found out that we still had the same problems as before," Karl said. "The vampire gang war, the Patriot Party trying to take over, a bunch of Slide-addicted supes knocking over grocery stores..."

"That reminds me, Rachel," I said. "You were looking into ways that magic might help with the Slide problem. Any luck yet?"

Rachel ran her hand over a face that looked like it would have benefited from a good night's sleep. Of course, I was pretty sure you could've said the same about mine. The only one of us who'd had any rest lately was Karl, and his was involuntary.

"On that front, I can report good news and bad news," she said. "Mostly bad."

"I could use some good news right now, even a little," I said. "So let's start with that."

"OK. Well, since Slide is a drug that affects only supernaturals, it is particularly susceptible to manipulation by magic. I've been able to develop a spell which neutralizes its effects. From what you've told me, there's a hallucinogenic phase, followed by a wave of euphoria, right?

"That's what the addicts say."

"Well, I've been able to render the small samples you gave me into something that should cause nothing but a mild headache, which is nobody's idea of fun."

"Rachel, that's fantastic!" I said

She made a face. "No, it's not."

Karl and I looked at each other, then he said to Rachel, "Sounds like there's something here we don't know about."

"On the contrary," Rachel said. "I've told you all there is to know about my experiments with the stuff. What you're not getting is that my results have *no practical value*."

I thought for a few moments, then told her, "I think I see where you're going with this."

"Well, I'm not too bright," Karl said, "so I wish somebody would fucking explain it to *me*."

"What I can do in my workroom doesn't affect what's going on out in the street, Karl," Rachel said. "I can hardly expect the... dealers, pushers, whatever they're called, to drop by so that I can render their product useless before they go out and sell it. From their perspective, it would be a pretty bad business decision, wouldn't it?"

"Oh," Karl said, followed a moment later by "Shit!"

"OK, it was worth a try," I said. "Thanks for giving it a shot, Rachel. Guess we'll have to deal with the Slide problem the old-fashioned way – by busting the dealers and trying to squeeze them into giving up their suppliers."

"Except we can't bust the fucking dealers," Karl said, "cause the shit they're selling isn't even illegal – yet."

"Well, yeah, there's that," I said.

"I sympathize with your plight, guys," Rachel said, "and I only wish..." Rachel stopped speaking, and I saw that she had a faraway look in her eyes, like somebody who's trying to think of three things at once. She dropped back into her chair, as if her knees had suddenly given way.

"Rachel? Are you alright?" I asked.

She didn't reply for a few seconds. "Me? I'm fine – apart from being a total fucking idiot, that is. Leave that out, and I'm doing just great."

I looked at Karl, and it was clear that he didn't know what was going on, either.

"*Sympathize*," Rachel said. "I told you that I *sympathize* with your plight."

"Uh, yeah," I said, just to be saying something.

"Sympathetic magic!" She slammed her small fists down on the desk's polished surface. "*That's* the fucking answer. Dear Goddess, I ought to have myself committed to an institution for the terminally stupid!"

"Rachel," Karl said, it'd be good if you'd stop beating yourself up long enough to tell us *what the fuck you're talking about.*"

"Alright, sure," Rachel said. The distracted look on her face was gone, replaced with something that looked to me like triumph.

"You guys know what sympathetic magic is, right?" she asked.

"More or less," I said. "You cast on a spell on some object that represents another object, or maybe a person. Kind of like voodoo dolls – stick a pin in the doll, and the person it represents feels a stabbing pain."

"That's essentially it," Rachel said. "I don't mess around with vodoun – a lot of it comes under the heading of black magic. But I know that for the spell to work, the doll must not only resemble the intended victim, but also has to contain something that was physically part of him – or her."

"You mean like hair, fingernail clippings, stuff like that," Karl said.

"Exactly," Rachel said. Then she turned to me. "You told me earlier that you had some baggies of Slide left, Stan. Do you still?"

"Yeah, two of 'em – they're in my desk," I said. "Are you telling me that you can cast a spell on a few bags of Slide, and that will affect *all* of the shit, no matter where it is?"

"Not by myself, I can't," she said. "Something like that, you'd need a great deal of magical power to make it work – a lot more than I possess." She grinned at us. "But I bet I know where I can get some help."

"The local coven, you mean," Karl said.

"Yep. Quite a few of my sister witches are as concerned as I am about what Slide has been doing to our town. I bet they'd jump at the chance to help render the stuff harmless."

"I want to be sure I'm following you," I said. "You think you can change Slide – all of it – into something that won't be addictive to supes anymore?"

"I would think so, yes," she said. "We'd be able to alter its molecular structure – always assuming we can make the spell work, that is. No guarantees in the Art, as you know."

"I'm no expert on magic," Karl said, "but that sounds fucking brilliant to me, Rachel. Way to go."

She shook her head. "Congratulate me if I can–"

"Don't say it, Rachel," I told her. "Just… *don't*."

As we walked back to the squad room, I said to Karl, "I just had the beginning of an idea. I think I'm gonna send an email to an old buddy of mine."

"It's always good to keep in touch with your friends, I guess."

"Well, we *used* to be friends – at the U, before I dropped out to join the cops. Turned out, this guy became a cop, too – even though he stuck around to get his degree first."

"He's on the force? What's his name?" Karl asked.

"Ted Kowal – but he doesn't live around here. After college, he moved to Philadelphia – I guess he's got family down there. Spent a couple of years doing this and that, then he joined the Philly PD. He's a Detective Second in their Organized Crime Unit, now. Or he was, last I heard from him."

"If you wanna talk to the guy, why not just call him?"

"Unlike you and me, he works days." I glanced at my watch. "He's probably in bed by now."

"OK, and you're gonna reach out for this dude because why?"

"Two reasons. One is Teddy probably knows as much as anybody – on this side of the law, anyway – about the Delatasso Family."

"The original one, you mean – that Ronnie D's old man controls."

"Uh-huh."

"I don't get it – you figure that by finding out about the old man, it'll somehow help us deal with his kid up here?"

"Something like that."

"You're being mysterious again, Stan."

"I prefer to think of it as enigmatic."

Karl looked at me. "*Reader's Digest*?"

"Yeah. The January issue, I think. Or maybe it was February."

"I must've missed that one. So *enigmatic* is like *mysterious*, huh?"

"Yeah, more or less."

After a few seconds, Karl said "Two."

"Huh?"

"You said you had two reasons for getting in touch with this Kowal guy. What's the other one?"

"Teddy owes me a favor – a *big* favor."

I got through the rest of our shift by drinking enough coffee to float a battleship. Fortunately, it turned out to be a quiet night – too quiet, like they say in the movies. It was as if the whole city was holding its breath – waiting. That's a worn-out cliché, I know. But sometimes even clichés are true. You could see the tension in the way people walked and held themselves, hear it in the way they snapped at each other over stuff that usually would get no more than a shrug.

When I got home it was still dark, but the birds in nearby trees were already chirping in anticipation of the sunrise. I checked my watch and estimated there was about half an hour until dawn.

Christine was sitting at the kitchen table, eyes focused on the screen of her laptop. When I walked in, she looked up at me, glanced down at the computer again, then did a double-take. Her welcoming smile quickly turned into a frown of concern.

"This may sound like pots and kettles coming from me, Daddy – but jeez, you look like death warmed over."

"And only lightly warmed over, at that," I said. I hung up my coat and went over to look in the fridge. "Oh, you got me some pineapple juice – thanks, sweetie."

"No problem, she said. "Would you like me to make some coffee to go with it? We could hook up an IV drip and put the stuff directly into your bloodstream."

"I've had more than enough coffee already," I said. "Besides, I'm done fighting sleep. In a little while I'm getting into bed, and sleep and me, we're gonna embrace like horny teenagers."

"Fatigue seems to make you poetic," she said. "Have you really been awake for two days straight?"

I sat down and had a big swallow of juice, closing my eyes in sheer pleasure as it slid down my throat. Getting my eyes back open took some effort. "Afraid so," I said. "A couple of things I had going didn't quite work out as planned."

"Like what?"

Knowing there wasn't much time until dawn, I ran it down for her as briefly as I could. Making myself focus was hard. It felt like my brain was swimming through a river of sludge.

When I'd finished, she said, "*Holy shit*," and shook her head slowly. "Poor Karl. Poor you, for that matter."

I lifted my shoulders in a shrug that took more effort than it should have. "It all worked out, eventually. Things are actually looking up, a little."

"What Karl did with the cross, though – that's just... fucking *awesome*. I can't wait to talk to him about it."

I gave her a crooked smile. "Guess you vampires aren't the spawn of the devil, after all."

"I never thought I was," she said, smiling back as she shut down her laptop. "I'm the spawn of Detective Sergeant Stanley Markowski, who's only devilish once in a while."

"Yeah, well, I've got the beginnings of an idea that might take 'devilish' to a whole new level."

"Really? I'd love to hear all about it." She stood up, glancing toward the window. "But now it's time all good vampires to go off to bed – and I'd say the same about one Detective Sergeant as well."

"No argument from me," I told her. "I'll fill you in on the rest at breakfast."

"I can hardly wait," she said, then bent over to give me a kiss on the cheek. "Goodnight, Daddy. Sleep well."

"I think that's pretty much a sure thing," I said. "'Night."

I set my alarm twice that day. The first time was for 11.00am so that I could put in a call to Ted Kowal in Philadelphia. Fortunately, I caught him at his desk in the Organized Crime Unit, and it didn't take much persuasion for him to agree to what I wanted.

"Alright, Stan – I'll send it to you as a Word doc attachment before I go off shift," he said. "You sure you want me to use your personal email address for this?"

"Absolutely," I said. "Christine nagged me into upgrading our home computer setup, so I've got a pretty good printer here."

"Uh-huh. And I suppose once I've sent it, you want me to delete the message from my 'Sent Mail' file, and then get amnesia about this whole conversation."

"Exactly. You're a pretty smart guy, Teddy," I said. "Makes me glad the Pittston cops never found out about that time in high school when you–"

"Oh, go fuck yourself, Stan."

"I tried that once – threw out my back something awful."

I reset the alarm clock for half an hour before sunset and went back to sleep. If I'd known what was waiting for me, I would've just stayed awake, exhaustion be damned.

I was chasing Patton Wilson, who looked the same as the last time I'd seen him – iron-gray hair, tan, slim build. He ran pretty damn well, too, for somebody in his sixties. I pursued the bastard all over Scranton, but it was a Scranton without people except the two of us – deserted streets, abandoned cars, all the buildings silent and dark. There were storm clouds above us with big, dark thunderheads. I was kind of amazed at my ability to keep up with Wilson for so long, but also frustrated because I wasn't gaining on him. He stayed about fifty feet ahead of me. He couldn't seem to find the speed to pull away, but I wasn't closing the gap, either. Fifty feet between us, all over town. Then Wilson started taunting me, throwing words back over his shoulder like mud balls.

"You'll never catch me, Markowski! You're too old, too slow, and too stupid!"

"I almost got your ass last time, in that warehouse!" I yelled. As devastating retorts go, it left a lot to be desired.

"Close only counts in horseshoes, you Polack cocksucker!"

I'd read that Wilson had gone to some fancy college years ago. Harvard, Dartmouth, one of those places. Apparently it hadn't helped him develop a refined vocabulary.

"Know why you'll lose, Markowski? Rules! You have to follow all those stupid cop rules, and I don't. I do what I want, when I want, to whom I want."

At least, he'd known enough to use "whom". A point for the psychopath. It occurred to me that Wilson was starting to sound like a James Bond villain, and I wished Karl was here to see it – he gets a kick out of that stuff.

He was right about the rules, though – damn his rich, crazy ass. But I was finally starting to run out of steam, and my lungs were burning. I'd have to stop soon, and Wilson would get clean away and finish his plans to get control of my city. One of the rules cops have to follow is that you can't shoot a fleeing suspect, if he's unarmed. You're supposed to catch and subdue him "using nonlethal means," as the manual puts it.

Well, fuck the manual – and fuck the rules, too. I reached under my jacket to draw the Beretta from my hip holster. And the holster was empty.

Ahead, Wilson came to a sudden stop and whirled to face me. He was holding my gun. "This what you're *looking for?"* he said with a smirk. *"Then, by all means, let me return it to you – one bullet at a time."*

He cocked the weapon and aimed it right in the middle of my face. His expression said, "I win again, sucker. I always win." Then he squeezed the trigger.

The alarm woke me up before I had the chance to die.

I sat on the edge of the bed for a few minutes, trying to shake what was left of that fucking dream out of my brain. Then I got up and checked my email. Teddy hadn't let me down. The document attached to his message was exactly what I'd asked him for, and I started printing it – all ninety-four pages' worth.

Over breakfast, I told Christine about the plan to pass on the news about Phil Slattery's verbal indiscretion to the *Times-Tribune*.

"That ought to have him spitting blood over his morning paper," she said.

"I hope so," I said. "Karl really wants to be the one to do it – maybe I should let him."

"Why's he so eager?"

"He thinks if he leaks the story, he can get the paper to refer to him as 'Deep Fang'."

She chuckled, then took a sip from her cup of Type O. "*Deep Fang* – if that isn't the name of some porno film, it should be."

"What do you know about porno films?" Sometimes it's hard to stop being a parent.

"Me?" She touched the fingertips of one hand to her chest, like some Southern belle in the movies. "I don't know a blessed thing about such matters, Daddy. I'm as pure as the virgin snow."

She gave me a wicked grin. "Or I was – until I drifted."

I decided this wasn't a topic I wanted to explore with my daughter, so I said, "Well, Slattery drifted, too – with some help from Karl."

"Think he's likely to drift far enough to sink his own flotilla?"

"Flotilla?"

She shrugged. "Just preserving the metaphor."

"No, that won't sink him – not all by itself," I said. "Fortunately, I have only begun to fuck with him."

"Good one, John Paul Jones," she said. "Are those the devilish doings you referred to last night?"

"Uh-huh."

"Tell me," she said.

So I did. It took quite a while.

When I was done, she sat there and looked at me for several seconds. "I knew you could be a tough son of a bitch, Sergeant – you have to be, in your job. But this kind of ruthlessness is something I haven't seen in you before. I'm not sure I like it."

"Yeah, well, extraordinary times demand extraordinary measures. Somebody said that once, although I forget who."

"No, don't hide behind clichés. That's for cheap politicians – and whatever else you are, you're no cheap politician."

"What do you want me to say? That I'm *happy* about it? That I rubbed my hands together and cackled fiendishly when the idea came to me, like some fucking mad scientist in the movies?"

She shook her head slowly. "I know you better than that. It's just that…"

"What?"

"I don't get to look myself in the mirror anymore," she said. "But you do – every damn day. Question is, will you still be able to do that, after this shit you're talking about goes down? Always assuming you can make it work, that is."

I rubbed one hand over my face, slowly. "I don't know, honey. I really don't. But I do know this much – I *won't* be able to look myself in the mirror again if I let this city go right down the fucking tubes, without doing everything I can to stop it. And I mean *everything*."

The mug she'd been drinking from had left circles of moisture on the table. She traced each one with her fingertip slowly, as if she had all the time in the world. Then she looked up and said, "Well, if that's the way it is, Sergeant, then all I can say is – *get out there and kick some fucking ass.*"

This time, I was the one who'd suggested the Brass Shield Bar and Grill as a meeting place. My motivation was basically the same one that had brought Louis Loquasto here the first time – safety, but a different kind of safety. Before, Loquasto had wanted to be close to all these off-duty cops as protection against the Delatassos' bombs and bullets. Now, I wanted to be seen talking to him in here, because nobody in his right mind would even think about engaging in a criminal conspiracy while surrounded by all these guys wearing badges. At least, that's what I planned to say to Internal Affairs, if it ever came to that – and it might.

We'd agreed to meet at eight o'clock, an hour before my shift was due to start. I figured that would be plenty of time – after all, how long does it really take to light a fuse?

The *consigliere* was punctual, sliding into the booth just as the clock over the bar reached the top of the hour. The room was full of the buzz of about two dozen half-drunk cops having what passed for conversation; I had to lean forward so he could hear me, and maybe that was just as well. I nodded toward the glass resting on his side of the table. "I ordered you a bourbon on the rocks, like you had last time. Don't drink it if you don't want to – it's just for show."

"Just as well," Loquasto said. He had to lean forward as well. We'd look like conspirators, except every other booth in the room featured the same thing. "As I recall, it isn't very good bourbon."

"I guess most cops don't have your refined taste in booze."

He raised an eyebrow at me. "I hope you had in mind something more interesting to talk about than your tiresome class envy."

"Yeah, I did, actually," I said. "How's the war with the Delatassos going?"

"We've taken some losses recently, but it's not over yet. I have no doubt that Mister Calabrese will ultimately prevail."

He was both a Mafia *consigliere* and a lawyer, so I couldn't tell that he was lying – even though I knew he was. Word on the street was that the Calabrese Family – what was left of it – was hunkered down in defensive positions, driven off their turf by the Delatassos' car bombs and superior firepower.

"What would you say," I asked him, "if I told you there was a way for your boss to get the Delatassos out of Scranton and out of his face – for good – in just a few days?"

He looked at me for a second or two, then picked up the glass of mediocre bourbon and drained it in two swallows.

"I would say, 'Tell me more,' naturally."

"It involves more work for your pet shark, John Wesley Harding," I said.

"I have no idea to whom you're referring ," he said. Loquasto was not only an expert liar but a grammar maven, too. "But do continue, if you wish."

"You know that Ronnie Delatasso is trying to take over in Scranton because he's probably never gonna head the main branch of the family down in Philly – his old man being undead and all."

"I believe *I* was the one who conveyed that information to *you*, Sergeant."

"I'm just trying to set the stage," I said. "OK, Delatasso Senior is undead – but that's not necessarily a synonym for 'immortal', as the number of vampires who have died in this town recently should demonstrate."

"Yes, I was aware of that very basic fact," Loquasto said. "Were you planning to tell me anything that I don't already know?"

"I was just going to point out to you that if something should happen to his old man, Ronnie would probably pull up stakes here – no pun intended – and go back home to take over the family business. He's the only son, right?"

"Yes." Loquasto chewed his lower lip for a moment. "But if you're suggesting that some hypothetical 'pet shark' of ours should be sent to

Philadelphia on a mission to assassinate Charles
Delatasso, you're wasting your time – and mine."

"Why's that?"

"If we did have some Boston hit man on retainer,
I would be fairly certain that he's never worked in
Philadelphia before."

"And that would be a major problem?" I already
knew the answer to that question, but I wanted
Loquasto to say it himself.

"Of course." He made an impatient gesture with
one hand. "A man like Delatasso is going to be well
protected. If there is a gap in his personal security,
even a local professional could take weeks finding
it. As for someone coming in from out of town,
who's unfamiliar with both the city and its criminal
element..." Loquasto's thin lips pursed for a second
before turning down at the corners in a frown.
"Let's say that the talents of such a man would be
better employed... elsewhere."

"Good as Harding is, he hasn't been able to stop
the Delatassos from kicking your asses so far."

"I would dispute your characterization of asses
being kicked, as you so elegantly put it," Loquasto
said. "Besides, as I told you, it's not over yet."

"But you agree that if Charlie Delatasso was
to run into the business end of a wooden stake
tomorrow, your troubles would be over."

"In theory, perhaps. But I find wishful thinking a
waste of time and mental energy, Sergeant."

"Yeah, me, too," I said. "I don't figure it would
come as a surprise to you that the Philadelphia
cops have been keeping the Delatasso family under
surveillance for years, waiting for the Don to make
a mistake so they can put him away."

"As you say, not much of a surprise." Loquasto maintained his poker face, but I was close enough to see the pupils of his eyes contract, which meant that I'd finally said something that interested him.

"What if this guy you never heard of, John Wesley Harding, got his hands on the Philly Organized Crime Unit's file on Delatasso? A file that lays out where the Don spends the day, the places where he does business, and the guys he hangs out with – including names, addresses, phone numbers, and even photos of Delatasso and his 'business associates'?"

Loquasto sat back in the booth and looked at me for a few seconds. "I'd say that kind of information would be of... considerable interest."

"There's one thing you were wrong about, earlier, Counselor."

I got the raised eyebrow treatment again. "Indeed?"

"Delatasso Senior's got bodyguards, sure, both for daytime and at night – but only a few, and they're not what you might call high-quality guys."

"Is that right?"

"Uh-huh. It's been more than ten years since anybody made a serious move against Delatasso. He's been top dog down there for so long, he's grown complacent. And so has his security."

"And you reached this conclusion how, exactly?"

"By reading the OCU's file – the one I told you about."

"I see." Loquasto stared into his empty glass as if it were a crystal ball. Then he looked up. "I believe I'll have another drink," he said. "Can I get you anything?"

"No, I'm good, thanks." I figured Loquasto wanted another shot of that bourbon about as much as I wanted another hemorrhoid, but if the guy wanted some time to think, I was happy to give it to him.

The service in the Brass Shield isn't what you might call speedy, so it was almost five minutes before Loquasto returned with his fresh drink.

He sat down, took a sip, and grimaced slightly at the taste. Then he leaned forward. "Alright, Markowski – what do you want?"

"Two things," I said. "One of them is information."

"Concerning?"

"Patton Wilson."

Loquasto's eyes narrowed. "That rich fool who was behind all the 'helter-skelter' nonsense last year? What about him?"

"I want to know where he is."

"Somewhere in Australia, the last I heard."

"Then your information is out of date. He's here."

Loquasto blinked a couple of times. "Here?"

"In Scranton. Or close by."

"What's the source of your information?" he said quickly.

"Sorry, that's confidential," I said. "But it's reliable." I didn't want to have to explain that I was working from deduction here, rather than cold fact. I wanted results from Loquasto, not an argument. Anyway, a guy named William of Occam once wrote something along the lines of "The simplest explanation that fits the known facts is probably true." And there was only one thing that made sense out of the chaos I'd been dealing with – Patton Wilson was back.

"I find it difficult to believe that Wilson could be in the area without any of our people even catching so much as a glimpse of him."

"Somebody with Wilson's money can buy a lot of concealment," I said. "Besides, you had no reason to look for him – until now."

"Alright," Loquasto said. "I'll have all our people start beating the bushes. If Wilson is in the area, they'll locate him. I hope you're not also expecting us to… deal with him for you."

"No, just tell me where he is – I'll take it from there."

"Very well. So, you want an address for Mister Wilson. What else is that file of yours going to cost us?"

I hesitated. What I'd done in the past twenty minutes or so had probably broken about six different laws, but what I was about to say now was really over the line.

"You ever hear of Dimitri Kaspar?" I asked him.

Loquasto thought for a moment. "Local vampire, isn't he? Not affiliated with the Family. Fancies himself some kind of politician, I understand."

"That's the guy. He's also Patton Wilson's candidate for the office of Supefather."

"For *what*?"

"Sorry. That's the name some of us use for whoever's the head of the local supernaturals."

"Like the late Victor Castle, you mean."

"Exactly."

He made a face. "Mister Calabrese has never paid much attention to the local power structure, such as it is. The Family makes its own rules."

"I figured as much. But plenty of others *do* pay attention, which is why Wilson is bankrolling

Kaspar. The guy's a militant supe-premacist –
humans are just walking blood bags, blah, blah,
blah. If he becomes head of our supe community,
he's gonna cause just the kind of trouble that
Wilson can take advantage of to spread his
helter-skelter bullshit."

"What do you expect us to do about it?"

I took in a deep breath and let it out. No turning
back now. "I want you to kill him."

My car was right where I'd left it – parked in
the shadows but with a clear view of the Brass
Shield's front door – and so was my partner.
As I slid behind the wheel, Karl turned off the
radio. The volume was so low that I couldn't
even tell what he'd been listening to, although
it was probably that Pittston station that plays
golden oldies.

"Everything go OK?" I asked him.

"Sure, no sweat. I was waiting near that big
fucking Caddie that Loquasto drives. When he
came out of the bar, I handed him the envelope.
He didn't seem too surprised."

"No, he was expecting you."

"I thought for a second that he was gonna pull
out his wallet and hand me a tip, but then I guess
he remembered where he was. He just gave me a
nod, got in his car, and drove off. He's been gone
two, three minutes."

"Good – and thanks."

"What kind of mileage you figure he gets in
that thing?"

"If you have to ask about the mileage, then you
probably can't afford the car."

"Ah, I wouldn't want one of them battleships anyway, even if I had the scratch. Too hard to park it."

"Lots of trunk room, though," I said.

"I was hoping not to spend any more time inside the trunk of a car – *anybody's* car."

"Good plan."

"So he went for it, huh?" Karl asked.

"Course he did. Otherwise I'd have called you and said sit tight with the envelope."

I could have started the engine and driven off then, but I didn't – maybe because I figured Karl wasn't finished yet. I was right.

"We're sailing on what your buddy Sherlock Holmes would call some dark fuckin' waters, Stan," he said finally.

"Damn right we are. But if you've got any better ideas, you should've told me about 'em before I went in there."

Karl turned his head away slowly to stare out the window at the night. I wondered what he saw out there with his vampire sight that I was missing. Whatever it was, it didn't seem to make him happy.

"No, I didn't have a better idea before," he said, "and I still don't. Sometimes, all the choices you have in life just fucking *suck*. You ever think that?"

"More times than I can count," I said. "But I also try to remember something else."

"What?"

"The choices may all suck, but that doesn't mean some aren't worse than others."

"Yeah I guess you're right." Karl reached for the strap and buckled his safety belt. A trip through the windshield at high speed probably wouldn't do him serious harm, but the law's the law.

"So, what do we do now?" he asked.

I turned the ignition key, then put the Toyota into gear. It was time to report for work. "Now we wait."

So we waited – for four days. I tried not to think about the fact that Loquasto was under no real pressure to fulfill his part of the bargain. He could just take our information and do nothing in return – what were we gonna do? Sue him?

I'd say that the suspense was unbearable, but Karl and I were too busy most of the time to think about it. All the cops on the Occult Crimes Unit had our hands full.

It didn't help that we had the full moon during that time, which naturally resulted in increased lycanthropic activity. Werewolves aren't more prone to criminal behavior than any other species – including humans – but those with violent tendencies seem to find encouragement each month in that round, glowing disc overhead. Of course, the Patriot Party was quick to point that out, as "proof" that supernaturals were inherently antisocial and needed to be controlled. They didn't have the nerve just yet to use the word they really meant – *eliminated* – but I figured that was only a matter of time, especially if that bunch of nuts won the upcoming election.

A couple of ogres in a downtown bar got into a fight over a female of the species. No humans were hurt but the property damage was substantial. Ogres are hard to subdue, so one of the responding cops called in the Sacred Weapons and Tactics unit. But by the time SWAT got there, the female had left in disgust, and the two male ogres, realizing there wasn't anything to fight about, were sitting at what was left of the bar, having a beer. I hear they went to County Jail quietly, although neither of them made bail.

There was an ugly situation involving a golem on Monday night. A member of Temple Beth Israel's congregation got the idea that Rabbi Jacobson was messing around with his wife. That turned out to be bullshit, but it didn't stop the guy from hiring a Kabbalistic wizard to get even in the traditional fashion. The golem had chased Rabbi Jacobson all over the inside of the temple and almost had him cornered when Karl and I showed up – SWAT was busy across town, where a bunch of Slide-addicted dwarves had tried to take down the all-night branch of Citizens Savings, but a teller had tripped the silent alarm before the little bastards had a chance to get clear.

The golem was at least eight feet tall, and single-minded in its purpose of pounding the rabbi into porridge. Nothing you can shoot a golem with makes a damn bit of difference, but I'd encountered one before and knew what to do. The thing is animated by a piece of paper in its mouth on which the wizard has written a *shem* – any one of the several Hebrew names for God. Remove the paper, you deactivate the golem. Of course, the thing is programmed to resist any attempts to grab the paper, and I'd have been crushed by its giant arms if I'd gotten close enough to try. Fortunately, my partner has vampire speed. Once I'd explained what needed to be done, Karl had the *shem* out if its mouth so fast, the golem didn't even have time to react before it crumbled into the big pile of mud that had been its original form. Rabbi Jacobson thanked us warmly for the great *mitzvah* we'd done him, but Karl and I said we'd just been doing our jobs. When we left, he was looking through the phone book for carpet cleaners who were open late.

When we got back to our car, there was a number ten envelope stuck under one of the wiper blades. I opened it and saw that Louis Loquasto had come through for us after all.

The message had been printed by a computer. It didn't waste words on social niceties, which was OK with me.

Resident of former Callaway home on Lake Scranton appears to be PW. Unable to determine with certainty, as grounds and house well-guarded, but this itself lends credibility. Other matters are well in hand, with positive results expected shortly.

It was signed – if that's the right word – with a simple "L".

"Huh," Karl said when he'd read it. "I guess 'other matters' means those two guys he's gonna hit, old man Delatasso and Dimitri what's-his-name."

"Kaspar."

"Yeah, him."

"Kaspar's a vampire, Karl."

"Yeah, you already told me. So?"

"So, I was wondering if you've got any kind of problem with him being taken off the board," I said.

Karl gave me a half-smile. "'Taken off the board.' Jeez, Stan, you're starting to talk like a Mafia boss yourself."

"You know what I mean, and don't change the subject," I said. "Kaspar's a vampire, and I asked Loquasto to have him killed. You're a vampire, so I was wondering if it bothers you."

"I'm a cop, too," he said. "And I was a cop before I became a vamp."

"I know that," I said. Who would know better? Christine had brought Karl over because I'd asked her to. It was either that or watch Karl die from injuries he'd received while helping me catch a killer.

"You were with Homicide before Occult Crimes," Karl said. "And a street cop before that. Right?"

"Yeah. Six years in uniform before I got my gold shield. So?"

"You ever kill any humans in the line of duty?"

"I think I see where you're going with this," I said.

"Well, did you?"

"Yeah – two as a street cop, and one while I was a Homicide dick."

Karl nodded. "Did it bother you?"

"Yeah. Some."

"Because you killed them – or because they were human?"

A few seconds went by. "I guess I'd probably say that you proved your point."

"Then how about you not ask me any more stupid-ass questions. Deal?"

"Deal. What do you say we go back to the station and see what we can find out about this Callaway place?"

"That's the second-best idea you've had tonight," Karl said.

"What was number one?"

"Letting me handle the fucking golem. Now I don't have to explain to Christine how you got yourself killed by an eight-foot pile of mud."

Lake Scranton. The house just had to be on Lake Scranton. It shouldn't have come as a surprise, really – there are lots of ritzy homes out that way, and I wouldn't expect Patton Wilson to hole up in a shack.

But some very bad shit had gone down a couple of years ago, in the pump house that controls the lake level – despite its name, Lake Scranton is a reservoir, not something made by nature. A number of people had died in the pump house that night, none of them pleasantly. Several others had come damn close to dying – including Christine, Karl, and me.

But the Callaway estate was almost a mile from the pump house, and I decided that I'd better stop thinking about old tragedies and start focusing on how to avoid a new one.

There was a lot of information about the place available online, including six photos showing the house, inside and out. The realty company had left the listing up, even though the word "SOLD" in red letters was prominently displayed on the page. I wondered why they'd even bothered.

The house was something called a Heritage Log Home, but it wasn't anything Daniel Boone would recognize. Instead, it looked like the kind of lodge you'd find at a ritzy ski resort. According to the

Realtor, the house sat in the middle of a two-acre lot, about a quarter mile from the intersection of Lake Scranton Road and Watres Drive. Four beds, three baths, four-car garage around back, surrounded by woods on three sides. The Callaway family had sold it last year for $460,000 to something called "V. H. Property Development." Four hundred sixty grand may not buy you much house, say, on Long Island. But in Scranton, it'll get you a mini-mansion, like the one Karl and I were looking at.

I googled "V. H. Property Development" and found exactly zip. Whatever properties they were developing apparently weren't available on the public market. Then something occurred to me.

"I bet I know what the 'V. H.' stands for," I said to Karl.

"What?"

"Van Helsing."

Karl snorted. "You're probably right. That sounds like something that would appeal to our buddy Patton."

We studied the property photos. "Check this out," Karl said. He picked up a pencil and pointed at the monitor. "A two-level veranda that goes all around the house. Three-hundred-sixty-degree view. Put people on each of the four sides, and it's gonna be pretty hard to sneak up on that place."

"Except at night, maybe."

"Sure," Karl said. "Unless the guys on the deck have night-vision equipment. Or they've got motion sensors on the grounds, or maybe body heat detectors. Motherfucker bought the place eleven months ago – think he might've installed stuff like that?"

"Who – paranoid millionaire Patton Wilson, who's got more arrest warrants out on him than John Dillinger ever had?"

"That's the guy."

"In a fucking heartbeat," I said. Staring at the photos on the screen, I said, "Still, some reconnaissance might not be a bad idea. Get an idea of what we're up against – if we can do it without getting caught."

"*We* can't, probably," Karl said. "But *I* can."

"You sure?"

"It's a vamp thing – you wouldn't understand."

I sat in the police-issue Plymouth, parked in some brush just off Watres Drive with the windows cracked a couple of inches each, and listened to the night. There wasn't a lot to hear, since all the insect life was already in hibernation, and whatever birds were still around this late in the season apparently went to bed early. What I was really listening for was Karl returning to the car.

I should have known better. One second there was utter silence, and the next Karl was opening the passenger door and getting in. "Drive," he said while fastening his seat belt. "No point in hanging around here any longer than absolutely necessary. I don't think they have patrols out, but I could be wrong."

There's nobody better than a vampire when it comes to sneaking around in the dark, a point Karl had made when explaining why he should recon the house alone.

"I can see in the dark, and you can't," he'd said. "I can move a lot faster and quieter than you, and even turn into a bat, if I have to. And if they shoot at me with anything but silver, they're shit out of luck."

"And what if they *do* use silver?" I'd asked him.

"Then I'm the one who's shit out of luck."

I slowly turned onto Watres Drive, then took a right, heading us back to the city. I drove without lights for the first half-mile or so, to avoid drawing attention to the car. It wasn't as dangerous as it sounds – my eyes were already adjusted to the darkness, and the almost-full moon gave enough light to see where I was going.

Still, I gave the road my full attention until it seemed safe to flick on the headlights. I blinked against the glare a couple of times, then asked Karl, "So, how'd it go?"

"Good news and bad news," he said. "The good news is that they didn't shoot me."

"I'd already figured out that part, kemosabe," I said. "Not that I'm not relieved."

"Yeah, well, the bad news is that they're in good shape to shoot the livin' hell out of anything else. I counted six sentries – four stationary and two rovers, all with automatic weapons."

"Sweet Christ."

"Two of the stationary guys are on the verandas with night scopes. Oh, and they all wear these little radios with headsets, so they can talk to each other. It looks like the same rig SWAT uses."

"Fan-fucking-tastic," I said.

"If we're gonna go in there and get out alive, we're gonna need some help. I'd recommend a couple platoons of Navy SEALs."

"When we get back to the squad, we better have a talk with McGuire."

"About what?"

"Getting some help."

McGuire sat behind his desk, looking like his ulcer might be kicking up again. Funny how he often had that expression when talking to Karl and me.

We'd been talking for about fifteen minutes when he said, "Let me be sure I have this right. You want me to ask the Chief to authorize a full-out raid on this place – this *heavily guarded* place – near Lake Scranton because you think Patton Wilson is in there."

I nodded. "Uh-huh."

"And your only source for this information is the *consigliere* of the Calabrese family, what's-his-name, Loquasto."

"Right," I said.

"And Loquasto provided you with this valuable intelligence because…?"

I hated to lie to McGuire. He's a good boss, and he's supported Karl and me at times when others were calling for our heads. But there was a limit to what he'd put up with, and I was pretty sure that one of his detectives engaging in conspiracy to commit murder was outside that limit.

"It's in his best interest," I said. "He believes, just like we do, that Wilson is behind the Delatassos' attempt to take over the Calabrese territory. If Wilson's out of the picture, Loquasto figures that Ronnie Delatasso will take his ball and go home. Eventually."

"It makes sense, boss, when you think about it," Karl said.

McGuire looked at Karl, then back at me. "So why don't the Calabreses just go after Wilson themselves?"

"It would take a pitched battle for them to overcome all the firepower that Wilson's got protecting him," I said. "Loquasto didn't come right out and admit it, but I'm pretty sure Calabrese hasn't got the troops to do the job. He's been hurt pretty bad in the war with the Delatassos."

"So he wants us to do his dirty work for him." Judging by his face, McGuire's ulcer had taken a turn for the worse.

"It's a win-win, haina?" Karl said. "We want Wilson bad as Calabrese does – maybe more. And if we can take him out of play before the election–"

"Which is eight days away," McGuire said.

"Which is eight fuckin' days away," Karl said, nodding, "it could make all the difference in the world."

"Or none at all," McGuire said sourly.

"We won't know for sure unless we can pull it off," I said. "But one thing's for sure, boss – if we *don't* do something, and quick, Wilson's gonna *own* this town, starting nine days from now. I don't wanna see that – do you?"

"You know I don't." McGuire ran a hand slowly through his thinning hair. "But there's a problem – make that two problems."

Karl and I looked at each other, but didn't say anything.

"For what it's worth, I believe you," McGuire said. "I think Wilson's hiding in that big house on

Lake Scranton. Shit, who else around here could afford that kind of security – and who else would *need* it?"

"Then what's–" Karl began, but McGuire waved him silent.

"But asking the Chief to send twenty, thirty cops out there, including SWAT, based solely on the unsubstantiated word of a known criminal... I just don't think it's gonna happen."

"It's still worth a try, dammit," I said. "If he says no, we're no worse off than we are now."

McGuire's expression had turned bitter. "You'd think so, wouldn't you? But, like I said, there's another problem."

McGuire moved around a couple of objects on his desk that didn't need moving, and that's when I felt icy fingers touch my spine. The boss doesn't usually hesitate to say what's on his mind – about anything.

"I've been hearing things, the last couple of weeks," he said. "Nothing definitive – it's what you'd have to call circumstantial evidence, but it still bothers me. Some people that the Chief's been seen having lunch with, a few things he's said at meetings, the fact that he's talking about retiring next year – *to Bermuda*."

"Holy fucking shit," said. "You think the Chief of Police is in Wilson's pocket."

"Can't prove a damn thing," McGuire said. "But, yeah, I do. So you see the problem. I ask the Chief to authorize a big raid out on Lake Scranton, and he's gonna turn me down flat – which he might well have done anyway. But more than that..." He let his voice trail off.

"He'll tell Wilson we know where he is," I said.

"Fucking Wilson'd turn that place out there into Fort Knox," Karl said. "You'd need an armored division to take it."

"Either that, or he'll just disappear again," I said. "And if he does, what do you figure the chances are we'd find the bastard again, before election day?"

McGuire snorted. "Snowball in Hell – if the odds are even *that* good."

"Which means we're fucked," Karl said.

"No," I told him. "It means we're *royally* fucked."

We got sent out on a call that turned out to be a false alarm. A woman living on Kaiser Avenue reported a werewolf prowling around her house. Karl and I didn't turn up any werewolves, but we did find a guy from the neighborhood – he could've used a haircut and a beard trim, but he was still human – who liked to peek through windows. We sent the jerk home with a warning that Karl reinforced with a little bit of vampire Influence.

It was about time for our break then, so we headed for Jerry's Diner, which was nearby. The mood I was in, I almost *hoped* somebody would try to stick the place up while we were there.

I was stirring sugar into my coffee when a thought occurred to me. "Karl, that Influence you laid on the peeping tom a little while ago...."

He put down his mug of Type O and looked at me. "Yeah?"

"Could you use it on Wilson's guards? Maybe get them all to drop their guns and take a nice nap?"

"All of them?" He shook his head slowly. "No way, Stan. If there's a technique for controlling a bunch of guys all at once, I never heard of it. I'd have to do them one at a time, and I don't think it would take long before the others tumbled to what I was up to. They'd open up on me – and since those fuckers work for Wilson, I wouldn't be surprised if they *are* packing silver bullets."

"Shit," I said. "Well, it was worth a try. I was hoping you could put them under your spell long enough for us to–"

"Wait – what did you say?" Karl was looking at me with an odd expression on his face.

"Just this crazy idea that you'd be able to–"

"I know what you meant," he said, and stood up abruptly. "I'll be right back."

I watched as he went to the rack near the front door where Jerry keeps all the free print material that's available for customers to take. I thought I remembered several books of realty listings, as well as the *Pennysaver Press*, a local rag that's full of cheap classified ads from people with stuff to sell. The Chamber of Commerce puts some of its publications there, too.

But when Karl returned to our table, he was carrying a copy of *The Weekender*, which bills itself as "The Wyoming Valley's #1 Arts and Entertainment Free Weekly." It's also the only such paper in the area, so the distinction of being number one doesn't mean too much.

Karl sat down again and began rapidly flipping the pages. He didn't bother to explain what the hell he was doing.

"If you're looking for the 'gentlemen's club' ads, I believe they're towards the back," I told him.

"Figured you'd know that," he said, without looking up. "But I'm pretty sure they also keep

track of what bands're playing at the local bars...
Yeah, here we go."

He began scanning the page he'd stopped at.
Then his eyes stopped moving. "Good – we're in
luck. They're still in the area. Got a gig in Wilkes-
Barre, starting tomorrow night."

"You're gonna let me in on this great discovery
sooner or later, right?"

"Sooner," he said, closing the paper and dropping
it on the table in front of me. "Our big problem is
all these heavily armed dudes guarding Wilson. We
can't fight 'em, so we've gotta find the way to get
the fuckers out of there."

"Tell me something I don't already know."

"OK, how's this – what would you say if I told
you I know where we can find us a Siren?"

The Banshees were beginning a two-night
engagement at the Palace, a club in South Wilkes-
Barre that looked like no palace I'd ever heard of.
We'd called ahead, and the manager had told us
that the band was expected to finish its last set
around 2am.

I hadn't been in Wilkes-Barre in a while, and
returning now made me feel kind of depressed.
Lacey Brennan lived here – or she used to, before
taking an extended vacation to visit her sister. I
wondered where Lacey was at that moment, what
she was doing, and how she was feeling. I also
wondered if she was ever coming back.

Then I told myself to suck it up and focus on the
job at hand. The stakes were too high for me to
fuck up now because I was feeling moony over a
woman. Even if the woman was Lacey.

The Palace's dressing room for performers was located in a basement that looked like it hadn't been swept out since Bush was President – the first one. It was ten after two when I knocked on the door, which was answered by the lead singer, who I remembered went by the name of some insect – Daddy Longlegs, that was it.

He looked at me and said, "What?" His voice sounded hoarse.

"We'd like a few minutes of your time," I said. Politeness pays, especially when you want a favor from some people who probably don't like you very much.

He stared a couple of seconds longer. "Hey – I know you."

"Yeah, you do." I held up my ID folder and let him see my badge. It was meaningless here, since Karl and I were out of our jurisdiction – but I was hoping a bunch of musicians wouldn't know about stuff like that. "Mind if we come in?"

"Yeah, OK. Sure."

He stepped back and let us into a twenty-by-twenty windowless room with concrete floors, harsh fluorescent lighting, and heating pipes running across the ceiling. There were some beat-up gray lockers, a couple of long benches, and another door through which I could hear water running.

The other two guys in the band looked up from the task of putting their instruments away. They didn't seem happy to see us, but nobody went for a weapon. That was about the best I figured we could expect.

I looked at Daddy Longlegs. "Where's your bass player – the girl?"

"She's in the shower."

"You mind getting her for me?"

He took a couple of steps toward the open door and called, "Hey, Scar! Come on out – we got visitors."

The sound of running water stopped. A minute or so later, the young woman – whose real name, I knew, was Meredith Schwartz – came out, using a towel to wipe down her buzz-cut blonde hair. Apart from the towel, she was naked, but the guys in the band showed about as much interest as if she'd been wearing a suit of armor.

She looked at Daddy Longlegs. "Hey – who called five-oh?"

"Nobody," he told her. "Guy said he wants to talk to us."

She turned to me. "What about?"

"Why don't you put something on first?" I said. I was trying to keep my gaze focused on her face, but one quick glance below told me that she had several more tats – besides the human heart on her arm that I'd seen before – and no pubic hair.

"How come?" She gave me an evil grin. "This ain't in public or nothin'."

According to the research Karl and I had done on the band the night before, Meredith Schwartz was an honors graduate of Mount Holyoke College, but she sure didn't act or talk like a typical Seven Sisters grad – at least, I hoped she didn't.

"We appreciate that you got the right to dress however you want in private," Karl said. "But we were hoping to have a conversation, and you're kind of... distracting." Then he gave her a big smile.

"Hey, you're a vamp!" she said with delight. "I didn't know there were any vamp cops."

"There's at least one," Karl said. "So, you mind getting dressed, or what?"

I couldn't tell if he put any Influence behind the request, but Meredith shrugged and said, "Sure."

She walked over to one of the lockers and pulled out a sleeveless T-shirt, jeans, and a pair of old Adidas running shoes. Without wasting time, she put them all on.

I, of course, didn't stare at her tight young body while all this was happening. I'm not some creepy old man. But I do have good peripheral vision.

Meredith finished tying her shoelaces and straightened up. "Better?"

"Less distracting, anyway," Karl said. "Thanks."

She gave him a look that said she might not be averse to distracting him again sometime, but turned toward me as I said, "We're not here to give you guys a hard time – about anything. Truth is, we need to ask you for a favor."

One of the other guys said, "Favor? What kind of favor?"

"We want to make use of your band's special talent – more precisely, Scar's ability to drive men into a frenzy by her singing."

"In a house near Scranton," Karl said, "there's a very bad dude holed up, surrounded by a bunch of guys with guns who aren't afraid to use them. If we went straight in after him, there'd be a bloodbath."

"Even assuming we could get authorization to go in after him," I said, "which we can't."

The beanpole who called himself Daddy Longlegs looked at me. "How come?"

"Politics," was all I said, but his nod seemed to say that he understood.

"So you want Scar to sing to these guys," he said, "so they'll run after her and forget all about guarding this bad guy you wanna bust."

"Yeah, that's about right," I said.

Scar looked at me, hands on hips. "So, what's the catch?"

"It could be dangerous," I told her. "Very dangerous."

Her challenging expression slowly changed into a wide grin. "Shit, man – that ain't the catch," she said. "That's the *fun*."

We'd borrowed the flatbed truck from Karl's cousin Ernie, who owned a John Deere franchise and used the vehicle to move heavy equipment around. Tonight it was being used to transport Banshee's amps and instruments, along with a portable generator I'd brought to provide power. When I'd suggested that Scar just sing a cappella, the other band members had insisted on being there. I'd explained why this gig might be more risky than what they were used to, and Daddy Longlegs had spoken for the others when he'd told me, "No way, man! We're a unit, an organic entity. Scar risks her neck, then we're gonna be right there with her!"

Organic entity. Right. Normally I don't like being called "man", but I was prepared to make an exception in the case of Daddy Longlegs, especially when he told me that he could drive a stick shift.

It was Wednesday night. Banshee had been committed to play at the Palace the night before, and although I'd offered to make up the eight hundred bucks they'd lose by not performing, they wouldn't even consider it. "It ain't just the money," Scar had explained. "We punt this gig with zero notice, word's gonna get around that we're unreliable. *Then* who's gonna hire us? We gotta think about the future of the band."

We've all got our priorities. Mine was to put this crazy scheme into action as soon as possible, before one of Wilson's pet cops found out what we were up to and warned him. If that happened, Wilson would be in the wind faster than a trailer park in a tornado.

But Karl had just come back from another scout of the Callaway estate, and he reported that all the guards were still in place, vigilant as ever. If Wilson had split, they wouldn't have bothered. Probably.

For a staging area, we used a construction site where some new apartments were going up, about a mile from the Callaway place. There were no houses close enough for anybody to be disturbed as the band did its sound check. I was glad to see that the gasoline generator I'd rented was putting out enough juice to power Banshee's big amps.

I also used the occasion to check my own hearing protection – it wouldn't do much good for me to get caught up in the Siren's song once it started. Vampire Karl was immune to it and didn't need special precautions, but I'd bought a set of those metal and plastic earmuffs that airport mechanics use. They look like old-fashioned stereo headphones but give you about four times as much protection from ambient noise. I watched from twenty feet away as Scar and the boys did a sound check, and I could barely hear a thing.

When they'd finished, I took off the earmuffs and walked back to the truck. In my pocket I had two

TracFones I'd bought at Vlad-Mart the day before. I handed one up to Scar. "Here, take this."

She looked at it and said, "I've got my own phone, man. It's lots better than this cheap piece of shit."

"I'm sure it is," I said. "But the only one who's got the number of that particular phone is me. Put it in your pocket, will you? When that thing goes off, you'll know it's time to start the party."

I went over to where Daddy Longlegs was sitting behind the wheel. "Once it starts, keep your eyes on the mirror. This works, a bunch of guys are gonna come bursting through those trees and make a beeline for the truck. They get within fifty feet or so, that's when you start moving."

"Keep the speed down to twenty or twenty-five," Karl told him. "The objective is to keep them following you, not lose them."

"I gotcha," Daddy Longlegs said. "Just like a bunch of dogs chasing after a bitch in heat."

"I heard that," Scar said from the truck bed. "Who're you calling a bitch?"

"Not you, baby," Daddy Longlegs said. "Purely a metaphor."

"Good thing," she said. Then she looked at me, and the evil grin reappeared. "Shit, I don't even *like* doggy-style."

That put an image in my mind that I tried to banish by focusing on the task at hand, and the risks it involved for all of us. That worked, more or less.

"OK, follow our car," I told Daddy Longlegs. "When we stop, come up right behind us and park. Then Karl and I are gonna drive down the road a little farther. Wait for the phone call, then crank it up. OK?"

"Got it. And thanks, man."

"For what?"

"This here's the most fun we've had in a long time."

"Glad to hear it. I hope you still think so an hour from now."

There was no traffic moving on Lake Scranton Road at two in the morning . Good thing, too, since there were now two vehicles driving on it without showing any lights.

After a while, Karl said, "Tree's coming up, 'bout a hundred feet."

We'd figured out the night before just where we wanted the flatbed to be, then marked the place by tying a handkerchief around the branch of a nearby tree. Karl touched the brakes, and we rolled to a slow stop. In my side mirror, I could see the flatbed inch up behind us until our bumpers were nearly touching. Daddy Longlegs turned the truck's engine off, and Karl and I continued on.

Between the big house and the road was about two hundred feet of woods. That was where we expected the guard detail to come bursting through. The house had a driveway leading to the road, but Scar had told me that the men would come to her using the most direct route possible, even if it meant fighting their way through heavy vegetation.

"They're gonna be outta their fuckin' minds," she'd said. "Trust me on that."

"I will." Then something else had occurred to me. "Those guys are all armed to the teeth. Are they likely to bring their guns with them?"

She'd thought about that for a moment. "Naw, they always drop anything they've got in their hands. These dudes are gonna become what you might call 'single-minded' real fast."

"What if some of them have a backup piece – a handgun in a holster?"

"If it's something they're wearing, I guess they'd still have it," she'd said with a shrug. "So what?"

"So, when they can't reach you, aren't you afraid they might shoot, out of frustration?"

"Don't you *get* it, man? They won't be interested in hurting me – they're just gonna want to *fuck* me. Like they've never wanted to fuck anybody in their lives."

I was giving silent thanks for the industrial-strength ear protection that I'd be wearing when she said, "I dunno – maybe after a while, we should stop the truck and let them have me. You said you wanted a diversion, right? What's more diverting than a gangbang?"

"*Scar–*"

"How many guards did you say there were – six? That could make for quite a party, dontcha think?"

"Now, *listen–*" I'd said, but she'd stopped me with a peal of laughter.

"Don't get your undies in a twist, man. I don't do gangbangs – well, except for that time in St Louis, and I was drunk then. I just said it cause I wanted to see that expression on your face. Priceless!"

I'd decided then and there: if Christine ever wanted to go to college, she was *not* going to Mount Holyoke. Not if I had anything to say about it.

Karl stopped the car again. We'd chosen a spot that gave us a clear view of the estate's driveway through the windshield and of the woods behind us through the mirrors. When the time came, we'd be taking the most direct route to the house – right up the driveway.

I turned in my seat, pulled a heavy canvas bag from the back seat, and put it between my feet. It contained a few things I'd persuaded Frank Dooley, the SWAT team commander, to let me have for the occasion. I know that Sacred Weapons and Tactics deals with supernaturals exclusively, but even *they* have to take down a door once in a while.

I put the earmuffs around my neck, ready to slip into place. Then I pulled out my TracFone and looked at Karl. "Ready?"

"Ready as I'll ever be. Do it."

I had the number of the phone I'd given Scar on speed dial, and all I had to do was push a button. So I did – *and nothing happened.*

I peered at the phone in the gloom, and saw that the call had gone through. I didn't expect Scar to answer, but I *did* expect to hear music. I cancelled the call and placed it again. Went through that time, too – but still no sound from the truck.

"Sweet fucking Jesus – what *happened*? Did Wilson's guards get to them already? It just isn't possible–"

Karl laid a hand on my arm and squeezed gently.

"The generator's noisy, Stan. The kids didn't want to get it going until you gave the word. And those amps of theirs take a minute or so to warm up."

I felt my heart, which had felt like it was about to burst through my chest, settle back into place. "Why the fuck didn't you *tell* me that?"

"I thought one of the kids already had. Sorry, I didn't – OK, here we go."

The sound of an electric guitar split the night, and I quickly put the plastic muffs over my ears.

After a few seconds I asked Karl, "What's she singing – anything you recognize?"

Karl pulled out his notebook, wrote busily, then showed the page to me. "A punk version of *Somebody to Love*, that old Jefferson Airplane tune. Grace Slick should be rolling over in her grave right about now, except I don't think she's dead."

"If she hears this, the shock might kill her," I said. "Hope she doesn't have a vacation home around here – I always liked that band."

A little while later, Karl nudged me and pointed toward the rear window. I turned in my seat, and there was enough moonlight to see a man on the road, running hard in the direction of the truck and its singer.

As I watched, another guy burst through the trees and followed him. Then two more. Ten seconds or so later, another man stumbled out onto the asphalt and took off running. This one was limping, as if he had twisted his ankle or something. But he still ran, as fast as he was able. Then another man fought his way out of the brush and headed up the road after the others. It didn't take him long to overtake his gimpy colleague, and he passed the limping runner without even a glance.

"OK, that's six," I said.

Karl held up his hand in a "Wait a minute" gesture. Good thing, too. A few seconds later, a seventh man burst out of the woods, with number eight right behind him. Like the others, they immediately took off in the direction the truck had taken.

"You said there were six," I told Karl.

Karl pulled out his notebook and wrote, "Said I *counted* six. Last two stationed behind house, maybe?"

With his vampire sight, Karl could see the men much better than I could. I was sure if one of them had been Patton Wilson he'd have said so, but I wanted to be one hundred percent sure.

"Was any of those guys Wilson?"

Karl shook his head.

"Positive?"

A nod this time.

"Guess that means he's still in there," I said. "Let's go get him."

We drove up the narrow driveway to the huge house. The ground floor was dark, but I could see some lights burning upstairs. We'd gone slowly, so no screeching tires. No headlights, either. If anybody inside didn't know we were here yet, I wanted to maintain their ignorance as long as possible.

I was reaching for the door handle when an idea struck me. "I know you've got extra-sharp hearing," I said to Karl, "but do you think a human would still be able to hear Scar and the boys from here?"

He listened out the window for a moment, then nodded.

"OK," I said, "how about this? Once I get the door open, let's leave it that way and wait outside. If Wilson can hear Scar, he should come running out, along with any other guys he's got in there with him. Save us having to go in after them."

Karl gave me a grin and a big thumbs-up. We left the car and walked rapidly to the house's immense front door, which looked to be solid oak. In the bag that Dooley had given me were a ten-pound sledgehammer, a small amount of plastic explosive for blowing locks, and a few other goodies. Karl could've probably torn the door off its hinges, but since he hadn't been invited in, he couldn't mess with the entranceway. Vampire shit is weird sometimes. Karl had been able to overcome his aversion to crosses, but the entry-by-invitation-only thing appeared to be more than just a psychological barrier.

I wanted to know just how solid the lock was, so I reached over and twisted the knob. But there wasn't any resistance – it turned in my hand, and the heavy door swung open on well-oiled hinges.

Karl and I looked at each other. When something like this happens in the movies, it usually means the hero's about to get jumped. But maybe Wilson had so much faith in his small army that locking the door seemed unnecessary. At least, I *hoped* that was the reason.

Standing to one side, I pushed the door open all the way and revealed nothing but darkness. Then Karl and I waited to see who inside the house would respond to the Siren's song.

Nobody came out. We stood next to the door for three or four minutes, then Karl started writing in his notebook again.

"Music playing someplace upstairs," he'd written. "Loud. Wagner? They can't hear Scar over it."

That explained a few things. It was disappointing that Wilson wasn't going to come running out into our arms, but on the other hand, loud music meant nobody up there would likely hear us until we were right on top of them.

I'd left my flashlight in the car, but didn't think it was worth fetching. I'd just step inside, invite Karl in, and with his vampire night vision we could creep up on Patton Wilson and whatever minions he might have left.

I took a couple of steps into the vast foyer and glanced around. Seeing neither light or movement, I turned back toward the open door to invite Karl inside. "Come on–" was as far as I got when somebody kicked me in the balls.

I gave a loud grunt and fell to my knees, clutching my groin. I know that a blow to the testicles isn't fatal – not even to your love life, usually – but for a few seconds the pain and nausea emanating from my crotch became the center of my world.

I was vaguely aware of the front door slamming shut in Karl's face. Then something hard hit me on the side of the head, and I pitched forward into blackness.

I hadn't had a lot to eat that day, since I'd been so busy planning my own little version of D-Day. Just as well – when I came to, the urge to vomit was strong. If I'd had food in my stomach, puking all over myself would have added messy insult to the injuries I'd already suffered.

My balls still hurt, though not as bad as before. My head throbbed where I'd been whacked – probably by a gun – for the *second fucking time* in eight days although not in the same place, fortunately. I tried to raise my hands to my aching head and found I couldn't – they were secured behind my back by something that felt a lot like handcuffs, probably my own. My brilliant plan wasn't working out too well, after all.

"I know you're awake," a woman's voice said. "Get to your feet."

A woman. That explained why someone was able to lurk in the dark foyer without being tempted to run outside after Scar. Women were immune to the Siren's song. I couldn't remember seeing any women around Wilson before, but then I'd only met him once.

I opened my eyes and saw that the lights were on now. Getting up from the floor with sore testicles, a pounding head, and no hands to help wasn't the easiest thing I've ever done, but I managed. Then I turned to face the lady who had just kicked my ass.

She was above average height, about 5'8", with broad shoulders under a short-sleeved T-shirt, with a pair of tight jeans below. The biceps revealed by the short sleeves said the lady had some acquaintance with lifting weights. Her brown hair was in tight curls and she wore it in a style that in a black woman I'd have called an afro. Under the hair was a round face about midway between plain and pretty, and its angry expression didn't exactly make me feel all warm and fuzzy inside. Neither did the big revolver in her right hand.

I drew breath to speak – I had in mind to say something along the lines of "Who the hell are you?" – but she waved me quiet with a slash of her free hand. "Don't talk until I tell you," she said. Seeing that I wasn't going to disobey, she went on, "I bet your ballsac hurts pretty bad, huh? I want you to think about how much worse it'd hurt if a put a bullet into it – which is just what I'm gonna do if you try to call in your vamp buddy from outside. Understand? Just nod."

I dipped my head a couple of times, because I had no trouble believing that she meant every word she'd said.

"Good," she said. "We're going upstairs now." She gestured with the gun barrel. "You first."

She walked me to a staircase that must have been twenty feet wide. It was made of highly polished wood, like everything else in my field of vision.

She stayed several steps behind me as we climbed the stairs – a good, professional distance. I wondered if she'd been a professional bodyguard, either private or government, at some time. I didn't try any TV hero shit on the steps, mainly because I had no desire to sing soprano for the rest of my life, however long that might be.

I hadn't been paying attention before, but now I could hear the music coming from someplace upstairs. I recognized Wagner's "Ride of the Valkyries," but only because I've seen *Zombie Apocalypse Now* three times.

We went up two flights of stairs and turned right, then right again. That brought us to a long hall with a door at the end that seemed to be the source of the music, which seemed really loud now. No wonder Wilson, or whoever was up here, hadn't been tempted by Scar's Siren song.

When we reached the door, the woman knocked loudly. She had to do it three times, but then the Valkyries' singing was suddenly cut off mid-note. From inside a male voice called, "What?"

"It's me, sir," she called. "We have a guest."

"Come."

She opened the door and motioned me inside ahead of her. I stepped into the kind of room you'd expect a rich fuck like Patton Wilson to hang around in – rich carpet, oil paintings, a big, overflowing bookshelf, and more polished wood. In the middle of it all was a desk that was probably some kind of antique, and behind the desk was the man himself.

If Patton Wilson was surprised to see me, he didn't let it show. "You're early, Markowski – by about a month. After the election, I was going to have you fired, preferably in disgrace, then kill you – right after you watched me stake that vamp bitch you call your daughter."

He looked at me as if waiting for a response, but I didn't want to get shot, especially now. So I turned to the woman, who was standing in the open doorway and raised my eyebrows.

She understood what I meant and said, "Yeah, you can talk now." She looked at Wilson and said, "I told him downstairs that I'd shoot him in the balls if he opened his mouth without permission."

He laughed with delight. "Sound idea. And you may get to do it yet."

He looked at me and said, "What do you think of her, Markowski? Quite formidable, no? Meet Sheila Barnard, formerly of the US Secret Service."

Turning to her, he said, "Sheila, this is Detective Sergeant Stanley Markowski, of the police department's Occult Crimes Unit."

"She beat me up downstairs," I said. "I figured that was as good as an introduction."

Karl was outside, somewhere. With his acute vampire senses, he might well hear me if I yelled for him to come in. Problem was, he'd get here just in time to see me dying on the floor with a bullet in my crotch.

"Would you care to tell me what happened to my guards?" Wilson asked me. "Not that it matters much – I'll be leaving here tomorrow, since the police apparently know about this place. But I am curious how you did it, Markowski – been polishing up your commando skills, have you?"

As long as we were talking, he wouldn't tell Sheila to kill me, so I'd talk all night and into the morning, given a chance.

"No, I'm not the commando type. I found a Siren."

He frowned at me. "A police siren? That doesn't make any sense."

"No, a *real* Siren – like in *The Odyssey*."

The frown got deeper. "Such creatures really exist?"

"They sure do. I found one singing in a rock band, and put her on the back of a flatbed truck, with the rest of the band and some amplifiers. Your guards were last seen chasing the truck down Scranton Road, and the singing won't stop until the last one drops from exhaustion."

"Thus giving me another reason why these so-called *supernaturals* need to be put down, like the dangerous dogs they are. And they will be, one day. Every last one of them."

"Helter-skelter," I said. "The great 'race war' between humans and supes."

"Exactly."

"You seem awful confident that humans are going to come out on top in that one."

"Of course we will. It's all part of God's plan."

Psychos. They all claim to know God's plan. Trouble is, none of them can agree on what it is.

"Uh-huh," I said. "And God told you to use the Delatassos – the same kind of creatures you say you despise so much?"

"*Vengeance is mine, sayeth the Lord,*" Wilson quoted. "But that doesn't restrict Him as to the tools he might use, does it?"

"And Slattery – he's one of your tools?" I said. "And that vampire, Dimitri Kaspar?"

"Don't be tiresome, Markowski. Of *course* they are. And very useful tools, too – for the time being."

Wilson pushed his chair back and stood. "Now, then. The last time you were my unwilling guest, I kept you alive because I thought you might be useful to me. I won't make that mistake again."

He turned to the woman. "Sheila, take him downstairs, if you would. When you're done, come back up here – I have another job for you." He looked at me then, and the hatred in his eyes was like a living force. "It involves Sergeant Markowski's daughter."

That was the worst mistake he could have made, because it pushed me into "nothing left to lose" territory. If I was going to die anyway, it might as well be here. Karl could settle up the score for me, and at least Christine would be safe. I quietly drew in a big breath, to be sure that my last words – *Come in, Karl!* – would be loud enough for my partner to hear through the wall.

"Goodbye, Markowski," Wilson said. "I wish I could say I've enjoyed our little talks, but frankly–"

That was as far as he got before the *bam* of a gunshot sounded from the hall – a shot that went into the back of Sheila Barnard's head and exited through the front in a spray of blood and bone.

The former Secret Service agent toppled forward onto her face – what was left of it, that is. A good amount of the tissue was now decorating the wall opposite where she'd been standing. Some of the gore had even splattered Wilson himself, ruining what I'd figured to be a five-thousand-dollar suit.

A blonde guy in his mid-twenties came in then, stepping over Sheila's corpse like it was an inconvenient mud puddle. He looked familiar, but I couldn't place him, at first. I was more concerned about the big automatic he was carrying.

It looked like Wilson knew the guy, too, judging by his stare – a mix of rage and disbelief. "Jernegan! What the fuck are *you* doing here?"

Then it came back to me. I hadn't known the guy's name then, but this Jernegan had been one of Wilson's fair-haired commando boys last year, when Wilson made his first attempt at starting a race war.

But then he had been possessed by the demon Acheron.

The possessed Jernegan had killed five people that night. I would have been number six, except Karl and Christine saved my ass at the last minute. Then the commando guy, and his demon host, had just walked away.

Was Jernegan still possessed, or had the demon moved on to somebody else?

"Me?" he said to Wilson. "I came in through the garage. One door was up – quite careless, really." He waved the barrel of the automatic in Wilson's direction. *"Now shut up, you crazy old cunt."*

Well, there was the answer to *that* question. The real Jernegan would never in his life have talked to Wilson like that.

He looked at me then. "Markowski! We do seem to keep running into each other at these crime scenes, don't we?"

I nodded. "Hello, Jernegen – or do you prefer Acheron?"

"Either will do, although the former name won't be appropriate much longer. I'm tired of this host and moving on shortly."

Did that mean me? Was he going to possess *me*?

"Keeping you alive all this time has been quite the chore, Markowski. I hope you appreciate my efforts on your behalf."

Some things were starting to make sense now.

"That was you who took out the Delatasso soldier – the one who was about to kill me that night in the warehouse district."

He gave a slight bow. "None other."

"And those three guys behind Jerry's Diner. That was you, too."

"They were going to kill you and make it look like a mugging gone wrong. Ronnie Delatasso sent them – but without consulting with Mister Bigbucks here, who apparently wanted you kept alive almost as much as I did. But for different reasons, of course."

"What *are* your reasons?" I asked him. "I mean, I'm grateful and all, but – *why*? Last time we met, you were going to cut my throat."

"Yes, that was short-sighted of me. I should have realized then that I needed you alive. Just as well your two blood-sucking friends intervened."

"But what did you need me alive *for*?"

"Isn't it obvious? To locate Mister Bigbucks here for me. He and I have some unfinished business, and I was sure the two of you would cross paths again soon."

"What unfinished business?" Wilson asked. Despite his tan, he looked white. Dead white.

Acheron went over to Wilson and slapped him hard across the face. "Did I not tell you to *shut the fuck up*? We'll *get* to you."

He turned back to me. "My, but I enjoyed that."

"That makes two of us," I said. "But if it won't get me slapped, I've got the same question – what business have you got with Wilson?"

"Isn't it obvious? It was on the orders of this septic excrescence that I was summoned from Hell."

"I know Scranton's got its problems, especially lately," I said. "But I still would've thought it's better than Hell."

"Oh, it is! Of course. Immeasurably better."

"Then why are you mad at Wilson?"

"Because he never *intended* to set me free – he planned to summon me, use me for his own purposes, and then send me back, just as he had so many of my brothers."

"Oh."

"Do you know who suffers the most exquisite tortures in Hell, Markowski?"

"There are degrees of pain down there?"

"Indeed, yes. And the very worst suffering is reserved for wizards, those who had the effrontery to impose their own will on the denizens of Hell. They all die in time, of course – and when they do, we are *very* eager to make them welcome."

The way he said that made me decide right then to start attending church more often. Assuming I got the chance.

"And that's what Wilson's got in store?" I asked him.

A slow nod. "Most assuredly."

"So that's what you're here for – to send him on his way."

"No, not just yet. I thought a taste of Hell on Earth would be a worthy prelude to his eternal damnation."

I hoped he wasn't going to possess Wilson and force the man to commit various atrocities on himself. I'd seen something like that once before, and it still gave me screaming nightmares.

The only thing worse than that would be making *me* do it. And, then, once Wilson was reduced to hamburger, forcing me to do the same thing to myself.

Getting shot in the balls was starting to look like a more attractive option than some of the other things that could happen. But I had to know.

"What have you got in mind?" I asked him.

"First, let's get you squared away."

He went over to the body of Sheila Barnard. There was a pistol tucked into the back of her jeans. It looked familiar.

Acheron pulled the gun loose and held it up. "Yours, I believe?"

All I could do was nod.

Then he walked over to me and touched one of my wrists. "Your own handcuffs?"

"Yeah."

"How embarrassing for you. Where do you keep the key?"

"Left side pocket."

A few seconds later, my hands were free and Acheron was handing the cuffs to me, followed by my Beretta.

"There," he said. "You'll need those to make your arrest."

"Arrest? Arrest who?"

"The killer, of course."

He pulled out the gun he'd shot Sheila Barnard with and tossed it underhand to Wilson. "Here you go, Moneybags."

Wilson's catch was clumsy, but at least he didn't drop the thing. I gaped – I couldn't help it. Why would Acheron give Wilson his gun?

Something changed in the room then. Jernegan groaned and put his hands to his head as if he'd been struck. A moment later Wilson screamed, "No, don't–"

That was as far as he got. Something in Wilson's face changed, a transformation I'd seen before. In Wilson's voice, Acheron said, "There, that's better."

He'd possessed Wilson now. Was a horror show still on the program? I hoped I wasn't about to watch Wilson cut himself to pieces.

Jernegan was staggering around, saying things like "Where am...?" And "How did...?"

The thing that used to be Patton Wilson said, "Oh, shut up," then raised the gun and shot Jernegan three times in the chest.

The gun going off in a contained space like the study had left my ears ringing. When I was sure I could hear again, I said to Acheron, "Not that you ever needed a reason to kill somebody, but I have to ask why you did that."

"Well, I had no more use for him, now that I've found these new accommodations, and he *was* starting to get on my nerves."

"Great. Just great."

"But more to the point, Detective Sergeant, you've just observed Patton Wilson commit cold-blooded murder, to which you can testify at his trial. Not to mention all the forensic evidence that can be introduced – gunshot residue on my hands, and so forth."

"Wilson didn't do it," I said. "You did."

"You and I know that – but no one else needs to, do they? And adding homicide to all the other crimes that Wilson is charged with should almost certainly result in a life sentence, since your state abolished the death penalty. Life without parole, of course."

Looking at Jernegan's corpse, I said, "Wilson's got enough money to hire half the lawyers in the world for his trial."

"Yes – but he won't."

I turned to stare at him. "Why the fuck not?"

"Because I'm going to stay around for a while. I think I can guarantee that Mister Wilson is going to put on a *very* inept defense."

"Jesus, how long are you planning to possess him for?"

Acheron winced. "I really wish you wouldn't use that name around me. But to answer your question, I think I'll stay with Mister Wilson past his sentencing – right up to the point where he's about to be gangbanged in the prison shower for the first time. Then I'll move on and let them have at him."

"He won't last long in that environment," I said. "He'll kill himself – I'd bet on it."

"Will he? Knowing what's waiting for him on the other side?" The smile that Acheron gave me was something I hope never to see again. "I'm quite certain that Mister Bigbucks here will prolong his life of misery as long as he possibly can – to postpone the eternal lessons in *real* misery that he will experience at the hands of my brethren in Hades."

I just looked at him, unable to speak. Finally, I said, "That's just... fucking diabolical."

"Thank you," the demon said. "I try."

It was just past 2.30am, and we were taking our break in Jerry's Diner, as usual. Tonight's shift hadn't been very busy so far, but Karl and I were both tired. Yeah, vampires get tired, too.

Karl drank some warmed-up blood and put his cup down. "Election's tomorrow."

"Yeah. I'll have to get up early, make sure I vote before going in to work. You gonna send an absentee ballot?"

"No need. With daylight savings time gone, it gets dark around 5.00 nowadays. Polls close at nine. I'll have plenty of time."

After a while he said, "Think the Patriot Party's gonna sweep?"

"A month ago, I'd have said 'Sure.' But with all the stuff that's been happening..."

"I know what you mean," he said. "You read the editorial in yesterday's *T-T*?"

"Yeah – they practically called Slattery and his boys fascists."

"They were practically right, too."

"You think anybody gives much of a damn what the *Times-Tribune* says anymore?" I said.

"Guess we'll find out tomorrow." Karl took another sip of Type O. "Streets are pretty calm lately – the PP can't bitch about that anymore. No car bombs the last two weeks. Supes have been quiet, too. Mostly."

"Mostly – except for somebody staking that Kaspar guy."

"I'm kinda glad we didn't catch that one," Karl said.

"Yeah, me, too."

The creamer at Jerry's comes in those little plastic containers, and I figured my coffee might just be drinkable if I added one more. Stirring it in, I said, "You hear the rumor about Ronnie Delatasso?"

"That he had his old man hit so he could take over the family business?"

"Makes a certain amount of sense, I guess. I mean, you look at a murder, what's the first question you ask?"

"*Cui bono*?"

"*Who benefits?* – damn right. And Ronnie seems to be the main beneficiary of this particular homicide. I hear the Philly DA's even talking about calling a grand jury."

"Tell you the truth," Karl said, "I wouldn't care if it was the fucking Girl Scouts who hit the old man, long as Ronnie and his troops went back home for good."

"Their war chest was probably running dry, anyway. Patton Wilson sure won't be giving them any more money, and now that the Slide trade has dried up, thanks to Rachel and her..."

The front door opened, and a couple of gnomes walked into the diner.

I felt myself tense up. "Karl," I said softly.

"I see 'em."

The gnomes walked up to the counter, no weapons in sight. No conical hats, either. They were acting perfectly normal – for gnomes. I couldn't hear what they said to Donna, but Karl could.

"We could have trouble here," he said.

"What is it?" I slowly pushed the right side my sport coat back, for easier access to the Beretta.

"They want a couple of coffees," he said. "One with cream and sugar, one just cream. And a toasted bagel, with butter. To go."

"So what?"

"Donna just told them she's out of bagels."

We watched as Donna prepared two coffees, bagged them, took money from the gnomes, and made change. They left without even glancing at the other customers.

"Guess the bagel wasn't such a big deal, after all," Karl said.

"Good thing, too. I've never shot anybody over a..." The phone in my pocket began playing "Tubular Bells". I checked the caller ID, and felt my stomach tighten. I told Karl, "I think I better take this."

He looked at me. "Something wrong?"

"I'll know in a minute."

I touched an icon and put the phone to my ear.

"Hello?"

"So, a zombie walks into a bar," a female voice said. "It's more of a shamble, really, but he finally gets to the back and orders a Scotch and water. The bartender brings his drink and says, 'That'll be twenty bucks.' So the zombie puts a twenty down on the bar and takes a sip of his Scotch. The bartender takes the money, rings up the sale, then says to the dead guy, 'You know, we don't get many zombies in here.' The zombie shakes his head, which almost falls off, and says, 'These prices... *uhhhh*... not surprised.'"

"Hi, Lacey," I said. "I missed you, too."

ACKNOWLEDGMENTS

Jeanne Cavelos, Director of the Odyssey Writing Workshop and sole proprietor of Jeanne Cavelos Editorial Services, provided her usual invaluable assistance when I ran into plot problems – which happened all too often.

Lee Harris, my editor at Angry Robot Books, deserves either sainthood or a knighthood for his patience with me – perhaps both. I'm not real tight with either God or Her Majesty, but I'm still going to see what I can arrange.

Miriam Kriss, my agent, provided invaluable advice and counsel – and no small amount of patience, either.

Linda Kingston made my life worth living. Seriously.

Terry Bear was always there for me.

ABOUT THE AUTHOR

Justin Gustainis was born in Northeast Pennsylvania in 1951. He attended college at the University of Scranton, a Jesuit university that figures prominently in several of his writings.

After earning both Bachelor's and Master's degrees, he was commissioned a Lieutenant in the US Army. Following military service, he held a variety of jobs, including speechwriter and professional bodyguard, before earning a PhD at Bowling Green State University in Ohio.

Mr Gustainis currently lives in Plattsburgh, New York. He is a Professor of Communication at Plattsburgh State University, where he earned the SUNY Chancellor's Award for Excellence in Teaching in 2002. His academic publications include the book *American Rhetoric and the Vietnam War*, published in 1993, and a number of scholarly articles that hardly anybody has ever read.

justingustainis.com

More investigations from the files of Scranton PD's Occult Crimes Unit

**Gods and monsters roam the streets
in this superior urban fantasy from
the author of *Empire State*.**

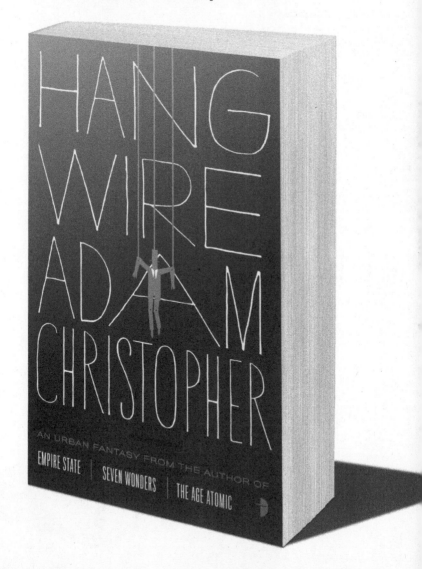

**Miriam is on the road again,
and this time she's expected...**

"Fast, ferocious, sharp as a switchblade and ****ing fantastic."
LAUREN BEUKES, author of *The Shining Girls*

THE
CORMORANT

CHUCK WENDIG

David Gemmel meets *The Dirty Dozen* in this epic tale of sorcerous war and bloody survival.

THE RAGE OF KINGS: BOOK ONE

THE IRON
WOLVES

Andy Remic

"A worthy successor to the Gemmell crown."
SFBook.com

"Pulse-pounding, laugh-out-loud funny and thoughtful."
Myke Cole, author of Control Point

**The quest for the Arbor
has begun...**

**Meet Matt Richter. Private Eye.
Zombie.**

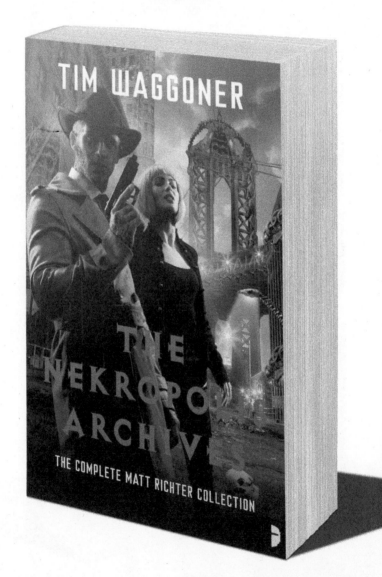

TIM WAGGONER

THE
NEKROPO
ARCHIV

THE COMPLETE MATT RICHTER COLLECTION

"You're missing out if you haven't bought this book yet. Pure and simple."
The Founding Fields